ALL OF
OUR
DEMISE

Tor Books by
Amanda Foody and
Christine Lynn Herman

All of Us Villains

ALL OF OUR DEMISE

AMANDA FOODY and
CHRISTINE LYNN HERMAN

**TOR
TEEN**

A Tom Doherty Associates Book
New York

ALL OF OUR DEMISE

Copyright © 2022 by Amanda Foody and Christine Lynn Herman

All rights reserved.

Map by Jennifer Hanover

A Tor Teen Book
Published by Tom Doherty Associates
120 Broadway
New York, NY 10271

www.tor-forge.com

Tor® is a registered trademark of Macmillan Publishing Group, LLC.

The Library of Congress Cataloging-in-Publication Data is available upon request.

ISBN 978-1-250-78934-1 (hardcover)
ISBN 978-1-250-78935-8 (ebook)

Our books may be purchased in bulk for promotional, educational, or business use. Please contact your local bookseller or the Macmillan Corporate and Premium Sales Department at 1-800-221-7945, extension 5442, or by email at MacmillanSpecialMarkets@macmillan.com.

First Edition: 2022

Printed in the United States of America

0 9 8 7 6 5 4 3 2 1

To Kelly and Whitney,
the other half of our team

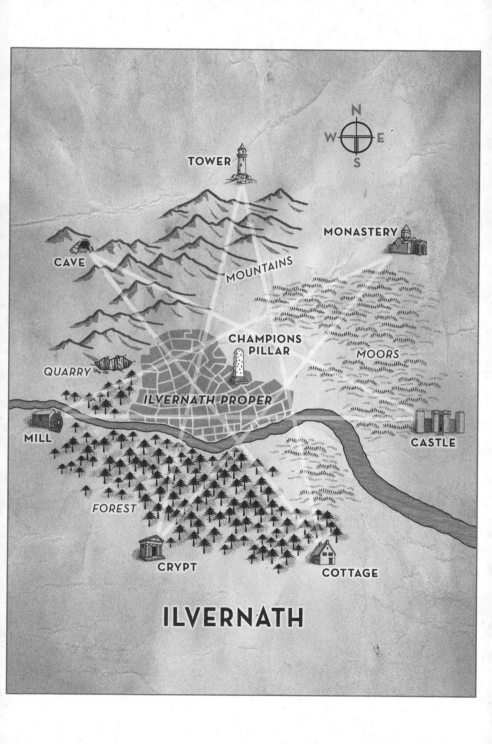

TOWER

MONASTERY

CAVE

MOUNTAINS

CHAMPIONS
PILLAR

MOORS

QUARRY

ILVERNATH PROPER

MILL

CASTLE

FOREST

CRYPT

COTTAGE

ILVERNATH

ALL OF OUR DEMISE

BRIONY THORBURN

Yesterday's events at the Champions Pillar have shown the citizens of Ilvernath that this year's tournament will not be fought safely beyond the Blood Veil.

The battle has come to us.

Ilvernath Eclipse, "Tournament Violence
Strays into Ilvernath"

The Thorburn family had always played the heroes in their town's ancient, bloodstained story, and no one resented that more than the Thorburn sisters.

The pair met at the door of the Tower, a historic structure of weathered brown stone twined with ivy and bramble, with a crooked peak like the point of a witch's hat. All their lives the Landmark had been a pile of rubble, yet now it stood proudly amid the hills overlooking the city of Ilvernath, a monument to the Thorburns' glorious triumphs.

Briony, the older of the two, had been raised certain that she belonged at the center of her family's stories. She was tall and muscular from a life spent in motion, her hands adorned with an arsenal of crystal spellrings whose power few others could wield. There was no challenge she wouldn't confront to meet her goals. No price she wouldn't pay for victory.

She was the perfect hero. Or so she'd once believed.

"I don't know what else to say," Briony started warily, "other than I'm sorry."

Innes crossed the threshold with a grimace. "I'm sorry isn't good enough."

"How about *I've changed?*"

Although the sisters shared the same fair, freckled skin and narrow features, they couldn't have been more different. Where Briony was brash, Innes was cautious. Where Briony was impulsive, Innes was calculating. Normally Innes would relent at any of Briony's apologies, but for the first time, she showed no signs of surrender.

Innes brushed past her and coolly examined the Tower's ground floor, her expression flickering with recognition. The interior of every Landmark adjusted to suit the taste of the champion who'd claimed it, and so, from the moment Briony had set foot inside, the Tower had decked itself in pastoral tapestries, cozy woolen rugs, and elegantly carved mahogany furniture, like a setting plucked out of a storybook. Briony had thought she'd feel right at home here, but instead she felt stuck inside a bizarre time capsule of her childhood fantasies.

Innes paused before the coarse stone pillar at the foot of the stairs. The pillar was the heart of the Landmark's magickal power, its front engraved with the names of hundreds of former champions, most of them crossed out. Three cracks cleaved through the rock, each pulsing with molten, scarlet light.

She touched one of the final names, etched in neat cursive.

Innes Thorburn

"I don't believe you," Innes said stiffly. "Nobody changes that fast."

Then she raised her left hand, revealing the pinky. An ugly, jagged scar marked the place where knuckle met bone.

A scar Briony had given her.

"Well, I'm trying to." Briony knew how pathetic that sounded.

"I don't care about your conscience. I'm not here for an apology."

"Then what *are* you here for?"

"Ilvernath has never had a tournament like this. Rules that have maintained the curse for centuries are breaking. Our family needs to know why."

"So they sent you to get answers." Briony tugged anxiously at a strand of chestnut brown hair that had slipped from her braid.

"I volunteered," Innes corrected sharply.

While most of the nation of Kendalle had embraced magickal and technological advancements over the past decades, the sleepy city of Ilvernath had begrudgingly crawled into the modern era. Its streets were still mazes of mossy cobblestones with minimal parking. Trendy department stores and chains had yet to overtake its quaint, local spellshops and restaurants. It boasted a puny airport, an up-and-coming art scene, and a charming—if unremarkable—reputation.

All of that changed one year ago, when an anonymously authored book catapulted Ilvernath into the international spotlight.

Magick came in two varieties: common magick, which, as its name suggested, was a plentiful natural resource, and high magick—powerful, dangerous, and extinct.

Except for a single surviving vein, kept secret by the seven oldest families in Ilvernath. Last year, the bestselling tell-all, *A Tradition of Tragedy: The True Story of the Town that Sends Its Children to Die*, exposed the appalling truth to the world: that these families had hoarded and warred over their town's hidden wellspring of high magick . . . until a brutal compromise was reached.

A curse that the families had cast upon themselves.

Every generation, each family sent a champion to compete in a tournament to the death. The victor won their family exclusive claim to Ilvernath's high magick for twenty years, until the next Blood Moon rose red in the sky, signaling that the cycle had ended and the tournament would begin anew.

Two weeks ago, the curse had started to unfold once more.

A curse Briony had always seen as an honor. A curse Briony had dreamed about being part of for her entire life.

A curse Briony was now doing everything in her power to break.

"I know why things are changing," Briony told Innes, who still stood at the foot of the spiral staircase. It wrapped around the pillar like a vise before curling up into the rest of the Landmark.

"Good." Innes stepped onto the first stair.

"We can talk about this down here." Briony hadn't been prepared to give her sister a grand tour. "Why—"

"Because I want to see what should've been mine."

With that, her sister began to climb. Wrought iron lanterns winked at Briony from the stone walls as she followed, as did the Tower's powerful warding spellstones lodged within the mortar. According to the Thorburns' many fairy tales, their first champion had embedded the crystals herself to defend against her enemies.

Briony and Innes had once cherished those stories. They'd been a source of comfort as they grew up shuffled from cousin to cousin after being abandoned as toddlers by their grieving mother. In those tales, Briony wasn't a lonely little girl whose only real home was her sister. Instead, she cast herself as the perfect Thorburn. The perfect champion. Someone who had proven that she *belonged*.

As Innes reached the landing at the top of the stairs, she turned to face Briony a few steps below. Her choppy brown fringe fell across her forehead, masking her eyes.

"It's just like we always dreamed," she said flatly. "You must be thrilled."

Briony winced. "I'm not."

Innes snorted. "Why? You care about winning this tournament more than anything. Or any*one*."

It was true that Briony had believed the tournament was her destiny. She'd believed it so strongly that she'd cut off Innes's finger so she could steal her champion's ring and claim her spot in the tournament. Yes, she'd genuinely thought Innes would die if she participated. But Briony has also envisioned herself as a legend, a breaker of an impossible curse.

Maiming her sister had seemed a worthwhile price for such a noble cause.

"You're right. That's how I used to feel," said Briony. "But I don't want to win the tournament anymore—I want to end it."

"Are you really still pretending you can do that?" Innes asked coldly.

"I'm serious. Cast a truth spell on me if you want."

Innes huffed. "Don't be so dramatic. Just . . . explain yourself."

By now, Briony could recite her plan flawlessly. She'd certainly had to explain it to enough people over the past day. But out of everyone she'd tried to convince, Innes felt the most important.

Like all curses, the tournament had been built within a septogram—a seven-sided star typically drawn on a spellboard, with an ingredient placed at each point and a crystal filled with an enchantment at its center.

Except the spellboard had been Ilvernath itself. The seven Landmarks, which came to life during the tournament, each contained a pillar that acted as a point of the septogram. And the Relics—seven items that fell intermittently throughout the three months of the tournament—were the ingredients.

"It's a curse that casts itself over and over again," Briony explained. "The Champions Pillar is the spellstone at the septogram's center. And the dead champions fill it with power, cycle after cycle."

Curses required sacrifice. And six lives taken countless times was a tremendous one.

As she recounted all of this, Briony watched Innes's expression, hoping for respect, or at least understanding. But her face didn't change at all.

"An interesting theory," Innes said noncommittally. "How do you actually plan to break it?"

"Each of the tournament families has a story about a specific Relic and Landmark," Briony offered. "You know ours. I—I tried to tell you, before . . ." Before she'd attacked her.

Innes touched one of the warding spellstones. The action reminded Briony of the two of them pretending to press crystals into the walls of the Thorburn manor home, mimicking the fairy tale.

"As though I needed another reminder of our story," Innes murmured. "But plenty of Thorburns have used the Mirror and claimed the Tower, and nothing's happened."

"It's not about claiming both. You have to pair the right Relic with its Landmark's pillar, and it activates a trial—a final defense to stop you from breaking a piece of the tournament. I know because we've already beaten one." By "we," Briony meant her and Finley Blair, a fellow champion. He was in the Tower, too, although he'd agreed to make himself scarce to give the sisters their privacy. "All this stuff our family's noticing? The cracks in the pillar, the Blood Veil between the Landmarks and Ilvernath disappearing? It's because part of the curse is broken."

When the tournament began, a magickal phenomenon called the Blood Veil descended over Ilvernath in a crimson shroud, separating the city from the tournament grounds and isolating them both from the rest of Kendalle. But after Briony and Finley had paired the Sword and the Cave, they'd unintentionally destroyed the internal Blood Veil. Although there was still no escape into the outside world, now champions could cross into Ilvernath, and anyone in Ilvernath could pass freely onto the tournament grounds—just like Innes had.

However, Briony left out a crucial detail: There was more than one way to break the tournament. She and Finley had begun to dismantle it piece by piece, which guaranteed the survival of the remaining champions after the curse fell. But the tournament could also collapse, taking down all five of them with it. And it was this possible outcome that terrified her.

Unlike the safer option, its collapse felt far beyond her control. The tournament was a story, a pattern that had reinforced itself over and over throughout its eight centuries of existence, and each time the champions deviated strongly from that pattern, the pillars cracked. Three deadly fissures already split through the side with the champions' names, compared to Briony and Finley's single victorious crack on its opposite surface, whose circle of seven stars represented the Relics. Their survival didn't hinge on a simple war—it was a race, one they were already losing.

"I guess that could be why all this is happening." Innes's voice was soft. "Do you really think you can end this forever?"

Briony took one hesitant step upward, then another, until they stood side by side. "I hope so," she answered. "I'll always regret what I did to you, but I'm trying to do the right thing now. I promise."

Innes sniffled, swiping at her eyes, and Briony's chest clenched. They'd spent a lifetime clinging to each other. It was impossible to ignore the instinct to comfort her—to reach for her, like she had hundreds of times before.

The moment her hand touched Innes's shoulder, she knew she'd made a mistake.

Her sister flinched away, and one of her rings shone white. A silver spark jolted through the air, then sizzled against Briony's hand. Briony yelped in pain and tripped down several stairs. She caught herself, barely, and pressed her back against the wall.

"What are you doing?" Briony croaked.

"Don't touch me." Furious tears glistened in Innes's eyes. "You don't get to try to fix things just to make yourself feel better. Maybe what you're saying about all of this is true, but I know you. You're still obsessed with playing the hero." She gestured angrily at the Tower walls, her voice rising with every word. "But you're the last person who deserves to. And even if you *do* end the tournament, none of that changes what you did to me. So don't try and use that to cover up your guilt."

Another of Innes's rings glowed, and spindly spectral hands scuttled along the walls before launching themselves at Briony. Briony threw up a Prismatic Protector spell before they could reach her. A diamond-shaped shield materialized in front of her, made of dozens of glimmering, kaleidoscopic pieces of light. The hands collided with it, then burst into wisps of smoke.

"I know what I did to you was awful," Briony choked out. "But we don't have to do this. *Please*."

"No, we don't," Innes agreed. "But I *want* to."

Innes had trapped her without even using magick. The stairs behind Briony were treacherously steep—and turning to run down them would give Innes an easy shot. If Briony had a Here to There spell, she could've teleported away, but she hadn't thought to wear one inside her own Landmark. Briony frantically tried to think of a way out of this that didn't end with one of them sprawled at the bottom of the steps with a broken neck.

Thankfully, Briony was at her best under pressure.

She cast a Signal Beam, then shaded her eyes. The spell, meant to act as a flare, sent a bright flash through the Tower's gloom. While Innes cried out in shock, Briony bolted up the stairs, shouldered past her disoriented sister, and burst through the door to the Tower's topmost room.

She barely had time to turn before another round of cursefire shot at her. Innes stumbled forward, blearily blinking away the effects of the spell. Briony hastily flung up her shield again.

"I thought you didn't like running away from a fight," Innes said.

"And I thought you hated starting them."

Innes's face contorted with rage. "*You* started this fight. When you left me unconscious in front of the Champions Pillar. When you cut my fucking finger off."

The words echoed off the stone walls. The ruby light streaming in through the three massive windows, tinted by the Blood Veil overhead, cast Innes in an eerie radiance.

"I've already told you how sorry I am." Briony's voice trembled. "I-I don't know what else to say."

Another of Innes's rings shone, and a wind began to whir around their ankles. It quickened and rose until it swirled around the room.

Papers rustled on the giant table in the room's center, and a crimson miniature, meant to symbolize one of the champions, fell over with a clatter.

"You'll never know how humiliating it was," Innes growled. "What it felt like to wake up and admit you'd taken the champion's ring from me. No Thorburn's ever been that *weak* before."

"You're not weak."

"Oh, please. You've always thought I was less than you. Less talented. Less capable." The wind strengthened. One chair toppled, then another, and Briony struggled to keep herself steady. "You were the only family I cared about, Briony. I would've done anything for you. But you chose a fairy tale over me."

The gusts roared with the strength of a storm, and Briony finally lost her balance. Her shield disintegrated, and she was thrown back until she collided painfully with the nearest window. Glass shattered beneath her shoulder, raining down below, and for one horrible moment, her body teetered on the sill's edge. The sharp rocks at the base of the Tower gaped at her like teeth in an open mouth. Her hands clamped down on the window frame. She yanked herself forward and collapsed onto the Tower floor, glass stinging her palms.

When she looked up, Innes was advancing toward her.

Maybe her sister *would* kill her. Right here, right now. Maybe she deserved it.

But no—ending this tournament was so much bigger than what Briony had done to Innes. Her mission was more important than her guilt, than either of them.

"What's going on?" demanded Finley Blair. He cut an impressive figure in the doorway, a Lightning Lance crackling in one hand, poised to strike. Briony had always thought of him as a modern-day knight—a strong, handsome spellcaster with dark brown skin, close-cropped coils, and a penchant for rugby shirts. But his greatest weapon of all wasn't his extensive training or his family's noble code, it was his tactical mind. He'd insisted from the beginning that this meeting was a terrible idea. Briony, foolishly, had insisted otherwise.

Innes twisted around and gasped. "You two are working together?"

In addition to being Briony's ally, Finley also happened to be her ex-boyfriend.

"Surprise," Finley said dryly.

"The fight's over, Innes," Briony murmured. "You can't take us both."

Her sister's cheeks flushed with fury. "You said you're different now. But I don't think you've changed at all."

With a *pop* and a burst of white light, she disappeared. A Here to There spell, Briony registered grimly.

Finley's gaze darted around the ruined room. "I take it this wasn't a warm family reunion?"

Briony shuddered. Innes might be gone, but her sister's words would haunt her. "My family had questions about why the tournament's changing," she said dully, yanking a piece of glass from her braid. "Innes volunteered to ask them. I guess they knew I'd let her in, but . . . I think she just wanted to punish me."

"Because being in a death tournament isn't punishment enough." Finley hurried over to where she sat slumped against the wall. "Are you hurt?"

"Not really." Her arms stung in a few places, but it was nothing a Bandage spell couldn't fix. "Well, not physically."

Finley cracked a smile. "That's the best we can hope for in here, right?"

Briony swallowed. "Right."

He reached out a hand. She took it, and as he pulled her to her feet, she was suddenly awash in memories of the day before, when they'd united the Sword and the Cave.

Briony pictured the Sword jutting out from where they'd stabbed it into the pillar. Rocks raining down into the lake, the two of them rushing madly for safety. And the triumph of its aftermath, the first time since the rise of the Blood Moon that Briony had truly known she'd done something *right*. Something good.

"Do you think she'll be back?" Finley asked.

"I mean, I obviously won't let her through the Tower's wards again." Briony sighed. "I . . . I told her about ending the tournament. She didn't seem to care whether I was telling the truth or not."

"It doesn't matter what she thinks. We have proof now. And we know what we need to do." Finley righted one of the chairs, while she collected the miniature crimson figurines and set them on the table. She reminded herself that while her family might not support her, she and Finley had at least one more ally in their corner: Isobel Macaslan, who would join them at the Tower after she recovered from their brutal battle the day before.

Once she arrived, their goal was simple.

Destroy the tournament—before it destroyed them all.

ISOBEL MACASLAN

Forbidden love? Champions Isobel Macaslan and Alistair Lowe spotted in a scandalous embrace.

Glamour Inquirer, "Star-crossed Romance
Leaves Ilvernath Swooning"

Isobel Macaslan woke tied to a chair.

The room was cramped and dark. Slivers of daylight sliced through the crack between the drawn curtains, illuminating speckles of dust suspended in the air. Along the walls, she dimly made out shelves cluttered with vials, jars, and plastic canisters. The air smelled of herbs and must.

As the fog in her mind abated, she realized she recognized this place: the back room of Reid MacTavish's curseshop. Or rather, one of the back rooms. There was a powerful enchantment cast over this space, swapping out its contents like slides on a projector.

Isobel frantically tugged at the magickal restraints on her wrists, bit at the gag tied across her mouth and knotted beneath her greasy red ponytail. In a panicked rush, she replayed her most recent memories.

The battle at the Champions Pillar. The curse that had struck her, one that should've been fatal.

Reid MacTavish, all too willing to nurse her back to health.

Her own spell that had let her peer into Reid's thoughts, glimpsing the truth of who he was, what he'd done, and what he still planned to do. Every one of the champions was in danger—

Something shuffled from beyond the room.

Isobel froze. Then, when no one entered, she yanked harder at her restraints, rubbing her pale skin red and raw. But the enchanted paracord didn't budge. All of the spellrings had been removed from her fingers. Her locket, gone.

Panic tore up her throat, yet no cry or whimper came with it. It took her several moments to realize that she wasn't breathing—she didn't need to. Her heart did not beat, was nothing more than a leaden weight in her chest. And she was cold, frighteningly cold, for reasons that went beyond the October chill.

Reid had explained what had happened to her, but still she couldn't believe it. Her father had promised that the Roach's Armor would *protect* her, and though it'd saved her life, he'd never told her the price she'd pay in return. Her body felt alien to her. She was broken.

Trapped.

Already as good as dead.

Isobel sucked in air through her nose in stuttered, forced breaths, so much that she coughed into the gag.

You are a Macaslan, her father's throaty voice rasped in her mind. *You are a survivor.*

He'd repeated those words to her a hundred times over, and even when imagined, they still grounded her. She willed herself to calm, to focus. Such a feat should've been impossible in this situation, but over the past two and a half weeks, Isobel had lost and regained her ability to sense magick, betrayed her former best friend, and condemned the boy she cared about to die.

Even before her heart stilled, she had been ice.

Isobel rooted around the floor with her feet. Her trainers smacked a piece of furniture—a desk, if she remembered the room right. She lifted one leg and swept it across the surface, kicking books and jars to the ground with a crash.

She paused for one moment, then two, three. Nothing: Reid must've cast a soundproof spell on this room to better hide her, exactly as she'd hoped.

Isobel threw her weight to the side. Her chair toppled, and she winced as her shoulder smacked the floor. She grasped around until her fingers closed over a shard of glass.

It was awkward work. Before long, her left arm went numb, and she'd accidentally cut into her palm. But eventually, the glass hacked through the restraints and the enchanted paracord vanished, glittery white magick winking around her wrists until it faded into the air. She scrambled to her feet, then tore the gag from her mouth.

Isobel went for the window first. She ripped back the black velvet drapes, squinting as her eyes adjusted to the daylight, tinted a muted red by the Blood Veil.

She was met with the sight of a mossy, gray brick wall only a meter away.

"If I make it out of this tournament alive," she muttered, "I'm never coming back to Ilvernath."

With no chance of waving down a passerby for help, she tried opening the window, but it was nailed shut, and hurling herself through it would only result in a three-story drop.

Isobel swiveled around and examined the newly lit room. She lunged for the spellstones on the counter, but one touch told her they were empty crystals, without any enchantment sealed inside. She could craft a spell or two—the room hardly lacked in ingredients—but that would take time, and Reid could return at any moment.

Fleeing was her only option.

Cautiously, she twisted the knob, peered through the crack in the door, and took in a narrow hallway with unpleasant floral wallpaper. Reid MacTavish decorated like her grandmama.

Whatever shuffling she'd heard earlier, it was silent now. She waited several more tense seconds before creeping into the hallway, her footsteps dampened by the beige carpet, and surveying either direction. To her right, bedrooms and a rattling radiator. To the left, a stairwell.

She tiptoed down the steps, whose walls displayed a gallery of framed family photographs. The oldest portraits were black-and-white or sepia, but there were more recent ones, too, snapped with a disposable camera. She spared a fraction of a second studying a toddler-aged Reid, her captor, straddling an orange tricycle.

The second story included a kitchen and living room, not unlike her own mother's flat above her spellshop. Microwave meal trays overflowed the rubbish bin.

"Stop. Calling. Me. How many times do I have to tell you that I'm not interested?"

Isobel stiffened halfway to the ground floor. That was Reid's voice.

"Yeah, obviously I saw the inner Blood Veil fall."

Isobel withheld a gasp. Though she knew the barrier separating downtown Ilvernath from the tournament grounds had been breaking, she hadn't realized it'd fallen entirely.

"What did people expect?" Reid continued. "Ilvernath's curse is eight hundred years old—of course it's unstable. And I for one don't give a shit."

In different circumstances, Isobel might've laughed at how ridiculous that lie was. Reid didn't just give a shit about the tournament—he was obsessed with it. After all, he was the anonymous author of *A Tradition of Tragedy*, the tell-all book that had catapulted Ilvernath from quaint vacation destination to notorious, international landmark. But only Isobel knew that.

Carefully, she peeked around the corner. Reid hunched over the front desk of his shop. With his back to her, Isobel could only see the stringy ends of his dark hair and his finger twisting around the coiled wire of the landline telephone.

"No, *no*, I don't want to meet in person. I—I . . . Why not? Because I have better things to do."

Her gaze ricocheted in every direction for a possible exit. Prior to being delivered to Reid for medical assistance, she'd only visited the shop once before, and she'd entered and left through the front, where Reid stood now. Then she spotted a hallway behind her that hooked around the stairs. Her hope lifted. That had to lead to a back door.

After double checking that Reid wasn't looking, she ducked beneath the banister. Past a bathroom and a broom cupboard. Then around the corner, a door.

Isobel lunged for it and twisted the handle.

Locked.

She crammed her fingers through the blinds, spreading them enough to glimpse a narrow alley. Behind a chain-link fence were several empty cars in a narrow parking lot. She didn't spot a soul.

"What does my age have to do with it? I'm the best cursemaker in the city!" Reid spat from the other room. "You know what? Whatever. Call Aleshire. Call Calhoun. Call whoever you want. I'm sure you'll find a spellmaker who'd love to give you their opinion."

She spun around. Maybe the key was stashed nearby. She rifled through the pockets of the coats hanging on the rack beside her. All she found were drained spellstones, crinkled receipts, gum wrappers, and a flyer for Ilvernath High School's Annual Autumn Bake Sale.

Cursing silently, she wrenched her hand from the last leather jacket. It slipped and crumpled to the ground, the zipper smacking the floorboards with a loud *clack*.

"I—I have to go."

Petrified, Isobel dashed toward the broom cupboard and threw herself inside, but before she could shut the door, Reid MacTavish's hand caught it. The dozen crystal spellrings on his fingers glimmered.

"Tried to slip out the back, did you?" He heaved the door open, exposing Isobel crouched amid winter coats and cleaning supplies. "I have the shop locked from the inside. A No-One-In No-One-Out. Clever, isn't it? People can only leave when I permit it."

Isobel's forced composure cracked like the brittle thing it was. But she refused to let him see her fear. Behind her back, she grasped a plastic handle—a mop. "You can't keep me here forever."

"Oh, I don't need to keep you here forever, princess. I'll only need you another hour."

A pompous sneer stretched across Reid's face. He loved how much she loathed that nickname, which only he used, as though they knew each other far better than they actually did.

Or maybe Reid just *thought* he knew Isobel Macaslan, the girl whose face had been plastered across news headlines for the past year. The whole world certainly thought they did. After being unwillingly announced as the first of Ilvernath's "Slaughter Seven," Isobel's identity had been reduced to the length of her heels, the brand of her makeup, and the hemline of her skirts. Pretty and popular, with stellar grades to match. The paparazzi starlet. Murderous Miss Perfect.

Truthfully, Isobel had sized Reid up in the same way. His tacky bad boy getup, ten renditions of the same black T-shirt, all of which hung shapelessly on his lanky frame. Eyeliner that made his fair skin look paler. A dozen necklaces of cracked, dead spellrings. A silver stud of a tongue piercing. Whatever other nonsense perfected the look of the eighteen-year-old punk wannabe who'd inherited his parents' curseshop.

Reid MacTavish was a greater villain than any of them had given him credit for.

"What happens in an hour?" Isobel asked warily. She slid her hand down the mop, getting a better grip on it.

"A finale," Reid said. "Even if it doesn't go the way I hope, I think it will make collapse inevitable."

Briony wanted to dismantle the tournament safely, piece by piece, letting all five remaining champions walk out alive. But Reid wasn't willing to be patient, or to leave the reward of Ilvernath's high magick to chance. He wanted to destroy the tournament, and let the curse take the remaining champions down with it. Then the high magick would be his to claim.

"What could possibly give you that in an hour?" she asked.

Reid grinned. "You."

As he reached for her, Isobel swung the mop at Reid's head. He caught it a hair's breadth from his jaw, then winced, his other hand clutching oddly at his side. Isobel grunted and aimed a kick between his legs, but before she could make contact, a curse shot out of one of his rings, white magick whirling through the air.

At *her*.

She cried out as the magick tangled around her like puppet strings, and her leg lowered back to the floor of its own accord.

"Come." Reid beckoned with his pointer finger. "I'll show you."

Isobel tried to resist the spell, but it was too strong. She was a passenger in her own body as she followed him to the front of his shop. Atop the desk rested a wooden spellboard, engraved with a seven-pointed star. Pewter rings and vials of ingredients had been shoved aside to make room for it, some of them strewn across the floor.

At the center of the spellboard was the Cloak. It was one of the seven Relics of the tournament, objects that fell from the sky like shooting stars, granting whichever champion claimed them unique and powerful high magick enchantments. The Cloak offered spells of invisibility and invincibility. Now it lay bunched in a wrinkled heap.

"You claimed this Relic," Reid said. "That means I need you here."

Staring at the Cloak, a clump of painful memories wedged in Isobel's throat. Alistair Lowe, gifting it to her. Alistair Lowe, whispering monster stories in the dark. Alistair Lowe, clinging to life, offering his own blood so she could reawaken the power she'd accidentally lost.

It took Isobel several moments to summon her voice. "Wh-what are you doing to it?"

"Sit," Reid said dismissively, ignoring her. Isobel's body slumped onto the wooden stool in front of the spellboard. He tapped the spellstone outlet beside the door. Automatically, the neon orange dragonfly in the window switched off. The curtains dropped, blocking the potential prying eyes of pedestrians and drivers amid morning rush hour. And the cardboard sign flipped over on the glass door. CLOSED.

Satisfied, Reid grabbed an aluminum fold-out chair, positioned it across from her, and straddled it. An intrusive thought of the tricycle photograph prodded at the back of her mind. "Have you ever cast a class ten curse?"

Enchantments came in two varieties: spells, designed for usefulness; and curses, designed to harm. Class ten was the highest class of any enchantment crafted with common magick. Daily life rarely required spells higher than class two or three, and most people never attempted any beyond class six. Most people didn't have reason to.

"You know I have," Isobel answered. The class ten Reaper's Embrace she'd cast on Alistair had come from a recipe in Reid's own family grimoire.

Something flickered across his features, and if Isobel didn't know better, she'd guess he was impressed. Until it vanished, replaced by a snide smirk.

"Right. How could I forget?" Reid nodded to today's edition of the Ilvernath Eclipse on a shelf to their right, where a massive photograph of Isobel in Alistair's arms dominated the front page, their lips pressed in a kiss. She imagined this week's Glamour Inquirer, the favorite national tabloid, would feature an equally scandalous cover story. "I've always found it romantic. 'A death cast with a kiss can never miss,' so the saying goes."

There had been nothing romantic about it.

Unlike most death curses, the Reaper's Embrace claimed its victim slowly, with each wrong committed. Although Alistair might still live and breathe for now, he was the cruelest of all the champions left in the tournament. Even Isobel, who'd seen the good in him, couldn't deny that. She doubted he'd last more than a few days.

Isobel blinked away useless tears. Even if casting that curse had broken her unbeating heart, she didn't regret it. The moment Hendry had returned, Alistair was lost to them. And if not for the Roach's Armor, Isobel would already be dead—at Alistair's hand.

She glared at Reid. He was goading her, and she wouldn't give him the satisfaction of knowing it was working.

"Is this when you start talking about whatever bad music you like?" she asked flatly.

He frowned. "This is when we drive the nail into your coffin. Together."

Even while she struggled against it, Isobel's left hand extended across the table toward him. With his smug expression locked on hers, Reid slid a tourmaline quartz cursering onto her fourth finger, like the most horrid of proposals, directly beside her champion's ring. Similar to most rings in his store, it sported an outdated pewter band and a distinctive oval cut to the stone.

"Your curse controls my body, not my mind," Isobel said. "You can't make me cast anything."

Reid squeezed her hand and turned his own over, letting his arsenal of ugly rings sparkle in the light of the fluorescent ceiling panels.

"Belladonna's Bane. The Iron Maiden. Guillotine's Gift," he drawled, naming each of them. "You can take your pick."

So he would force her, no different than holding a knife against her throat.

"You wouldn't," Isobel said, thinking again of the pictures. Of the upholstered furniture and the floral wallpaper and the once upon a time happy family home.

Reid examined her incredulously. Her bold words scarcely matched her blood-splattered, preppy pink velour tracksuit.

When he finally spoke, his voice was grave.

"Wouldn't I?"

Without her heartbeat, her own fear felt alien to her. It made it harder to swallow down.

"F-fine," she stammered. "What curse am I casting?"

"An Inferno's Wake, directly on the Cloak. I realize that high magick doubles the class of any casting, and so being made of high magick, the Cloak ranks even higher than class ten. But since you're the one who claimed it, that should be nullified. I think."

"You *think*?"

Ignoring her, Reid fished in his pocket then pulled out another stone, this one a delicate rose quartz, and placed it atop the Cloak.

No glow emanated from it, neither the white light of common magick nor the red of high magick. It was empty.

"What's that for?" she asked.

He clicked his tongue, as though she were a petulant child. "So many questions. You need to focus. If you fail at casting a class ten curse it could rebound back at you—or worse. And don't bother casting it on me instead. I'm wearing a shield of equal class, and this Guillotine's Gift would sever your head from your shoulders before you even had a chance to feel sorry."

Isobel *had* been considering just that but, unfortunately, she believed him. He wasn't foolish enough to slide a cursering on her finger without being prepared to defend himself.

But casting an Inferno's Wake on the Cloak would destroy it, and that would ruin everything that Briony and Finley had planned. Without the Relics, the only way to break the tournament's curse would be to sacrifice themselves, so that no champion walked out of the Blood Veil alive.

Her stomach roiled with panic. She wanted to resist, to survive, but not at the expense of her allies. And if Reid's plan worked, then Isobel would die anyway.

The choice should've been obvious. Surely it was better to die nobly now than as a coward later. Briony or Finley would. Even Alistair, as cruel and lost as he was, had risked himself for what was important to him—for her.

Her composure finally shattered with a sob. She was so tired of impossible choices. She wanted to go home, wanted her bed, her mother. She wanted her body to feel like hers again. She wanted to stop feeling so wretched and afraid.

As Isobel considered her death, a terrible thought occurred to her. If she let Reid kill her, who would claim the Cloak? Per the rules of the tournament, only champions could claim Relics . . . but the tournament was already breaking. It shouldn't be possible for Isobel to be here, in Ilvernath proper. Yet she was. As a noncompetitor, Reid shouldn't be able to speak to her, to hurt her. Yet he could.

If Reid killed her, who was to say that the Cloak's ownership wouldn't pass to him, and then he could destroy it himself? It might've been unlikely, but Isobel wasn't Briony or Finley or Alistair.

She couldn't risk her life just because it might be right to. Maybe that meant she was damning the others. Or maybe, once Reid let her go, she could find a way to fix this.

It was the only choice she had.

"I'd lean back, if I were you," she choked.

Then she cast the Inferno's Wake.

White flames exploded over the Cloak. Its beautiful silky fabric shriveled as though no thicker than tissue paper. A powerful stench wafted up, like burning hair, and the Relic's three spellstone clasps cracked one by one, the red light of high magick gradually fading from within each of the fissures.

As Reid had warned, it was dangerous for Isobel to lose her concentration. But Reid's gaze never wavered from the Cloak, and the firelight danced in the dark of his eyes.

Then the empty spellstone resting atop the Relic blazed scarlet.

Isobel gasped. Not only was Reid destroying the Cloak, but he was stealing its high magick. He shouldn't have been able to do that—the tournament's rules forbade it. But she had no time to dwell on the impossible.

Tentatively, she twitched her fingers. She was right. Distracted, Reid had dropped the puppeteer spell.

As carefully as she dared, Isobel slid whatever cursestones she could onto her lap and stowed them in her pocket.

She had no chance to celebrate her paltry success. A moment later, the Inferno's Wake fizzled out, leaving nothing more of the prized magickal artifact than a pile of dust.

As Reid plucked the stone from the Cloak's pyre, Isobel wiped the tears from her cheeks and asked, "What are you going to do with that?"

"Add it to my collection, of course." Reid lifted the stone to eye level and marveled at its crimson radiance, his tongue piercing flicking over his lips. "Thanks to us, Briony's plan is doomed to fail. The tournament is one step closer to collapse, and soon Ilvernath's high magick will be mine to claim."

Isobel white-knuckled the rim of her stool. High magick could level mountains, could summon or quell a hurricane with a single enchantment. What would Reid MacTavish, who'd plotted and lied and now destroyed the only hope they had, do with that power?

"I-I've done what you wanted." Isobel's voice quivered. "Now I'd like to leave."

"Leave?" Reid tilted his head to the side with mock curiosity. "Who said anything about leaving?"

A new curse spun from one of his rings. Isobel's first instinct was to lift her arms to shield herself, to brace for the gory end that he'd promised. Instead, she felt only a prick on her finger, and everything faded into blackness.

ALISTAIR LOWE

Eyewitnesses claim a seventh person took part in the confrontation at the Champions Pillar, but whoever they were, they did not appear in any photographs.

Ilvernath Eclipse, "Tournament Violence
Strays into Ilvernath"

Three Lowes wandered the woods, hand in bloodied hand.

The one at the lead was in a foul, murderous mood. As he stalked through the underbrush, the trees and shrubs contorted out of his path. Plausibly, it could've been the wind's doing. But Alistair Lowe preferred to imagine them cowering, scuttling to flee from him. He loved monster stories, after all, and he was undoubtedly the monster of this tale.

"Do you know where you're going?" his older brother, Hendry, whispered behind him.

The two boys resembled each other: dark hair that had gone too long unwashed and uncombed, faces chiseled with sharp lines, eyes of asphalt gray. But where Hendry's fair skin was freckled and warmed from afternoons napping in sunshine, Alistair's was pale, almost sallow in the red of the daylight. Where Hendry's features were soft and boyish, Alistair's widow's peak was needle-thin as a spindle. Whereas Hendry freely gave his smiles, Alistair's lips rested perpetually in a sneer.

"We're going home," Alistair answered. "A new home."

Mere hours had passed since Alistair and Hendry had returned to the Lowe estate to exact their vengeance. Alistair wondered if the bodies had already been discovered. Their uncle, sprawled in his four-poster bed. Their grandmother, lying prone beneath the grim ancestral portraits that covered the parlor walls. Their mother, slumped over her bathroom sink.

Alistair could still hear the echoes of her scream, as though she'd spotted a ghost in the mirror. Even as he shuddered, he hoped to never forget it.

"What if I don't want a new home?" asked the third Lowe, eight-year-old Marianne Jr. She was a fright of a child, dressed entirely in black except for the white lace trim of her socks and the repugnant bubblegum pink of her backpack. Her favorite things included toffee candy, Saturday morning cartoons, and collecting the bones of dead animals, especially teeth. Her least favorite thing was Alistair. Since her toddler years, Alistair had often awoken to find her looming at the threshold of his bedroom, as though she'd been infesting his sleep with nightmares.

"No one asked you, Maggot," Alistair grumbled.

Hendry shot Alistair a warning look, which he ignored. If Alistair had his way, then Marianne would be spelled unconscious on the stoop of Mayor Anand's home, with a postage stamp slapped on her forehead like the ghastly parcel that she was. But Hendry had insisted the remaining Lowes needed to stick together. Alistair would rather keep a pet skunk.

In response, Marianne stabbed her black-painted nails into Alistair's hand. Even through his woolen glove, Alistair was certain she'd drawn blood.

Above them, the treetops rustled as a crow cawed and took flight. Alistair jolted, and his Vampire's Stake ring brightened, a weapon readied. Withered leaves fluttered around them like flakes of dead skin.

Hendry, too, stiffened. But as the seconds passed and no new horror emerged, he spoke softly, "It's nothing, Al."

It was his brother's nickname for him, not his instincts, that made Alistair relax. A lifetime spent preparing for the role of champion had honed Alistair into a blade, and only Hendry had ever seen him as something more, something human.

They trekked on, and soon the forest opened into a clearing, where a stubby stone cottage slouched on a slant. Seven historic structures known as Landmarks were scattered across the tournament grounds on the wild outskirts of Ilvernath, each offering unique, powerful attributes to the champion who claimed it. The Cottage was the least coveted of them, as it only held the basic necessities of survival, like food and water. But having spent the past two weeks subsisting almost entirely on dried instant noodles and protein bars, Alistair wouldn't decline a good meal.

However, that wasn't why he'd chosen the Cottage. He'd picked it because not once in the tournament's history had any Lowe champion claimed it.

"No way," Marianne whined. "I want the Crypt."

"You can have first pick of the beds," Hendry told her.

Appeased, Marianne scampered toward the entrance, crushing the flowers of the charming garden beneath her patent Mary Janes. But when she twisted the doorknob, she called back, "It's locked!"

Alistair started after her, holding his breath. Only champions could control the Landmarks, and even then, each could only command one at a time. Sixteen days ago, Alistair had claimed the Cave. And though the Cave was destroyed now, he had no idea if the Cottage would accept him, or where what remained of his family would go if it didn't.

Thankfully, as soon as Alistair grasped the wooden knob, the power of the Cottage thrummed at his touch, and overhead, scarlet wards descended around the clearing in a misty shroud. The door swung open, revealing a cramped kitchen of clay pots, assorted pickling jars, and cast iron skillets. The fire roared to life, a welcome heat in the coolness of October. The curtains opened. The tea kettle whistled.

As they walked inside, Hendry swiped his index finger down the window, leaving a streak across the grime. "This place is filthy. I thought Landmarks adjusted to their champion's taste?"

It reminded Alistair of a witch's cottage, the sort from the frightening stories their mother used to whisper to them before bed. Alistair had once clung to those stories. He'd spun his identity out of them—someone heartless and wicked. After all, he grew up fearing the very tournament he was being raised for, but in the Lowes' tales, the villains always won.

But he couldn't want that anymore. He and Hendry had slain

the true villains. Yet the Cottage didn't change, as though taunting Alistair that he hadn't either.

Alistair dispelled the dread from his mind, and after taking in their new, humble home, he paused in front of the fireplace. A gigantic slab of stone jutted from its mantel and through the ceiling—the pillar, the heart of the Cottage's magick. Etched on one side had been a circle of seven stars, one for each of the seven Relics. However, three of them had since descended to stone's bottom, indicating the Relics that had already fallen: the Sword—now destroyed—the Cloak, and the Mirror. The opposite side listed the names of each of the champions; slashes cleaved through those of the dead.

~~Carbry Darrow.~~ Sweet, naive, studious. Pierced by a dozen arrows. An accident, Briony Thorburn swore.

~~Elionor Payne.~~ Cunning, ruthless, stubborn. Thanks to Alistair's curse, her body had burst like a popped balloon. And it'd been no accident.

Alistair thoughtfully traced one of the three cracks that severed the coarse gray stone, this one only a few centimeters below Elionor's name. Each of the fissures bled with hazy, ominous scarlet light, as though the tournament was leaking high magick, the very power that held it together. A single crack splintered the pillar's other side.

Four cracks in total, a fallen inner Blood Veil—the tournament really was breaking.

But Alistair didn't care about that anymore.

Behind him, the faucet sputtered, and he turned to watch Hendry wash their family's blood from his hands in the kitchen sink. When he finished, he faced Alistair with a cold expression. It didn't suit him, but it did match the gruesome white line etched across his throat, the scar that made even charming, good-natured Hendry Lowe look like a monster.

"How do you feel?" Alistair asked him warily.

"Alive."

That was all that mattered, because only two days ago, Hendry hadn't been.

Alistair scooped Hendry's discarded backpack off the floor and dumped its contents onto the dusty table. At least a hundred spell- and cursestones scattered across it, all raided from the Lowe estate.

Alistair's gaze caught on a particular onyx crystal, and he lifted it in his gloved left hand, letting its grooves glitter in the firelight.

A Demon's Pyre. His grandmother's favorite.

"You can't use these, Al," Hendry said. "Not any of them."

"Because I'm above that now?" Alistair scoffed. The two of them had exacted their justice, but that didn't make him noble.

In the other bag, wedged among a fresh collection of crossword books, Alistair retrieved a wooden spellboard and set it on the table in front of them. In the center, he placed the empty Demon's Pyre.

"No," Hendry said. "If you do, your curse will only worsen."

Unable to help himself, Alistair stretched down the neckline of his sweater, as he'd done constantly, anxiously over the past two days. After their family reunion this morning, the bleach white stain of the Reaper's Embrace had crawled from his fingertips to his shoulder.

Alistair recoiled and let go of his collar. He hated to look at his cursemark, to dwell on the death inevitably coming for him.

"I know how the Reaper's Embrace works," he said heatedly. "I helped Isobel craft it, didn't I?"

He ripped the cork from a glass vial and dumped it over the spellboard. Raw common magick eddied through the air, white and glittery like flecks of stardust. Once a spellmaker imprinted an enchantment into a stone, the stone needed to be filled with raw magick before it could be of use. And raw magick was simple to find, easily purchased at any local supermarket or corner pharmacy, or collected by anyone industrious enough to go looking for it themselves. Magick often settled into quiet places, like cemeteries, forests, or attics. A few speckles of it even shimmered in the Cottage, winking within the kitchen sink.

Alistair tried to coax the raw magick into the cursestone with impatient jabbing motions. Raw magick was supposed to be handled tenderly, but the mention of the Reaper's Embrace had flared his already cross mood like gasoline doused on a fire. It *hurt* to remember what Isobel Macaslan had done to him, the first person other than Hendry who'd seen him as something more than a villain, more than a Lowe.

Or so he'd pathetically believed.

Today, their star-crossed kiss was the front page story of the *Ilvernath Eclipse*. Tomorrow it would surely be his murdered family.

He pictured how the headlines would cast him: the troubled son, the bloodthirsty champion, the monster. He pictured them piecing the appalling truth together, the truth that Alistair himself hadn't managed to uncover in his sixteen years growing up in that home, the truth of why the Lowes won so many tournaments. Every one of their triumphs had been bought with a sacrifice—a death used to fuel an unspeakable, ultimate weapon.

This generation, that sacrifice had been Hendry.

The grimness of the Cottage soured further. The kettle over the fire bubbled, thick and mucky, like swamp water. The shadow of a rodent scurried across the floor.

Hendry reached for Alistair. As he moved, a streak of red light trailed behind him, as though there was a lag to his image. Because even though Hendry was real enough to breathe and sleep and cast enchantments, he was only alive thanks to the high magick of the tournament. And if the tournament broke the way Briony and the others wanted—the way Alistair had once wanted—then Hendry would go back to being dead.

Hendry swallowed. "I want you to win because I want you to survive. But what if you win the tournament, and I'm gone anyway?"

"That won't happen," Alistair snapped, his voice betraying his panic.

"Al, you don't know—"

"I do. Because when I win, the high magick will belong to the Lowes. And that's . . ." For the second time, he banished the phantom sound of his mother's scream. "That's just us now."

Hendry squeezed Alistair's hand tightly. He smiled one of his real sunlight smiles, and Alistair could almost imagine that the tournament was far behind them, that they'd already escaped Ilvernath together, just like they'd always dreamed.

"I hope you're right," Hendry murmured.

"I am." Alistair had spent his entire childhood studying his family's high magick. He was sure.

"But how can you possibly win? If you kill the other champions, the curse could consume you."

"I don't see another choice."

"And what if they kill you? You nearly died once already."

"That was before. Everything is different now." Alistair slipped his newly filled cursestone onto his fourth finger, watching the onyx shine with sinister white light. He would wear his grandmother's favorite toy like a trophy now. A reminder that even if he'd rejected the Lowe name and everything it stood for, he was still the most formidable champion in the tournament, the one whom all the others knew to fear. "Now I have something to lose."

GAVIN GRIEVE

Thanks to everyone who filled out our tournament survey and mailed it in! Although the overwhelming majority of our readers predicted that Gavin Grieve's death at Alistair Lowe's hand would be the first blood of the tournament, so far, he's outlived two of the other champions. Complete our updated bracket for a chance to win a FREE class four ring from Aleshire's Spellmaking Emporium!

Glamour Inquirer, "The Slaughter Sweepstakes!"

Gavin Grieve stood in the Castle dungeon, staring between the corrugated iron bars at his prisoner slumped within the cell. When Gavin had first claimed the Landmark, with its gleaming suits of armor and massive throne room, he'd felt like a king. It was proof that he was a true contender in the tournament, instead of the afterthought he'd been his entire life. But over the past two weeks, he'd learned that glory and grandeur wouldn't grant him the tale he craved—one that ended with six champions dead, and himself victorious.

Here in the dungeon, amid the filth and rot, lay the key to his survival.

"Wake up," he ordered his prisoner. The squat pink-skinned man jerked upward with a start. Flickering torchlight illuminated the panic on his features. Gavin hoped he enjoyed the view—moss-encrusted walls, stagnant pools of cloudy liquid on the dirt-packed floor, animal bones and broken manacles scattered outside his cell.

Yet as the prisoner took him in, his discomfort ebbed far too quickly for Gavin's liking. The man adjusted his tie, straightened his cufflinks, and rose to his feet.

"So, you've kidnapped me, you've hypnotized me, and now you're interrupting my sleep?" Osmand Walsh sauntered over to the bars. "What do you want, exactly?"

Gavin despised his false bravado, his reedy, condescending tone. Walsh was a spellmaker who openly mocked the Grieves every chance he got, never missing an opportunity to remind the world that they were the only family whose champion had never won. Just like Ilvernath's other spellmakers, he'd refused to sponsor Gavin with enchantments for the tournament. But Walsh had been particularly cruel when he'd turned Gavin away, uncaring that a seventeen-year-old boy was being sent off to die.

Even now, he seemed to consider Gavin more of a nuisance than a threat. Gavin had spent a lifetime learning to channel his anger into workouts and studying instead of losing his temper. But the spellmaker was testing his limits.

"That's none of your concern." He stepped closer to the bars, until he loomed over Walsh. Gavin was tall and broadly built, with ragged blond hair, muddy green eyes, and a fair-skinned face that could have been handsome if it wasn't so haunted. Though he might've been the least talented spellcaster of the remaining champions, his ruthlessness was as lethal as a class ten curse, even if no one else knew it. He raised a hand, displaying the crystal that glowed ominously on his forefinger. But before he could cast the Devil's Maw, which would temporarily glue the man's mouth shut, Walsh cut in.

"Wait!" *There* was the panic, Gavin noted with a rush of satisfaction.

"Why should I?" Gavin questioned coolly.

"Because I have a theory about what you're doing." Walsh tugged at his ripped shirt, displaying the cut Gavin had left on his collarbone. It'd scabbed over in the night, dried brown blood crusted at the edges. "You're stealing my life magick."

Gavin swallowed, remembering the curl of white that had emitted from the wound as he sliced into the man's skin. How it had sunk into Gavin's arm, easing the ache he'd carried for weeks. Most spellcasters filled their crystals with raw magick, but Reid MacTavish had turned Gavin into a vessel—a spellcaster who could only draw on his own life magick as a source of power. It made each enchantment Gavin wielded stronger. It was also slowly killing him, sucking away years of his life. But since the tournament had begun, he'd uncovered a loophole: Gavin could draw on others' life magick instead of his own. It was a desperate and despicable thing to do. Yet after years of being tortured by Walsh, it had only seemed fair that Gavin return the favor.

"If you know I'm taking your life magick, then you know how much danger you're in."

Walsh grasped the rusted iron bars and leaned forward.

"You misunderstand, Grieve. I'm not upset." The spellmaker bared his teeth in an unnerving approximation of a smile. "I'm impressed."

It was the last thing Gavin had expected him to say. "You're *what?*"

"I'll admit, I was a bit disarmed at first," Walsh continued. "But once that hypnosis spell you cast on me wore off, and I realized where you'd taken me . . . Well. I've always wanted to see what it's like inside a Landmark. And I assume my being here means the curse is . . . changing."

The curse *was* changing, but Gavin wasn't about to give the spellmaker all the details. Even so, Walsh's words reminded him of the day before, when three of the champions had decided to try and end the tournament for good.

Gavin didn't think they could pull it off.

Briony's half-baked theory had come from Reid MacTavish—the same person who'd warped Gavin's magick. The cursemaker obviously couldn't be trusted. Besides, according to the cracks on the pillars, the odds of all the champions perishing were three to one. And if the options were all of them dying or one of them living, he'd do everything he could to be the lone survivor. Walsh's imprisonment was proof of that.

"You underestimated me," Gavin told him. "Now you'll pay for it."

"You're certainly right that I misjudged you." The spellmaker's tone was oily and flattering. "But instead of punishing me for it, consider that I may be able to help you."

"You *are* helping me." With that, he cast a Hold in Place, and Walsh's hands froze around the bars, his body stiffening as though in rigor mortis. Gavin's arm twinged with familiar pain. His scowl deepened as Walsh's eyes darted to the hourglass tattoo peeking out from the sleeve of his T-shirt.

Each time Gavin used his life magick, sand trickled from the hourglass's top bulb into the bottom, indicating how much power—how much life—remained.

"So that's how it works," the spellmaker murmured, seemingly unconcerned that Gavin's spell had paralyzed him from the neck down. "Fascinating."

Gavin felt another rush of fury. "You're lucky I need you alive."

"You *do* need me alive, but not for the reasons you think. Consider this, Grieve. Life magick sucks years away, but how many of those do I really have to give? I'm far more valuable as a source of knowledge about your condition."

"Why should I believe you? You'll say anything to keep yourself alive."

Something moved at the corner of Gavin's vision—a rat. It scuttled through the bars of the cell, then across Walsh's frozen foot. The spellmaker's face twitched with momentary horror.

"It's true that I'm no expert on life magick," Walsh admitted. "But your casting visibly injures you, and you use life magick regardless—even though something as trivial as freezing me here is a waste of that power. Which leads me to believe this must be your *only* source of magick. Yet you seem to have no comprehension of how it works."

It *was* true that Gavin had a vague notion of life magick at best. Reid MacTavish hadn't exactly provided him with an instruction manual when he'd given him the tattoo.

"I've understood enough to survive this long."

"Yes, but for how much longer? Let's say you drain the rest of my life away, then waste it chasing the other champions. What happens then? You take a new victim?"

"What happens is that I win the tournament."

"And then what? The prize is high magick—magick you won't even be able to use."

The spellmaker's words wounded him, more painful than a torturous curse. Because Walsh was right—Gavin's magick was so mutilated that even if he *did* win the tournament, he wouldn't be able to use the power it would grant him.

He'd never truly allowed himself to think about that before. In this horrible moment, in the dungeon's gloom, he finally admitted why: because when it came down to it, he'd never truly believed he would live. Not even Gavin had been willing to bet on himself.

And why should he, when no one else had ever bet on him? He'd spent his entire life isolated from the rest of the Grieves, snubbed by the other families; even his friends vanished after the tournament became public knowledge. The other six champions had either been trained for this since birth, or were so talented that it hardly mattered. They could cast at a level most people never achieved in a lifetime, and thanks to their sponsorships with local spellmakers, they had all the enchantments they could ever want.

Becoming a vessel had felt like Gavin's only option to close the gap between himself and his competitors. If he sapped Walsh's life magick, he could endure a while longer. But it would take more than enduring to earn the victory he deserved. He needed a better long-term strategy, and the strength to see it through.

Gavin dropped the Hold in Place. Walsh unclasped the bars and shook out his hands, looking relieved. Another of Gavin's rings flashed—the Silvertongue, a truth spell. The spellmaker gasped and jerked his head up as a glimmering line drew across his throat.

"You said you could help me." Animal bones crunched beneath Gavin's trainers as he stepped toward the bars. "Does that mean you can cure me?"

"I would have to consult with a few other spellmakers," the man said, truth loosening his tongue. "And then we'd undoubtedly need to examine you. We'd also need time to run tests and concoct a solution. Becoming a vessel is incredibly rare, but Ilvernath has some of the most powerful spellmakers in the world. If there's anyone who might have a chance of helping you, it's us."

"Let's say I had any interest in your offer," Gavin said. "What's in it for you?"

"Well, I'd be free to go, wouldn't I?" Walsh gestured at the mildewed walls. "But your condition is also a once in a lifetime opportunity for study. I believe there's much my colleagues and I could learn from your life magick."

"If you're willing to make this deal, I'll need an oath spell." Two champions couldn't cast oath spells on each other, as allies inevitably turned enemies by the tournament's end. But an outsider like Osmand Walsh wasn't bound by such limitations.

"I'd expect nothing less," the spellmaker said smoothly.

"And if it'll take time to find a cure, I still need the means to defend myself against the other champions. So I don't really see why I should set you free."

"Why not capture another champion?"

"They're all in alliances. It's not that simple."

"All of them?"

"Two of them are dead. Three are allied. And then . . ." Gavin hesitated.

"That leaves one other champion vulnerable, correct?"

"Not exactly. His brother's joined him." Gavin had vowed to kill Alistair Lowe, but he couldn't do that without understanding what kind of a threat Hendry posed to him. "He's not a champion, though. He's . . . he shouldn't even be alive."

"What?" Walsh rasped. "How?"

Gavin explained as best he could. How Alistair had possessed a terrible cursering crafted from the death of his brother. How the two of them had buried it together in the Castle's courtyard. How the next day Hendry had returned, somehow alive, bound to the tournament's high magick.

"Fascinating," Walsh breathed. "*That's* how they win so frequently. That cursering must've been filled with the boy's life magick."

Gavin had never thought of it that way. But he supposed the spellmaker was right. Everyone had life magick inside them—while they were alive, it sustained them; when they died, it turned to common magick and dispersed at their burial. He'd assumed that Alistair's cursestone was filled with the magick that had come from Hendry after his death. But if it'd been siphoned all at once when Hendry was still alive, then it was life magick.

"So then Hendry . . ." Gavin said slowly. "Hendry's made of life magick *and* high magick."

"Do you see what I see, Grieve?"

"That he must be incredibly dangerous?"

"No. He's an opportunity." Walsh licked his lips. "He could be the source of power you're looking for. Or the key to your cure. If you bring him to me . . . we could learn more about him, about you. It would almost certainly help us find a solution to your problem."

"And what makes you think other spellmakers would be willing to work with you?"

"This tournament is our legacy, too," Walsh said. "You'd be providing us a valuable window into understanding it better—and learning more about magick."

Gavin's Silvertongue spellring shone. "Say that again."

Walsh gulped and nodded as that same line traced across his throat. Gavin knew he needed to be careful, as casting a truth spell over and over again could damage someone's mind. But verifying this was important.

If Gavin teamed up with Walsh and his spellmaker friends, there was no guarantee they'd actually be able to fix his magick. But should Hendry prove to be a real lead, he could go a long way toward Gavin being cured. Unfortunately, following that lead would mean attempting to ingratiate himself with Alistair Lowe—the very champion he'd fantasized about murdering for over a year.

But if Gavin could ally with him, if he could get close to Hendry . . . maybe he could cure himself. And when he was finished with them, he'd destroy them both. He did have something Alistair wanted, too—the Mirror. Perhaps he could use that as a bargaining chip.

Gavin locked eyes with Walsh. "I'm willing to work with you, but I'll still need that oath spell."

"We can go back to my shop. I have plenty to offer you—"

"You're not going *anywhere* until we make this deal."

Walsh scowled. "Understood."

Gavin left the dungeon and hurried upstairs. Without an oath spell on hand, he had no choice but to craft his own, using an amethyst the same color as a bruise. As he carried the finished spellstone back to his prisoner, he hoped he was starting a new Grieve story. One that ended in triumph instead of tragedy.

ISOBEL MACASLAN

TRIPLE HOMICIDE OF THE LOWE FAMILY—LOWE CHAMPION THE PRIME SUSPECT
Ilvernath Eclipse

Isobel was growing tired of waking tied to a chair.

She squinted into the early morning light streaming through the windows, taking in the familiar view of the brick wall. This was the same room, though the space had been magickally altered, the clutter and shelves swapped out for a guest bedroom with all the hominess of a prison cell. The furniture was outdated without the charm of being vintage. The mattress on the wooden bed looked barely thicker than a blanket. And the hideous patchwork quilt had a red stain on the corner, like fruit punch.

Also unlike last time, Reid MacTavish was with her.

He slept in the bed, wearing a pair of drawstring sweatpants, an oversized band T-shirt, and a pair of black-framed glasses. From his position, Isobel guessed he hadn't meant to fall asleep. He sat against the headboard, a CD player in his lap. His earphones had slipped off and rested around his neck, and the music must've stopped, because the spellstone in the CD player's center wasn't glowing. It'd run out of magick.

Staring at him, Isobel was struck by how young he looked. It was easy to forget he wasn't even two years older than her.

She hardly dared to move, lest she wake him. Her head pounded, and she realized with bewilderment that she was dehydrated, that her body that lacked a heartbeat still lived in ways that didn't make sense. But Isobel had no time to dwell on that now.

Judging from the sunrise, another day had passed since Reid had taken her prisoner. Why hadn't Briony and Finley come for her? Had they already tried, and failed?

Or worse—had they abandoned her? Isobel logically knew they needed her help, that her sickbed heart-to-heart with Briony two days ago had seemed too sincere to have been deception. But Isobel had once attacked Briony and locked her in the Castle's dungeon. She'd cast an unbreakable death curse on the boy she cared about. Neither Briony nor Finley knew that Isobel had let Reid destroy the Cloak rather than sacrifice herself, but maybe they'd already decided there was no room for Isobel in their heroic story.

A story Isobel had possibly doomed.

Regardless of what they thought of her, Isobel *was* committed to ending the tournament, and so all that mattered was escaping and telling the others what Reid had done. If they worked together, maybe they could find a way to break the tournament without the Cloak, a way that wouldn't kill them all.

She twisted her hands through the rungs of the back of her chair, awkwardly feeling for the three cursestones she'd stolen yesterday, tucked beneath the plush layers of velour in her pocket. Her middle finger grazed one, and she sensed the enchantment inside. Some sort of nature manipulation curse. With more flexing, she determined that the other two included a sickness curse and a bludgeoning curse.

Bludgeoning would work fine.

Isobel didn't bother to consider what it would do to Reid. She was the prisoner; she was the one in danger. So she didn't waver as a gigantic, menacing club materialized in front of her, radiating white light.

Reid's eyes blinked open, but he had no time to react. The club struck his head with a sickening *crack*.

The cursemaker slumped across the pillows.

"Shit," Isobel murmured. She might've killed him. A crimson stain bloomed across his pillowcase, and she reminded herself that Reid was no longer the boy on the tricycle from that photograph. He was the man who'd published the book that'd ruined her life. Who'd kept her prisoner. Who'd destroyed the only hope the champions had at a happy ending.

She still needed to get out of the chair. And so she cast a second curse.

The rocking chair writhed beneath her. Wood severed into strips of bramble, dagger-like thorns jutting from every groove. Isobel swore loudly as they stabbed into her back, her thighs. Then the chair collapsed. She landed in a heap of briar, blood oozing from several gashes in her tracksuit.

She clambered to her feet and sprinted to the bathroom.

The next ten minutes were a blur.

Isobel untied her restraints while she peed, cutting through the paracord with a pair of scissors from the drawer below the sink. Then she staggered downstairs to the kitchen. Filled a glass from the faucet and gulped down one, two, three pints of water. She tore through the pantry for food and ravenously stuffed an entire bag of crisps, then trail mix down her throat. None of it sat well in her empty stomach, and she clutched her abdomen as it twisted with a cramp.

From the living room, the television blared.

"No, I've never doubted my daughter. Not for a second."

Isobel froze. She would've recognized that voice anywhere, yet the sound of it here, now, was surreal enough to make her dizzy.

"But kissing another champion?" asked someone else. "And not just any champion, but Alistair Lowe, who many believe to be disturbed, who was supposedly her rival—that hardly sounds like the Isobel we all know, does it?"

Isobel crept into the living room as a blurry video clip played on the screen. The camera, clearly fallen on the ground, had an awkward but clear vantage on Alistair kneeling, Isobel lying weakly in his arms, their lips pressed in a treacherous kiss.

The moment Isobel had cast the Reaper's Embrace.

The moment the world would never let her forget.

The clip ended, and the screen returned to today's broadcast of *Wake Up Ilvernath!* Her father leaned back into the talk show sofa, one arm stretched across the pillows, one ankle resting on his knee. His red hair was slicked harshly back, and his smile gleamed brighter than his expensive, gaudy gold watch.

He was *smiling* while his daughter was cursed. Heartbroken. Fighting for her life.

"It's strategy," Cormac Macaslan said smoothly.

"Strategy?" repeated the show's host.

"Look, here's the thing that the protestors and all those government agents sniffing around like to forget. Isobel isn't a normal teenager—none of them are. They've prepared for this their entire lives. For the seven families, it's more than a tradition. It's who we are. Fighters. Survivors."

Isobel trembled, a moment away from screaming at the television. But she couldn't ignore her nausea any longer, and she fled to the bathroom. She shakily rummaged through the medicine cabinet and drawers for an antacid spell. But all she found were a Zit Zapper, several generic brand Stain Lifters, a basic first aid kit, and some useless cosmetic enchantments.

She groaned in frustration, then—despite trying desperately to avoid it—caught her reflection in the mirror. Her skin had the bluish tint of something dead. Her lips, too, had paled, and an oily sheen glistened on her forehead and in the roots of her hair. Flecks of Elionor Payne's blood still clung to her clothes.

If any tabloid reporter took a photo of her now, they wouldn't recognize her. Her own mother barely would.

Isobel lurched to the toilet and retched.

Afterward, she undressed and staggered into the shower. She cried as she teased the knots out of her hair. Vanity was worthless in the tournament—obviously it was better to live cursed and broken than not at all. But her father had *lied* to her. He'd claimed the Roach's Armor was a family heirloom, that it would protect her. Instead, it'd left her permanently suspended on the cusp of death. That wasn't safe. That wasn't whole.

Unwilling to rewear her blood- and sick-stained clothes, Isobel wrapped a towel around herself and wandered into the closest bedroom.

Reid's bedroom.

Isobel had expected cheap posters and shelved vinyls. She was mistaken.

A map of Ilvernath's tournament grounds was splayed above the disheveled bed, pins connected with crisscrossed string jutting out from each Landmark. A junk pile towered in the room's far corner: discarded spellstones, notebooks, cardboard boxes full of hardcovers of *A Tradition of Tragedy*. Tacked behind the wardrobe door were printouts of each champion's face, including her own. Elionor's and Carbry's were crossed out.

Feeling as though she'd disturbed an aspiring crime scene, Isobel dashed to the dresser and yanked out a pair of joggers and a black T-shirt—not exactly her usual ensemble. Nevertheless, she dressed, eager to get the hell out of there, but her gaze snagged on a framed photo of Reid atop the dresser, his arms slung around the shoulder of a pale, obviously sick man. Father and son. They both grinned.

Swearing under her breath, Isobel nervously returned to the spare bedroom, where Reid lay exactly as she'd left him.

If she wanted to be kind, she could call the emergency hotline and abandon him for them to find. But it wasn't her conscience that truly gave her pause—it was her practicality. The MacTavish family were the oldest and most esteemed cursemakers in Ilvernath, and Reid had quite literally written the book on the tournament. If anyone could reverse the damage that Reid had done, it was Reid himself.

After snatching the first aid kit, Isobel sat on the bed beside him. Her fingers shook as she brushed aside Reid's hair and felt for his pulse.

It was there, faint but there.

How strange that Reid had one when she didn't.

Gingerly, she tilted his head to the side, exposing the wound. She rooted through the kit until she procured the most basic of healing spells—enough to stop him losing any more blood, but not enough to revive him. Not yet.

After she'd patched him up, she stumbled into the main shop to ransack his wares. It didn't matter how tacky the rings were; she grabbed whatever she could find and stuffed them into her clothes until her pockets bulged and the inside of her sleeves rattled with stones. In his back office, she found the Macaslan enchantments Reid had taken from her. She slipped the rings on her fingers and left the locket behind. Though she'd always held it for comfort, a reminder of her mother, she neither needed nor wanted the two curses the necklace carried. The Roach's Armor demanded a sacrifice that Isobel could no longer pay. And though it was powerful, she couldn't bring herself to cast the Reaper's Embrace ever again.

But the true prize lay in the safe beneath the desk. She broke the enchantment on it easily with one of Reid's own lockpick spells, then pulled out the spellstone full of high magick that he'd siphoned from the Cloak, glowing scarlet.

In this story, the princess would take a prisoner of her own.

GAVIN GRIEVE

"Bleeding hearts across the world have claimed these champions
kill only out of necessity. But if Alistair Lowe really *did* murder
his family, it proves they're all dangerous, inside or outside the
tournament."

On-site reporter, *SpellBC News*

Gavin stood at the edge of the Cottage's clearing, staring at the
misty crimson wards along the tree line. A champion was inside the rickety stone building, and if Gavin's hunch was right,
that champion was Alistair Lowe.

Gavin found it hard to believe that the same boy who'd boasted
about his so-called lair would willingly camp out in this most humble
of Landmarks—the traditional Grieve Landmark, in fact, if only because no one else wanted it. But the Cave was gone, the Tower surely
claimed by Briony Thorburn, and the other Landmarks vacant. There
was nowhere else Alistair *could* be.

Maybe Alistair was hiding because of what he'd done. Gavin
thought of the slightly damp edition of the *Ilvernath Eclipse* he'd
found trampled in the woods. He'd read the cover story twice, but
the words had yet to sink in.

Alistair Lowe was the prime suspect in the slaughter of his own
family—as though he hadn't been monstrous enough before.

If not for the possibility of what Hendry's life magick could provide, and Walsh's guarantees that other spellmakers *were* willing to
meet with him, Gavin would've abandoned all hopes of an alliance.
As it was, he couldn't shake the feeling that he was about to write his
own death sentence.

Gavin sent a Signal Beam at the wards, trying not to wince at the
corresponding pain that coursed down his arm. He still had the life

magick he'd stolen from Walsh, at least. And he had some new spell-work, again thanks to Walsh, who'd given him supplies after Gavin had set him free, far nicer than anything Gavin could afford or craft on his own. All it'd taken for him to get a spellmaker sponsorship like the other champions was kidnapping and extortion.

"Come out, asshole," he muttered. Then the curtains drew open, and a small round face the color of milk peered out through a grimy window. Not Alistair—someone much younger. Gavin frowned, confused. Then he remembered; there had been one survivor of the massacre—a child.

The door swung open a moment later, and Alistair strode out.

Despite the fact that Gavin had summoned *him*, as Alistair approached, Gavin couldn't help but feel like a rabbit spotted by a wolf.

Alistair's dark, disheveled curls fell every which way across his forehead, the sharp line of his widow's peak emphasizing features both handsome and cruel in equal measure. There was something feral about his red-rimmed eyes and stalking gait, and the crimson mist of the wards cast him in an ominous glow, as though he'd been spun from the very fabric of the tournament itself.

Oddly, Alistair wore a black glove on his left hand, which meant he was armed with half as many spellrings as usual. Gavin wondered if it was meant as an insult to him—that Alistair thought so little of his power.

"Grieve?" Alistair paused at the edge of the wards, until only two meters of withered grass stretched between them. "What are you doing here?"

"I didn't come to kill you."

Alistair smiled insincerely. "Obviously. You couldn't dream of succeeding without the element of surprise."

Gavin refrained from responding with an insult. He needed to win Alistair over, not provoke him, but it was hard to hold back when every conversation with Alistair felt like a competition.

"The others insist they can break the curse without anyone else getting hurt," Gavin started. "You and I are the only ones who know they're delusional."

Alistair chuckled, but there was no mirth in it. The wind rustled in the trees around them, as though it were laughing at Gavin, too. "Ah. So that's what this is."

"What do you mean?"

"You do realize that the last time a champion begged me for an alliance, they betrayed me?"

"I wasn't going to beg. I have something you want." Gavin pulled the Mirror from his jacket pocket. "It belongs to you now that Elionor's dead."

Alistair studied the Relic, then dragged his gaze back to Gavin, his expression steel. "Tell me, why would I strike a bargain with you when it'd be just as easy to strike you down?"

Gavin had been trying to answer this question himself for the past day. The Mirror was an incentive, but Alistair could simply try to kill him and retrieve it from his dead body.

"Because the other three champions are allied now," he answered. "Having someone else on your side gives you better odds."

Alistair flexed his ungloved hand, his stacks of curserings glimmering threateningly. "You call the others delusional, but I don't think they are. The Cave is destroyed. The pillars are cracked. So either you have some other brilliant explanation for all of that, or you don't care."

But Gavin *did* care. He'd weighed the odds and made his choice: not just survival, but a cure, a legacy, a lifetime of power and respect. All at the expense of four other lives that would likely be lost anyway.

"I don't think they can end it in time. You saw how much faster the pillars are cracking on the wrong side. So if it comes down to all of us dying, or one of us living . . . I want to walk out of here a winner. Don't you?"

Alistair smiled to himself, as though Gavin's offer was a joke. "What a toll it must've taken to drag yourself here. You've always hated me. Don't bother trying to deny it."

"My opinion of you has nothing to do with this," Gavin said derisively. "It's a solid strategy. Us against them."

Alistair's countenance clouded. Then his face set into cold, cruel certainty. "Maybe it's true that we share the same enemies, but you're worth far more to me dead."

One of Alistair's curserings flared. Gavin barely had the chance to throw up a Spikeshield before a tree root curled into the air and lashed against it like a whip, and he stumbled backward, his jagged silver armor embedding into the trunk behind him.

"We don't have to fight!" Gavin called desperately, yanking himself free.

"But it's exactly as you said," Alistair sneered. "We're the only ones still playing. So let's play."

Gavin fumbled for his Here to There, but another root punctured his armor and slashed his shoulder before he could cast it.

A million thoughts raced through Gavin's mind—could he somehow find a way to lie and ally with the other champions? Could the Castle hold against Alistair's siege? Was there any point in fleeing the inevitable?

He decided that there wasn't. Not only did Gavin need Hendry to win the tournament, but after angering the other champion, Alistair would surely give chase. And Gavin would rather die fighting than die cowering in his Landmark.

"Fine." Gavin turned tail and bolted through the underbrush, knowing Alistair would follow. If he *was* going to stand a chance against the other champion, he'd need to draw him away from the protection of the Cottage. A fireball whizzed over his head, then another, igniting the drooping branches of the oak above him. Gavin ducked as pieces of the canopy snapped and crashed to the ground, smoldering.

He inventoried his spellrings—a Spikeshield, for armor. The Chimera's Bite and the Iron Fist, both formidable curses. His Here to There. And, in his pocket, the Triumph of the Fallen, a death curse Walsh had crafted specifically for him. Ranked at class ten, it was undoubtedly strong enough to slay Alistair, but Gavin struggled to cast anything higher than class seven.

Gavin rolled behind a briar bush, only for it to erupt into flames a moment later. He swore and crawled away, frantically patting out a few embers on his shirt.

"Come out, come out, wherever you are." Alistair's voice drifted through the woods, sounding straight out of a nightmare. Smoke clouded Gavin's vision, and fire surged through the underbrush. Alistair seemed willing to burn down the whole forest if it meant drawing him out.

Gavin sprinted to the right, unwilling to cast curses at random until he had a clear line of sight on Alistair. The smoke dissipated and Gavin held still, listening, as he took in his surroundings. He'd found his way to a small clearing.

He watched the direction he'd come from, waiting, tensing. A twig snapped nearby, and the earth buckled before him in a wave. He lunged out of the curse's path as it sent the forest floor quaking, trees groaning and swaying. Then he cast the Iron Fist.

The curses Walsh had given him felt different than any he'd wielded before. Unlike basic retail spellwork, they were sleek and high quality, masterfully crafted. Two metal hands appeared in the air before him, each the size of Gavin's torso. When Gavin opened his left hand, the corresponding Iron Fist mimicked him. His arm throbbed, but the pain was worth it for such power.

He clenched his hands and sent an Iron Fist hurtling toward the nearest tree. With an ear-splitting *crack*, the trunk severed cleanly in two and timbered to the ground.

"Now it's your turn to stop hiding," he called out.

Finally, Alistair emerged in the distance, a glossy, brown-plated shield hovering before him, as though the exoskeleton of a beetle. "Planning to punch your way out of this? How uninspired."

In response, Gavin slammed a magickal fist against the shield, then another, pummeling Alistair with blow after blow. With a final strike, the enchanted plates split apart, chitin shrapnel exploding through the air. Gavin hoped the champion now regretted confronting him with only half an arsenal.

Before Alistair could counterattack, Gavin's Iron Fist seized him around the torso. Then he hurled Alistair to the ground, hard enough that the *thud* of his body reverberated through the clearing. The curse sputtered out, and Gavin's tattoo ached so painfully that tears welled in his eyes. He pushed away worries of how much precious life magick he'd spent. A little suffering didn't matter, not when he was so close to finishing this.

"Not as easy to kill as you thought I'd be, am I?" Gavin snarled, stalking toward the other champion. Alistair coughed and rolled over, his eyes widening as Gavin loomed above him. Dirt coated his cheeks, and clumps of moss and broken twigs clung to his sweater and mussed hair. Across his forehead, a scrape oozed, blood trickling down the slopes of his brow and nose.

Gavin had fantasized about this moment a hundred times. How it would feel to look Alistair in the eyes and see not just respect, but fear. How Alistair's cruel face would slacken as Gavin drained the life from him. Yet no matter what he pictured, he could never get Alistair's death quite right, each different brutal end somehow unsatisfying. But that didn't matter now. It was finally here.

He pulled the Triumph of the Fallen from his pocket.

Below him, one of Alistair's rings blazed. Gavin threw up a Spikeshield again, sending a row of silver thorns protruding toward the other boy's chest, and Alistair paused his casting to shield his face with his gloved hand. As he held it there, panting, Gavin spotted a tear in the wool. The skin below it was not just fair—it was white as bone.

Then Gavin did something he'd never dreamed of in any of those fantasies. He hesitated.

"Well, Grieve?" Alistair growled. "Finish it. Or are you too—"

"Shut up." Gavin reached forward and tugged the glove off, revealing the most brutal cursemark he'd ever seen. It engulfed Alistair's hand entirely, from his fingernails to his wrist, before disappearing beneath the ragged sleeve of his sweater.

"You're cursed," he said. "You're, um . . . *really* cursed. How?"

"Why do you care?" Alistair ripped his hand away and buried it in the grass.

Why *did* he care? Alistair was far more vulnerable than Gavin had realized—he should seize the opportunity and kill him. Yet in his fantasies, Alistair was at his strongest, and Gavin bested him anyway.

But the truth was, Gavin had no shot of besting Alistair at his strongest. Even weakened, he could effortlessly cast enchantments that Gavin himself had never dared to attempt. He was a vicious prodigy who'd killed his own family in cold blood. This was no time to worry about whether Gavin had earned this victory or not.

The Triumph of the Fallen had already filled with Gavin's life magick, and so he focused on the sickly green quartz. But before he could even begin to cast it, his arm twinged with a pain so severe, it made him dizzy. His armor vanished, and he struggled to regain his balance.

Alistair was on him in an instant. A line of roots whipped from the forest floor, knotted around Gavin's ankles, then yanked back. He tumbled to the ground, head smacking against the dirt. He groaned woozily, but before he could scramble to his feet, the roots twined around his arms and wrenched him to the ground.

He'd wasted his chance, and now he was going to die, just like every other Grieve. Gavin tried to ready himself for the end. He could at least die with dignity—no begging, no screaming. Instead he smiled, hoping his fear didn't show. Hoping it made Alistair angry.

Maybe that smile tripped him up, because instead of casting a curse, Alistair froze, studying him carefully.

"Everything you cast hurts you, doesn't it?" Alistair asked. "Why?"

Gavin's temper flared. "Yeah, my magick's all fucked up. Congratulations, you figured it out. Now get this over with."

With a deep, shuddering breath, Alistair closed his eyes, and one of his curserings shone. It was a large, nasty-looking stone, its pale yellow crystal marbled with black veins.

Suddenly, the shadows along the ground seemed to darken and grow, as though they'd been given new dimension. A creature unspooled from them, made entirely of negative space, like it had carved a hole in the air and crept from it. Claws curled from the ground and scuttled up Gavin's prone body. He gasped in horror at their cold, slimy touch against his skin. They lunged for his neck—and then, with an awful *screech*, the curse split off, dozens of tiny shadow fragments swirling into the air like bats.

Alistair shouted in surprise. The curse binding Gavin in place weakened, and Gavin seized his chance. He broke free and pulled the Chimera's Bite from his pocket, and at his touch, it automatically filled with his life magick. Pain lanced down his arm once again, but this time, he wouldn't fail.

Hissing filled the air. Green smoke twined around Alistair's wrist and arm, then solidified into a snake, scales gleaming; he tried to throw up a shield as the serpent's head reared back, fangs bared, and dove for his neck.

Without warning, another force collided with it, and the snake dissolved into smoke. Gavin felt the curse break like a blow to the stomach, and he collapsed to his knees as Hendry Lowe burst into the clearing, covered in soot. The once dead boy looked just as unnerving as he had when they'd fought at the Champions Pillar. A scar sliced across his throat like a menacing second smile, and a flash of red lagged behind him as he moved.

"Al!" he cried out. "Are you all right?"

Gavin forced himself up. The brothers stood together, Hendry glaring at him as Alistair sagged beneath his arm.

"Step back," Hendry warned his brother. Alistair uttered a noise of protest, but Hendry gestured until the other boy staggered away.

Perhaps Gavin had traded death at the hands of one Lowe for another. Left with no recourse but to flee, Gavin attempted to cast his Here to There, but he was too weak.

Hendry fired another curse, and this one landed, a barrage of tiny thorns that sent agony surging through Gavin's veins. He collapsed to the ground again, groaning.

Dimly, he registered the brothers crouched over him.

"You can't do this." Hendry's voice was as soft as wind rustling through fallen leaves. "You know you can't."

The Lowes exchanged a grave, meaningful look. Scarlet shimmered at the edge of Hendry's silhouette, reminding Gavin of all the blood the brothers had spilled. After what they'd done to their family, surely Alistair was more than capable of finishing him off himself. But . . . that cursemark. There was something else going on here.

It was all Gavin could do not to black out as Hendry pressed his fist into Gavin's neck. Each crystal and knuckle bit painfully into his skin.

Alistair uttered something that Gavin didn't hear. The hourglass tattoo on his left arm screamed in agony. He couldn't tear his gaze away from Hendry, who was staring at the forest floor, his chest heaving.

"No." Alistair seized Hendry by the shoulder and wrenched him back. Gavin gasped for breath on the ground. "He can't kill me. Isn't that right, Grieve?"

It took Gavin a few beats to respond. He coughed, rolled over, and forced himself into a crouch. "Can *you* kill *me?*" he gritted out.

"I could," Alistair snapped.

"But you won't."

Alistair's expression froze. Hendry shot him yet another pointed look, but the other boy shook his head. Even if Gavin didn't understand their exchange, he knew an opening when he saw one. "Then why . . . fight?" Gavin wheezed. "I'm still willing to . . . talk . . . if you are."

Alistair grimaced, not at Gavin, but at his brother. "Fine. Let's talk, champion to champion."

BRIONY THORBURN

THORBURN FAMILY SEEKS TO DISMISS REPORTER
LAWSUIT, CLAIMS BROKEN CAMERA EQUIPMENT
THE RESULT OF "IRRESPONSIBLE CURSE-CHASING"
Glamour Inquirer

A grand table sat in the center of the Tower's top floor, carved with a map depicting Ilvernath and the tournament grounds in breathtaking detail. Briony stood beside Finley, staring at the crimson miniatures scattered across it, each representing a champion. Two of the miniatures had been removed from the map—the dead. Two more were hostile, one placed on the Castle, the other as far away as Briony could put it without chucking it off the table. And two clustered together atop the Tower, back to back, their tiny faces gazing at the challenges that awaited them.

Briony clutched the seventh figurine in her hand.

"It's been too long," she murmured. "Isobel should be here by now."

Finley sighed with frustration. "I think it's time we talk about what that means."

It'd been two days since Briony's fight with Innes, and although they'd received a brief update from Reid their first night in the Tower, reassuring them that Isobel was still recuperating, the messages they'd sent since had gone unreturned.

"Maybe she's still healing," Briony suggested weakly.

"Maybe. But she wasn't injured enough to need this much recovery time."

"Well . . . something could've happened to her. Maybe Alistair attacked the curseshop."

"Her name's not crossed out on the pillar. And Reid would've told us if there was an emergency."

"We should go check on her," Briony said.

"Or . . ." Finley's voice was delicate. Gentle. The same way he'd spoken to her in the aftermath of her fight with Innes, before she'd shut herself in her room, inconsolable. When she emerged later, she'd found the window repaired, the glass on the floor gone, as though the battle had never happened at all. Finley's spellwork had been perfect, but when Briony peered closely at the glass, she swore she still saw cracks.

When Briony didn't respond, he spoke again, more firmly this time. "Or we can accept that she's chosen not to join our cause."

The two figurines standing on the Tower suddenly looked a lot lonelier to Briony—surrounded by Gavin and Alistair and an unpredictable Hendry Lowe.

"She told me she wanted to break the curse." Briony's shoulder brushed against Finley's as she turned to face him—she hadn't realized how close they were standing. His shrewd gaze bored into her, and although he'd surely noticed their proximity, too, he didn't move away.

She was reminded suddenly of the first time he'd ever looked at her like that. In their advanced magick course, when she'd cast two class eight spells simultaneously. It'd earned her a nosebleed, and an A.

"You made it look easy," he'd told her as he escorted her to the nurse's office.

"It was," she'd said. "I could've handled three."

That was also the first time Briony had made him laugh. Before that, the two of them had barely spoken—but when she came to class the next day, he was waiting at her desk.

"I need someone to train with," Finley had said, without preamble. "Someone who knows why it's important. And you're the strongest caster in school."

He'd been competition, technically. Briony had said yes anyway. She was susceptible to flattery—and, as it turned out, to Finley's broad shoulders and the slight quirk at the corner of his lips and the low, soothing timbre of his voice.

"Maybe Isobel lied," he said now, his serious tone jolting Briony back to the present. "I know she was your friend, and you want to believe the best of her—of everyone. But this is still technically a fight to the death. We can't forget that."

"You're right." She clenched the figurine until it dug painfully into her palm. "She *was* my friend. But the tournament changes people."

Isobel had turned on her mere days ago, back at the Castle. Briony had wanted to believe they'd moved past it, that Isobel understood the importance of breaking the curse. But maybe Briony had been naïve yet again, relying on old bonds instead of the facts in front of her. She considered Isobel once more—not the girl she'd known, but the champion who'd locked her in a dungeon. Cold. Ruthless. Pragmatic. The last thing she'd ever believe in was a happy ending.

Briony said as much to Finley, who looked grim.

"Have you ever wondered why I didn't invite Isobel to be in my alliance?" Finley asked.

Briony *had* wondered. They'd known each other, too, after all, both as classmates and through their connection to Briony. "I thought it was because of her family."

"It's because I knew she wouldn't hesitate when the time came to turn on each other. She was too big a risk. Maybe . . . maybe she still is."

Unease swelled in Briony's chest. She'd been so willing to accept Isobel's apology because of their old friendship. And she'd allied with Finley because of the relationship they'd shared before the tournament, too—but how much of that was real? How much of that still mattered?

"If she's not with us, we're outnumbered," she said worriedly. "And she has the Cloak." Suddenly, everything felt insurmountable—three powerful opponents, six Relics and Landmarks left to destroy, and a tournament that was already collapsing in a way that could kill them all. She dropped the figurine onto the table with a clatter.

Finley picked it up and placed it beside Elionor's and Carbry's. "We'll make another plan. We'll find another strategy."

"Maybe," she mumbled.

"The theory we tested, the theory we *proved*," he said intently, "it's worth fighting for. Together."

Briony clung to his words. Maybe neither of them were the people they'd been before the tournament, but they both wanted the same thing now. That was what mattered. Ending this, whether the other champions helped them or not.

"So let's fight," she whispered.

Then Briony felt a bone-deep twinge—her defensive enchantments. "The wards," she said with a gasp. "Someone's trying to get in."

They rushed to the windows. A figure with an unmistakable shock of red hair stood at the base of the Landmark.

"Let me in!" Isobel called frantically. Someone else was slumped beneath her arm, but Briony couldn't make them out from this distance.

She gathered the Tower's wards in her mind, felt their power pulsing through her. She could dispel them with a mere thought. But instead, she hesitated.

"Do you think we can trust her?" she asked Finley.

He paused. "I don't know. But she needs help. For now . . ."

"We let her in?"

He nodded.

Briony dropped the wards as they rushed downstairs. When she threw the front door open, Isobel stood before her, looking wretched. Normally, the other girl didn't leave the house without coordinating her lipstick color with her trendy outfit. Now she wore an all-black getup, wrinkled as though snatched from a hamper. Her wet hair hung down her shoulders. Her face looked terrible, sallow and sunken, her skin seeming to barely cling to her bones.

In one hand she clutched two disposable bags, bulging so heavily with spellstones that their sharp edges had begun shredding the flimsy plastic.

Her other hand clasped Reid MacTavish's limp arm. The cursemaker lay on the ground, unconscious, drool dribbling from the corner of his mouth. Dried blood was matted in his dark hair and down his neck.

"What happened to you two?" Briony asked, stunned, while Finley hauled Reid over his shoulder.

"I'll explain inside," Isobel said.

Briony reactivated the wards, and a shimmering crimson mist appeared between them and the outside world. Then she stepped aside for Isobel to pass and slammed the door shut behind her.

Isobel dropped her plastic bags onto the kitchen table, her gaze flitting from the tapestries to the old wooden furniture. Finley laid Reid on a couch and began examining the wound on his head. The cursemaker looked as though he'd been attacked in his own bed, and without his typical ensemble of ripped black jeans and a studded leather vest, he seemed fragile. Skinny. Young.

"Were you attacked?" Briony asked. "Was it Alistair—"

"Yes, I was attacked! By *him!*" Isobel pointed a quivering finger at Reid. "Reid isn't who we thought he was. He lied. He's been lying since the very—"

"What are you talking about?" Briony asked, as taken aback by her tone as her accusations. Isobel was normally collected and matter-of-fact, even in a crisis. "Why would he—"

"Just *listen to me.*" Isobel's voice hitched. "It wasn't some Grieve who wrote *A Tradition of Tragedy*—it was him. This whole time, he's been manipulating us. He's the one who told you about breaking the curse. His advice led me to Alistair. For two days, he's kept me imprisoned in his shop, all so he could destroy the Cloak."

"He did *what?*" Briony demanded.

"Slow down," Finley said, the only calm one of the three. "Tell us what happened."

As Isobel recounted the hell of her past two days as Reid Mac-Tavish's prisoner, Briony's distress mounted with each word. If Isobel's story was true, then Briony had abandoned her when her old friend needed her most.

But Isobel could also be here under false pretenses, just like Innes. Maybe she'd attacked Reid and hidden the Cloak somewhere. Because she'd known that even after all they'd been through, Briony would still let her in.

"You're sure he destroyed the Cloak?" she rasped.

Isobel hugged her arms to herself. "Of course I am. He made me do it with a death curse aimed at my . . ."

She trailed off and raised a trembling hand to her neck, where a silver line traced across her throat. Her red-rimmed eyes widened. "You . . . you cast a truth spell on me?"

"I didn't—" Briony protested.

"We had to be sure," Finley said gravely, one of his spellrings winking out.

Briony stared at Reid MacTavish, bloodied and unconscious, and an unfathomable rush of horror roiled inside her. She'd sacrificed so much to get this far. If they couldn't destroy the Relics and the Landmarks . . . if the tournament shattered . . .

All of them would die. *All of them.* She stalked toward Reid, shaking with fury.

"He started all of this," she snarled. "I risked everything, I . . . I hurt Innes, and if he's really damned us all . . ."

Spellcasting had always come easily to Briony. Restraint did not. Her Ten of Daggers ring flared, and blue light crackled through the room, then solidified into tiny blades, winking like shards of broken glass. Each of them hovered mere centimeters above Reid's unconscious body.

"Wait!" Isobel's hand closed around her wrist, her grip strangely cold. "Believe me, I want him dead as much as you do. But we need Reid. *Alive.*"

"Need him for what, exactly?" Briony snapped, wrenching away from Isobel's grasp.

"To fix the Cloak," Isobel said tersely.

"Fix a broken Relic?" Panicked thoughts whirled through Briony's mind too quickly for her to catch her breath—if she should be preparing for the tournament to revert to how it had always been, if the three of them could even call themselves allies anymore, if . . .

Finley. She couldn't bear to think of his gaze leveled at her not with warmth, but with brutal resignation.

"I don't know if it's possible," Isobel said, "but Reid knows more about the tournament than we do—more than anyone. He's the only one who can fix what he's broken."

The daggers winked and spun and inched just a *little* closer to Reid.

"Bri . . ." Finley said warily.

Part of her wanted to do it—end him here the way he'd tried to end them all. But furious or not, Briony knew killing the cursemaker would do no good, however much he might deserve it. She dropped the spell, and the daggers dissipated into common magick. Beside her, Isobel's shoulders sagged with relief.

"And how exactly will we convince Reid to help us?" Finley demanded. "If we threaten to kill him, he'll know we're bluffing. He'll know we need him."

Both Briony and Finley turned to Isobel for an answer, and Briony realized that Isobel's panic had disappeared, replaced by something stony and wary. Briony was pretty sure there were more rings on her hands than there had been a few moments before.

"I have an idea," Isobel said coolly. "If you're both willing to trust me."

"Of course." Briony felt a rush of guilt, even though she wasn't the one who'd cast that truth spell. But hopefully Isobel was pragmatic enough to understand.

Isobel ripped open the nearest grocery bag. A hoard of crystals spilled out, each in the signature MacTavish oval cut. Isobel retrieved a particular rose quartz glowing a deep, impossible red.

Briony gaped. "Is that high magick?"

"That doesn't make sense," Finley said. "We shouldn't be able to see it, unless it's part of the tournament."

"But it is." Isobel clutched the stone tightly. "This is the high magick Reid siphoned from the Cloak. If he helps us . . ." Her voice was laced with a threat. "We might be able to craft a replacement Relic."

"You think that will work?" Finley asked.

"I don't know."

"And if it doesn't?"

Isobel scrutinized him, then Briony. "I don't think you need a truth spell to guess the answer. Now, one of you heal him while I prep the magick."

Briony cast another dubious glance at Reid, whose head had lolled back. He somehow looked both evil and pathetic. "Just because I'm not going to kill him doesn't mean I want to heal him."

"I can do it." Finley moved to the couch, where he tentatively touched Reid's shoulders. Magick shimmered around his hands. "It'll take a few minutes before he's recovered, though."

Briony wondered how Finley could so willingly offer his aid to someone who'd done his best to doom them all. But then again, Finley was practical enough to cast that truth spell on Isobel, to know they needed Reid alive if they wanted any hope at salvation.

If Briony considered how slim a chance that was, about what would happen if this didn't work, she'd fall apart. She shoved those thoughts away and sat beside Isobel.

"Can I help?" Briony asked her.

"You can bring me some dirt," Isobel said.

"Um. Excuse me?"

Isobel frowned at her impatiently. "Well, obviously I need to extract the raw high magick. Since this high magick comes from the tournament, we should be able to see it, and I assume it'll work like any other spellstone—"

"Got it." Briony understood now. The easiest way to nullify a spellstone was to bury it in earth, which dissolved the enchantment inside and sent any residual magick floating back into the air. She hurried to the corner, where an emaciated potted plant drooped beneath an ivy-covered window. When she set it on the kitchen table, Isobel had already fetched a flask to collect the high magick.

"This will work," she grunted, surveying the soil. Then she shoved the stone at Briony. "You bury it. I'll bottle the magick."

Briony nodded, holding the stone carefully. She'd never interacted with high magick like this before. The spellstone radiated power in her hand, giving her a heady, fizzy feeling; she couldn't sense the enchantment inside, like she normally would. She tugged off her other spellrings, lest she accidentally break them, pushed the plant's withered leaves aside, and dug a hole in the dirt with her nubby fingernails.

"I'm sorry about what you've been through," she told Isobel. "And I'm sorry we didn't believe you."

"I killed Alistair, for this. For you," Isobel said darkly. "I know I needed proof from you, but I've proven myself, too."

Briony stiffened, unsure how to answer. She knew she'd failed Isobel. She'd wanted her old friend to join them—only to abandon her by accident.

But she couldn't forget what Finley had said, that Isobel wouldn't hesitate to do what needed to be done. She certainly hadn't hesitated when it came to Alistair. And Briony had the distinct sense that if they couldn't fix this Relic, their tenuous alliance would be *very* short-lived.

"You have," Briony said. *For now,* she didn't add.

"Good," Isobel said. "Now let's hope this works."

Briony pressed the spellstone into the divot she'd made and brushed dirt over it. Isobel's guess had proven right—the moment the crystal was completely covered, fragments of red glitter rose in the air in a hazy, hypnotizing swirl. Throughout her childhood, Briony had dreamed of using high magick after she was crowned winner of the tournament. Even now, wonder surged in her at the sight of it.

She scooted back as Isobel bent over the flowerpot, coaxing the magick into her flask.

"Huh," Isobel murmured, and then, sharply, "*Shit.*"

Briony caught the problem a moment later. Instead of pouring into the flask, the magick was rapidly dissipating, vanishing into thin air.

"What's going on?" Finley called from the couch.

"It's disappearing," Briony answered, panicked. Isobel tried to beckon the remaining high magick into the flask, while Briony scrabbled for anything that might help. Their only shot at repairing the Cloak was slipping away, and Briony didn't know how to stop it. Unless . . .

"If Reid put it in a spellstone before, maybe we can do that again." Briony reached for the nearest pile of MacTavish curses. "We need to find one that's already been made. Something that might help us."

Isobel dropped the flask, shoved the planter aside, and began rifling through the other cursestones. Finley joined them, abandoning Reid on the couch. Briony hastily discarded a fire enchantment, then a gaseous curse, then a stone with a sleek illusory curse inside that felt like touching a nightmare. She shuddered and picked up another—an oath spell. At least class eight.

"I have an idea!" she cried out, brandishing the translucent piece of quartz. Finley shoved a wooden spellboard in front of her. She slapped the stone down in the center. The remaining bits of high magick shimmered in the air, then funneled toward it. A faint red light shone inside the crystal. "Look—it's actually going in!"

"What is it?" Isobel demanded, clutching a fistful of cursestones.

"It's an oath spell—it can bind him to us. Then either he helps us fix this, or he dies, too." As Briony spoke, the high magick's movement quickened into a vortex, whirling into the stone.

"That won't help us make the Relic," Isobel warned.

"We don't have time to try another," Briony said desperately. The light inside the quartz now blazed vibrantly.

"She's right," Finley said.

"Fine," Isobel breathed. "Just do it. Whatever you can."

The last few embers of high magick vanished. All that remained glowed within the stone—their one spell. Their one shot. She reached for it, and it quivered in her hand, a tiny bit of high magick leaking from the crystal.

"We need to cast it. *Now*," she snapped. "I don't think this spellstone can hold it for very long. Is Reid . . ."

"He's stable," Finley said. "I put him under a sleep spell."

Briony gripped the enchantment tightly. "Then let's wake him up."

One of Finley's spellrings flared, and Reid shot up on the couch, letting out a great, tortured gasp. He scrambled back, eyes darting between them like a frightened animal. Blood still trickled down his temple.

"Where am I? What the hell did you do to me?"

"Nothing yet," Briony said, with malice. Then she took a deep breath and cast the curse.

Briony had cast class ten spells before, but nothing compared to wielding high magick. The garnet spellstone in her palm pulsed violently, and Briony's heart pulsed in time with it. Blood rushed in her ears and power thrummed through her, from her toes to her palms to the crown of her head. Scarlet light twined through the room, wrapping around Reid's throat, his neck, his fingers. He hitched his breath, looking as though he might heave.

Then the magickal cords yanked him up from the couch and dragged him toward the pillar, step by tortured step. Briony would've thought he was trying to run if not for the way he strained against them.

"What's going on?" Finley demanded. Red shone inside the pillar's cracks, then along Reid's body, as though high magick had infused his very veins.

"I don't know." It was all Briony could do to maintain her focus. The crystal in her palm burned, nearly too hot to hold. "Reid MacTavish—do you swear to help us, or die trying?"

Reid cried out in pain.

"It's too strong," Isobel shouted. "It's out of control—"

"It is *not* too strong for me," Briony growled. Crimson coiled around Reid's hand and wrenched it toward the pillar.

"What are you doing?" he wailed, and then, "*No!*"

A knife materialized in his fist, its image winking in and out of existence. His hand traced across the stone, and a letter appeared on the pillar—a large, wobbly R.

Briony gasped. Isobel let out a choking sound of disbelief.

"The high magick isn't just binding him to us," Finley said with awe. "It's binding him to the tournament."

Briony held on to the curse with everything she had as Reid's hand continued dragging across the pillar. Each new letter of his name felt like justice. Like retribution.

When he finished, the pillar flared in a massive, blinding burst of light. Briony blinked, eyes watering, as the stone began to rumble. The pulsing of the crystal in her palm finally ebbed, and she collapsed to her knees, spent. The floor quaked beneath her and the walls trembled too, until fragments of weathered stone tumbled to the ground.

A *crack* split through the uproar. Briony's stomach lurched as a fault line spread from Reid's name toward the side of the pillar, joining the three others. She'd cracked it on the wrong side. Come one step closer to killing them all. But there was no undoing it now. Briony could only hope her choice had been worth it.

The light faded. The rumbling stopped. Reid slumped against the pillar, his bonds unraveled. Then he tipped his chin up and glared at Briony.

"What have you done?" he snarled.

"You've always wanted to be part of this story." Briony's voice echoed through the quiet. "Well, now you are."

Reid raised a shaking hand. A small gold ring glinted on his left pinky finger, a red stone embedded in its side.

The ring of a champion.

ALISTAIR LOWE

"Despite rumors circulating about seventeen-year-old Hendry Lowe's death, the police who investigated the crime scene did not uncover any evidence of his passing."

SpellBC News: Wake Up Ilvernath!

Alistair stretched down the collar of his bloodied sweater and grimly examined his cursemark. The Reaper's Embrace now spread as far as his clavicle.

"Al . . ." Hendry's gray eyes bored into him, so gentle and expectant.

Before the tournament began, Hendry had told Alistair that if he wanted to confess his fears, he would listen. But by the time Alistair had been ready to admit his weaknesses, weaknesses the Lowes had methodically tried to burn out of him, Hendry was already gone.

Yet even presented with this precious second chance, Alistair couldn't bring himself to speak. He couldn't admit his own fears about dying to his once dead brother. He couldn't admit he was weak when they both needed his strength more than ever.

A chill wind blew, and Alistair shivered and let go of his sweater. Around them, the Cottage's neglected garden rustled and writhed. Thorny vines had overtaken the plant beds, strangling herbs and flowers until they'd wilted to ashy straw. Mushrooms polyped over the drooping trunk of an apple tree. Stone gargoyles, hunched and grotesque, stood guard along the winding path to the Cottage's front door.

Behind Hendry, Marianne peered at them, sitting primly atop the wrought iron bench in the garden's center. How uncannily she resembled their grandmother, her namesake. As though her specter haunted Alistair through the small girl's body.

"We can't just leave him in there," Hendry said.

At that moment, Gavin Grieve sat at the kitchen table inside the Cottage, along with three cups of earl grey that had probably long gone cold.

"I know." Alistair paced back and forth, brittle autumn leaves cracking beneath his trainers. "I don't trust him, and I don't want another alliance."

"Then why did you bring him here?" Hendry asked pointedly.

"Because if I kill anyone, I could die. That isn't the case for him."

"Exactly, which means he could kill *you*."

"Something's wrong with his magick. You saw it."

"So, again, *why did you bring him here?* Last time you allied with—"

Alistair groaned and kicked a loose stone in frustration. He didn't want to think about Isobel. The wound she'd carved into him was still raw and bleeding. And maybe that was for the best. Better he hated the champion who'd betrayed him than falter when they next faced each other on a battlefield. But he didn't trust his judgment anymore, thanks to her.

"You think I don't know that?" he snapped. "I can't stand Grieve. He's had it out for me before we ever laid eyes on each other, and he's always looking for a fight. But Briony? Isobel? Finley? They're strong, and you and me alone can't—"

The Cottage's front door flung open.

"Get in here!" Gavin shouted. "Something's happening to the pillar!"

Alarmed, Alistair and Hendry ran inside. A horrid scratching noise screeched through the Cottage, raising the hairs on Alistair's arms. Hendry cringed, and Marianne covered her ears.

On the pillar that jutted from the fireplace mantel, amid the endless list of crossed-out names of champions long past, a new name began to etch itself into the stone, each lopsided letter bleeding sanguine light.

Reid MacTavish

Alistair blinked several times in disbelief, but the name never disappeared. It was real, as real as those of any of the other champions.

"No, *no*." Gavin clenched his fists. "This doesn't make sense. Why *him*?"

"The cursemaker?" Alistair recognized the name—he'd probably met the man the day his grandmother had summoned all the spell-makers of Ilvernath to the Lowe estate to present their tithes. But all he recalled of that afternoon was the spellmaker he'd accidentally blinded, Bayard Attwater, bloated and purple like a corpse drowned in wine.

Before anyone could answer, the dishware on the shelves began to rattle. A shriveled potted plant crashed down from the window-sill. And an earsplitting *crack* tore through the air. A gash like a bolt of lightning cracked down the pillar from the tail of the R, slicing through the names of dozens of dead champions.

When the shaking finally ceased, Alistair eased his grip on the table's edge. His mouth was dry. "Another champion. How is that possible?"

"We already knew the tournament rules were breaking," Hendry said.

"Yeah." Alistair gestured at the crack, the fourth on that side. "And now they're breaking *more*."

"The cursemaker caused enough trouble when he *wasn't* a champion," said Gavin darkly.

For the first time in the last hour, Alistair forced himself to look at Gavin directly. It was impossible to do so without reliving their battle.

When Alistair had hesitated, suddenly nauseous at the thought that casting the Demon's Pyre made him no different than his grand-mother.

When Alistair had lain aching and beaten on the forest floor, forced to consider that Gavin Grieve's infuriating face was the last thing he'd ever see. The heinous way the sunlight gleamed off his blond hair. The ridiculous size of him, making Alistair feel small and insignificant even though he was supposed to be the most dangerous champion in the tournament.

When Hendry had stepped in to kill Gavin for him.

Alistair couldn't admit it to his brother, but that moment was the real reason he'd agreed to speak with the other champion. Not the Reaper's Embrace. Not Briony and the others. But the thought of Hendry, who'd already suffered enough, who was *good*, fighting Alistair's battles for him.

"So you know MacTavish?" Alistair asked Gavin.

"We're acquainted," Gavin grumbled.

"Then what do you think this means? Did he do this?"

"Willingly volunteer for the tournament? Even he isn't that sick. The other champions . . . They must've done this somehow, but I have no idea why."

"Which means there are now four champions trying to break the tournament." Hendry cast a wary glance at his brother. However MacTavish had become champion, he was another person to kill. Another chance for the Reaper's Embrace to claim Alistair.

"And three of us," Alistair added, earning an appraising look from Gavin.

"*Four* of us," Marianne corrected indignantly.

"Go outside, Maggot," Alistair said. "The grown-ups are talking."

Marianne propped her hands on her hips. "You're not grown-ups."

"Outside. Now," Alistair snapped, and Marianne stormed to the garden. Then Alistair slid into one of the chairs at the kitchen table and peered into his cold cup of tea. A fly floated on the surface, unmoving. "So, Grieve, what did you do to yourself, to warp your magick like that?"

Gavin claimed the seat across from Alistair, then, with a resigned sigh, rolled up the left sleeve of his shirt, revealing a strange tattoo over his brawny bicep. It was an hourglass, most of its sand piled in the upper bulb. Colors eddied around it, green and violet like a marbled bruise.

The sight was so hideous that Alistair had to refrain from grimacing. Beside him, Hendry's breath hitched.

"When I use spell- or cursestones, I have to fill them with my own life magick," Gavin said. "This tattoo keeps track of how much I've got left."

At first Alistair thought he'd misheard. Life magick, though indisputably real, was the stuff of horror movies, of monsters who manipulated their bodies into something unnatural, of serial killers who sucked the magick from their victims until the corpses resembled withered husks. Not even the Lowes, in all their wicked creativity, dared to dabble in a power so obscene and unstable.

While Hendry recoiled, Alistair found himself leaning forward, oddly curious about this new version of Gavin Grieve. Details stood out to him he hadn't noticed before: the way every angle of his face protruded from sunken cheeks; the lack of warmth in his skin, making the absinthe green of his eyes unnervingly bright in comparison; the veins threaded through his arms and neck bulging like worms.

"You *have* to use life magick?" Alistair asked. "You can't use common magick?"

A muscle in Gavin's jaw clenched. "No."

"That isn't how it works in comic books."

"Well, if it's not that way in *comic books*." Then, bitterly, he added, "The process went wrong. My magick is fucked now, basically."

"Did your family do this to you?"

Gavin scoffed. "They have no idea what I did."

"But you didn't manage it yourself."

If possible, he looked even more tense. "Reid MacTavish did it, but I don't think he wanted to help me. He just needed someone to experiment on."

"Interesting." Alistair's gaze flickered back to the pillar, trying to understand how the cursemaker fit into all of this. Even if MacTavish's intentions had been pure when he'd swooped in to rescue Gavin, no one would accept such an offer unless they were truly desperate.

"Did it hurt?" Hendry asked, which struck Alistair as a useless question.

"It's agony," Gavin answered flatly. Not was—*is*. He wrenched down his sleeve. "Your turn. What are you hiding underneath that glove?"

Once Alistair revealed the Reaper's Embrace to Gavin, his enemy, there was no taking it back. But while he deliberated, Hendry cut in, "Why should he tell you? You're offering us an alliance, but what use do we have for an ally who's mutilated themself?"

Alistair stiffened at the words *us* and *we*. The tournament wasn't their fight—it had always and only been Alistair's.

For several moments, Gavin narrowed his eyes, calculating.

Finally, he lifted his hand, as though examining the few spellrings dotting his knuckles. "I have an arrangement now with a spellmaker in Ilvernath."

Alistair *had* noticed during their fight that Gavin carried a far more impressive arsenal than the last time they'd compared wares. Granted, that time, Alistair had been deeply drunk. But Gavin had seemed little more than a pest then, hardly worth his attention.

Sourly, Alistair realized he'd underestimated the Grieve champion.

"Among us champions deemed to have a chance," Alistair taunted, "we call those sponsorships."

"That's not what it is. He's going to help me fix my magick."

"Can he?" Hendry asked curiously.

"I don't know, but he's going to get more spellmakers to help."

Alistair's chest swelled—a foolish mistake. Judging from the smug glimmer in Gavin's eyes, Gavin had certainly noticed it. He leaned back in his chair, his arms crossed, suddenly comfortable and at ease—the way no Grieve should feel in the presence of a Lowe. But Alistair refused to concede the upper hand.

"And what are they getting from you in return?" he demanded.

"They want me to win," Gavin answered smoothly.

Despite the unlikelihood of anyone betting on a Grieve, Alistair believed him. Even from his brief interaction with Ilvernath's spellmakers, he'd found them spiteful and proud. Of course they'd side with any champion over the Lowe.

"And so you've come to me," Alistair said, "the only other champion playing to win."

A sneer widened across Gavin's face. "Yeah, I need an ally. But you need me more, don't you? That's what you're thinking: If the spellmakers can cure me, maybe they can cure you, too."

Alistair's pride shriveled, because every word Gavin spoke was the truth. Alistair still didn't trust him, didn't like him, but he needed him.

"Well?" Gavin goaded, making Alistair's composure slip a fraction of an inch.

Ignoring the warning in Hendry's eyes, Alistair tilted his head to the side and yanked down the collar of his sweater, exposing the lethal white of the cursemark.

"It's called the Reaper's Embrace," he bit out, careful not to look at it. "With each wrongdoing, it creeps over me more and more. Once I'm fully consumed, I'll die."

Gavin hissed out a breath. "Did your family cast that on you when you . . . ?"

His voice trailed off. He glanced nervously between the two brothers.

He knew.

It shouldn't have stunned Alistair that the world had discovered the crime scene so quickly—no doubt reporters had been hounding the Lowes every day for comment since the tournament began. Already the forensics team would've invaded his home to discover the bodies carelessly strewn across the estate. They'd overturn Alistair's bedroom, and Alistair cringed imagining what conclusions they'd draw from his belongings. His years of study materials. The trove of completed crossword books stacked beneath his bed. A childhood's worth of monster crayon drawings, still in the box at the top of his cupboard.

Dimly, their mother's screams echoed. His composure slipped once more, and a hysterical laugh bubbled from his throat. "Just say it, Grieve."

"So. You really did kill them." Gavin sounded unsurprised.

"We did," Alistair replied.

"We had to," Hendry added quietly. "And no, they're not the ones who cursed him."

As the silence dragged on, Alistair scanned Gavin's face for judgment. But either he hid it well, or there was none to find. Maybe Gavin understood. After all, Gavin had watched him bury the ring that contained the Lamb's Sacrifice, the curse crafted from Hendry's death.

"So who *did* cast the Reaper's Embrace?" Gavin asked.

"Isobel. The *Eclipse* even caught it on camera."

Realization dawned on his face. "The kiss."

Alistair wracked his brain for an explanation that didn't make him sound pathetic, that he had somehow seen it coming, that it'd meant nothing to him.

Thankfully, Hendry spared him from responding. "So using your magick hurts you and makes you weaker. Even if the spellmakers *can* cure you, that's a heavy disadvantage until they do. How will you protect yourself in the meantime, when it's six against one?"

"Gavin isn't—" Alistair started to argue, because no matter what Hendry thought of this alliance, they were in no position to challenge Gavin. But then Hendry continued.

"And with every curse Alistair casts, the Reaper's Embrace consumes more of him. With five champions to slay, that's a huge risk, even with me beside him." Hendry paused, giving Alistair a meaningful look. Hendry wasn't trying to fight this alliance—he was trying to seal it. "Either way, we're outnumbered. But together, we have a chance to make it to the end of the tournament. Especially if your magick is fixed. And if . . . if . . ." He trailed off. Even Hendry Lowe couldn't sugarcoat this last request.

"If your spellmaker friends heal me, too," Alistair finished for him.

Alistair braced himself for that same smug smile. Gavin's magick might've been ruined, but Alistair was far from the formidable ally he'd been looking for. Alistair was desperate. So desperate that, as the silence stretched on, he frantically considered what else he could possibly offer Gavin. The hoard of curses he and Hendry had stolen from the Lowe estate would hardly tempt a champion with the backing of multiple spellmakers in Ilvernath. The Mirror rightfully belonged to Alistair, but it would be worth far more to Gavin if he killed him and claimed it as his own. Flirting had worked for Isobel, and if left with no resort, Alistair might be forced to consider—

"All right," Gavin said.

"That's it?" Alistair asked wildly. "Just like that?"

Gavin's gaze slid from him to Hendry. "Yes. I can't make promises on their behalf, but I'll take you to them. I swear it."

He reached his hand over the table to shake.

Alistair sucked in his breath. This was too easy. There had to be something he was missing—just like he had with Isobel.

"I have another condition," he blurted.

Gavin cocked a brow. "What?"

"You stay here, in my Landmark." The Castle was the Lowes' traditional Landmark of choice, and Alistair had no desire to step foot in it again. Plus, if this *was* a trick, staying here would make it harder for Gavin to murder him in his bed. "There's only two bedrooms, and seeing as Marianne has claimed one all to herself and Hendry and I have the other, you can have the broom cupboard."

Gavin glanced at the crooked door with pursed lips. "Fine."

"Fine," Hendry echoed, looking both relieved and dismayed.

"I . . . All right then." Alistair shook Gavin's hand. "We work together."

"Until the other champions are dead," Gavin finished seriously. His words sounded as much a promise as a threat. And Alistair wondered if Gavin was already picturing it, the final duel between a Lowe and a Grieve. He wondered if such a finale had ever happened in the tournament before.

Hendry stood from the table, smiling victoriously. "I'll reheat our tea."

Alistair jolted awake, his forehead slick with cold sweat. Even as he blinked blearily in the direction of the mucky Cottage window, vestiges of his nightmare still squeezed him in their grasp. A man, with skin and hair consumed by a chalky, unnatural white. Dull eyes that seemed to sink within their sockets. Fangs peeking out over thin lips. A monster.

Him.

Shuddering, he rolled over, then froze when he didn't bump into Hendry beside him. He groped across the sheets and realized with panic that his brother was gone.

"Hendry?" he croaked, pushing himself up. "Hendry?"

An instant later, Hendry materialized on the bed, exactly where he should've been. His eyes were closed. His chest rose and fell gently with each breath.

Alistair lay down and tried to calm himself, but his pulse wouldn't slow. Finally, he gave up and crept out of bed.

It was easier to breathe outside. He slumped against the base of an alder tree at the edge of the Cottage's clearing, his knees pressed against his chest, a wool blanket draped around his shoulders. In his hand, he clutched the Mirror.

Like all the Relics, the Mirror granted its owner three enchantments. The first Alistair had seen used before: a powerful defensive spell, one that reflected curses of any class back at the caster. The second was the ability to spy on the other champions.

And the third was to ask three questions and be shown the truth.

Alistair could think of hundreds of questions to pose. Had he imagined everything between him and Isobel? Had he been wrong to kill Elionor, even if she'd tried to kill him? If it had been justice to slay the Lowes, why had the Reaper's Embrace crawled so much farther up his skin?

But since his handshake with Gavin a few hours before, a treacherous thought needled in the back of his mind, one that threatened to undo him.

If the spellmakers could find a way to heal Alistair, could they heal Hendry, too?

The prospect kindled a hope in him so fervent that it burned. If the magick that sustained Hendry could be untangled from the tournament's power, everything would change. Alistair would find the other champions again, to see if they could repair all that had broken between them. They might not succeed in destroying the curse, but if Alistair did die, he wouldn't do so at the hands of a ruthless ally of necessity, of the Reaper's Embrace, of the perils of battle. He would die knowing that despite where he'd come from and what the world thought of him, he'd fought for something good.

His hand trembled as he lifted the Mirror higher. His Lowe gray eyes glistened.

"Can Hendry survive without me winning the tournament?" he rasped.

The Mirror shrouded in fog, then, gradually, it dissipated, revealing nothing but blackness. The ruby glow of one of its spellstones dimmed, his query spent.

Alistair fruitlessly, foolishly waited several heartbeats more. When nothing changed, a low, wounded howl erupted from his throat. He slammed his fist against the earth. He kicked out at nothing. He furiously wiped his tears against the sleeve of his sweater, but his lips still tasted of salt and snot.

After minutes passed and his pain had barely abated, he lifted the Mirror a second time.

"Show me Isobel Macaslan."

The glass rippled, and an image appeared: a shape almost like a face, distorted in a red haze. Isobel was protected behind a Landmark's wards.

And yet, he stared anyway, letting his malice swell and fester. Yes, she had tricked him, but this pain was his fault. Because despite all the horrific training he'd endured, his heart remained a soft and brittle thing. He'd let her hurt him. And his weakness would get him and Hendry killed.

Alistair had thought he was done with his family when he'd

driven a stake through his grandmother's heart. But he was wrong. If he was to win and save them both, he couldn't repeat his old mistakes. He couldn't squabble with his paltry conscience. He couldn't delude himself into caring for another champion, an enemy. He couldn't poison himself with hope that he would ever become something more than the villain the Lowes had raised him to be.

Winning would demand all the cruelty he had.

"Grins like goblins," he whispered to himself. "Pale as plague and silent as spirits."

He needed to carve those words into himself, just like he'd carved his name into the Champions Pillar. And though the thrill they'd once stirred in him had faded, it hadn't disappeared entirely. Likely, Alistair had been kidding himself that it ever would.

"They'll tear your throat and drink your soul," he finished, and he felt—almost—right.

A twig snapped, and Alistair straightened, a cursering shining on his thumb.

"Why are you out here alone?" Hendry asked, shivering and hugging his arms to himself.

"I've been thinking." Alistair's voice betrayed none of his emotion from moments before, and he thanked the dark of night for hiding his swollen, bloodshot eyes. He didn't want Hendry to worry about him.

"So have I." Hendry sat cross-legged beside him and leaned back against the same tree. "What happens if the spellmakers can't cure you?"

"Ilvernath has some of the best spellmakers in the world. If anyone can—"

"That's still an if. What happens if you and Gavin are the last champions left, but you're still cursed? Killing him could kill you."

"We don't know that," Alistair said quietly. "Not for sure. And I thought you changed your mind about the alliance. Inside, you made it seem—"

"I still don't like it, but curing you is the best chance we have. I see that. But if it doesn't work, you and Gavin will eventually have to turn on each other, and I . . ." Hendry plucked a dried leaf from the ground and twisted its stem between his fingers. "I want you to know that I'll do it. I'll do it for you."

Alistair turned to him in horror. "No, absolutely not."

"Why?" Hendry challenged.

Because Hendry wasn't like Alistair. He dozed through studies and seized every opportunity to leave the Lowe estate, to dream of elsewhere. He had sunlight smiles and strawberry seed freckles. He got drunk on a single beer. He cried during happy endings, and it had never once occurred to him that they wouldn't get one. And Alistair couldn't bear it if he changed.

But instead of voicing all that, Alistair managed only to grunt, "You're no good at curses." Hendry's specialty had always been healing spells.

"I saved you today, didn't I?"

"Yeah, but—"

"I'm capable. I know I don't have your training, but I'm not weak—no matter what our family seemed to think. If I can't fight for you, then I really was worth more to you dead than alive."

"That's *not* what I meant," Alistair said sharply.

"Then what did you mean, Al?"

"I just meant— You're not— You're not killing anyone."

Hendry's voice turned quiet and grave. "I already have."

Unbidden, Alistair's memory of the prior day resurfaced in stark, gruesome clarity. The two of them creeping toward the bedroom door. Hendry lunging ahead of him to grasp the knob first, leaving Alistair to watch silently as his brother cast the curse that killed their mother, as he slit her throat just like she'd slit his. But it hadn't been her scream that made his hair stand on end; it'd been Hendry, his hands bloodied, his expression twisted into one Alistair didn't recognize.

He wanted to tell himself that had been different—that was vengeance, justice. But he knew that wasn't true.

"Don't make me ask you to fight my battles for me," Alistair pleaded. "If I'd been a proper Lowe champion from the start, the tournament might already be over by now, and you and I would be . . ." He swallowed. "Somewhere else. Anywhere else."

Hendry tilted his head until it touched his. "You know that what they did to me wasn't your fault, right?" Alistair didn't answer. "Last generation, Aunt Alphina murdered all the other champions in four days. You think *she* wasn't a proper Lowe champion?"

"She used the Lamb's Sacrifice," Alistair muttered. "So I guess we'll never know."

"Grandma would never have been satisfied. She started your training when you were seven, and she never stopped testing you till the end. When I think of what she put you through, what you've already gone through in the tournament, I'm so angry that I . . ." Hendry squeezed the leaf in his fist, letting it crumble. "In some ways, I'm grateful that I'm here with you. I never wanted you to fight alone."

Alistair didn't trust himself to speak. He merely glared at the sunrise bleeding across the horizon.

Then Hendry lifted his hand and opened his fist before Alistair's mouth. "A wish."

Like a sigh, Alistair's anger diminished. Even if their family had changed them both in irreparable ways, the core of who they were remained: brothers.

Alistair blew, wishing for the impossible—wishing for forever. The crumbled leaf bits scattered.

He leaned his head on Hendry's shoulder. "We'll need to be careful. The Grieve is smarter than you'd think."

"I know. I don't like the way he looks at you."

"Like he wants to kill me? I'm used to it."

"Like he despises you, and not just because you're both champions."

Alistair laughed mirthlessly. "Trust me when I say that's better than the alternative."

Hendry fiddled with the curserings on his hands, raided from the Lowe estate, every bit as lethal as Alistair's. "Will you be okay when Isobel is gone?"

"Yes," Alistair said, though it was true only because it had to be.

"What about the others? You were helping them before."

"They don't matter to me. But slaying them won't be easy, especially if they have MacTavish. It doesn't make sense to rush into a fight without the Grieve and I trying to heal ourselves first." As he spoke, Alistair was surprised to find it felt good to strategize—normal, grounding. The role of champion fit him as it always had. "Isobel currently has the Cloak, but knowing their plans, they'll pair it with its Landmark soon—that's good. Let them destroy their weapons for us. It will only make it easier to strike."

"And then? With the Grieve?"

"If he shows any sign of betrayal, kill him."

Alistair stood and stretched out his hand to his brother, who took it and clambered to his feet. Side by side, their shadows stretched long and gaunt across the grass. In the shade cast by the alder behind them, the topmost branches reached over their heads, crowning them in twin pairs of pointed, briary horns.

"And if all goes to plan," Alistair added, "I'll kill him myself."

ISOBEL MACASLAN

"I'm not surprised that bets for Isobel have plummeted. Kissing a boy during the tournament? Really? That girl needs to sort out her priorities."

Call-in on *Champion Confidential*, WKL Radio

The next morning, Isobel dragged a chair across from Reid and straddled it, mimicking his own position two days before in his curseshop, when he'd wielded all the power and she'd had none.

"We're in a predicament," she started coolly, her voice amplified by the stone walls of the Tower's cramped bedroom. "We can't safely dismantle the tournament without the Cloak, but you destroyed it."

Reid sat on the edge of the stiff, hay-stuffed mattress, glaring at the Warden's Shackles that encircled his wrists. His crimson champion's ring glittered on his clenched hand.

"You told me it was only a matter of time until the tournament collapses and takes all of us with it, which means the clock is ticking. You and I need to find a solution, otherwise . . ."

Reid grunted something unintelligible.

"I'm sorry. I didn't catch that."

"I said there *is* no solution. Without the Cloak, you're all . . ." His voice hitched. "*We're* all doomed."

Isobel scrutinized the brown blood still crusted along the side of his neck, the defeated hunch in his shoulders. But after everything he'd done to her, she had no pity to spare him.

"We'll see about that." She laid her hand over his. He jerked away, but it was too late. The white mark of the Divining Kiss already stained his skin, in the shape of her own lips.

Isobel braced herself as she waited for the spell to take effect. The last time she'd peered into Reid MacTavish's thoughts, she'd found his mind a disturbing place.

But as the seconds trickled past, she realized the enchantment hadn't worked.

"What's going on?" she demanded. "The Divining Kiss never fails. Three days ago, I saw your—"

"None of your attempts will work, no matter how hard you try."

"I don't understand. We removed all your spellstones. How are you blocking me out?"

When Reid didn't answer, still didn't even look at her, Isobel groaned with frustration and leapt out of her chair. Through the trio of narrow lancet windows, outside the Tower's wards, an intrusion of reporters thronged like cockroaches. The fall of the inner Blood Veil had provided some benefits—namely, access to new enchantments and resources—but the champions had forfeited their privacy in return.

She drummed her fingertips against one of the windowsills. She didn't like to rely on truth spells, as, if used often enough, their side effects were far more dangerous than the simple Divining Kiss. But without another recourse, she faced him and cast a Truth or Treachery. The amethyst ring on her right index finger glowed, and a hazy silver line encircled Reid's throat.

"Tell me how to repair the Cloak," she commanded.

"That won't work either," he answered flatly. "And I already told you—I don't know how."

Isobel frantically wracked her brain. Why would both telepathic and compulsion spells fail on him? When she chose to save herself and let Reid destroy the Cloak, she'd staked all her hope on the high magick he'd stolen. But now that magick was gone. And without it, without *him*, she had no idea how they'd fix what he'd broken.

"I don't believe that," she snapped, unable to hide her desperation. "You know more about the tournament than anyone, so you—"

"Do you honestly think I'd lie now?" He finally dragged his liner-smeared, bloodshot gaze up to her. "I'm tied to a sinking ship, and I can't . . . I can't . . ." He yanked uselessly at the champion's ring, even though he knew as well as Isobel that it wouldn't budge. "Believe me, I want to live as much as you do."

"Do you?" Isobel paced back and forth, reaching instinctively for her mother's locket, only to remember she'd abandoned it in Reid's shop. "Because I know everything you've done to make the tournament collapse. All your secret research and planning. The kidnapping. The lies. Your bedroom looks like a serial killer's den. Your house is sad and creepy and empty. As far as I'm concerned, you're a freak. Why shouldn't I believe you'd die for a cause you've clearly spent years obsessing over?"

Reid held his head in his hands. "Maybe I'm just a coward, all right?" He spoke so vehemently that spittle sprayed onto the ground. He seethed and restlessly jerked his leg, all dramatics. It was too much. She didn't believe it for a second.

"Maybe you are, but I'm not convinced you're telling the truth."

"Oh, you have me all figured out, do you? You've been in my house and worn my clothes, so you must, right?" Isobel stiffened as Reid glanced up, a feral glint in his eyes. He took in her new, athletic outfit, borrowed from Briony, then he smiled ruthlessly. "How's the Roach's Armor treating you? You look terrible, princess."

Isobel had avoided mirrors since yesterday, but with the curse's effects compounded by an entire night tossing and turning without sleep, she probably looked worse than terrible. Whenever she'd come close to drifting off, she kept imagining what her parents would say if they saw her.

Honora Jackson, the fashionable free spirit who owned one of Ilvernath's trendiest spellshops, would cup her daughter's cold face and sob. *Oh, Isobel, my sweetheart. What have you done to yourself?*

Her father, meanwhile, would sneer, *Don't blame me for not telling you the price of the Roach's Armor. What, would you have chosen death instead?*

Isobel banished them from her mind. Panicked or not, she couldn't relinquish the upper hand. There were more ways to pry answers out of someone than enchantments, and after everything she'd sacrificed for Briony's plan, Isobel wasn't above threats.

"If I were you, I'd be more careful choosing my words. You're only alive because you're useful." She pressed her knuckles against the side of his neck, letting the sharp points of her curserings bite into his skin. He flinched and craned his jaw up, whimpering. The bed beneath him creaked as he tried to lean away from her. "Would you rather I kill you now?"

"No, but I—"

"I don't want to hear you tell me it's impossible. This is *your* mess. You're lucky I'm giving you the chance to fix it. So *will* you?"

Reid grasped at her wrist, prying her hand away from his throat. "I'll fix it. I'll fix it." He clutched her so tightly, Isobel felt his pulse drumming against her skin.

The sensation startled her, and she wrenched away from him.

"Y-yes, you will," she forced out. Then she stalked toward the door, wondering if she could truly rest her hope on a self-proclaimed coward.

She had never been one for hope.

As she walked into the stairwell, Briony yelped from a few steps below.

Isobel frowned. "How long have you been standing there?"

"Not long," Briony squeaked, eyeing her warily.

Isobel already knew that Briony and Finley didn't wholly trust her—the truth spell they'd cast on her had proven that. And though it'd hurt to know that she couldn't rely on her old friend, it was the wake-up call she needed. They weren't *friends*; they were allies. If Reid failed and this all went to shit, Briony and Finley would choose each other, and Isobel would be alone.

"Why are you looking at me like that?" Isobel asked sharply. "I had to threaten him. Or would you rather I'd said please?" How very like Briony to ride in on her Thorburn high horse.

"What? After what he did to you—to all of us—you can torture him for all I care." Briony chewed on her bottom lip. "I only came to tell you that Finley wants to ask you something. It was his idea, but . . . I don't think it's a bad one. I think you should hear him out."

"Why?" Isobel asked nervously.

"It could really help us. Come on—he's upstairs. He'll explain it better than me."

Briony brushed past her, and Isobel took her time following. Shakily, she reached into her pocket and slipped on several more defensive spells. Hope might not be lost yet, but if this was a trick, she needed to be prepared. She didn't want to take Briony and Finley down, but she could, if she had to. After what she'd done to Alistair, there was nothing she wasn't capable of.

On the top floor, Finley waited with his palms braced against the strategy table. As lifelong classmates and Briony's ex, Isobel knew him well enough. But his typical easy charm and golden boy aura had vanished since the tournament began, replaced by a firm, calculating set to his brow. She didn't blame him for changing. Without her perfectly styled hair and ever present lip gloss, he probably barely recognized her either.

"Any luck with MacTavish?" he asked.

"I didn't get much out of him. He's resistant to mental spells. Compulsion ones, too."

"What? How?"

"I don't know, but I threatened him into agreeing to try to fix the Cloak, which means someone will probably have to go to his store and get some supplies. Research materials. Grimoires . . ." Isobel's mind drifted to the back room of his shop, her prison cell, and she shuddered.

"It doesn't have to be you," Finley told her gently.

"Oh, um. Thanks." She didn't know how to react to kindness from a boy she'd thought about killing moments prior. "What did you want to ask me?"

"Right. So, all those reporters outside? We think you should do an interview with them."

"*What?*" Isobel shot Briony an accusatory look, who tugged anxiously on her braid. She could've warned her.

"We've been thinking a lot about this, and we don't need to break the curse by ourselves. Not anymore. If we're transparent about our plan, maybe Ilvernath can help us. Maybe the other families will offer up the stories about their own Relics and Landmarks."

Isobel cringed at his palpable optimism. There was nothing handsome, likable Finley Blair hadn't been given the moment he'd asked for it. "And we can't just ask them privately?"

"Not all of them will help us—not without a little public pressure."

"Let's say Ilvernath does help us, for argument's sake. None of it matters with the Cloak destroyed."

"I know, but you said Reid's on it, right? So this is what we'll do in the meantime. We'll find more answers."

"We'd do the interview ourselves," Briony said apologetically, "but, well, you've been the face of the Slaughter Seven for nearly a year—"

"Yeah, because of *you*!" Isobel growled, and Briony at least had the decency to cringe. "I never asked to be famous. I never asked for any of this!"

"We know, we know," Finley said hastily. "And we're going to be part of this interview, too, but it makes sense for you to lead it. The world knows you better. And you've heard the reporters outside. They all want to hear about the kiss with Alistair."

Though Isobel couldn't fault their logic, she felt acutely that they'd ganged up on her, plotted behind closed doors. The thought of donning a slimy, false smile to match her father's made her ill.

"N-no," she stammered. "You want to give them a story? How about *you* kiss each other in front of the whole city?"

Briony flushed. "I— That wouldn't be . . ."

Finley cleared his throat awkwardly. "We're sorry to ask, we really are. But it could help us a lot, and we'll support you the whole time. The three of us are a team. And we're going to end this—together."

Isobel hated how soothing and sincere his voice sounded, how easily it wormed its way inside her. Maybe she'd been wrong about them. Maybe she was the only one already planning her escape in case of the worst. She didn't know what that made her.

"Fine," she gritted out. "I'll do it."

Thirty minutes later, Isobel had no choice but to examine herself in the mirror.

"Don't worry about it. You're in a death tournament." Briony sat atop the toilet lid as though they were primping for a school dance. "It shouldn't matter how you look."

That was easy for Briony to say, with her silky straight hair that didn't frizz at the mere suggestion of rain, with her unblemished cheeks that didn't need concealer for every spot and scar.

"Yeah, well, remember that tabloid that ran a story on my weight last summer? Because I do." Isobel pinched her cheeks, then grimaced as no pink flushed beneath her pallor.

Briony fiddled with her spellrings. "I'm really sorry about that. About all this."

"You don't need to keep apologizing."

"I feel like I do."

"Well, don't. I'm just being..." Vain, probably. Because even though Isobel didn't doubt a gossip column would gleefully rail on how abysmal she looked, her own mind was harsher than some disillusioned journalism major could ever be. Being pretty shouldn't have mattered to her, but it had, and now, because of the Roach's Armor, she barely recognized herself. She felt broken, disgusting, dead. The sight of her reflection made her want to claw off her own skin.

But she didn't tell Briony that her father had lied to her about the true nature of the Macaslans' traditional enchantment. Isobel had spent the past year defending her family to the world, and she was ashamed by how right everyone had been—everyone but her.

So she changed the subject. "What am I supposed to tell them about Alistair that doesn't make me look terrible?"

"He cursed you first," Briony pointed out.

"Sure, but I'll live, and he won't. We're supposed to be the good guys, aren't we?"

Briony paused, then: "Maybe we don't tell them you cursed him. I mean, who are they going to believe—the Lowe champion, or you?"

And so, resolved to do just that, ten minutes later Isobel opened the Tower door.

All at once, the reporters stirred and skittered, leaping up from the grass and shouting at each other through their tents. Isobel hadn't even taken a step before the first camera flashed.

"Isobel!" one of them called. "What made you decide to ally with the Blair and Thorburn champions?"

"What happened between you and Reid MacTavish?"

"Is the Lowe champion here as well?"

Isobel grimaced and reminded herself that she could do this. She'd sat for countless interviews as Ilvernath's murderous starlet, and though she hadn't asked for her fame, after a while, she *had* grown to like it. Her friends and classmates might've abandoned her in disgust, but at least the world loved her. And the Macaslans, once distant relatives, had welcomed her in a way they never had before. Even when the press felt incessant, even when she found graffiti smeared across the windows of her mother's spellshop, it hadn't been all bad.

She marched across the rocky hillside, Briony and Finley trailing behind her.

"I'm here to offer an interview to the *Ilvernath Eclipse*," she announced. Finley had selected the newspaper for its legitimate reporting and local familiarity. "Their reporter may step through the wards."

Amid a buzzing of chatter and competitive offers, a young man in an ill-fitting button-up and slacks raised his hand.

"Th-that's me," he stammered, as though he wasn't quite sure himself. He bumbled toward them and squeezed his eyes shut as he passed through the hazy red wards. Isobel's forced smile wavered more and more with each step he took. Despite the brisk weather, his ruddy forehead glistened with sweat, and he gawked as he examined her up close. "You look . . . I mean . . . You want to do an interview?"

"We have some information about the curse that we'd like to share with the city," Isobel said. "Can you make sure it's printed tomorrow morning?"

"I don't really have control over that, but I'm sure my editor will say yes."

"Great. This is Finley Blair and Briony Thorburn. And I'm—"

"Oh, I know who you all are, obviously. I'd be surprised if anyone didn't at this point, especially you. Your family took out ads in our paper to sell official Isobel Macaslan merchandise. They're very, well, supportive, I guess."

Isobel tried hard not to cringe, picturing some kind of heinous foam finger with her name on it. No doubt her father made a nice profit off it all. "That's . . . nice."

"This conversation is off the record until we say it isn't," Briony cut in. Isobel shot her an irritated look. She shouldn't just blurt things out because she thought they sounded official.

"How about we talk inside?" Finley suggested smoothly.

The three of them led him into the Tower, where they'd made an effort to tidy up the ground floor. He gaped at the pillar, then stumbled forward when Isobel gestured for him to sit with them at the table.

"What is your name?" Isobel asked him.

"I'm Ed Caulfield." He pulled a notepad out from his briefcase. "So who exactly, um, resides here?"

"The three of us," Isobel answered. "And Reid MacTavish, who kindly offered his help. He'd join us, but he's caught up in his research at the moment."

"His name appeared on the Champions Pillar yesterday," Ed ventured. "Does that mean he's a champion now, too? Did he volunteer, or—"

"We'd like to start by making a statement, on the record," Finley said.

"Oh. Oh yes, sure, whatever you like. But will I get to ask questions after that? If not, I understand. But I know my editor will want—"

"You can ask your questions later," Isobel assured him. Then she reached for the words that she, Briony, and Finley had rehearsed. "The three of us don't want to win the tournament. We want to end it. For good."

Ed's eyes widened, and he hurriedly scribbled onto his notepad. "You want to break the curse?"

"Yes, and we have proof that it can be done." Isobel explained Briony and Finley's theory and how they'd already united the Sword and the Cave.

Ed's gaze darted wildly between them. "If you really did manage that, then where are the other champions? Why wouldn't your boyfriend help you?"

"Alistair Lowe is *not* my boyfriend," Isobel said, a little too sharply. If there was one rule her father had drilled into her about publicity, it was the importance of being liked.

"Oh, I didn't mean . . . Would you like to publicly comment on the status of your relationship, then?"

Isobel steeled herself—then forced out a dramatic sigh. "I . . . I don't know. I always knew he was dangerous, but when we were allied, I guess I let him trick me, or I let the pressure of the tournament get to my head. I thought he cared about me and—I'm sorry. This is so humiliating."

For the first time, Ed seemed to realize he was the only adult in the room. He once again took in Isobel's frightful appearance, his nerves slackening into pity. "No, it's all right," he told her kindly. "Go on."

"The truth is, I was wrong. I kissed him, but h-he cursed me." She added a faux wobble to her voice. "I'm lucky to be alive."

"Wow, that's . . . Well, that's dreadful, indeed." He shifted awkwardly in his chair. "But I must say, that doesn't sound like you. Your father claimed on *Wake Up Ilvernath!* that the kiss was strategic."

Originally, Isobel had been horrified by that interview. Her father had so proudly twisted her character into someone conniving and ruthless, but now, hearing Ed state it so plainly, she realized her father was right. Brokenhearted or not, the kiss *had* been a ploy. Romance, a tactic. Even now, she smiled his same false smile, lying through her teeth.

What right did she have to be ashamed of her family? She was a Macaslan, through and through.

"They say love makes fools of us all, right?" she said weakly.

Isobel knew she had him fooled when Ed flashed her a rosy, sympathetic smile. "That it does, that it does. And I can't imagine how this must all feel to you now, after the murder of the Lowe family."

Isobel, Briony, and Finley jolted.

"What? What murder?" Isobel rasped.

Ed stared at them blankly. "Well, the entire Lowe family was found dead in their home two days ago, except for the youngest kid, who's gone missing. The Ilvernath PD already questioned some of the other families—it was all in yesterday's edition."

"Holy shit," Briony murmured.

"Right now, the prime suspect is Alistair Lowe. You three wouldn't happen to know anything about that, would you?"

"No," Isobel whispered, shocked. After what the Lowes had done to Hendry, of course Hendry and Alistair would want revenge. But the idea that they'd slaughtered their own family . . . it was unspeakable, even for them.

Finley cleared his throat. "We'd like you to print a message from us to the other families. We need to ask them if they have any stories about favored Relics or Landmarks buried in their histories."

"Tell them to reach out to us," Briony said boldly. "We know they'll want to help."

Ed took in Briony with interest. "You're the Thorburn champion, the one who took her sister's place at the last minute. Your family said that Innes caved under the pressure. How does it feel to be in her spot?"

Briony withered in an instant at his words. "It doesn't feel good, obviously. None of this is right, or good, or okay. That's why we need to end it."

"First you save your sister, then you save everyone," Ed remarked, sounding impressed. "That's quite the story." He scribbled eagerly onto his notepad.

"Well, when you put it like that, I guess—"

"And Isobel was your friend before this, and Finley your boyfriend. That makes you the glue of this little team, doesn't it?"

Briony seemed to shrink several centimeters as she slumped in her chair. "I . . . I think we should stay focused on the tournament's curse. That's what's important."

"Mhm, mhm." Ed barely paused his scrawling as he flipped to a fresh page of his notepad. "There's a lot of speculation running throughout the city—throughout everywhere, really. So the inner Blood Veil has fallen. Is that because of this tournament-breaking business?"

"Since Briony and I destroyed the Cave with the Sword, the tournament has been thrown off kilter," Finley told him.

Ed nodded, then he paused for several moments, seeming lost in thought as he scanned his sloppy writing. When he finally met their eyes, resolve flushed across his cheeks. "This has all been tremendous—really, I can't thank you enough for this opportunity. This is a headline story we have here. But there's just one more question that I know my editor would want me to ask—which champion killed Carbry Darrow?"

All three of them stiffened. Briony began to speak, but Isobel cut in. "Gavin Grieve." If Briony objected to the lie, she didn't voice it. They needed the other families to help them, including the families of the champions already slain. And when it came down to it, the Darrows were more influential than the Grieves.

Ed's brow furrowed with concern. "Would you consider him a threat to your mission?"

"Absolutely," Isobel replied. "The curse *can* be broken, and we've provided proof. Any champions who claim otherwise are disregarding the evidence because they'd rather there be bloodshed."

"You're risking everything for this," Ed said with awe. "What happens if time runs out, and you've failed?"

Now it was Briony who cut in, "Then all of us die, no one wins the high magick, and our families—and the whole world—have to do this again in twenty years. And it keeps going, generation after generation. That's why we need to stop it."

"And you believe you can?"

"Yes, of course. All of us do."

Isobel swallowed but held her tongue.

Ed's face broke into a smile. "My editors will *love* this. Thanks very much for your time, Miss Thorburn, Miss Macaslan, Mr. Blair." He tucked his notebook away and earnestly shook each of their hands, as though he were thanking them for their selflessness, as though he truly regarded them as heroes. "And for the record—I'd like to personally wish you good luck. I think you're all very noble, for what you're trying to do."

GAVIN GRIEVE

Given that the mystery figure sighted at the Champions Pillar matched Hendry Lowe's description, the rumors circulating about his death are clearly sensationalized.

Glamour Inquirer, "Three Bodies Discovered
at the Lowe Estate"

Walsh Spellmaking Emporium reminded Gavin of a museum, with its polished tile floor and carefully curated selection of spellwork displays. Enchantments winked coyly from wall-mounted shelves and glimmered strategically on rotating exhibition tables, showing off every angle of their perfectly cut stones. Walsh's assistant had told the three boys the spellmakers weren't ready to meet with them yet, so they roamed aimlessly, peering into glass cases at each increasingly expensive arrangement.

Alistair frowned at a cluster of class seven defensive spells nestled on a plush cushion. "What do you think the meeting will be like?"

"Depends on how well they remember you," Hendry said darkly.

Alistair pursed his lips. "It's not like that day is easy to forget."

Gavin's stomach, already knotted with nerves, twisted tighter. He'd known going into this agreement that Alistair and Hendry would be a tough sell—the last time Alistair had met with Ilvernath's spellmakers, he'd blinded one of them, a headline that had seemed atrocious at the time. Next to the Lowe massacre, it now seemed almost quaint.

What he *hadn't* known was that the spellmakers had gone so far as to sabotage Alistair's enchantments for the tournament. Learning that had made Gavin respect the spellmakers all the more . . . and made him seriously regret agreeing to bring the Lowe boys along, leaving Marianne to play gargoyle tea party all by herself. But if

Hendry really did hold the key to curing him, it was worth the risk. It was even worth sleeping in a broom cupboard and putting up with Marianne's creepy antics.

"All we need to do is convince them we're worth helping," Hendry said.

"We are," Alistair said firmly, as though trying to convince himself.

A *crash* rang out from across the room, and Alistair jolted back as the shards of a display case he'd knocked into scattered across the floor. A mournful alarm began to blare.

"How did you even *do* that?" Gavin asked incredulously. "Now you'll really get us kicked out."

"He's clumsy," Hendry volunteered, while Alistair stepped awkwardly away from the carnage. The wooden door behind the sales counter slammed open, and Walsh's assistant hurried out. Gavin recognized her vaguely—she'd been a few years ahead of him in school.

"Sorry about that," Hendry said, but she didn't respond. Instead, she hastily shut off the alarm and set about mending the glass.

"You should probably let me do most of the talking," Gavin said flatly. "I'll— I don't know—charm them or something."

Alistair shot him a dubious look. "*You?* Charm them? I'll believe it when I see it."

"Mr. Walsh and his associates are r-ready for you," Walsh's assistant stammered. "But you'll need to surrender your spellwork first. And if you miss anything, they'll know."

When the assistant finished tidying up, she escorted them to the counter, her gaze darting nervously between Alistair and Hendry as the three of them piled various cursestones into a basket. Once they'd finished, she set the basket atop the counter, beside a stand of the most recent issue of the *Glamour Inquirer*. Its front-page headlines promised a deep dive into the Lowe family murders.

Gavin grimaced and turned away, then caught Hendry staring at it, too.

"Do you think we should read it?" Hendry whispered.

"No," Alistair said tightly. "I don't."

"They've dropped the wards. You can head inside," the assistant squeaked, gesturing at the door before fleeing toward the spellwork displays.

Gavin squared his shoulders and stepped into the lead.

"You asked me to bring you here," he hissed at the Lowe brothers as he twisted the doorknob. "So don't mess this up."

The spellshop felt like a museum open to the public, but the room beyond it had the air of a private collection, curated only for those powerful enough to be welcomed inside. Paneled mahogany walls stretched up to a domed ceiling where Ilvernath's muted sunlight filtered through a mosaic of stained glass. Gavin's trainers sank into plush rugs piled over weathered stone as he breathed in the scent of leather and something crisp and biting, like a breath of bracing winter air.

A display case to his left contained a spellstone embedded in an enchanted, unmelting block of ice. Another held a statue of a hand, each knuckle studded with an identical yellow crystal. And a taxidermied owl with glimmering ruby spellstones for eyes was perched above the hearth.

But Gavin's focus was reserved not for the curiosities, but the people who'd clearly selected them. Three spellmakers sat beside a glimmering green fire—a clever illusion that blew specks of common magick into the air like smoke. Each of them was among the most influential people in Ilvernath; combined, they were as powerful as any of the seven families.

"Grieve." Walsh rose to his feet. The last time Gavin had seen him, he'd been covered in sweat and grime. Now he wore a fresh suit and a full arsenal of spellrings. A glass of amber liquid swirled in his hand. "How kind of you to join us."

All posture, all performance. Yet again, he was behaving as though this were a business transaction instead of a deal he'd struck under duress.

"How kind of you to honor the terms of our agreement, you mean?" Gavin shot back.

Walsh tensed. One of the spellmakers beside him chuckled—a middle-aged woman wearing deep purple lipstick that matched the long folds of her dress, with dark brown skin and box braids piled in an elaborate knot atop her head. She lifted her own glass to Gavin, as though toasting him.

"I never thought I'd see the day," she said. "A Grieve outsmarting a member of the Ilvernath Spellmaking Society board. I'm Diana

Aleshire—we knew as soon as Walsh told us about you that we simply had to meet you."

"It's nice to meet you, too," Gavin said. For his entire life, these people had ignored him. Now they were treating him as an honored guest.

"Liam Calhoun," boomed the man beside her, who wore so many spellrings, Gavin had no idea how he could bend his fingers. He was burly and broad, fair-skinned, with a thick brown beard, and even sitting, he towered over his two colleagues. "Aleshire's right. This was far too interesting to pass up. Although I'm not sure why we're introducing ourselves when we've already had such a *memorable* introduction."

This was directed not to Gavin, but to the Lowe brothers, who both lingered behind him.

"Hello." Hendry stepped forward carefully. High magick lagged in the air behind him as he moved, and the spellmakers all leaned forward, rapt with attention. Calhoun looked intrigued. Aleshire, perturbed. But Walsh . . . for the briefest moment, before the spellmaker's face relaxed into polite curiosity, Gavin swore he saw a flash of hunger.

"We're here in good faith," Alistair added quietly. "We don't want any trouble."

"Oh, there won't be any trouble here at all." Walsh closed the distance between them. Alistair stiffened at his approach. "I daresay this room is just as warded as any Landmark."

"You'd know, wouldn't you?" Calhoun joked. Walsh's hand clenched tightly around his glass.

"Well, now that we've all been introduced," Gavin said. "Should we get started?"

"Just a moment." Walsh set his glass on the adjacent end table. "There's something we need to clear up. Since our last encounter, I've been informed that some of the other competitors are trying to end this tournament for good."

Gavin had no idea how he'd found out. He gulped and tried to look like an appropriately intimidating, victorious champion. He realized a moment later that he was mimicking Alistair's stance yesterday as the other boy threatened him at the edge of the Cottage's wards.

"That shouldn't matter," Gavin said coldly. "You swore to help me win this tournament, to the best of your ability."

"But *we* didn't swear anything," said Aleshire. The owl's ruby eyes shimmered ominously above her head. "It's true that we're intrigued by the chance to study your life magick. But if the tournament ends forever, then high magick would return to all of Ilvernath. Which would obviously be quite beneficial to us. So why should we help you win instead?"

He vowed silently to convince them. He hadn't come this far to be turned away.

One of Aleshire's spellrings shone. A truth spell took hold of Gavin, sending a light, heady feeling spreading through his chest.

"There's information the other champions are conveniently ignoring," he said, then went into the explanation he'd already given Alistair and Hendry. The truth spell tugged at him further, but he refused to reveal the possibility that the tournament could also break and leave all of them dead, lest the spellmakers decide *that* was their preferred outcome to this situation. She'd asked why they should help them, not why they *shouldn't*.

"What about MacTavish?" asked Calhoun. "How the hell did he get his name on that pillar?"

"We have absolutely no idea."

The truth spell faded. Gavin rubbed at his throat, relieved.

"Thank you for your candor," Aleshire said, as though he'd offered it freely.

"So?" Gavin asked. "Will you help us or not?"

The two spellmakers exchanged glances. Walsh went very still.

"As you may have noticed, the Ilvernath Spellmaking Society has quite an interest in magickal anomalies," Aleshire said. "Lucky for you, all three of you qualify."

"And we've all been around for a tournament or two," added Calhoun. "We've seen what your families do for high magick. We have no interest in watching the general public join in on that bloodbath. It'd be far neater for everyone if the tournament continued, and so long as it does, we benefit—in status, in money, in power."

The other two nodded. Gavin searched each of their faces for deception, wishing he could cast a truth spell of his own. But their word would have to suffice.

"That's a yes?"

Aleshire smiled. "Yes."

"Thank you," Gavin said, trying not to display his nerves. Beside him, Hendry mumbled his own thank-you, while Alistair stayed notably silent.

Then, before they could move on to what they'd come for, the door banged open behind them. Gavin whipped around as a girl about his age stomped inside, while Walsh's assistant protested behind her. One of the girl's spellrings glowed, and the door slammed violently shut.

She was pretty, strikingly so, with dark hair that fell in a choppy pixie cut, light brown skin, and an elaborate gold choker with a spellstone at the center that peeked through the collar of her Ilvernath Prep uniform. At the sight of them, her face contorted with disbelief, though Gavin had no clue who she was—he would've remembered her if they'd met before.

"You!" Walsh sounded startled. "You weren't invited."

"It's really true." She gasped, rounding on all of them. "You're helping Alistair Lowe."

Alistair regarded her with cool disinterest. The clumsy boy who'd knocked over a display case had vanished, his face set in the same haughty expression Gavin had seen him wear countless times before, as though even without a single spellring, he knew he was dangerous.

"And who are you?" Alistair asked.

"Diya Attwater-Sharma. You might remember my grandfather, Bayard Attwater? He'd be here today, but he's still recovering from when you *blinded him*."

Hendry blanched, and even Alistair's stoic demeanor faltered. Gavin cautiously examined the other spellmakers. They hadn't seemed to care about what had happened to their colleague. But maybe this would make them reconsider.

"Well?" Diya demanded, seemingly unperturbed by both Alistair's appearance and his reputation. "Don't you have anything to say for yourself?"

A muscle in Alistair's jaw clenched, as though he was chewing on his words before he spoke. Finally, he breathed, "You won't believe me, but it was an accident. And I'm sorry for it."

His voice sounded oddly soft. Gavin had no idea if it was an act or not.

"You were right," Diya said sharply. "I don't believe shit."

"Listen, Diya," Walsh said. "This is none of your concern."

"I was voted into my grandfather's spot on the board, fair and square. I belong here just as much as the rest of you. If you're giving your support to champions—especially *that* champion—I should know about it."

"This isn't official board business, darling," said Aleshire.

"And we're here for the Grieve," added Calhoun. "Consider the Lowes . . . a side project."

"A side project?" Alistair muttered, while Gavin felt a jolt of satisfaction. The other boy had mentioned something about comic books back at the Cottage—Gavin hoped he was absolutely loathing being treated like a sidekick.

Hendry elbowed him. "Don't push your luck."

Diya crossed her arms. "Well, now that I'm here . . . I'd love to hear how all of you convinced my colleagues—" Walsh coughed at that word. Diya glared at him. "To help you."

Gavin repeated his argument, and then each of them presented their cases one by one while the spellmakers examined them. When Hendry confirmed the rumors of his own death by gesturing to the scar on his neck, Aleshire let out a horrified gasp. When Alistair removed his glove and explained the Reaper's Embrace, Calhoun cast something on his hand that enveloped it like a second skin. He pulled the enchantment away, looking disturbed.

When Gavin's turn came, he rolled up his sleeve to reveal the hourglass tattoo, sending the room into an uneasy hush. He sat steadfastly in an armchair as they hovered over him, muttering. Reid MacTavish had made him feel like a lab rat. He'd hoped this would be different. But it was as though he'd been locked inside one of their fancy display cases, another curiosity. Until Diya elbowed past Aleshire and Calhoun, then perched on an ottoman beside the armchair. She held up a blue spellstone with striations inside it like veins.

"I want to verify that you're actually using life magick," she told him. "Which means I need to see how you look when you cast. Internally, I mean."

"Internally?" Gavin echoed nervously.

"Yeah. Here—" The spellstone flared, and Gavin gaped as his bicep turned translucent, muscles and veins spiraling beneath invisible skin. Diya grinned. "That *never* gets old."

"Do you make a habit of this?" Gavin asked.

Diya clutched the blue spellstone fondly, the gold of her nose ring shimmering in its radiance. "Not a habit, exactly. But I'm sort of a fixer—broken spellstones, unintentional enchantment side effects, old grimoire recipes that need translations and updates. And if I'm going to fix something, I need to understand how it works."

"The thing in question being . . . my arm?"

"Exactly."

"Fair enough," Gavin said. "But I'm willing to bet you've never solved a problem like this."

"No," Diya admitted. "But I'd like to try." Then she leaned in close and whispered, "I like the idea of a Grieve coming out on top, for once."

A smile snuck onto Gavin's face. "Me too." He cast Alistair a glance, unsure if he'd heard or not, only to realize the other boy was staring intently at him. Their eyes locked, and the room suddenly felt suffocatingly small.

"Ready to cast something?" Diya procured another spellstone. Gavin hastily returned his gaze to her.

"Sure." The other spellmakers crowded around as Gavin's life magick automatically filled the stone.

Beside him, Diya sucked in a breath. Green and purple clouded beneath Gavin's skin before slowly dissipating into flecks of white magick. Nausea roiled in him as he cast the spell. A tiny sparkler looped in the air before dive-bombing into the emerald flames.

"So it's true," Diya breathed. "You really are a vessel. The way everyone always talked about it, I thought it was just a myth." She dropped her enchantment. Gavin had never been more relieved to see the skin on his arm again, tattoo and all.

"Not a myth," Calhoun said. "Rare, though. How did you manage to do that to yourself?" He sounded impressed, albeit horrified.

"I didn't." Gavin dropped the spellstone into Diya's hand before it could refill again. "Reid MacTavish did."

"The cursemaker?" asked Calhoun. "I always knew that family was up to something—"

Aleshire frowned. "Is that how he joined the tournament, do you think—"

"Leave it to the MacTavishes to dabble in things far beyond their capabilities."

"Enough!" Walsh's voice, magickally amplified, cut through the chatter. "Are you prepared to make an assessment?"

One by one, the spellmakers nodded.

"We'll begin with Gavin." Aleshire gestured toward the armchair where he still sat. "What Reid did to you was . . . irresponsible, to say the least. By cutting off your connection to common magick, not only has he made your body's life magick your lone power source, he's also stopped it from regenerating."

"Life magick can regenerate?" Gavin asked. "I thought I was literally taking time off my life with each spell I cast—shouldn't that be something I can't get back?"

"As long as you're alive, you can generate life magick," Aleshire said. "Siphoning it quickly, the way you are now, could remove decades off your life. It could even kill you. But if left undisturbed, it *will* regrow. If we can find a way for you to use common magick again and sever your connection to your life magick as a power source, you have a chance at recovery."

True hope clawed at Gavin's throat like a wild animal. If he could cast spells with common magick, he'd no longer need to drain his own life force to fight.

"Do you actually think you can do that?" he asked.

"Thanks to Diya, yes, I do."

"You're welcome," Diya said cheerfully.

Aleshire sighed and gestured to the tattoo. "You've only been using magick this way for a few weeks. You haven't fully adjusted to the change yet—that's why you have that disturbance beneath your skin, why you're in pain each time you draw on your life magick. Your body's still trying to reject what MacTavish did."

His body was still fighting. Gavin clung to that fact with renewed vigor.

"This seems like a good start," he said. "But what now? What next?"

"Now, we do more research," Walsh said smoothly. "We run some tests. And we get back to you when we have something tangible to discuss."

"This should tide you over in the meantime." Calhoun tossed him a book.

Gavin barely caught it. He turned it over, frowning. "Is this a textbook?"

"It's a training regimen to make you a better caster. We think it'll lessen the strain of your life magick. I've marked some exercises for you to try. It won't stop you using your life magick entirely, of course, but it could mean you waste less of it."

Gavin got to his feet, feeling triumphant. First he'd cemented an alliance with Alistair and Hendry, and now these spellmakers had committed to helping him. It was more than he'd ever dared to hope for.

"Thank you," he told the spellmakers. "I won't forget this once the tournament's done. You have my word."

"What about us?" Alistair asked impatiently.

Aleshire grimaced. "You're . . . trickier. The Reaper's Embrace is an unfamiliar enchantment to us, but we've dealt with class ten curses before."

"There's a chance it can be cured," Calhoun said. "Maybe."

"Are we so certain it's a bad thing that he can't hurt anyone?" muttered Diya.

"I don't *want* to hurt anyone," Alistair said sharply. "All I want is to save my brother."

Aleshire raised a brow. "Shall we verify that with a truth spell?"

"It hardly matters what he believes to be true," Walsh said. "We all know what he's capable of."

There were murmurs of assent throughout the room. Alistair's gloved hand flexed into a fist.

"And what about Hendry?" he gritted out, each polite word clearly an effort.

Hendry shifted uncomfortably beside him. "Al, you already know—"

"Ah. Right." Walsh cleared his throat. "Regarding Hendry . . . well, while there are recorded cases of class ten death curses, and even the rare account of humans becoming vessels . . . we have no idea how you came to be, Mr. Lowe. Our best guess is that the curse that your family made from you was crafted with life magick, and they siphoned it away in the moments of your death." Though Walsh had already told Gavin as much, this news was clearly a revelation to the brothers. Each of their eyes widened—not quite in surprise, but resigned horror. "Thus, you were resurrected because your life magick and the high magick of the tournament have interacted in a

way none of us have ever heard of—perhaps if we knew more about
high magick itself, we'd have a better theory. But right now, I'm afraid
there's nothing we can do. We won't give up, though."

"I understand," Hendry murmured.

Gavin watched Alistair struggle, face flushed, to keep his anger under control. Gavin knew a lot about rage. How hard it could be to rein
it in without a lifetime of practice. How it could eat you up inside.

If Alistair lost control here, he'd ruin everything for all of them.
But he didn't. Instead, for the briefest of moments, his expression
faded into something softer and sadder, before he glared at the floor.

"Let's go, then," he said gravely. Hendry reached for his arm, but
Alistair shrugged him off and stalked toward the door.

The spellmakers looked unimpressed, while Gavin felt nothing
but confusion. Alistair had killed his own family and Elionor Payne.
He was cruel to his core—he had to be.

Gavin didn't follow, at least not right away. Instead he sighed and
cornered Walsh in front of the hearth. The other spellmakers clustered near some of the display cases, although Gavin was sure he saw
a Listen In shimmer around their heads.

"They may owe me nothing more than empty reassurances," he
told Walsh. "But you owe me far more than that. Don't forget it."

Walsh smiled wanly. "I'm very committed to your cause, Mr.
Grieve. Don't you fret."

"You don't need to play polite. I want to know what you really
think about Hendry. Can he help me or not?"

"He's promising," the spellmaker murmured. The green flames lit
his face in a sickly sheen. "As I said, we need to run some tests first.
But the fact that we can see his high magick at all is astounding."

"I'll expect something from you soon, then," Gavin said. Common
magick wafted from the fire and drifted around him, an unhappy reminder of what he couldn't use, couldn't have. "If all of this is so *promising*, I'll be . . . disappointed if you don't generate results."

"I assure you, I'm doing all I can on that front," Walsh shot back.
"Now then. There's one more thing you should know before you
leave."

"What?" Gavin asked suspiciously.

"I've received a tip that the other champions are also seeking outside assistance. You may want to prepare for that."

"You mean MacTavish?"

"No, not him," Walsh said evasively.

"You swore to help me to the best of your ability. If you're omitting something—"

"That's all I know. I swear it."

Per the oath spell, if the information put him in direct danger, Walsh would have to tell him. Gavin had no choice but to accept this for what it was—vague assistance at best.

"Well, if you learn more, you tell me," he said brusquely.

But as he strode toward the door, Gavin realized it didn't matter what the other competitors were planning, or who they were working with. His allies were more powerful than anyone else in Ilvernath.

He pictured his tattoo fading along with the red sky above them, diluting with the death of champion after champion until only he remained. And for the first time since the Blood Veil had fallen, his face split into a true smile.

ALISTAIR LOWE

"The curse *can* be broken, and we've provided proof. Any champions who claim otherwise are disregarding the evidence because they'd rather there be bloodshed," said Macaslan, speaking of Lowe and Grieve.

> *Ilvernath Eclipse*, "Could This Tragedy
> Have a Happy Ending?"

*"HOW MANY PEOPLE HAVE TO DIE
BEFORE YOU ANSWER FOR YOUR CRIMES?"*

With his gloved hand, Alistair smeared away the grime on the kitchen window and peered outside. Beyond the glimmer of the Cottage's wards, a few dozen figures congregated in the forest, their silhouettes clouded in the morning fog.

"What's happening?" he demanded.

"Reporters have started prowling about," Hendry said behind him. "I saw their cameras."

"Yeah, but these aren't just reporters. They're protestors. And they're protesting . . . *us.*" Many amid the crowd brandished cardboard signs, but he couldn't discern their writing save for the garish, blood-red paint. "This doesn't make sense. Something must've happened."

Gavin snorted. "No one ever wanted you to win. I'm only surprised they didn't swarm around here sooner."

Alistair hardly needed another reminder that the world hated him. Even grieving, he'd noticed the glares he'd attracted at the tournament's opening banquet, how they'd prickled like barbed wire against his skin. When each champion's name was called, the protestors so seemingly appalled by the curse had silenced when it came time to defend him.

Alistair stared at the other two boys and Marianne coolly. They sat at the kitchen table, Hendry's dense, burnt attempt of a bread loaf resting in a cloche between them. *A peace offering*, Hendry had told Alistair, though he still glared at Gavin as though hoping he choked on it.

"Yesterday, your spellmaker friend mentioned the other champions had help from the outside world. And now the outside world is here." Alistair reached over Marianne's shoulder, took a crumbly bite of toast, then tossed it back on his plate. "I'm gonna go chat with them."

"That's a bad—" Gavin started, but Alistair was already striding out the door and through the wilted garden.

At his appearance, the chanting paused, as though the protestors didn't believe their eyes: the shape of a boy, shoulders hunched against the cold, hands shoved in his pockets, slinking through the mist like an apparition. Then, as he neared, the shouting resumed and crescendoed to a raucous roar. The few people who'd been sitting on the grass lurched to their feet, waving their signs with renewed fervor. One of them even wielded a pitchfork.

"AFTER ALL THE BLOOD YOU'VE SHED
YOU SHOULD BE THE NEXT ONE DEAD!"

Alistair halted at the edge of the wards, staring his guests down through the hazy crimson veil. With a single lethal glare, their cries quieted, and the crowd took three collective steps back.

How easy it was to play the villain. As though he'd never removed the costume at all.

"You have ten seconds to explain why you're here"—Alistair raised his hands—"before I leave all of you in pieces for the next flock to find."

When no one dared respond, Alistair began lowering his fingers. "Ten, nine, eight—"

"W-we support Briony!" someone stammered. "How could you still want to play out the tournament when all of you could survive?"

Alistair struggled not to betray his surprise. When Walsh had told Gavin the others were seeking external help, Alistair assumed he meant the families. Had they gone to the public, instead?

Then he spotted today's edition of the *Ilvernath Eclipse* clutched in one protestor's hands.

"I'll take that," he told him coolly. When the man hesitated, Alistair barked, "Now!"

Like a rodent, the man scurried to the edge of the wards, lay the newspaper on the grass, and fled. Alistair stretched his hand across the barrier and snatched it. Below a gigantic, beaming portrait of Briony Thorburn, the headline on the front page blazed "COULD THIS TRAGEDY HAVE A HAPPY ENDING?"

Alistair's gaze darted from photograph to photograph. Him snarling at a reporter in the Magpie pub before the tournament began. Him carving his name into the Champions Pillar. And, once again, Isobel draped in his arms, their lips locked in a kiss.

The others had told the world about breaking the curse. They'd told them *everything*.

When he'd finished the article, Alistair folded it closed and tucked it beneath his arm. Rage roiled in his stomach, but he couldn't reveal that in front of so many cameras.

"*Monster*," a woman hissed.

A mere day ago, the comment would've cut him in the same place where he'd been cut far too many times before. But today, he'd gladly accept such an insult as a trophy. How nice it would look beside all the high magick he'd claim alongside his victory.

"Also," he said, casting a Come Hither, "I want that."

The spell wrenched the pitchfork from the protestor's grip and tossed it to Alistair. He caught it, rested it against his shoulder, and stalked back to the Cottage, ignoring the flashes of cameras behind him.

His false composure lasted until the moment he threw open the door. It slammed against the wall, yet Hendry and Gavin paid him no mind.

Marianne was telling a story.

". . . born under the light of the full moon," she whispered. "It's a sign of evil. Because when the night is bright, it means you cast a bigger shadow."

Alistair had heard this tale before. His mother loved to tell it on Alistair's and Hendry's birthdays because, according to her, every member of the Lowe family had been born beneath a full moon. From the moment they took their first breaths, they made the world a little darker.

"Children of the full moon are stronger, too," Marianne went on. "Especially after dark. Some people think that's because you can see magick easier then. But others believe it's when their instincts are best. At night, they think better. And they have a stronger urge to kill."

"You have it backward." Alistair leaned his pitchfork against the wall and rested his gloved hand on her chair. "In the story, the night muddles their thoughts. It distills their identity down to bloodlust and nothing more."

Marianne craned her neck to look at him, but she didn't wear her usual glare. Alistair's voice had gone hushed and ominous, as it always did when he told stories.

"Some children of the full moon try to reject their powers," he continued, sliding into the lone empty seat. "They sleep and wake early to avoid the night. But running away from who you are has consequences. They'll find themselves unlucky. Doomed to be hurt more often, to lose people they care about, to never know anything but misfortune.

"You can tell a child of the full moon by their eyes. On full moon nights, their true eyes are covered in darkness, making them appear as little more than empty sockets. But if you look at their shadows—the eyes of their shadows glow. So if you meet one after sunset, run. You won't escape, but it's preferable to die when your back is turned, so you can't see their curse coming."

With the story finished, Alistair admired the faces of his audience. Hendry, the corner of his lips tilted up in nostalgia. Marianne, entranced and twirling a lock of hair around her finger.

Only Gavin looked less than enraptured. "You're disturbed."

Alistair laughed darkly. "Oh, I think you'll prefer my stories to the ones the other champions are telling about *us*."

He slid the *Ilvernath Eclipse* toward them. Then he propped his shoes on the table and snatched his half-eaten slice of toast.

"What is this?" Hendry asked, flinging open the four-page spread.

"This is *not* good," Gavin breathed.

"You see what they're saying about me," Alistair said, unbothered, sniffing a dusty, suspicious jar of fig preserves. "That I'm 'unstable' and 'destructive.'"

Across from him, Marianne lifted the photo of the Lowe estate crime scene, horror twinging across her face. Hendry hastily ripped the paper from her grasp.

"I see I'm a murderer now," Gavin commented dryly. "I bet that's the most they've reported about me during the entire tournament, and it's not even true."

"A lot of details were left out," said Hendry. "It's never mentioned that Isobel cursed you."

Alistair smeared the jam across his toast. "Or that I helped her craft the curse she used on me. Or that the Payne attacked first. It's all very convenient, isn't it?"

"That's one word for it," Gavin said scathingly. "So what does this mean for us? Will there be protestors screaming at us day and night? Protecting the other champions? Cursing us the moment we leave the wards?"

"It *is* a predicament, isn't it?"

"I don't get it," Gavin snapped. "Why aren't you angry?"

"Because it's bullshit. These people claim to be self-righteous, that they're fighting against all that the tournament stands for, but if I died violently tomorrow, they'd celebrate. They're already proudly saying so." He chewed on the last piece of crust and brushed the crumbs off his hands. "So welcome to the bad guys' club. You learn to get used to it."

Gavin stared at Alistair so long that Alistair wiped his mouth on the back of his glove, figuring he had jam dabbed on his chin.

Finally, Gavin said, "Fine. Then we give an interview of our own."

Alistair scoffed. "Did you hear anything I just said? Even if I wasn't . . ." He gestured at himself, figuring his appearance served as explanation enough. "Isobel has been the media's favorite for months. Now, they're obsessed with Briony. It'll be a disaster."

"Why? Your—*our* story is the truth."

"They don't want the truth."

"I don't know . . ." Hendry said. "Even if most of the world doesn't believe us, it'll at least muddy the others' story, right? And it's like you said—if we have to worry about protestors breaking in here and calling it justice, then anything is worth a shot."

Alistair narrowed his eyes. Hendry never took Gavin's side.

"What do you both propose I do? Pretend that I'm a lover scorned? That I'm the secret victim in all this?" He faked a pout. "What happens when they ask about Mum and Grandma and Uncle Rowan? Will they give us a pat on the head? Remind us that nice boys don't run around killing their families?"

"Al," Hendry said warningly, glancing at Marianne. She hadn't heard. She was too busy smearing a jammy mustache on a picture of Alistair.

"If you told them the truth of it, all of it," Gavin said quietly, his eyes flickering to the white line across Hendry's throat. "I bet you'd be surprised what people might think."

Alistair didn't grace that with a response, because he knew Gavin was only trying to coerce him with bogus compassion, and he refused to fall for it. But Hendry's gaze bored into him, and when Alistair met it, his brother gave him a pleading look.

Alistair considered ignoring it—despite Hendry's unfailing optimism, no amount of honesty would change anything.

But it couldn't hurt.

"I can't believe I let you talk me into this," Alistair muttered as Gavin wiped away the earthy blood mixture splattered across Alistair's trainers. "You look ridiculous, by the way."

Gavin glanced at his sweatshirt and joggers. "This is what I always wear. Besides, it worked on the spellmakers."

"I think I look dashing." Hendry adjusted his turtleneck to cover his scar. Then he walked to Alistair and smoothed down yet another errant curl. They'd spent the better part of a half hour combing Alistair's hair into side part submission. "You should practice smiling."

"Why?" Alistair demanded. "What's wrong with my smile?"

When Gavin looked up to hand Alistair his now pristine left shoe, Alistair flashed him his best, golden boy grin.

Gavin cringed. "Don't do that during the interview. We need you to look nice."

"I'm not sure I can. What about my murderous instincts? The *Eclipse* was right, you know. They're so *hard* to suppress. And what about cackling? Devious monologues? Or—"

"I'm trying to suppress *my* murderous instincts right now," Gavin muttered, then he thrust Alistair's shoe into his chest. "Let's get this over with."

The moment Alistair stepped out of the Cottage, the wind swept his hair into the mess it'd once been. But Gavin paid it no mind, effectively pushing Alistair toward the reporters while he and Hendry rearranged the benches in the garden.

As per usual, the protestors resumed their chanting at Alistair's approach.

"Hello, everyone, beautiful weather, isn't it?" Alistair asked, smiling no matter Gavin and Hendry's ridiculous judgment. The closest reporter foundered back, tripped on a stone, and tumbled to the forest floor. "Are any of you gracious reporters from the *Glamour Inquirer?*"

He named the tabloid which had most extensively—and scandalously—covered Isobel prior to the rise of the Blood Moon.

A woman raised her arm. Unlike the protestors around her, she hadn't dressed for camping. Instead, she wore a pair of cheetah print heels and bubblegum pink lipstick. Her brassy blond hair didn't budge no matter how much the wind blustered.

"That would be me," she said, almost with a giggle. She held a tape recorder to her lips. "And whatever you're about to ask, *yes.*"

She strutted confidently toward the wards, and Alistair relaxed them for a single second, allowing her to pass. Once she stood beside the boys, she spun around and waved at the crowd of gawking protestors. She'd willingly entered the dragon's lair.

"My name is Barbara Scott. Call me Barb." She inspected Alistair, from his extra shiny shoes to the dark Lowe spellrings on his right hand. "I can already tell this is going to be delightful. The red light suits you, you know."

Alistair had expected fear, not playfulness. "Oh, um, all right," he said awkwardly. Then he led her to the garden's wrought iron bench, ignoring Marianne's beady eyes watching them from the window.

"Thank you so much for speaking with us," Gavin told her, his voice so schmoozy that Alistair had to fight an eyeroll. "It means a lot that we have a chance to tell our side of the story."

"Well, aren't you boys polite? The pleasure is all mine." She turned back to Alistair. "So let me guess, your girlfriend said some things that weren't fair, and you want to have the last word." Seeing that Alistair was too taken aback to respond, she added, "I've been doing this a long time. I know how these situations go."

"A situation like this one?" Alistair asked, genuinely baffled.

She laughed. "You're funny." Then she patted the bench beside her. "You can sit. I don't bite." When the four of them arranged themselves into a circle, Barb pressed the green button on her tape recorder, and the spellstone at its top flashed on. "So you've just read everything Isobel Macaslan spilled to the *Ilvernath Eclipse*. What was your reaction?"

Across from him, Gavin raised his brows expectantly, as though reminding Alistair that this was the part that counted.

"Sh-shock, honestly," he stammered. Gavin's expression squirmed as he struggled to keep a straight face. Admittedly, the voice crack might've been pushing it.

Barb tsked. "Now don't get carried away. You don't strike anyone as an honest person. So why do you say shock?"

Alistair faked fiddling with his curserings. "I know what the world says about me—no one thinks I have a heart. But the truth is, deep down—very deep down—I do. And Isobel broke it."

Barb scooted closer to him, so close that Alistair could smell her overpowering neroli perfume. "Now wait just a moment. According to the interview Isobel, Briony, and Finley gave to the *Eclipse*, you chose to work against them. You nearly killed her. Shouldn't Isobel be the heartbroken one?"

"That's not the full story," he said.

"Then do tell, what *is* the full story?"

He hesitated. He could start on the night that he and Isobel had met, rival champions in their favorite pub. Or the morning after the tournament began, when Isobel had staggered to the Cave and begged him to help her. But it was harder to find the words than he'd anticipated. Because what mattered most wasn't where their story started, but where it went wrong—if it had ever been right to begin with.

"Al," Hendry prodded.

"Al," Barb repeated thoughtfully. "That's a cute nickname. You're Hendry Lowe, I take it?"

Hendry nodded.

"There are *quite* the conspiracy theories flying around, about why and how you faked your death. If you were trying to escape being named champion. If your family did it as some kind of ploy—"

"*Faked* his death?" Alistair bit out, his scorned lover façade instantly vanishing. Gavin shot him an annoyed look. "The world thinks Hendry faked it?"

Barb's coy smile wavered. "What *did* happen?"

Alistair glanced at his brother, who closed his eyes and gave an almost imperceptible nod.

Alistair began the tale at the Lowe estate. He described the house in vivid detail, from its haunting collection of family portraits to its weathered graveyard. He recounted the ghastly training montage that was his childhood. How his mother had loved monster stories. How she'd tortured him with them. How the tournament had only ever been described like a fairy tale, like an honor, and Alistair had known he would be champion from the time he was seven years old.

Barb didn't interrupt him, not even as he approached the rise of the Blood Moon. The first time she spoke up was when he reached the part where the Lowes killed Hendry to craft the Lamb's Sacrifice.

"Th-they *killed* you?" Barb asked Hendry. "They really did?"

Rather than respond, Hendry wrenched down his turtleneck, exposing the lethal scar across his throat. His expression remained unerringly calm, but his other hand white-knuckled the arm of his chair.

"And so you killed them," Barb said, understanding dawning on her.

Alistair and Hendry nodded.

"You realize this is a confession, don't you? What's to stop the authorities from arresting you?"

Truthfully, Alistair hadn't considered the repercussions when he killed his family. He hadn't considered anything except vengeance.

"It's illegal to interfere with curses like the tournament," he replied.

"It's illegal to murder, too," Barb pointed out. Then she tapped his knee lightly with her pen. "But don't worry. You're both underage, and I'm no lawyer, but I already spy a hundred different holes in the case. And with all of Kendalle chattering about high magick possibly coming back, the police have bigger problems. Go on, go on."

From there, Alistair recounted the tournament. The night Isobel had appeared outside the Cave, defenseless and shivering in the rain. How they'd helped each other. How he'd gifted her the Cloak, how Alistair had nearly died helping her craft the Reaper's Embrace.

Alistair understood why some described honesty as brutal now. Even when so carefully crafting his story, every word he drew out felt like extracting a knife from his own back.

Eventually, Barb's questions extended to Gavin, too, who talked about witnessing Briony kill Carbry Darrow, how the others had lied and blamed it on him. How Alistair had saved Briony *and* Isobel, yet both of them had turned on him when he only asked that they save Hendry, too.

Allies or not, rehearsed or not, it was strange to hear Gavin back him up, to consider that Gavin Grieve and Alistair Lowe could ever be on the same side.

"And Reid MacTavish, the cursemaker who's supposedly helping them?" Gavin said. "A few days before the tournament began, I met with Reid. He promised me he could make me stronger, and as a Grieve, spellmakers weren't exactly lining up outside my door to sponsor me. So I said yes. Except . . ."

He bunched up the sleeve of his sweatshirt, exposing his ghastly hourglass tattoo. His veins distended around it in a swollen lattice.

"*Please* tell me you got a refund," Barb said with a tight laugh.

"He didn't just give me this. He warped my ability to cast enchantments. Whenever I touch a spellstone, it fills with my life magick. It's the only type of magick I can use."

Barb gasped. "B-but that's . . . It's been years since someone's been arrested for experimenting with life magick. Decades, even."

"Are you from here?" Gavin asked her.

"No, I came here after I finished school."

"Then you should know by now—all the fucked-up fairy tales in Ilvernath are true." He rolled down his sleeve. "So you see, the story is more complicated than the other champions made it seem."

"It is, but I'm still curious—I know why *they're* fighting to win the tournament." She nodded at the Lowe brothers. "But what about you? Your history with MacTavish aside, shouldn't you want to break the curse, too?"

"A part of me does," Gavin said smoothly. "But as much as I wish it were possible, I don't believe it is. And maybe this isn't what the other champions would consider good, but I won't sacrifice myself for a one in a million chance. Contrary to what . . ." He faltered as he chose his next words. "Contrary to what my family believes, I'm not expendable."

"Of course not," Barb said in a quiet voice, like his grim story had genuinely bothered her. Alistair had to hand it to Gavin—he played the sad, pathetic boy well.

After several moments of silence, Gavin added, "Thank you again for doing this. You didn't have to." He chewed on his lip as though he were fighting back a smile, and even Alistair could begrudgingly admit that maybe, just maybe, Gavin's ridiculous strategy wasn't so ridiculous. This interview had gone far better than he'd imagined. He still didn't think it would change anything, but he was glad he'd given it. When parents tucked their children into bed with the blood-curdling tale of Alistair Lowe, at the very least, Alistair wanted that story to be *true*.

"Hold up—I'm not finished just yet." Barb shoved the recorder toward Alistair's lips. "When you face Isobel on the battlefield, what will you do? Will you be able to kill her?"

Alistair's mouth went dry. "I, uh . . ."

"Come on. You must've thought about it. This girl played you for weeks, taking advantage of your grief and vulnerability to eliminate you as a threat. I'd be angry, if I were you."

"I *am* angry," Alistair replied.

"What if she said she did care for you, after all? What then?"

Across from him, Gavin subtly shook his head. Alistair's irritation piqued. No matter what impression Gavin had gotten from this plan, Gavin wasn't his handler. Either he wanted Alistair's honesty, or he didn't.

"Isobel could apologize to me with her last words," Alistair said gravely, "but she never mattered to me the way Hendry does, and I don't appreciate being made a fool. The world has spent the past month calling us rivals, and, well, I'll admit I'm looking forward to Isobel finding out what that really means."

"Oh, you're even *better* than I thought you'd be," Barb said. "You really are a fascinating character, aren't you? A boy or a monster?"

Alistair had zero idea how to respond to that—or to Gavin's furious glare.

"And don't let Isobel bother you too much," Barb said, standing to leave. "It's their loss, I usually say."

*   *   *

"What was that?" Gavin demanded the second they returned to the Cottage. All of his petty smiles were gone, replaced by aggravation. "You went off-script."

"What happened?" Marianne asked.

"Quiet, Maggot," Alistair snapped, advancing on Gavin. "You wanted the truth. What did you expect me to say? That I'd hold back? That I'd let Isobel kill me?"

Gavin didn't answer, and Alistair groaned and turned toward his brother.

"What did you think of it? Should I have played a wounded puppy that Isobel kicked?"

"I don't think anyone would've believed that," said Hendry.

Gavin stalked to the couch and sat, his elbows on his knees, his fingers steepled. As though Alistair's honesty was a problem he needed to solve.

"Oh, come off it," Alistair growled. "If either of us has the right to be angry, it's me. It's a wonder I can walk straight after you spent that whole time with your hand up my ass, trying to manipulate me like a puppet."

Marianne clapped her hands to her mouth and giggled.

"I wasn't saying . . ." Gavin shook his head. "Never mind. Forget it. You literally brought a pitchfork in here—I don't know why I thought you'd be able to get the media on your side."

Alistair bristled, and along the walls of the Cottage, dust sprinkled like snow from the ceiling, the Landmark descending into deeper states of squalor. He'd done a lot of terrible things in his life, some of them accidents, some of them every bit by choice. But when tomorrow's papers declared him a monster, he refused to let Gavin blame him for it.

He spun back to Gavin. "Kill or be killed. Those are our options. Or, wait, let me correct myself—those are *my* options."

"What's that supposed to mean?" Gavin asked.

"You know what I mean."

Behind them, the floorboards creaked—Hendry shifting from side to side. Alistair knew nothing could be gained from goading their only ally, but as far as he was concerned, Gavin's promise of the spellmakers' aid hadn't gotten him anything. Sure, Gavin might've been given a reason to hope, with his ridiculous magick exercises, but Alistair wasn't cured.

Gavin stood, and Alistair always forgot how much bigger the other boy was until they were chest-to-chest. In a fist fight, Gavin would beat him bloody, but Alistair didn't care. It would feel good to land a single hit, to smack that infuriating condescension off Gavin's face.

Gavin sucked in a breath, like he truly did expect Alistair to strike him.

"How do you plan on killing me?" Alistair asked instead.

Hendry made a strangled noise and choked, "Marianne, do you want to go outside?"

"No," she answered.

"Oh, well, we're going anyway."

After Hendry dragged Marianne out to the garden, Gavin fixed Alistair with a steely stare. "What are you talking about?"

"After we're miraculously cured, after we defeat all the other champions and our alliance is finished, how do you plan on killing me? I know you think about it."

"Why would you think that?"

"Because *I* think about it. Constantly." Alistair drew out his words in a long, skin-crawling hiss. He smiled wickedly when he noticed the goose bumps prickle across Gavin's arms, then he lifted his hand to brandish his curserings. "The Shadows' Talons was a favorite of my uncle's—in fact, you've already met it. It uses the victim's own shadow against them, breaking it into dozens of fragments, each of them solid and deadly. They tear you into so many pieces that your family would have to put your corpse together like a jigsaw puzzle."

Gavin didn't reply, but judging by the muscle flexing in his jaw, he was picturing it.

"Or the Wraith's Screech, my mother's preferred choice. It summons a vortex that sucks every speck of air from your lungs until your chest collapses." Alistair still remembered how it felt to slide the ring off his mother's corpse. The cruelest of mementos. "Or the Demon's Pyre. My grandmother loved this one. Because there's nothing left of the victim. Not even ash."

"Why are you so angry with me?" Gavin asked.

"Because I don't give a damn about the rest of the world's judgment, but I refuse to take yours. You think *I'm* cold? That I'm the greater villain? You've always been the most ruthless competitor in the tournament, and I'm the only one who's noticed. Does it bother you that I'm the one who gets all the credit?"

"I don't *want* to be a villain."

"You want to be a winner. That's the same thing."

Gavin shook his head. "You've never thought about killing me, not once."

"What makes you say that?"

"Because you've never thought I was important enough to kill before. All you did was rattle off the curses you took from your family—if you hated me enough, you'd have planned it all out. Chosen something original." Gavin's voice *did* betray an emotion now. Rage.

Alistair didn't think it was possible for Gavin to say something to infuriate him more, but he had. Because it was true. Alistair had never fantasized about killing Gavin before, but he certainly would tonight. He would lie in bed and stare at the ceiling, envisioning a death that Gavin Grieve deemed original enough for him. Because, for reasons Alistair couldn't explain, when he did kill Gavin, he didn't care if Gavin died afraid or angry or even sorry. Not so long as he died impressed.

"Oh, so you deserve something better?" Alistair challenged. To his right, the kitchen sink gurgled, mucky bog water spewing from the drain.

Gavin's voice changed again, the fury gone, that same cool tone back in place. "What do you want me to say? Sorry about your shitty childhood? At least yours came with a real chance of making it out of here alive. My family's been planning my funeral from the moment I was born."

Maybe the sad, pathetic boy act hadn't been an act at all.

Alistair would've preferred it if Gavin *had* struck him. In the awful concoction of feelings he had about Gavin—namely, irritation and loathing—he didn't want to add shame among them.

Gavin sighed. "This was pointless. I'm going for a walk."

"And if the protestors attack you?"

"Then I'm sure you'll be very disappointed that they beat you to it."

He threw open the door, only to collide with Hendry creeping behind it, a Listen In spell shimmering around his ear. Cursestones pulsed on Hendry's knuckles, poised and ready.

"Subtle," Gavin said flatly, then he stalked past him through the garden.

Hendry watched Alistair warily. "We still need him if—"

"Don't," Alistair snapped, then he shook his head. "Sorry. Sorry. I know we need him. I just have to think."

Hendry retreated, closing the door behind him.

Defeated, Alistair lay down on the rug in front of the fire. And when he did stare at the ceiling and fantasize, he didn't conjure any scenarios of death or torture, not even of Gavin. Instead, the fantasy that felt most tempting, most unreachable, was a pleasant one. Where a happily ever after for one person didn't spell doom for everyone else.

BRIONY THORBURN

"She redefines bravery," says Malvina Thorburn, one of the oldest and most respected members of her family. "We'll support Briony in every way we can."

SpellBC News

The Thorburn estate sat at the very edge of Ilvernath, a sprawling property surrounded by thick stone walls. Briony had always thought of its grand main house, elaborate gardens, and ancient amphitheater as a corner apart from the rest of the world, kept under meticulous control. But there was nothing controlled about the reporters and protestors crammed outside the gate, yelling questions and jostling for the perfect paparazzi shot.

"What does it feel like to be Ilvernath's new favorite champion?"

"The whole world's talking about you—what do you have to say to them?"

"Briony! Finley! Give a shout-out to your fans!"

"Just wanted to say thank you!" Briony called back awkwardly, grateful for the wards and the wall of stone separating her from the public.

The *Ilvernath Eclipse* had run their interview just two days ago, but instead of talking about the champions as a unit, they'd lauded Briony Thorburn as the poster child for ending the tournament. Headlines labeling her a hero were plastered on the front page of every tabloid and broadcast on every news station. The Thorburns had seized on the attention, giving interview after interview about how much they believed in her. They'd even invited all of her allies to the estate for a press conference and a meeting with the other families, promising the stories the champions sought . . . so long as they chatted with the media. And came in cocktail attire.

The message was clear: If Briony wanted to break the curse, she'd have to play the hero after all. No matter how little she felt she deserved it.

"How much longer do you think we have to do this?" Briony muttered to Finley. Behind her, various Thorburns beamed at the press.

"It's not so bad, is it?" Finley muttered back, waving at the crowd. He looked confident and comfortable, impeccably dressed in a suit delivered by a local department store. Everyone was all too happy to send gifts to the newly anointed heroes of Ilvernath. "They're here because they support us. And you've never been the type to shy away from attention."

"Neither have you," Briony shot back. She tugged at the hemline of her dress, tight and gold and glittery. When they'd left the Tower, she'd been struck with a memory—the two of them heading off to a school dance. The thought reminded her of their former selves, and she added, teasingly, "Finley Blair, class president, team captain, perfect attendance—"

"Champion," he said, in a tone that made Briony realize she'd hit a nerve, and then, "Do you see those signs over there? Seriously?"

Briony followed his gesturing hand. Pictures of Alistair and Gavin bobbed above the crowd. The people holding them wore FUTURE MRS. LOWE T-shirts; a boy next to them with a MR. LOWE variant cast a spell that made the signs glow menacingly. "Murderer!" they shrieked at Briony, before breaking into boos.

"I can't believe them," Finley said. "Alistair killed his entire family, and he gets a fan club."

"There's at least one Blair banner over there," Briony pointed out, elbowing him.

Finley straightened his tie and squared his shoulders. "Well. It's good to know *some* people have taste."

Though the *Ilvernath Eclipse* was firmly on their side, Alistair's interview in the *Glamour Inquirer* painted him and Gavin as tragic victims of circumstance who'd been wronged by the other champions. A small but passionate faction had taken up their cause. They hated Briony and Finley, but they hated Isobel far more, decrying her as a bitter ex-girlfriend.

As for Reid, the media hadn't known what to make of him, especially after Gavin's accusations. Both he and Isobel had remained behind today. No matter what they'd told the reporters, Reid was still a prisoner, and Isobel was worried about sparking yet another headline that belonged in the gutter.

Briony and Finley answered a few more polite questions, avoiding eye contact with Alistair and Gavin's supporters, until at last Elder Malvina Thorburn, the unquestioned matriarch of her family, emerged in front of the gates. She was ancient, with wispy white hair, wrinkled pink skin, and a wardrobe that made her look ready for a formal event regardless of the occasion. She greeted Finley warmly, then wrapped Briony in an embrace perfectly angled for the cameras.

"Thank you all so much for coming!" she called to the crowd. "But I'm afraid our honored guests have important business to attend to. Please don't hesitate to reach out to our PR representatives for more official quotes from the heroes of Ilvernath."

The Thorburn gardens felt uncomfortably familiar. Just a few weeks ago, Innes's champion-crowning party had been hosted here. Briony had spent the entire celebration sulking like a petty, jealous child, until Reid showed up and set her down the path to taking Innes's place by any means necessary.

Briony's heart seized at the thought of her sister. But in a seemingly endless sea of smiling Thorburns, Innes was nowhere to be found. Maybe it was better that way. Briony had no idea how to face her now.

She and Finley were led to the main courtyard in the gardens, where tidy clusters of chairs had been arranged in front of a podium. Families milled about, chatting politely, along with a few local spellmakers and some people Briony didn't recognize. It had been late summer when Innes was crowned champion. Now burgundy and orange leaves scattered across the hedgerows like flower petals, and the afternoon air had just enough of autumn's bite in it to make Briony shiver.

"We should find my family," Finley told her. She nodded, but before she could follow him into the crowd, Elder Malvina caught Briony's arm with her withered hand.

"We're so grateful you could come, darling," she said. "It's important to every Thorburn that you've chosen to work with us for the betterment of all of Ilvernath—and, perhaps, the world."

"The world?" Briony echoed, and then, her voice lowered, "Every Thorburn? What about Innes?"

Elder Malvina's grip tightened. "Your sister understands the importance of what you're doing. She also understands the way it reflects on all of us. Do you?"

Briony thought of Innes's fury with a rush of unease. It was hard for her to believe that her sister had come around, but . . . the Thorburns had done all of this for Briony. She was in no position to ask follow-up questions. "Of course I do."

Elder Malvina smiled at her, false teeth gleaming in the pink light. "Then I believe we understand each other perfectly. Now, come, come, let me introduce you to some very important people."

Briony was ushered into a smaller, more secluded part of the garden. She recognized the woman in a pantsuit with fair skin and a low black bun—Agent Yoo, of the Kendalle Parliament's Cursebreaking Division. Beside her stood a sharply dressed man in a suit and a pair of spellstone cufflinks.

"You may recall that our family has a special arrangement with the Cursebreaking Division," Elder Malvina said. Briony *did* recall. The government had chosen Innes as champion over her, then sworn both of them to secrecy with a powerful oath spell. "I'm pleased to report that thanks to your heroism, we've been able to find new ways to support each other."

"It's a pleasure to see you again, Briony," Agent Yoo said. A powerful cloaking spell fell over them a moment later. "Allow me to introduce you to my colleague, Agent Ashworth. He's stepped in to supervise this case."

Briony shook the man's hand. He was tall, thin, and pale, with a gaunt face and a buzz cut. One of his spellrings dug into her palm, painful enough that she suppressed a gasp.

"We know you're an intelligent young lady," Agent Ashworth said. "And we appreciate this service you're doing, for your city and for all of Kendalle. We're looking forward to watching you break the curse."

"Thanks," Briony said warily.

"I'm sure you've given some thought to what might happen in Ilvernath after the tournament ends," said Agent Yoo. "We're here to reassure you: The Cursebreaking Division has that situation under control."

Briony honestly hadn't given an *after* much thought. They had so much left to do, and from within the Tower walls, it was easy to forget the rest of the world existed. Now, she let herself truly think about it for the first time. The tournament ended. Briony and her friends alive. And the power that had made the tournament possible now freed from its enchantment, accessible to everyone.

"You're talking about high magick, right?" she asked.

"Of course," said Agent Ashworth. "We all know how dangerous it is. And since it seems that ending the tournament will mean returning this ancient and unpredictable power to the world, it needs to be properly regulated. While you handle things in front of the cameras, we're working on safety precautions behind the scenes."

Before high magick had been depleted, it had torn through history, igniting brutal wars over its immense power and potential. Briony realized with a twinge of unease that her and her allies' mission wasn't just about breaking the curse—it was about making sure that whatever followed was better than the violence that had come before.

"What kinds of precautions?" Briony asked.

"We're still working out the details," said Agent Yoo. "But we want to make sure there's a formal system for obtaining high magick, with reasonable laws surrounding its use."

"All of that sounds good." Some of Briony's misgivings about the Thorburns melted away. "I appreciate you telling me."

"We know you might get some questions about it from reporters," said Agent Ashworth gruffly.

"And we want you to feel confident in what you're fighting for," Elder Malvina added. "*Hero* is a big word. The world is watching to see how you live up to it. Don't forget that, Briony."

"I won't," Briony said solemnly. She and Elder Malvina returned to the crowd.

"You should get started," the older woman told her. "The other families have been waiting patiently."

"I need to find Finley," Briony said, looking around. She didn't spot him, but someone *did* call her name from a meter away.

"Briony!" She turned to find Isobel's mother, Honora Jackson, staring at her with concern. Briony had always liked her—she was a spellmaker who owned an indie store in town, and she'd let Briony and Isobel sample as many of her wares as they'd wanted. But Briony hadn't spoken to her since she'd pushed Isobel into the spotlight. She imagined the woman must hate her now.

"Isn't Isobel coming?" Honora questioned.

"Um . . . no. She couldn't make it."

Honora's face fell. "Your family said all of you would be here."

"I'm sorry." Briony hesitated. "Is there anything you want me to pass along to her?"

"Just tell her that I want her to come home safe," the woman pleaded. "And for whatever it's worth, I'm proud of her—and you all. I think you're doing the right thing."

"Thanks," Briony choked out, then stepped away. A group of Darrows watched her with disapproval as she walked toward the podium. One of the most controversial parts of Briony's story was Carbry's death—to the *Ilvernath Eclipse*, it was a tragic accident; to the *Glamour Inquirer*, it was proof of Briony's hypocrisy. Thinking too hard about either opinion made her head feel like it was about to explode.

In front of the Darrows sat a few Paynes, whispering to one another. A woman on the end of the row with a sleek blond bun and deep green eyes watched Briony with particular care. Briony recognized her as Gavin's sister, Callista, recently married to a Payne. Briony had attended the wedding because Thorburns were invited almost everywhere, and she'd wanted to scope out her competition.

She'd found Gavin unimpressive then. Now she found him confusing. If his magick really was as twisted as he'd claimed, shouldn't he have more reason than anyone to want this curse broken? There were no Grieves in attendance, but Briony figured the Thorburns wouldn't have thought to invite them. And the Lowes were no longer an option. Which only left . . .

"My family isn't here." Finley reappeared at her side. Although his expression was calm, his tone betrayed his agitation.

"You're sure?" Briony asked worriedly.

"I'm sure." He blew out a breath. "I don't understand. They must've been invited."

"They definitely were." But before she could say anything more, a screech of audio feedback rang through the air.

"Attention, everyone!" called Elder Malvina, tapping the spell-stone set into the microphone. The crowded courtyard fell into an expectant hush. "Allow me to introduce two of Ilvernath's heroes— Finley Blair, and our own Briony Thorburn!"

The Thorburns broke out into raucous cheers, while the other families clapped politely. Briony strode to the podium, eerily reminded of the night they'd all cheered for Innes as she treaded up to the Champions Pillar. Briony had wanted nothing more in that moment than a do-over, a world where *she* was the one carving her name into that scarred, ancient stone. Now she clenched her hand into a fist and stared at the champion's ring on her pinky. Then she turned her gaze to the crowd.

"Thank you for coming, everyone." Her magnified voice made the words sound more important, like she really *was* the hero of some grand homecoming. "It's an honor to be here."

"We have so much appreciation for the families who've joined together to end this curse for good," Finley said. "We know that after generations of sacrifice, it must be difficult to imagine a possible future for this tournament that doesn't end in tragedy. But we've found a new way forward. And we'll do everything we can to see it through."

There was another smattering of polite applause. Three people rose from the crowd: a Darrow, a Payne, a Macaslan. Each of them presented Briony and Finley with a thin book—the Paynes' frayed and tattered, the Macaslans' so ancient it looked like it might crumble in her hands, the Darrows' gleaming and beautifully preserved. Briony's alliance knew Isobel's family story already, of course, but the Macaslans had made the gesture anyway. Based on the way they held up the book for the reporters, Briony could tell they wanted their family to stay on the press's good side as much as the Thorburns did.

"With the gift of your stories," Briony said, "we'll be able to right this wrong and bring peace to Ilvernath."

In the back of the garden, Briony caught a flash of a choppy brown fringe. Her heart leapt into her throat—but it wasn't Innes, just one of her cousins, leaning over to whisper something to another.

The world had decided Briony Thorburn made the perfect hero. It was everything she'd ever wanted.

If she forgot there was a broken Relic. Or that her sister was mysteriously absent. Or that Innes's words echoed through her thoughts every night—*I don't think you've changed at all.*

"I need to see my family," Finley said to her quietly as they left the podium behind. "I need to know why they didn't show up. And it might get kind of intense, and, well . . . it would mean a lot if you came with me."

Finley had grown up in a brownstone on a bustling city street, near the heart of Ilvernath proper. Briony had spent time there during the four months they'd dated, but she knew the moment the door swung open that this would be a very different sort of visit. Despite sharing a similar dark brown complexion, a favorite rugby team, and a penchant for princess-cut spellrings, Briony had always considered Finley's mums to be somewhat opposites—Abigail short where Pamela was tall, Abigail casual where Pamela was glamorous, Abigail effusive where Pamela was quiet. Right now, though, the two women wore identical, somber expressions as they stood in the foyer.

"Hi, Mum," Finley said. "Mother."

Abigail took a half-step forward, then hesitated.

"Go on, then." Pamela sighed. "You might as well."

Abigail engulfed Finley in a massive hug, and he squeezed her tightly. "You shouldn't have come," she told him solemnly as she pulled away.

Finley's voice went soft. "What?"

"You heard her," Pamela said. "But since you're here, we should get inside before any stray cameras find us." She gestured away from the front steps, then added, "You too, Briony."

Briony trailed behind as Pamela led them through the ground floor. Even though their welcome had been chilly at best, Briony's impression of the brownstone hadn't changed since the first time she'd visited—that unlike the various drafty houses she and Innes had grown up in, this place actually felt like a home.

The exposed brick was charming, the plaster accent wall painted a soothing eggshell blue and decorated with photos of Finley and his extended family. They weren't stately oil portraits like the Thorburns; they were actual pictures of people who looked like they were having fun. Several pieces of art depicting the Blair family code hung between them, all proclaiming the same three words: HONOR. VALOR. INTEGRITY.

Back when they'd dated, Briony had teased Finley that he couldn't get through a single conversation without discussing the code. But as she gazed at a needlepoint of the words with a decorative sword at the bottom, she couldn't remember the last time he'd brought it up.

Cries of surprise and delight rang out as they entered the living room, where two girls in Ilvernath Prep uniforms sprawled out on a comfy leather couch. She recognized them both—although Finley was an only child, he was close with his cousins.

The oldest one, Gracie Blair, had been friendly with Innes. She was nearly as short as Abigail, with warm brown skin and green spell-rings that matched the trim of her blazer. While she also wrapped Finley in an enormous hug, Briony was besieged by an intrusive thought of her sister. Innes was an open wound that she had no idea how to close.

"You're both, like, famous," babbled Ava, the younger one, eyes widening. "What's it like in the Tower? Is it scary?"

"Not in there, no." Finley caught Briony's gaze and beckoned for her to stand beside him.

"What about everything they're saying on the news?" Gracie asked. "Is it true that—"

"Gracie." Abigail's tone was gentle, but firm. "Why don't you take your sister to the study?"

"I want to stay." Gracie frowned at her.

Pamela's voice left far less room for protest. "I'm afraid that's not an option."

Gracie huffed with frustration, but she grabbed her backpack and slung it over one shoulder. "Come on, Ava," she muttered, ushering her sister through a door on the left. She shut it emphatically, not quite a slam, but not quite polite, either. A moment later, a telltale twinkle of light crept beneath it—some kind of Listen In. But if either of Finley's mums noticed, they didn't say a word.

"Now then," said Pamela. "Would you like to explain what you're doing here?"

Finley had seemed so sure back at the Thorburn estate. But now he coughed and stared at the floor, then at the walls. Anywhere but at his mums. The silence stretched on for an uncomfortably long time, until at last, he blurted, "Why weren't you there?"

"Finley . . ." Abigail said wearily.

"I know you were invited to the press conference. Every family was there, showing support. Everyone beside the Grieves—and *you*."

Abigail flinched. Pamela regarded them both coolly, with a stare that Briony recognized well. It was the same calculated look Finley got while planning out a rugby play or talking through tournament strategy.

"Perhaps this should be family only," Pamela said tightly. "I'm sure you can understand, Briony."

"Of course," Briony said.

But Finley shook his head. "She stays."

"Very well. You want to have this conversation in front of company? Let's have it." Pamela lowered herself into the nearest armchair. "What's another broken rule, when you've shattered so many?"

"Are you talking about the tournament?" Finley asked, sitting on the couch. Briony joined him, cognizant of the way he shifted nervously beside her. "Because I believe trying to break it is a good thing."

"We know exactly what you're trying to do." Abigail emphasized *trying* in a way that made Briony wince. "And your mother's not just talking about the tournament, Finley. She's talking about our code."

Finley looked utterly stricken. When they'd agreed to try and break the curse, he'd told Briony that his family's code wasn't enough to justify the tournament anymore. But Briony knew what a hold her own family's stories had on her, even now. And just as she'd striven to impress the Thorburns, Finley had once talked endlessly about wanting to impress the Blairs.

"So that's what this is about," he said bitterly. "Three words on a wall."

"You know they're much more than that," Pamela scolded. "Our family chose to participate in this curse because the alternative was war. The Blair code brings meaning to that decision and the responsibilities that come with it. Ignoring your commitment is dangerous—and dishonorable."

"Trying to stop this *is* the honorable course of action," Finley retorted. "It's the right thing to do. It's the only thing that makes sense. Other families can see that!"

"The families have the same goal they've always had," Abigail said bluntly. "They want power. And with the Lowe family no longer a threat, they've sensed an opportunity to claim it. Those whose champions have failed possess a vested interest in high magick returning to Ilvernath. Others are working with the government, playing both sides." She shot Briony a pointed look.

"I know the Thorburns are working with the government," Finley said defensively. "Briony told me."

"And it doesn't bother you that you're serving their—and her— self-interests?" Briony bristled as Abigail pressed on, ignoring her, "Not only that, you've allowed her to use you for the sake of the press—"

"It was my idea to ask for help," Finley snapped. "I'm the one who pitched that story in the *Eclipse*. But I guess it was ridiculous to think that after centuries of pretending we're not using our code to justify slaughtering people we care about, you'd suddenly change your minds."

"People we care about?" echoed Abigail, finally acknowledging Briony. "If this is some misguided lovers' pact . . ."

Briony decided she'd endured enough of this. She started to rise to her feet, but Finley grabbed her wrist. She swallowed, feeling horrifically awkward, but stayed.

"This is so much bigger than either of us," Finley said firmly.

"On that, at least, we agree," said Pamela. "Our expectations for you haven't changed, Finley. You've trained for this your entire life. The Lowes are dead. Instead of allowing high magick to slip through our fingers, you should win the tournament and secure a new legacy for Ilvernath, one where the victor's family wields their power responsibly in a way the Lowes never did. And if you believe the other families' intentions are any more honorable than ours . . . consider that we're proposing you earn us high magick for twenty years. *They're* trying to stake a permanent claim to it."

"They're trying to make sure nobody dies for high magick ever again," Finley argued.

"I encourage you to be less naive," Pamela told him. "You too, Briony. Both of you chose to become champions of your own free will, with full understanding of the task that awaited you. Other champions have tried to change the rules, too. All they did was prolong the inevitable."

Finley's expression hardened. "No one becomes a champion of

their own free will. But it's clear that I can't reason with either of you, so I'm done here. Come on, Briony. Let's go."

As soon as they left the front stoop, Finley started shaking. Briony didn't want to burn a Here to There, but he couldn't walk to the Tower in this state. So she steered them both to the nearest alleyway and cast an Undetectable. A cocoon of silence enveloped the alley, cloaking them both. Any potential spectators would suddenly feel their attention drawn elsewhere, leaving them to their privacy.

"I'm sorry," Briony said as he sagged against the wall, tears on his cheeks. "Do you need a minute?"

He nodded, looking utterly wretched.

"I can leave you alone if you want—"

"You know that's not what I want." His voice was gruff. A moment later, his trembling hand clutched hers.

"Hey," Briony murmured, stepping closer to him. She remembered how he'd wrapped his arm around her in that illusory blood lake, holding her while she panicked. Maybe he was merely seeking comfort the same way he'd comforted her, but it was hard to touch him without her mind wandering back to familiar, dangerous territory. But she didn't let go of his hand, not even as a shiver ran down her spine. "I'm here. I'm *here*."

She hadn't seen his gaze so unguarded since that day she'd knelt on the moors and asked him to kill her. Then, he'd looked furious. Now he seemed shaken to his very core.

"I thought I'd given it up," he whispered.

"Given what up?"

"Trying to make my family proud." He shuddered. "When we decided to end this, I told you it didn't matter what the other Blairs thought, but I think deep down I knew I was lying to myself. When I asked the world for help, I hoped it would convince them that what I was doing was right."

He choked on the last word.

Briony's heart twisted painfully. "Do you still think it's right?"

"I haven't changed my mind," Finley said quickly. "But you're lucky. Your family actually listened to you."

"I know. Maybe yours will, too. Eventually."

She thought of the Blairs' warnings that none of the families had abandoned their pursuit of power. She believed them. It was just that the Thorburns were being up front about what they were getting out of the deal—political leverage and good PR. If it meant they gave Briony and her friends the stories they needed, was that really so bad?

"Maybe." Finley sounded as though he didn't buy it. "It's just that my whole life, I've known what I was supposed to do. And I've always been good at it. School, rugby, spellcasting—easy. Getting people to like me? Also easy."

"Telling people how charming you are is a great way to charm them," Briony quipped.

Finley raised a brow. "I charmed you, didn't I? With all my class president bullshit?"

So Briony *had* struck a nerve back at the Thorburn estate.

"I don't think it's fair to call it bullshit," she said. "Or easy. You worked hard to balance everything."

"It *was* a lot of pressure." Finley freed his hand from hers and tugged at his tie, loosening it. "But it was pressure I was prepared to deal with. Since I've realized the tournament can end, everything feels different. For the first time in my life, I . . . I'm on my own, without my family backing me."

"You're not on your own, I promise. And maybe we won't be able to break the curse, but hey, maybe we will." Briony tapped gently on one of the storybooks, which he clutched in his free hand. "After today, I like our odds a little better."

His shoulders relaxed. "At least we got what we came for."

"Are you ready to go back now?"

"I think so," he said softly. "Thank you."

"Don't worry about it." And then, before her brain could catch up with her mouth, she added, "For what it's worth . . . I didn't want to date you because you were class president. Or rugby team captain. Or any of that other stuff."

For a moment, he looked startled. Then he took a step closer to her, his gaze lingering on her dress before rising to meet her eyes. Again, she was reminded of that school dance—and how they'd ditched it to make out in an abandoned classroom.

"Why *did* you date me, then?" he asked softly.

The words came to her easily—too easily. "Because you pay attention to the things most people miss. You're kind. You're loyal. You pretty much never give up. And when we were together, I felt—" she broke off. Not because she didn't know what to say next, but because she knew she wouldn't be able to take it back. Because her feelings for Finley weren't in the past anymore. Maybe they never had been.

All Briony's life, she'd felt as though she needed to prove herself to her family, prove she was good enough to be champion, prove she belonged. But Finley had always made her feel as though she was enough—not for him, but for herself. She hoped she'd made him feel that way, too. And she could no longer deny that she still wanted him. But the thought of telling him so felt impossible, dangerous, even. Even if he did return her feelings . . . there was no guarantee they'd succeed in their quest. The tournament could very well revert to the way it had always been, leaving them on opposite sides of the battlefield.

She could already lose her life. She didn't want to lose her heart along with it.

So she choked back her longing with a chuckle, then stepped away from him. "I felt like I could always out cast you. I mean, yeah, you're good . . . but I'm better."

Finley swallowed, his Adam's apple bobbing. Then he snorted. "You want to test that when we're back at the Tower?"

"Wouldn't that be a waste of magick?"

"Sounds to me like you're afraid to lose."

They walked through the city streets, still bantering. Briony kept up the Undetectable so passersby avoided them. It was a relief to be hidden from the cameras. For a moment, it made her feel hidden from all the expectations heaped upon her.

In the Thorburns' stories, the hero never faltered. Never doubted.

But one of the Relics was broken. Briony had plenty of reason to doubt. And all of Ilvernath—no, the entire world—would notice if she faltered.

GAVIN GRIEVE

"Viewership of Ilvernath's local news stations has skyrocketed over the last few weeks. Thousands of people from all over the world called in for the *Glamour Inquirer*'s latest poll about the tournament. Seventy-three percent of them think the death curse afflicting Alistair Lowe was cast unfairly."

SpellBC News

So," Alistair asked, rubbing his hands together gleefully. "What do we have today?"

Gavin dumped the newest delivery of fan mail on the rickety kitchen table. "Love letters, spellstones, homemade biscuits . . ."

Alistair smirked. "The usual, then."

The mail had begun the day after Alistair and Gavin's interview ran in the *Glamour Inquirer*, and in the week and a half since, it hadn't stopped. The external Blood Veil that still cut off Ilvernath from the rest of the world limited the full spectrum of support, but even within the city, the volume of messages was overwhelming. So far, Gavin had tallied over a hundred enchantments and handwritten notes, along with several pastries that were far better than Hendry's attempts at baking.

After Gavin's argument with Alistair, he'd feared the interview had been a massive miscalculation. But each message bolstered Gavin's pride at how well his gambit had paid off. He'd won over the spellmakers. He'd cemented his alliance with Alistair and Hendry. Now, total strangers were flocking to their aid.

For the first time in Gavin's life, people cared about his fate.

"Those look delicious." Alistair reached for one of the aforementioned biscuits. Their red sprinkles resembled droplets of blood.

"Don't eat those yet," said Hendry worriedly from beside him, stuffing a letter back into an envelope. "They could be poisoned."

Alistair stopped, the biscuit hovering in front of his mouth. "Aren't we screening for that?"

He sounded flippant, but Gavin noticed an undertone of anxiety. There were always cursestones mixed in with the spellstones, usually targeting Alistair. Gavin and Hendry had taken on the task of identifying them and burying them in the backyard, draining them of their enchantments. It was a sobering reminder that there were still plenty of people who considered them the bad guys.

"We are," Hendry said. "But . . . sometimes things get through." He looked uneasily at the envelope.

"What is that?" Alistair asked.

Hendry hesitated. "I don't want to worry you—"

"Give it to me." Alistair snatched the envelope, pulled out its contents, then scanned them with a frown. "Someone's accusing you of murder?"

Hendry's gaze was fixed on a stain in the table's corner. "To be fair, a lot of people have accused us of murder over the last week."

"Yes, but those were the murders we actually committed!" Alistair slammed the envelope onto the table. Gavin peered at its contents. Someone had written to Hendry about their missing husband, convinced he was behind the man's disappearance. At the end, in big block letters, were the words ANSWER FOR YOUR CRIMES, KILLER.

"Why do they think it was Hendry?" Gavin asked.

"Because they don't know what to make of me," Hendry said flatly. "I'm a living ghost story. Of course they think I'm dangerous."

Gavin refrained from pointing out that a triple homicide was also a pretty good reason to consider someone dangerous.

"That's not fair," Alistair grumbled. "*Maggot's* more of a menace than you."

"I am!" the girl piped up from her armchair, where she was busy gluing together a rat skeleton she'd found in the garden.

"Thanks," Hendry muttered. He grabbed one of the biscuits and cast a class four Poison Detection spell. A warm golden light twinkled across the batch. "You can eat them if you want, Al."

But Alistair had seemingly lost his appetite. He pushed the plate away, instead reaching for the nearest spellstone. He cast it, and an old-fashioned scroll materialized over the table, facing Alistair. It unfurled, revealing scrawled cursive embellished with cartoon hearts.

"Someone wants me to record myself telling a monster story and then leave it outside the wards." Looking puzzled, Alistair set the spellstone down, and the scroll faded. "As a present?"

Gavin rolled his eyes. "Oh, don't pretend you don't know why they'd want that."

"Because I'm a masterful storyteller?"

"Because . . ." Gavin couldn't bring himself to say it. He settled for, "Because it's part of your tragic backstory. Your, uh, bad boy appeal."

Alistair chewed on his lower lip, as though unsure whether to be flattered or unnerved.

Gavin had pushed Alistair to give that interview because he'd thought it would elicit sympathy—it'd worked well enough on him, back when they were playing drinking games at the Castle. What Gavin hadn't expected were the people lining up to take Isobel's place, as though Alistair hadn't ended his interview talking about how much he wanted to kill her. He found it incredibly disturbing.

Gavin doubted any of them could handle the Alistair Lowe who'd murdered Elionor Payne with one of Gavin's own curses—a curse far beyond his own meager strength. Who'd threatened Gavin with a series of brutal, excruciating deaths.

That Alistair Lowe was the champion he'd have to fight at the end of all this, not some broody, misunderstood heartthrob. As it was, he felt as though he lived with some sort of comical in-between, with an Alistair who'd put his shiny new pitchfork in a place of honor by the fireplace, who mumbled about souls and goblins and whatever other nonsense when he thought no one was listening.

The broom cupboard, alas, had extremely thin walls.

"Is there another one for me?" Marianne called from her rocking chair.

"No, there isn't," Hendry said hastily. A few people had written in about their concerns regarding an eight-year-old in the care of a death tournament champion—including Child Protective Services.

Marianne pouted as she fiddled with the rat skull. "Rude."

Alistair gestured to a letter—the last one left unopened. "I think that's from your spellmaker friends, Grieve."

The envelope was thick, made of paper that felt luxurious. Inside was an elaborate piece of stationery.

"Greetings from your spellmaking colleagues . . ." Gavin began. The letter was flowery and pretentious and clearly written by Osmand Walsh. After a lot of pontificating, the message finally took an interesting turn. "They think the healing Relic might cure us. The Medallion."

As he spoke the words aloud, Gavin felt a cautious glimmer of hope.

"Let me see that," Alistair said immediately. Gavin passed him the note. "They . . . they think it might be able to reverse the Reaper's Embrace, and maybe even help Gavin. What do you think, Hendry?"

"It makes sense, doesn't it?" Hendry asked. "With high magick imbued inside it, its spells are—"

"Higher than class ten," Alistair finished softly. He clenched and unclenched his gloved hand.

"Look what I did," Marianne declared, holding up her finished skeleton. A spellring shone on her finger. The rat's tail began to twitch. Red dots appeared where the corpse's eyes used to be, and then it scuttled up her arm. She grinned viciously as Gavin shuddered.

"That's very impressive, Marianne," Hendry told her gently. "But wouldn't you rather play with something nicer? We want you to be happy. We could get you action figures or dolls or—"

"No. Skeletons," she grunted.

"Shocker," Alistair muttered, and Gavin inwardly agreed.

Hendry's smile twitched. "But skeletons aren't very nice—"

"*You're* not very nice," she snapped.

"Just leave her be," Alistair told his brother. "She's clearly content—"

Ignoring him, Hendry rose from the table and carefully approached their cousin. "That's all right, then. Would you like to have a tea party? It'll be fun, and we can leave them to their grown-up talking."

He held out his hand, crimson light flickering between his fingers. Gingerly, Marianne took it and let Hendry lead her away to her room, leaving Gavin and Alistair alone.

"Well, Grieve?" Alistair asked. "What do you think?"

The Medallion was far more likely to cure a class ten death curse than fix his magick, but Gavin could tell from that meeting that the spellmakers' allegiance still lay with him. Although it was a calculated risk, healing Alistair would make the Lowes feel secure. It was part of the reason he'd taken on the job of protecting Alistair from those cursestones, why he'd agreed to sleep in a broom cupboard—he needed to win them over, particularly Hendry.

"When the Medallion falls, the other champions will chase it," Gavin said. "Right now it's four versus three, and none of *them* are cursed. Fighting them in our current state is a massive risk. It's only a risk worth taking if it'll get us closer to being at full strength—but I think we should give it a try."

"And if we have to wait a long time?"

"Then we hope the spellmakers find some other, better cure. For all of us."

"What about those exercises they gave you?" Alistair asked him. "Are they helping?"

Gavin had spent the past week and a half training furiously, mostly in the garden. The exercises were meant to show a spellcaster how to conserve common magick and focus their talents to handle stronger enchantments, but the spellmakers had annotated suggestions for how he could adapt them for life magick. He'd been working on breathing and visualization exercises, with some supplemental stretches.

"Yeah, they're helping," he answered. "I still have to use life magick when I cast. But I can ration it now in a way I couldn't before."

"Will you show me?"

Gavin hesitated. Alistair was still an opponent, alliance or no alliance. However, he wasn't really sure how they could put a battle strategy together without him being honest about his capabilities.

"I'll need a spellstone," he said at last.

Alistair stood and rifled through one of the kitchen drawers. Rain pelted against the windows behind him. "What kind hurts you the least?"

Gavin had thought Alistair would care the most about the strongest enchantments he could manage, not the effect casting them would have on him.

"Something simple," he replied. "A spell, not a curse."

Alistair fished out an orange stone. "Will this work? It's a class three Levitate."

"That should be fine, yeah."

Alistair returned to the table and slid the stone over to Gavin.

"Watch my tattoo," Gavin explained, his hand hovering over the enchantment. "Before, when I picked up a spellstone, it automatically filled with my life magick. But now . . ." He concentrated, then scooped up the crystal.

"It's not changing," Alistair said, sounding impressed.

"Exactly. The stone's still empty. I can control how I fill it. And when I do fill it . . ." Gavin took a deep breath, held it, then exhaled slowly. The stone began to shine faintly. His arm twinged with pain, but it was far less than he was used to. "It doesn't take me as much life magick to fill a spellstone as it did before. The more I practice, the less power I waste."

Alistair's stare bored into him, calculating and sharp. "Managing your magick like that must take a lot of control. And strength."

Gavin had never expected Alistair Lowe of all people to call him *strong*. The rain came down harder on the thatched roof, and the fire in the hearth cast Alistair's contemplative expression in a soft glow. With his curls falling across his forehead and his features framed in gentle light, Gavin could almost understand all that fan mail.

And then an ear-splitting shriek rang out from the other room. Marianne stormed into the kitchen a moment later, her face streaked with tears.

"I want to go home!" she wailed at Hendry, who dashed after her.

"We will, one day. A new home." Hendry knelt beside her. "This place, it's only temporary—an in-between. Soon you and me and Al will go somewhere brand new, like a really big city, or the ocean. Don't you want to see the ocean—"

"I want to go *home*!" The girl sounded shrill, dangerously so, and Gavin caught that look on her face that he'd noticed when she saw those pictures in the newspaper. "I want Dad! Why can't I see him?"

"Mag—Marianne." Alistair rose from his chair, his voice wobbling. "Your dad isn't . . . He's . . ."

"He's gone," Hendry told her softly.

"No!" The rat on Marianne's shoulder quivered, then launched itself at Hendry, skeletal claws scratching. The boy yelped, and Alistair rushed to him. He yanked it off and threw it aside, sending bones scattering across the floorboards. Marianne shrieked all the louder. "You killed Dad! I hate you! I hate you both!"

Then she dove beneath the table. Gavin felt a viselike grip on his leg and realized that Marianne was clinging to him. She screamed until her breath ran out, and then she screamed again—over and over.

Alistair's chest heaved, and anguish bloomed across Hendry's face.

"Hey," Gavin said to Marianne awkwardly, reminded of his brother Fergus's tantrums when they were younger. "Hey, uh—it's okay." But he could tell she was barely registering the words as she rocked back and forth, howling herself hoarse.

Gavin thought of the stories Alistair had told the reporter and knew he hadn't been playing up how horrible the Lowes were. Their childhoods really *had* been some kind of dark, demented fairy tale.

Alistair squeezed his brother's shoulder. "She can't stay here." It was hard to hear him over the girl's wails.

"She's family," Hendry bit out. "She stays."

"This isn't good for her. *We're* not good for her."

Hendry shoved him aside. "Family is supposed to mean something."

"I know," Alistair murmured. "But do you really want it to mean this?"

Marianne still clung to Gavin's leg. Her screams had finally dissipated into whimpers.

"Fine," Hendry snapped. "But where could we possibly take her? I don't want the newspapers getting hold of her."

Gavin's mind whirled, then landed somewhere unexpected.

"I have an idea," he said quickly. "Somewhere she'll be safe, where the press can't find her. I promise."

Marianne was inconsolable when he cast the Here to There spell, too angry to say goodbye. Alistair and Hendry both tried, but she scratched and spit at them like a wild animal. Gavin looped her pink backpack over one shoulder, hoisted her into his arms—she weighed almost nothing—and let the Cottage melt away.

The Payne estate cut an imposing image in the rain. It was a jagged, strange building—Gavin hoped that it would remind Marianne at least a little bit of home. He knocked on the door until a butler answered. The man seemed startled but recognized him immediately, and waved him and Marianne into a parlor. Gavin sat on an uncomfortable chaise longue, Marianne hiccupping beside him. Framed pages from various grimoires hung on the walls, along with displays of spellstone jewelry not unlike the ones in Walsh's store. Which made sense, since the Paynes were the family who focused most on spellmaking.

They waited in awkward silence until Callista Payne, formerly Callista Grieve, walked through the door, wearing a long white nightgown and rubbing her eyes. Gavin's older sister was far shorter than him, with shiny blond hair that hung in a curtain down her back and small, pinched features.

The two of them had never been close. She'd always wanted to leave their family behind—so much so that Gavin suspected her of being the anonymous author behind *A Tradition of Tragedy*, which was filled with bitterness and pain. Gavin had often wondered if she felt guilty for how much she'd distanced herself from him while doting on Fergus. If there was ever a time for that guilt to matter, it would be now.

"Hello, Gavin," she said cautiously. "I must admit, I never expected to see you again."

"See me alive, you mean," he corrected, pushing down a pang of anger. Gavin had years of practice ignoring his family's cavalier attitude toward his impending mortality.

His sister's fair skin flushed. "Well. Yes."

"How's the marriage going?"

"Well enough." She cast a glance at Marianne. The butler had used a Freshen Up spellstone to dry their hair and clothes, and she'd stopped crying, but Gavin didn't know how long that would last. "You've procured a . . . child?"

"She's a Lowe," he said.

Callista sucked in a horrified breath. "I read the articles about her family. That poor thing."

"She's a bit eccentric, but she needs a safe place to stay, at least for a little while."

"You want her to stay here?"

"She's got nowhere else to go."

Callista regarded Marianne warily.

"What's your name?" she asked her, her tone far more soothing than it had been moments before. Marianne's grip hurt Gavin's arm, and her eyes were wide with fear.

"My family says not to talk to strangers," Marianne said suspiciously.

"Well, I'm Gavin's sister," Callista said. "He's not a stranger, right?"

Marianne sniffled. "I guess not. I—I'm Marianne Lowe."

"Nice to meet you, Marianne. I'm Callista."

"Where . . . where am I?"

"Somewhere safe," Callista said.

Gavin had wanted her to care about Marianne's plight, but it still pained him to see how kind she could be to a child she'd never met before, when she'd greeted him like a corpse who hadn't had the decency to stop breathing yet.

Beside him, Marianne reached wordlessly for her backpack. Gavin slid it off his shoulder and handed it to her. She clutched it tightly in her lap, her tiny sneakers treading dirt on the white carpet. Callista didn't seem to mind.

"Have you ever had a sleepover?" Callista asked her. "With friends?"

Marianne looked bewildered. "What's a sleepover?"

"Oh. Well . . . it's fun. You spend the night in a new place, and you tell scary stories, and you eat all the snacks you want."

"Scary stories?" Marianne sounded a little brighter. "Do you know any good ones?"

"Of course I do. But we should pick out a bedroom first, if you want to stay here for a little while?"

"I don't want to go back to the Cottage."

"Well, then. Let's take a look."

Gavin walked awkwardly beside Callista up a set of stairs and down a long, gloomy hallway. She pulled a ring of keys out from a pocket in her nightgown, each with a spellstone embedded in it, and unlocked room after room. One was full of stacks of dusty grimoires. Another opened into a strange workshop where her husband sat slumped over at a desk, gently snoring. Spellstones glowed in cages of iron and steel like beating hearts.

Callista shut the door gently. "I'm still getting used to this place. It's a maze."

"What was all that?" Gavin asked.

"Many of the Paynes are inventors, Roland included. He's currently trying to upgrade our home security system." She spoke matter-of-factly, as though she was some kind of tour guide.

"Home security system?" Gavin echoed. "I heard something about a person going missing . . ."

"Two people," Callista said briskly. "It's not in the news yet, just rumors. But Ilvernath's small. Stories spread. So we're being cautious."

The next room Callista opened looked far more modern. Marianne flitted inside, past a giant jewelry stand and a precariously balanced pile of spellboards. Gavin took one step through the doorframe and found himself face-to-face with a ghost—a series of photos of Elionor Payne tacked up on the walls. Someone had gathered sympathy cards and flowers on an end table below them in a makeshift memorial.

Gavin had never known the other champion. Never cared for her. All he'd really registered about her were her spellstone gauges and the way she'd fought past the point of reason, right up until she died horribly at Alistair's hand.

Now, he was pretty sure he stood in her bedroom. She was clearly missed, clearly mourned. His stomach twisted painfully.

"Not this one," he said hastily, ushering Marianne out.

The next door Callista opened was at the very end of the hallway. Marianne rushed inside and immediately let out a delighted yell. Gavin followed her into a spacious bedchamber with dark purple sheets and an intimidating iron bedframe. The single lightbulb in the cobwebbed fixture flickered when he turned it on. A wardrobe in the corner looked like it could grow a mouth and swallow him, and the windows had an ominous view of the rainy forest.

"Oh, dear," Callista murmured. Marianne clambered onto the bed, still clutching her backpack, still wearing her dirty shoes. "This belonged to my husband's great-great-aunt, and it hasn't been updated since . . . I don't know when."

"I love it," Marianne declared. Gavin was deeply unsurprised.

"Well, if you love it, you can certainly stay here." Several of Callista's spellrings flared in quick succession. An invisible duster swept neatly across the floor, while the pillows fluffed themselves out. Gavin wondered if he should tell her to leave the cobwebs intact. "Do you need any snacks? Any more clothes?"

Gavin had a sudden memory of being around Marianne's age

and knocking on Callista's door, crying. He'd had a nightmare, and he wasn't a strong enough spellcaster yet to drown out his parents' screaming. But when she finally cracked open the door, it wasn't to provide comfort.

"They yell at each other every night," she'd hissed. "Go back to sleep."

It wasn't her fault, he'd told himself. Until she started tucking Fergus in every evening to help with *his* nightmares, and he realized she favored him the same way their mother did. That just like everyone else in their family, she'd decided Gavin wasn't worth the trouble of caring about.

"I want a scary story," Marianne declared. "That's what you said happens at sleepovers, right?"

Callista hesitated. "Once upon a time, there was a beautiful unicorn—"

"No." Marianne crossed her arms. "No. I want a *scary* story."

"She's not kidding," Gavin said.

Callista sighed. "Well, I'm sure you know a lot of stories about your family. But do you know any stories about mine?"

Marianne shook her head, looking expectant.

"Then I have a tale for you." Callista lowered her voice. "The tale of the very first Grieve."

"What?" Gavin blurted. He'd assumed she was about to discuss the Paynes. "We don't have a story."

"Yes, we do," Callista said.

"But Mum and Dad said we didn't." Gavin had only been brave enough to ask them once, and their reactions had been so humiliating he'd never tried it again. "And it isn't in any records . . . just that we hid in the Cottage a lot."

Just like you're doing now.

Marianne glared at him. "You're being rude."

"You *are* interrupting," Callista said, although her voice was far gentler than Marianne's. "But the story of the first Grieve does start in the Cottage. It's our traditional Landmark, you know. Not to *hide*—" She cast Gavin a glance. "But to rest."

Callista had abandoned him long before she fled the rest of their family. She had no right to know this story when he didn't. She had no right to talk about the tournament at all. But for Marianne's sake, he stayed silent.

"Resting isn't scary," said Marianne.

"It is when the stakes are life and death," Callista said. "Outside the Grieve's doors, a terrible battle raged beneath a blood-red sky. People cast curses more powerful than anything you can imagine—strong enough to level mountains or turn a river into a flood. No one and nowhere were safe."

The words echoed through his skull, a painful reminder of what it truly meant to be a Grieve champion. In the thrill of spellmaker alliances and fan mail and Lowe protection, he'd almost been able to push down the fear that had haunted him all his life. Now, though, reality rushed back in. From the moment his family had chosen him to die, nothing was safe.

Until the tournament was finished, nothing ever would be.

Marianne curled up on the bed like a cat, her eyes watchful. "So what did the Grieve do?"

"Well, he had something very special. A Relic called the Shoes. Allies turned each other to piles of ash, and on the drawbridge of the Castle, a deadly curse sucked the life from anyone who challenged its wielder. But because of how fast the Shoes could run, he escaped them all. He was faster than the wind, stealthier than a shadow."

Marianne yawned, her eyes fluttering. "I want shoes like that."

Gavin couldn't keep a quiver from his voice. "What, he wasn't strong enough to fight?"

"He used the strengths he had the best way he could," Callista shot back. "He was smart enough to choose the Cottage as his destination. It was well hidden and stocked with provisions. The perfect place to plot your next move."

Gavin thought of the Cottage as he knew it, claimed by Alistair Lowe. He felt the story closing around him like a trap, but he had no idea how to escape it. The first Grieve certainly hadn't.

"He had a grand plan to destroy his enemies," Callista continued. "But he also knew that if he waited long enough, most of them would destroy themselves. His opponents chose bigger targets—the Castle. The Tower. While the Grieve kept his hearth warm and his belly full. Until one day, a terrible misfortune befell him."

Gavin expected a gleeful reaction from Marianne at the words *terrible misfortune*, but none came. Instead, he heard a tiny snore. The girl had fallen asleep.

"Let's go," he whispered to Callista. The two of them crept carefully out of the room. Gavin hoped Marianne wouldn't be too terrified when she woke up. "Try to take care of her, okay? Don't tell the press where she is."

"I'll do my best," Callista said as they returned to the parlor. Lightning flashed outside the windows, strange and muted through the filtered sky. "Don't you want to know how the story ends?"

"You mean, the story about our champion being weaker than everyone else and fleeing from battles?" Gavin had meant his words to sound like a joke. They didn't. "Let me guess, a Lowe brutally murdered him."

"Nobody murdered him at all, actually." Callista met his eyes, her gaze slightly pitying. "He was too hasty and took a step in only one of the Shoes. He was torn in half."

Gavin wanted to scream, or cry, or curse. Instead, he just glared.

"That's the most depressing thing I've ever heard."

"That's what I said. But Dad was drunk when he told me, so maybe the details are a little messed up, I don't know. I was planning on changing the ending, for Marianne's sake."

"If anything, you probably could've made it gorier. Maybe you could make our family sound even more pathetic, too—although I guess you've already done that, haven't you?"

"What are you talking about?" Callista asked.

"The book," Gavin said. "*A Tradition of Tragedy*. I . . . I've always suspected. But the way you told that story . . . the way you clearly hate our family . . ."

"You think I wrote it?" Callista stepped backward, her key ring jangling. "I had nothing to do with it. I promise."

He thought briefly about asking for a truth spell, but the expression on her face felt like proof enough.

"Then who did?" he asked harshly. "Mum? Dad?"

"I don't think it was a Grieve at all," Callista said softly. "I think someone set us up to take the fall."

Gavin decided she had a point. He didn't know exactly why, only that his gut told him that there had *always* been something wrong with it all. Maybe if he lived long enough, he'd find the answer.

"I guess it doesn't really matter, anyway," he muttered. "I should get going. Thank you for taking Marianne in."

"Wait." Callista cleared her throat. "I read your interview. In the *Inquirer*. Gavin . . . you know there's another way out of all this, right? The Thorburns are trying to gather stories. I was at their press conference—Briony and Finley are really trying to help."

Gavin gritted his teeth. "If you read my interview, then you know exactly how I feel about their chances."

"But—"

"No." Gavin's control finally snapped. "You don't get to tell me what choices to make. You said it yourself, you never thought I'd live this long."

"That's not what I—"

"Then what *did* you mean?"

She paled. "I . . . it's just that we all know the odds."

"Yeah, one in seven," Gavin said. "The same as every other champion."

Before Callista could respond, he stormed for the door. Another Here to There spell would be a waste of his life magick, so he walked back to the Cottage instead, swiping furiously at the tears that dripped down his cheeks. It was a long way to go in the cold and dark.

Gavin had spent his whole life wishing his family had a story. He'd tried to tell one of his own during this tournament, one where he was finally a victor. But Grieves never got what they wanted, not even in their stories. No matter how well they fooled the world. No matter how much they sacrificed to survive.

Gavin wished he'd never heard the tale of the first Grieve. And he vowed to never tell it to another living soul.

ISOBEL MACASLAN

It seems Isobel Macaslan has more weapons at her disposal than curses.

Glamour Inquirer, "The Scarlet Starlet"

Isobel grimaced at the photograph splashed across the *Glamour Inquirer's* front page: a six-month-old still of her on *SpellBC's* national morning talk show, printed beneath the searing headline: "THE SCARLET STARLET—WAS SEDUCTION HER STRATEGY FROM THE START?"

"You shouldn't look at those," Briony told her gently from the chair beside her.

"Or what? I might feel sorry for myself?" Isobel bitterly tossed the tabloid across the table, among the teetering towers of Briony's and Finley's fan mail. "How considerate of you to take my feelings into account."

Of course the *Glamour Inquirer* had chosen a photo from *that* interview. The one that marked the dreadful turning point of her fame.

Before: Isobel Macaslan, worldwide fascination, the face of Ilvernath's curse.

After: Isobel Macaslan, evil media whore.

The public had deemed the skirt she'd worn too short for a proper young lady, even one training to kill six of her peers. Crude letters began to arrive in the mail. A stranger harassed her at a restaurant, screamed that he hoped she lost, hoped she died. That night, tearstricken, Isobel had burned the skirt in her father's fireplace. She hadn't intended it to be short. Being tall, most clothes on her were.

But even those hellish months hadn't prepared her for the backlash of Alistair's interview.

"Poor, heartbroken Alistair," she said sarcastically. "Who murdered Elionor right in front of us. Who struck me with a *death curse.*"

"It's bullshit," Briony agreed.

"He makes it out like I'm some sort of . . . *temptress.* Like I tricked him! As though he wasn't the one who betrayed us all the moment he saw Hendry again."

"Asshole," Briony muttered.

"Now the whole world thinks I'm terrible, when in reality it nearly killed me to curse him. And I'm still living with it, with what he did to me. I'll always be . . ." Isobel sniffled, stopping herself. She still wasn't ready to tell Briony about the Roach's Armor. "I'll never forgive him for this."

"I'm sorry," Briony said.

Isobel wiped her eyes and glared at her. "Stop doing that. This is your and Finley's fault as much as it's his." Briony winced, but Isobel didn't care if she'd wounded her. Even though Briony had apologized for submitting Isobel's name to the papers as the first champion last year, all Isobel's old ire felt fresh now. Because once again, Briony got to walk out of her messes unscathed. Even the truth about Carbry's death hadn't swayed her admirers. Though regrettable, they said, such dire mistakes could be forgiven when considering the nature of the tournament.

Unless, of course, the victim was hot.

While Briony made a pathetically poor show of concentrating on the books the Darrows and Paynes had given her, Isobel snatched up another magazine with a headline even more vile than the last: "A NEW CASUALTY OR CO-CONSPIRATOR?"

After a passerby reported spotting Macaslan with Reid MacTavish in his curseshop, we have to ask—has Macaslan moved from one dastardly male champion onto another? Or, even more scandalous, has this new champion been part of the story from the start?

Isobel snorted and flashed Briony the article. "Oh, how silly of me. Here I was, traumatized, thinking I was a hostage in Reid's curseshop. Turns out, we were on a date!"

At least Isobel wasn't the only one the public loathed. Since Reid's unmasking as a dabbler in the forbidden arts of life magick, conspiracy theorists debated over how to cast his character: the mad scientist, the troubled delinquent, and now, apparently, her amorous co-conspirator.

While Isobel pored over the pictures of Reid—including a blurry photo of him flipping off a journalist and an oddly normal, smiling senior portrait—she pretended not to notice Briony's eyes going bloodshot. Because even though Isobel's anger was justified, a voice prickled in her mind, accusing her of being terrible. After all, not a single day had passed since the Cloak's destruction when she hadn't considered betraying Briony and Finley.

Maybe she'd been wrong to curse Alistair.

Maybe she was cruel to Briony, who hadn't meant to hurt her.

Maybe she deserved this.

"Why do we even care about our reputations anymore?" Isobel tossed the tabloid aside. It collided with a tower of fan mail, which toppled and scattered across the floor. "We already have the families' stories. Literally all we can do now is wait for the Relics to fall. Which means we don't need these reporters, the love letters, any of it."

Technically, they only had five of the families' stories: the Darrows with the Monastery and the Hammer, the Paynes with their Medallion and Mill, the Macaslan Cloak and Crypt, and, of course, the Thorburn Tower and Mirror. Process of elimination had left the Grieves and the Lowes, the Castle and the Cottage, and the Crown and the Shoes. Laughably easy to guess.

"Being the favorites has its advantages." Briony nodded to the pile of spellstones gifted to her and Finley from their admirers.

"Maybe you and Finley *should* stage a kiss then," said Isobel.

"Don't."

"But think of the hoard of useless class three spells we'd accumulate."

"*Don't.*" Briony flushed. "Just because we have to wait doesn't mean we have nothing to do. Is Reid making any progress on the Cloak?"

Isobel cleared her throat. The Cloak was the last thing she wanted to discuss.

"Judging by the way he threw me out of his room last night, no."

Itching for a distraction, Isobel stood and examined the heap of gifts, from brown paper parcels to loose spellstones to gingham-covered wicker baskets. A neatly wrapped package caught her eye, with a bow stapled on top—maybe someone had remembered her birthday two days prior. Isobel had told Briony she didn't want to celebrate, but she wouldn't turn down a gift.

"Have you already checked all these for curses?" Isobel asked.

"Yeah, they should be safe."

Satisfied, she opened the box, which, to her surprise, contained an elegant soy candle of lavender wax with a spellstone embedded in the jar—the sort she might display in her bedroom at home. And when she lifted it to her nose, she gasped. It *smelled* like home. Like the invigorating bubblegum scent of her mother's spellshop, of her favorite brand of shampoo, of the fresh brewed coffee from the café she visited every morning before school. A mixture of comfort and homesickness settled over her like a weighted blanket.

"A candle?" Briony said with bewilderment. "What else did they send us, bath salts?"

"No, smell it." Isobel passed it to her, and Briony frowned and sniffed. Instantly, her face softened. "It smells like a field of grass. No, cinnamon. No, like—" She cut off, blushing.

"It must have a different scent for each person," Isobel said. "It's . . . nice."

"It is," Briony admitted, setting it aside. "We'll put it downstairs in the common room."

A little mollified, Isobel sifted through the other gifts, wondering if anyone would've been thoughtful enough to send them instant coffee, or deodorant. Her gaze caught on a pretty cushion-cut spellstone, colored a deep umber, with a treacly light barely visible within its depths.

"Wait," said Briony. "I don't recognize—"

But it was too late. As soon as Isobel picked it up, a white light flashed from within the crystal, then something red and wet exploded over her. Briony yelped. Isobel didn't, only squeezed her eyes shut as the hot mystery liquid dribbled down her forehead.

"Are you okay?" Briony scrambled out of her seat. "Let me—"

"I'm fine," Isobel snapped. She peeled her eyes open and dabbed at a dollop on her face. Crimson glistened on her fingers but faded in mere seconds. She glanced down, and the speckles receded into her tank top, not even leaving a stain behind.

Except for one section.

On her left arm, a vulgar word was scrawled across her skin.

Isobel whimpered and scraped at it, desperate to smear it away, but as she did so, her skin began to swell. Scarlet pustules bubbled in the shape of each letter. One of the boils along the C engorged until it burst, splattering pus across her chin.

Briony gasped. "I'm so sorry. I didn't see that one. I don't know how it got in—"

"Well, how could you see it?" Isobel sneered. "It was buried underneath all your fan mail." Tears pooled in her eyes, and her breaths stuttered out, useless but rote. She couldn't even cry right anymore. She felt violated. Mortified. Furious. Why did Alistair get the world's sympathy while she suffered its scorn? Why did Briony get to play the darling while she played the damned?

Briony stammered, "I-I have a healing spell—"

"I don't want your help."

Isobel fled down the stairwell to the bathroom. With a strangled sob, she closed the door and pressed her back against the wall. The rash glared at her from the mirror, red and ugly, perfectly suited to her horrid, dead reflection.

Maybe it didn't matter whether she was good or evil. Maybe the world would hate her no matter what.

Forty minutes later, Isobel entered the coffee shop she'd so dearly missed. Thanks to her Undetectable, the gazes of the other patrons slid off her like oil over water, yet she still kept her eyes downcast. Not only would it be awkward—even precarious—to be recognized, she couldn't bear for anyone to see her like this, with her puffy face and fading rash and icy, unsettling pallor.

She claimed a quiet corner table and braced for her company to arrive.

Cormac Macaslan showed up several minutes late, as per usual. He wore a dark overcoat, a white silky shirt, and a plastic pin that read BLOW A KISS FOR ISOBEL. After ordering black iced coffees for the both of them, he scanned the café, and Isobel relaxed her spell so that only he would notice her. He beamed, his gold tooth gleaming.

Despite how furious Isobel was with him, the sight of her father still filled her with relief. She stood and hugged him. He reeked of cigarettes. "Thank you for coming."

"Of course. I dropped everything when I got your message. Even brought you some stuff. Not exactly the most exciting birthday presents I've ever gotten you, but I thought they should be discreet." As he stepped back, he handed Isobel her drink and emptied his pockets, scattering spellstones, candy bars, and some miscellaneous cosmetics across the table—including, Isobel noted gratefully, deodorant. "Wild times, aren't they? First the Blood Veil vanishes, then all these people disappear."

"People are disappearing?" Isobel repeated, alarmed.

"Oh, it's just the latest whispers. The *Eclipse* won't print anything about it—they call it gossip, people caught up in the buzz of the tournament. But it's been chaotic, to say the least, which is why I'm glad we're finally speaking. I would've reached out to you sooner, but I didn't want to risk exposing whatever it is you're planning."

"What do you mean?" She sat and stirred her straw anxiously in her drink.

"Well, you're with the Thorburn and Blair champions, aren't you? I think it's brilliant. Getting close so you can slay them, exactly like you did the Lowe. The kiss was a stroke of genius, by the way. I'll admit, I was confused when I saw the photographs, but as soon as I read his interview, I said, 'Aha! I *knew* it! That's my girl, that's my Isobel.' It's just like the saying, isn't it? A death cast with a kiss can never—"

For the second time that day, Isobel burst into tears.

Her father hastily slid into the seat across from her and squeezed her arm. "What is it? Are you hurt?"

"*Yes*, I'm hurt. Can't you tell?"

"I, uh . . . Do you need a healing spell? I know a guy. Has a business on the side, sells prescription-grade enchantments for a fraction of—"

"Why didn't you tell me what the Roach's Armor would do to me?" Tears streamed down her cheeks. She had never been more grateful for the Undetectable. "My heart doesn't beat anymore. I'm cold all the time. I don't breathe. And *look* at me."

"So you've used it then," Cormac said mournfully. He cast a shifty glance over his shoulder at the other patrons, then lowered his voice.

"Well, a powerful curse requires a powerful sacrifice. Though if it makes you feel better, I didn't notice anything."

"How? I look half-dead!"

"Now, now, I know my daughter, and you didn't ask to meet with me just to throw a tantrum. The Roach's Armor is our family's traditional curse for a reason. Not any old enchantment can stave off certain death. And I, for one, am grateful you're alive. That's what matters, isn't it?"

Isobel wiped her eyes. "Yeah, I know."

"Now tell me why you really asked me here. I want to help, in any way I can."

She'd practiced her words carefully on the walk here, but then, she hadn't been crying. She stared at the chalky, handwritten menu behind the bar simply to have something to focus on. "I . . . think Briony and Finley are trying to do the right thing—I really do." She sniffled. "But I'm scared they won't succeed."

"Of course they won't. They're a pair of teenagers who think they can destroy a curse that's lasted for centuries. This isn't some class project. This is the real world." Cormac slid his grip from her arm to her hand. If he noticed the coldness of her skin, he didn't comment on it. "Is this about all the limelight? Because I'll admit it—your reputation has definitely been sunnier. But for what it's worth, it's been great for business. Your cousins sell loads of merchandise about you—they play every angle. So anything else you need, you tell me, got it?"

It was no surprise that the Macaslans would capitalize on her fame, even by besmirching her. She wondered if any of the signs the protestors waved outside the Tower came from her own family.

"No, I have plenty of spellwork, really," she said tightly. "It's that *I* want to do the right thing. I don't want to kill my friends. I didn't want to curse Alistair. And I don't want the world to hate me. But I think you're right about the curse—they can't break it. I guess I just wanted to hear you tell me that . . . I don't know. That I'm not a monster."

Cormac scooted his chair closer to her, knocking into the table and making her drink wobble.

"Listen to me, Isobel. The rest of the world will cast their judgments, but they're not the ones wearing a champion's ring, are they? The only right or wrong that truly matters is what's right for *you*." He jabbed his finger into her chest. "Remember, you're a survivor."

As always, his words trickled through her like sap, gluing her broken pieces back into place. He was right. And if the world would hate Isobel no matter what she did, then she might as well live. A future after the tournament was all she had left to hope for.

"You haven't spoken to your mother, have you?" Cormac asked.

"No." As much as Isobel wanted to see her, to let her mum hold her and listen to her cry and run her fingers through her hair, Honora had always despised the tournament. She wouldn't understand.

"Good. I'm not going to tell your uncles about our little chat. As far as they're concerned, you've taken out the Lowe, and the Blair and the Thorburn are next. Now . . ." He glanced at his clunky gold watch. "There's a funeral in twenty minutes. They'll wonder if I'm not there . . ." He stood and kissed Isobel on the cheek. "You know how to reach me."

He left. Isobel finished her coffee and departed a few minutes later. As she walked down the bustling street, her enchantment concealing her from the other pedestrians, she passed the pastel green awning of her mother's spellshop. A sign dangled from its door.

BE BACK SOON!

Her mother was on her lunch break, then.

After a moment's deliberation, Isobel grasped the knob. White shimmered around the brass—the security spell recognizing her. It unlocked, and she stumbled inside, forcing in a breath just to inhale the bubblegum-scented air, better than any candle aroma could capture. As she wove through the aisles of trendy, beautiful spellstones, her reflection stalked her in the gilded mirrors along the walls. But not even its enchanted glass could improve her lifeless complexion. It stamped rouge like bullseyes on the hollows of her cheeks, filtered her skin an unnatural orange rather than a beachy glow.

She slid open the glass case of cosmetic spells—her mother's specialty.

Isobel hated to steal, even if her mother would freely give her any of these. It was slimy, and one of her father's worst traits, who shoplifted for the rush of it rather than true necessity.

Yet this felt like one. Almost.

She grabbed the full set: Flawless Base to paint over the gray of her skin; Lovestruck for blush to bloom on her cheeks; First Kiss to plump her chapped, crusted lips. She applied spell after spell until she finally recognized her reflection. Here was the girl who pulled all-nighters with Briony at their weekly sleepovers just because they could. The girl who dreamed of traveling and attending an impressive fashion school. The girl who'd never thought herself terrible.

Almost.

When she finished, she stuffed the crystals into the already bulging pockets of her baggy joggers. Part of her wanted to sneak to the flat upstairs, to steal some of her clothes, even to lay in her own bed—if only for a moment. But she didn't have much time until her mother returned from the local deli.

She left, and Honora Jackson's eyes glided over her daughter as they passed each other on the sidewalk.

By the time Isobel returned to the Tower that afternoon, she'd made up her mind. She would kill the others in their sleep, swiftly and painlessly.

Tonight.

But as she climbed the stairs to her room, seeking out solitude to plan, she noticed the door to Reid's room hung ajar. She peeked inside, finding her supposed new lover sitting cross-legged on the floor, hunched oh-so-dreamily over an ancient grimoire. Its crabbed, handwritten text had faded to little more than a shadow across the yellowed parchment, and wrinkles, grooves, and fissures threaded the leatherbound cover in a weblike lattice.

Reid parsed through the tome as though expecting it to disintegrate beneath his fingers, and even with the Warden's Shackles still binding his wrists, his touch looked as gentle as a caress.

"You've already read that one," Isobel pointed out. "I saw you read it four days ago."

Reid jarred, but he didn't look up at her. He'd made a point never to look at her—which suited her fine. His death was the only one she wouldn't mourn. "I might've missed something. The language is archaic. It barely resembles how we speak today."

"So you've made no progress, then?"

"What do you think?" He turned to a fresh chapter, where a diagram of the moon cycle stretched across a two-page spread. Then he gingerly closed the grimoire and reached for another from the pile beside him. This one had no cover at all, its paper held together by sinews of frayed twine. "If we're going to craft a replacement Cloak, we need high magick, and that's not exactly easy to come by, is it?"

"Alistair once told me that there's tons of it beneath the Lowe estate, in a vault."

He traced his index finger down the table of contents. "I'm sure there is, but as you all probably realized before you frantically bonded me to you, there's a reason I siphoned the high magick of the Cloak directly into a spellstone. Unless you're from a victor's family, raw high magick is too unstable to work with—we wouldn't even have been able to see it if it hadn't come directly from the tournament's curse. So whatever stores the Lowes have are worthless right now."

"So we're screwed, is what you're saying."

"Yeah. I think so."

"Then why are you still bothering?"

Reid flipped through the pages a little too quickly, making several swing loose from their binding. "Because I refuse to accept it. Because books *always* have the answers, somewhere. If you look hard enough."

"Is that why you wrote one?" she asked bitterly.

He didn't reply.

"*A Tradition of Tragedy* ruined my life, you know. It ruined all our lives." Even a year since its publication, the nightmarish details of the first day it hit shelves still felt painfully fresh. The reporters who'd camped outside her father's house. The cruel graffiti dripping down her locker. The searing glares from her classmates.

"My book didn't ruin anyone," Reid said. "Your families ruined themselves when they created the tournament."

"You're talking about something that started hundreds of years ago. My parents and grandparents had no more say in this than I do."

"And yet they kept the high magick a secret." Finally, Reid dragged his attention from the grimoire to her, his eyes bloodshot from squinting. He looked strange in his glasses and without his typical smudges of eyeliner. More like the child in the photographs in his family's flat. Isobel wished she hadn't seen them. She had every right to hate Reid MacTavish, and she didn't want the burden of making that hatred complicated. Especially not now, as she planned his demise. "Do you know what good that high magick could've done, had you all not hoarded it for generations? The lives that could've been saved? The people who—" Reid's voice hitched, and he wrenched his gaze back down to the page.

"My family hasn't won the tournament in thirteen generations."

His fingers curled around the edges of the manuscript. "Do you really think I spared a thought for *you*? Some random popular girl at her prep school? All I cared about was telling the truth."

"Yet you purposefully wrote it as though you were a Grieve. You *lied*."

"It was protection. I was a seventeen-year-old emancipated minor living alone in my parents' flat. You think the Lowes would've hesitated to dispose of me if they knew who I was?"

From the whispers Isobel had heard about Marianne Lowe, she didn't put it past the woman to have made Reid disappear, even if Reid was barely older than her grandsons.

"If you're so noble, then why did you experiment on Gavin Grieve's life magick?" she asked. "It was true, wasn't it? What he told the *Inquirer*?"

Reid scoffed. "He can complain all he likes, but if it wasn't for me, he'd already be dead."

Isobel wasn't sure why she still lingered. None of these questions changed her decision, and any closure they gave was paltry at best. Most likely, she was stalling.

"What about since you published the book?" she asked. "You must be rich now. You could leave. You could go anywhere."

Reid barked out a hollow laugh. "Why am I not surprised you'd say something like that?"

"What's that supposed to mean?"

He shook his head. "I'm digging the new makeup, by the way. Very subtle. What are you going to tell Briony and Finley? They've got no clue about your whole corpse problem, right?"

"How do you know that?" she demanded.

"They're chatty babysitters. Briony says she worries about you."

"Worries about me how?" Briony couldn't suspect her—she'd been careful. Hadn't she?

Reid cast her an odd look. "I meant *for* you, obviously. What did you think I meant?"

Isobel hugged her arms to herself; she was just being paranoid. "I'm going to tell them I've been sleeping better."

"Brilliant. I'm sure they'll believe that. After you essentially murdered your ex-boyfriend and became a pariah, it makes sense you'd be sleeping like a baby."

Isobel didn't think she'd ever so utterly despised someone. But before she could retort, Finley's voice echoed up the stairwell. "Briony! Isobel! Come look at this!"

Abandoning Reid to his research, Isobel hurried down the stairs, where she found Finley and Briony both gawking at the pillar on the ground floor. Of the seven stars engraved into the stone, two twinkled crimson. *Two*, descending in an arc to join the three others on the pillar's bottom. Which meant two Relics were falling simultaneously, and from their positions, Isobel knew which ones: the Hammer and the Medallion, which corresponded to the Darrow and Payne stories.

"*Two* Relics? At the same time?" Briony remarked with a gasp. "Has that ever happened before?"

"Maybe it's because the tournament is breaking," Finley said, that familiar calculating tone seeping into his voice. "We'll need to split up. Two of us go after the first Relic, one goes after the second."

"But what if the others show?" Briony protested. "We'll be outnumbered. And whoever goes alone—"

"I'll go alone."

"No, definitely not. If it has to be one of us, it should be me."

Isobel tuned them out, too panicked to listen to them bicker about who should or shouldn't play martyr. Because now her plan had been derailed. If she wanted to take advantage of their alliance to slay them, then for now, she had no choice but to join them on their pointless quest. But wherever the Relics fell, Alistair would be there, waiting for her. She knew he would—felt it like a lead weight in her gut.

Isobel can apologize to me with her dying breath, he'd declared in his interview.

No, survival came one day at a time, and fleeing now was the only option that ensured she'd live to see morning.

"While the three of you were arguing . . ." Reid appeared at the curve of the stairs with arms full of spellstones. "I grabbed our supplies. We need to hurry if we don't want the others to claim the Medallion and Hammer first."

Isobel stiffened. "What makes you think *you're* coming?" Beside her, Briony and Finley exchanged a wary glance, clearly agreeing with her.

"It'll be four against three," Reid answered, dumping the crystals onto the couch. "We need those odds."

"I don't know . . ." Finley said.

"Don't give me that bullshit. You think I'll turn on you? Where would I go, with this ring on my finger? What choice do I have other than to fight?"

"I still don't think that's a good idea," Finley told him.

Reid stared at them, wringing out his hands, still bound by the Warden's Shackles. "You can't be serious. You tie my survival to this and you don't even let me help? You just keep me locked in this tower waiting, for what? To die? You know what will happen to all your families if you die? They'll go on, even if they don't deserve to. You all have parents or siblings or cousins. But I'm all that's left of my family. If I'm gone, their legacy is gone. You have to let me come with you."

Isobel stared at him. He'd just told her that they were screwed, so why would he want to fight? It had to be a trick, but when she examined Briony and Finley to see if they were moved by Reid's impromptu speech, to her irritation, reluctance clouded both their expressions. At least Alistair had never bothered to squabble with his conscience.

Then Reid reached into his back pocket and pulled out the most recent issue of the *Glamour Inquirer*, which he must've found on the top floor. He pinched the magazine between two fingers as though it were tainted.

"Besides," he sneered, "what would the press think if Isobel left without her new boyfriend to protect her?"

Isobel cringed. "Charming, isn't it?"

"I would've said 'psychotic.'"

"Fine," Finley muttered. "You can come along. But only because we could use you—not because of . . ." He gestured at the magazine. "That."

Over the next ten minutes, they frantically replenished their enchantments—Isobel most frantically of all. She sprinted around her room, cramming whatever stones she could into her pockets. She would go with them, playing along until the last moment. Then she'd use a precious Here to There spell and flee to the Crypt. After experiencing her family's traditional curse, she had little desire to claim their traditional Landmark as well. But she couldn't pass up its defensive enchantments for something as trivial as comfort.

Once finished, the group started out of the Tower, where two stars traced ruby trails across the rainy sky. One veered to the right, toward the forest, and the other to the left, toward the Monastery.

The four of them huddled together, each in rain jackets and hoodies.

"Reid and I will go toward the moors," Briony told them. "You two can take the forest."

"Got it," Finley said.

"Got it," Isobel echoed, relieved. She had far fewer qualms about abandoning Finley than her former best friend.

"All right," said Finley. "Three . . . Two . . ."

Reid cleared his throat. "Forgetting something, darling?" He smiled at Isobel insincerely and lifted his arms. The shimmering chains of the Warden's Shackles clamped around each of his wrists.

Isobel gritted her teeth. "Right." As she released the spell, the chains dissipating into puffs of smoke, Reid leaned toward her.

"Forget what I said earlier," he hissed into her ear. "I haven't given up, and you shouldn't either."

When he pulled away, Isobel studied him, stunned. His expression looked strangely pleading.

"Three . . ." Finley resumed. "Two . . . One."

Finley hooked his arm around Isobel's. A moment later, they each cast their Here to There spells, and with a *pop*, reality momentarily winked out. Then the shadows of trees loomed into view, surrounding them on all sides. Rain pattered against the canopy.

Above them, scarlet light shone molten through the leaves, growing brighter and brighter as it neared the ground.

Isobel froze. This was her chance.

Yet she couldn't shake Reid's words from her mind. She still didn't like him, didn't trust him. But if Isobel abandoned the others now, the world would be right about her. And even if she agreed with her father that she shouldn't care what the world thought, she still cared about what she thought of herself.

Which left only one frightful option: to fight.

"It'll only be another minute now," Finley breathed, craning his neck skyward. He glanced at Isobel, who couldn't meet his eyes. "If Alistair is here—"

"I know," she said tightly.

"I just want to say that I've got your back. All this stuff that's been happening to you? It's shit, and I'm sorry about it. But for what it's worth, I'm glad you're here. Briony—well, both of us—need you more than you realize."

Isobel cursed him in her mind. Perfect Finley Blair with his charm and goodness, who had no idea the abhorrent thoughts she'd just been entertaining. If only it was possible to hate him—he should certainly hate her.

"Thanks," she answered awkwardly.

The light of the Relic flared above them, so close and bright that Isobel had to squint.

"Come on," he said, and they tore through the woods, mud splashing beneath their trainers. They followed the falling star to a thick grove of trees, then halted, Finley panting, Isobel still, as it crashed down. A *boom* thundered, so loud Isobel clamped her hands over her ears, wobbling as the ground quaked. Dirt and pebbles blasted in all directions, pelting her cheeks.

Then the dust cleared, revealing a crater cleaved into the earth. A necklace hovered within it, doused in otherworldly red light. Its three gigantic spellstones winked as it spun in a slow circle, beckoning a champion to claim it.

The Medallion.

Something rustled in the trees ahead of them.

Finley took a step forward.

"Wait," Isobel warned, but he didn't listen. Not even as a figure appeared through the forest, staring at them from across the crater.

Without a moment of pause, a curse shot toward them.

And the world exploded.

ALISTAIR LOWE

"Oh, I don't know if I could change him," said twenty-year-old Addison Partridge, the president of Lowe's fan club, "but wouldn't it be fun to try?"

Glamour Inquirer, "The Unexpected Phenomenon of Ilvernath's Most Eligible Murderer"

Alistair shuddered as his cursestone snuffed out.

Smoke smothered the forest, so dense that he lost sight of Isobel and Finley in the distance. He choked and lifted the collar of his sweater to his mouth, breathing through the scratchy wool. His instincts urged him to duck for cover behind a tree, to wait until the enemy gave away their position. But his legs seemed to move of their own accord. He wandered the haze like a ghost, a single word lodged, unspoken, in his throat.

Above him, the canopy rustled, birds scared by the explosion cawing and taking flight.

As the smoke gradually dissipated, red radiance bathed the woods. The Medallion, waiting to be claimed.

Alistair quickened his pace toward the light. The forest floor dipped beneath him into a muddy crater, sloshed with damp leaves and mulchy, uprooted underbrush. Then he caught sight of it—a large necklace, floating at eye level. It was ethereally beautiful, an item seemingly plucked out of a fairy tale. The intricate knots in the metalwork could've been mistaken for lace, and its trio of gemstones shone, engulfing the Relic in a crimson halo.

As Alistair moved toward it, a silhouette appeared through the smoke. He froze, and the unspoken word burst free from his grasp.

"Isobel?"

Then the figure stepped into the light, the scarlet rendering the green of their eyes unnaturally gold and piercing, like a fox.

Gavin stiffened as he took in Alistair, then he pointed at something behind him. "Look out!"

As Alistair ducked, Gavin cast an Impenetrable Fortress, and a white wall shaped like an outline of a castle sprung up behind Alistair a mere heartbeat before the curse could strike him. The enchantment battered off the shield, shooting like a firework into the sky. Its path carved a hole in the treetops, and orange smoldered through the leaves like fire through parchment.

Gavin reached for the Medallion, but Alistair caught his wrist. "Don't. Once we claim it, they leave."

"Once *we* claim it, you mean," a voice said haughtily, and Finley Blair approached the wall. A blue lance shimmered in his right hand, crackling with electricity.

Alistair relaxed his shoulders. He'd faced Finley twice, and each time, he'd outmatched him. Even with the Reaper's Embrace limiting his cursework, Alistair knew they'd prevail.

"I'll guard the Medallion," he told Gavin quietly. "You take him out."

Gavin nodded, stalking ahead of him.

Finley raised the lance and hurled it at the Impenetrable Fortress. It shattered, shards winking out amid the smoke. The weapon rematerialized in Finley's grasp, and he barreled toward Alistair, rearing the lance for another strike.

Gavin summoned an Earth Tremor, and the ground beneath Finley lurched. Finley was thrown backward and rolled across the bramble. Alistair watched Gavin advance toward him. He didn't prowl as Alistair might, with shoulders hunched and careful, quiet steps. Instead, he walked with his chin high, his chest back, each of his strides steady with purpose. Finley looked up, leaves matted against his clothes, his eyes widened in alarm. He pushed himself to his knees, but before he could clamber to standing, the earth quaked again. The tree above him teetered and groaned, and he scrambled out of the way as it crashed to the ground.

Gavin hopped over its fallen trunk, disappearing from Alistair's view.

And it was for the best—Alistair needed to focus. He hadn't seen

Hendry since the explosion went off, and any of Finley's allies could lurk in the darkness.

In another scenario, Alistair would cast an Artisan's Deception, an enchantment that used his own imagination to paint his surroundings like a canvas, allowing him to hide his and the Medallion's presence completely. But if the other champions believed that Alistair had claimed the Relic and run, Alistair and Gavin would lose this chance to slay them.

Which left him no choice but to wait, standing guard, the Medallion's high magick beaming like a beacon behind him.

Seconds stretched into minutes, and the minutes stretched into an eternity. Alistair shifted from side to side, his gaze catching on every shadow in the Relic's light, on the full moon looming overhead. The scratching of branches against one another reached an eerie, unnatural pitch. The gnarled roots resembled the hands of corpses clawing out from beneath the dirt.

Suddenly, lights flashed in the distance—a barrage of spellwork. Alistair squinted, trying to discern the casters, but it was too far, and he couldn't leave his post.

A twig snapped to his right, and he whipped around, his chest heaving. "Who's there?"

No one emerged from the darkness.

As a precaution, he cast a protective Shark's Skin, and he suddenly wished he'd brought the Mirror for its defensive enchantment, even if that risked the other champions stealing it. Goose bumps prickled up his arms. He swore someone was watching him.

"Come out. I know you're there."

Finally, Isobel emerged from behind a tree. At first, Alistair hitched his breath, struck by how similar she looked, how pretty he'd always found her. Every detail of her brimmed with memories, some real and some fantasized. Her hands clasping his in the dark. Her lips and how ruinous they'd tasted. Her brown eyes, wide and wanting, reflecting his desire in equal measure.

But the longer he stared, the more differences caught his notice. The faint threads of purple veins like spiderwebs plaiting her cheeks. The severe slant of an expression he'd never seen her wear before.

Since she'd betrayed him, Alistair had imagined this moment countless times, yet his carefully planned vengeance fractured in an instant.

"Is this it?" he asked hoarsely, readying his stance. "Our duel?"

Her countenance was steelier than his, even as her eyes dropped to his glove. "It didn't have to be."

"And whose fault was that?" He hated the vulnerability in his voice. "I trusted you. I nearly sacrificed everything for you. And you *cursed* me."

"You cursed me first," Isobel snapped.

"I never meant to. When I realized what happened, I was so scared that I'd . . ." He swallowed. The memory of that morning still felt fresh. "Doesn't that count for anything?"

"You almost killed me." She stepped into the crater, and Alistair stiffened. He knew her tactics. If she hadn't confronted him with a curse, then she'd hoped to deceive him—with words, with touch. But he wouldn't fall for the same tricks twice. "You have no idea what it took to save myself. You think you deserve forgiveness because I'm alive?"

He did. Because if the two of them had hurt each other, he was hurt worse.

"I deserve an explanation," he said. "Was it all a trick?"

Frustration flashed across her features. "You can't possibly believe that."

Alistair's heart stuttered. How easily he latched onto her words, even now. "What other explanation is there? The person with me in the Cave, that wasn't someone who could do this to me. No one could hurt someone they cared about so much."

A cool wind tore through the woods, and the canopy swayed above them. Isobel hugged her arms around herself. Alistair's words had finally struck somewhere true.

"Of course I cared about you," she said harshly.

"And how am I supposed to believe that?"

"I thought you would kill me, when I went to the Cave and asked you to help me. You were supposed to be this . . ." She gestured at him. "Monster. My rival. Instead, you were just lost, even more than I was. But when we were there, and we couldn't even tell if it was day or night, and you gave me the Cloak, and you would tell those stories . . . It felt like we were somewhere else, somewhere where the only thing I had to be afraid of was in our imaginations. And even now—especially now—I miss that place. I miss you."

As though she'd laced an enchantment into her voice, Alistair was frozen as she took a step closer to him. A tear slipped down her cheek, glinting like a ruby in the light of the Medallion.

Alistair didn't know if he believed her—if he even wanted to. He thought the truth would console him, but instead it would torture him, always. What they could've been. What he couldn't have.

"You once wanted to end the tournament," Isobel murmured. "Do you still believe it's possible?"

"It's not about that, not to me."

"But . . . do you still believe it can be done?" Something heavy weighed in her voice, though Alistair couldn't discern what it was.

"It was never me who doubted," he said pointedly.

Isobel swallowed and took another step closer, so near that, if she reached out, she could just barely touch him. And despite every shred of self-preservation he had, Alistair wanted her to.

"Then what if it's not too late? What if you could—"

"Don't," he snapped. He would never regret saving his brother.

She didn't flinch at the venom in his tone. If anything, it emboldened her. She gently placed her hand against his chest. But it was her words, not her touch, that undid him the most.

"It doesn't have to be like this."

Alistair's knees wobbled. It felt as though she had peeled back every layer of his desire and laid them bare to the night's chill.

Then, when he gave no resistance, she leaned closer and spoke into his ear.

"I never thought you were a monster, Al."

The nickname struck him from his trance. After everything they'd done to each other, it felt discordant, wrong. And as it hung there, burdening what little space remained between them, a streak of red light winked in the underbrush behind her, vanishing in an instant.

Hendry.

They had her flanked, though she didn't realize it. Which meant that this was the perfect opportunity to strike.

Anguish lashed through him. He couldn't do it. He couldn't kill her, no matter what his weakness would cost him.

Then a worse realization washed over him.

"If you really cared about me, why did you curse me?" he murmured.

Her brow knotted. "Because you chose your brother over—"

"No, why did *you* have to curse me? It could've been Briony. It could've been Finley. If it hurt you so much, why did you do it?"

Isobel's lip quivered, but Alistair didn't trust it, nor the tears pooling in her eyes, the wretched look on her face. "I . . ."

Alistair moved closer, until not even the wind could slip between them. With a trembling hand, he intertwined their fingers. Her touch was strangely, jarringly cold. A ring shimmered on his thumb, one he'd brought to this battle especially for her, but she didn't notice. Her gaze had caught on his neck, at the bone white that inched just above his collar.

He cast the spell, and Isobel's most recent thoughts poured into his mind. A trace of fear, the sight of his cursemark summoning the memory of the Payne's mangled corpse, the photos she'd seen of how he'd left his family. Heartbreak—she'd meant it when she said that damning him had hurt her. But it was muted, buried beneath emotions far uglier than Alistair had braced himself for. Doubt, unshakably heavy. Deceit, though not of him. Resentment, endless and sharp, a thousand needles that Isobel lived with in her skin. Revulsion at herself, at something wrong with her. Grief that—

Alistair wrenched away from her, gasping. The ivory mark of the Divining Kiss ghosted Isobel's wrist in the shape of his lips.

"This whole time, I thought it was my fault you couldn't believe in me," he rasped. "But you can't believe in anything, can you?"

Isobel staggered back as though he'd struck her. Her expression changed, returning to the same harsh stone, and as Alistair gazed wildly at her clenched fists, her lips, the warm brown of her eyes—he realized Isobel Macaslan had always been more of a fantasy to him than reality.

Before she could respond, a curse shot across the clearing, and Alistair swiveled around toward the Medallion. A young man he dimly recognized crouched at the edge of the crater—Reid MacTavish. While Reid ducked to avoid the curse, Hendry tore out from the underbrush, sprinting in the direction of the Relic. He seized it, but the Medallion's glow never dimmed, as it would when claimed by a champion.

Rather than stop to fight MacTavish, Hendry kept running and disappeared into the trees.

Alistair's gaze whipped back to Isobel, and with a single, uncertain look, she raced after his brother. Alistair swore under his breath and followed.

The woods blurred past in the darkness. He might've run faster if he didn't trip on every stone, root, and slope of the forest floor, but he never lost sight of Isobel in the distance. He didn't spare a moment to glance over his shoulder, but the sound of footsteps warned him that MacTavish wasn't far behind.

Ahead, Isobel slowed to a stop, and Alistair didn't realize why until trees ended at the riverbank, the Ilvernath skyline glittering in the distance. Then she shrieked and ducked as a flash of a Salamander's Tongue fired from her right. Its sparks whizzed over her before sputtering out, raining embers on the pebbles.

Hendry advanced from the shallows.

Apart from when Hendry had intervened during Alistair's duel with Gavin, Alistair had never seen Hendry fight. At home, Hendry had been spared from their mother's gruesome lessons, instead encouraged to nap away his afternoons or indulge in sweets from the kitchen. Hendry's only battles were waged in the realm of make-believe.

Now, his face bathed in the crimson light of the Medallion hooked around his fingers, Hendry Lowe looked more than capable of spilling blood.

Except when he cast his next curse, it wasn't aimed at Isobel—but at MacTavish, tearing through the forest behind Alistair.

MacTavish grunted as the Kraken's Whip knocked into him with the force of a kick. Clutching his stomach, he blew the greasy strands of hair out of his eyes and looked between the brothers with a crooked smile. "Is that all you got?" he goaded. "Tell me, how's my family's curse treating you?"

Alistair's mind whirled. Even after weeks studying the Reaper's Embrace with Isobel, he had no idea it was a MacTavish recipe. But he had no time to respond. Isobel had climbed to her feet, several of her rings flaring white. Swiftly, he cast a Griffin's Maw, forcing her to deflect it with a shield. The curse's golden feathery darts ricocheted into the water with a splash.

"I'll hold MacTavish off," Hendry told Alistair, brushing past him toward the cursemaker. "You focus on her."

Nerves fluttered in Alistair's gut. Hendry was gifting him a precious opportunity, one Alistair might never have again: to right the wrongs Isobel had done to him.

And so, while Hendry shot one, two, three new curses at MacTavish, Alistair approached Isobel, his heart hammering. It would hurt to slay her. It would be agony. But whatever false bond they'd shared was gone; they were not allies, not lovers, not friends.

They were champions, and her life still stood between Alistair and his prize.

"I'm not afraid of you," Isobel told him, raising her chin.

Alistair cracked his neck. "Oh, but you should be."

A spell flared from her palm like a strobe light, and Alistair winced, shielding his eyes. Isobel seized the moment to bolt to the left, but Alistair wouldn't be evaded so easily. Squinting, he cast the Dragon's Breath. Fire burst from his mouth, sputtering aimlessly in all directions, and the forest around them burst in hot, orange brilliance. A flaming barricade encircled the pair of them on all sides, cut off only by the river.

"Nine letters," Alistair said, prowling forward. "A word for retribution, justice."

"If you kill me, you could die," she warned.

Alistair knew that, but he'd murdered his grandmother, his uncle, and the Reaper's Embrace still had much of him to claim. He was flirting with peril, but it would be worth it, when the champion who haunted him most no longer stood in his way.

He cast the Wraith's Screech.

A torrent of wind rose up from beneath Isobel's feet, and she stumbled as a cyclone consumed her from all sides. Her clothes whipped and rumpled. Her hair ripped from her braid. Her face raised skyward, and Alistair watched, wretched, as his mother's favorite curse tore her last breath from her throat in a piercing, torturous scream.

Yet as he waited, she never collapsed, never drew her hand to her neck as she suffocated, never knelt as the strength fled her body. Finally, unable to maintain the curse any longer, he let it recede, and as the winds died down, Isobel stood taller than ever.

"You once swore you could never kill me," she said steadily, as though his curse had had no effect on her at all.

"How did you survive that?" he asked, astonished.

Behind him, MacTavish's voice cut hoarsely through the dark: "What the *fuck*?"

Alistair stole a glance behind him and spotted his brother with a gaping hole through his abdomen and right arm. Hendry wobbled, and the Medallion slipped from his grasp, clunking onto the river stones.

"*Hendry*," Alistair breathed, running toward him on instinct. But the second he spun around, pain burst across his back, and his knees buckled. He fell, stifling a scream as agony quaked through him. Still, with two palms flattened against the ground, he looked up at Hendry. Red light shone through his center, and his form gradually began to piece itself together.

MacTavish lunged for the Medallion, but Hendry snatched it with his left hand. As he backed toward Alistair, still reforming, he whimpered, "I'm sorry. He's stronger than I am."

Alistair's chest heaved, and as he tried to regain his concentration, he caught sight of the blood dripping from his sides.

"Th-the Medallion," he choked. If he claimed the Relic, he could heal himself. He could fight for them both. "Hendry, I need the Medallion."

Hendry's face contorted in terror, and he turned to run the last few meters toward him. But before the brothers could reach each other, a hazy shield appeared between them. Isobel's Burial Shroud.

"Surrender," Isobel said from behind him. Each of her steps splashed in the riverbank. "We'll let you live."

No, they'd let Alistair and Gavin live. Hendry they'd willingly sacrifice, no different than the Lowes.

Alistair dug his fingers into the pebbles and grit. Then, scrunching his eyes shut, he cast the Giant's Wrath. The ground beneath him rose, then slammed down with seismic force. A blast wave of magick shot in all directions, tearing through the Burial Shroud, the trees, the water. The sound thundered like an explosion, and as Alistair crumpled onto his side, his hearing dimmed. His vision blurred. His whole body throbbed.

Then someone seized him by the shoulder and hoisted him up. Alistair leaned deliriously into them, even as it dawned on him that someone was Gavin Grieve.

"Can you stand?" Gavin asked.

"Where's Hendry?" Alistair rasped, wrenching himself away. Panicked, Alistair looked around their dusty surroundings. It was eerily silent. He swayed. "No, *no*. He can't get hurt. I can't have—"

"He's there. He's there." Gavin twisted Alistair around. The red, distorted shape of a boy gleamed in the distance. Alistair shuddered with relief and, once again, pried Gavin's fingers off him. "Now *listen* to me. Can you stand?"

"Obviously." The pain made his stomach lurch, and he hunched over slightly, one hand braced on his hip to hold himself steady.

"What about run?"

"Of course."

Gavin muttered something under his breath, then, without warning, he hooked his arm around Alistair's and turned, their backs pressing together.

Briony Thorburn skidded to a halt atop the pebbles along the riverbank. In her right hand, she wielded the Hammer, large and weighty enough to shatter a man's skull. Panting, her gaze locked on Alistair's. Only a few weeks ago, Alistair had freed her from the Castle's cell and told her—told himself—that he believed in her when no one else did. And that even then, he couldn't be the hero of this story. If anyone could play such a role in this tale, it was her.

Now those weeks divided them like a chasm. She'd accepted his faith and given him none in return.

And as much as Alistair wanted to make her pay for that, he couldn't. A heartbeat later, Finley and MacTavish appeared beside her. Apart from some scrapes, MacTavish looked steady. And judging from the sounds of splashing in the shallows behind them, Isobel, too, had survived Alistair's class eight curse.

He and Gavin were surrounded.

Alistair frantically inventoried his enchantments. His class six Conjurer's Nightmare *might* provide a distraction, but it required concentration, creativity, and all of Alistair's focus had been reduced to his injured back. Even the brush of his sweater felt agonizing.

In the distance behind Briony, Hendry staggered, his face and legs once again solid, the rest of his body little more than a projection of scarlet light.

"If you surrender," Finley told them, repeating Isobel's words from earlier, "we promise not to hurt you."

Alistair barked out a delirious laugh, his gaze fixed on Isobel. "There's not much more you could do to me."

With a howl of fury, Isobel cast a Bog's Innards—not at them, but at the ground. The soil beneath them sank, and Alistair and Gavin stumbled to regain their balance. Brown oil-slick sludge puddled beneath their shoes, bubbling like yeast. Puffs of noxious fumes wafted in the air, and Alistair's vision blurred. He teetered, his consciousness waning.

"Shit," Gavin breathed weakly behind him. A bubble of sludge had splattered across his bare arm, and Alistair felt Gavin's weight tip against him. Alistair wheezed trying to hold them both upright. Never had Gavin seemed more ridiculously bulky. If not for adrenaline, Alistair would've collapsed face-first into the muck.

"Your Here to Theres," he hissed at Gavin, who grunted as Alistair elbowed him. "How many of us can you take right now?"

"*Two*," he answered, slurring.

"Don't be—"

"I said two!" he growled, then he pulled away from Alistair and planted his feet wide, as if daring the very storm to strike him down.

Alistair didn't know whether he believed him, but he didn't have a choice. Nor would he let Gavin outmatch him.

"Grab them," Isobel said, but before either Finley or Briony could venture into the poisonous mud, Hendry ran.

Alistair bit down hard on his tongue, steeling his concentration. Then he cast a Come Hither. The spell grabbed Hendry, and he howled with surprise as an invisible cord yanked him limply through the air, past Briony and toward Alistair and Gavin. As Hendry slammed into the other two boys, Alistair dizzily fired whatever enchantments he had remaining—an additional Griffin's Maw, another Dragon's Breath, and a Shadows' Talons. But before he could tell if any of them had met their marks, Gavin seized Alistair by the wrist and cast two Here to Theres.

With a *pop*, the world blinked in and out of existence.

They landed inside the Cottage's wards, Hendry materializing beside them a moment later. Gavin, though he'd performed true to his word, crumpled immediately to the ground, his fall cushioned by the grass.

As the heat of battle gradually faded, Alistair panted and looked at his brother, at the horror of his still reforming features. Alistair's agony, too, had begun to fade, and spots smeared across his vision. "Did it hurt?"

The shape of Hendry's chest heaved. "I didn't feel a thing."

Alistair relaxed, the remnants of the Here to There fluttering around them in white flurries. Then, with a quiet groan, he finally collapsed, falling with a thud at Gavin's side. At least he'd held out longer than him.

The last thing Alistair saw before he blacked out was the glittery magick of the spell, caught like snowflakes in Gavin's eyelashes.

BRIONY THORBURN

"Who wore it better? Call our hotline and tell us whether you prefer Briony Thorburn or Isobel Macaslan's champion banquet outfits. Press one for Briony, two for Isobel! And be sure to tune in at the same time tomorrow for the next installment of *Champion Confidential*, where we share the hottest tournament gossip until the Blood Moon rises."

Champion Confidential, WKL Radio

Briony collapsed on the riverbank, the Hammer clutched in one hand, the crimson sky above her warped by her pain-blurred vision. Agony shot through her left leg, from her ankle to her shin. She'd dealt with athletic injuries before, but nothing came close to this. It was as though a parasite had burrowed beneath her flesh and was devouring it from the inside out.

"Help," she grunted.

"Briony?" Isobel knelt beside her, grasping her arm. Her grip was freezing. "What's wrong—"

"Leg," she managed, panting. The Hammer slid from her hand as she curled into a fetal position, gritting her teeth through another spasm of pain. "One of their . . . curses . . ."

Finley, who'd been a step ahead of them, dropped to her side. "Bri! Which one of them did this to you? Did you see—"

"I . . . I don't . . ." Briony tried to replay the last few moments of the battle, but her thoughts were foggy and half-formed. She dug her nails into the loamy dirt of the riverbank, whimpering.

"It's going to be okay," Finley muttered, as though trying to convince himself. One hand clasped her shoulder, the other wiped sweaty strands of hair from her forehead. His touch felt like an anchor. "We'll get you fixed up—let's just take a look."

Finley cast the Guardian's Glow, and three golden orbs circled the clearing. Briony blinked blearily into the light. She fumbled for his hand and squeezed, choking back a sob.

"This might hurt," Isobel said gently. Briony heard a tearing sound as Isobel ripped her leggings. The feel of fabric raking across her wound was excruciating. Blood seeped into the water beside her, eddying into the river.

But even that dreadful sight didn't compare to the horror dawning on Finley's face.

"Wh-what is it?" she murmured, craning her neck to glimpse the injury.

"Don't look," Isobel told her hastily—too late.

Nearly a dozen spindly creatures carved of shadow engulfed her leg, their mouths latched onto her flesh like leeches. Each of their bodies was engorged with blood.

An awful cry rang through the air. It took Briony a second to realize it had come from *her*. Dark spots bled at the edge of her vision as she watched a new creature materialize, as though the night had birthed it, and sink into her upper thigh. Finley caught her by the cheek and turned her away from the curse. He looked tender and terrified in equal measure.

"Can you cure it?" Briony sniffled.

His hand, still cupping her face, gently wiped away her tears. He leaned down and pressed his forehead to hers.

"Of course I can." But the fear in his voice hadn't faded.

Isobel cast a healing spell on her leg, but any soothing sensation was obliterated by the vicious throbbing. Even the wind seemed to lash at her wound. Finley's enchantments joined Isobel's a moment later, one of his rings glowing, then two.

Briony had wanted to save the other champions, and *this* was how they'd repaid her. But she wouldn't let her story end here, with so much left unfinished. She was stronger than this curse. She had to be.

"Is it working?" But before she could hear any response, her vision faded out, and she sank into oblivion.

She came to propped against a boulder, Finley's hand still clasped in hers. The rushing of the river mixed with a pattering drizzle, and mist hung in the chilled forest air. As she lifted her head, stirring, Finley loosened his grip.

"You're awake," he breathed. "How do you feel?"

Briony stretched her leg out hesitantly. It was warm and comfortably numb. "A lot better." She glanced up at the sky—pure darkness had fallen. "How long was I out?"

"At least a half hour," Isobel said, appearing above her. The bags under her eyes were violet and puffy.

"I was unconscious that whole time?"

"Asleep," Isobel corrected. "Once you fainted, it felt cruel to keep you awake for the rest of it. Finley and I traded off on healing you."

Reid stalked out from the tree line. "I think I deserve a little credit, too, don't you?"

"Wait. Did *you* help heal me?" Briony eyed him suspiciously. Sure, he'd fought with them tonight, but she and Reid had been a tense and awkward team while retrieving the Hammer. After what she'd done to him, she didn't blame him for hating her—and after what he'd done to all of them, she was hardly fond of him, either.

"He helped us figure out how to break the curse." Isobel sounded begrudgingly impressed.

"It was a powerful physical and illusory enchantment," he said. "Class eight. Bespoke Lowe, probably. You could've died—you're welcome."

"Th-thank you. All of you." Briony dared to look at her leg again. Raw pink flesh now stretched where the nightmare had been. She twisted her ankle from side to side. It ached, but it was mobile. "Is everyone else okay?"

"More or less," Isobel said. "A few scrapes and bruises."

Briony had a vague memory of Isobel being struck with a horrible curse. But if the other girl said she was fine . . . she probably was, at least physically. She wanted to ask if she was all right after coming face-to-face with Alistair, but now definitely wasn't the time.

"Are you feeling well enough to travel back to the Tower?" Finley asked. "We didn't want to move you."

"The Tower?" Briony swiveled around, taking them all in. "No. No, we shouldn't go back yet."

"What?" Isobel asked nervously. Briony frowned. While Reid's and Finley's breaths fogged in the cold air as they spoke, Isobel's didn't.

"We have a Relic," Briony argued. "We should pair it with its Landmark, right now."

"Bri . . . you were *really* hurt, and our healing spellstones are drained—"

"She's got a point," Reid said. "Although I think we should chase down the others, not go after a trial. It's four on three, and Alistair's injured. We know where their Landmark is—we could get the Medallion back."

"No, we couldn't," Isobel shot back. "The Medallion is the healing Relic. Alistair's probably fine by now, and . . ." Panic flashed across her face, and she immediately turned to Reid. "The Reaper's Embrace."

Reid swore under his breath. "The high magick *could* cure him. Maybe. I don't know for sure."

Isobel still looked panicked. Reid, grim. Finley's eyes darted across the clearing, as though he expected Alistair and Gavin to emerge from the forest and attack them again.

Briony knew all four of them were lucky to be alive. She didn't want to push too hard, but she could sense that their alliance was fraying. They needed a win, not just because of their near miss, but because of the tension that had plagued all of them from the start.

"All the more reason for us to do this now, then," Briony said sharply. "Before they get even *more* dangerous."

"Briony . . ." Finley's hand slid from her grasp. "Those trials are no joke. You know that. Are you sure you're up to it?"

In answer, Briony rose to her feet and walked to the Hammer. It was gigantic, the sort of tool intended to summon lightning strikes or construct monuments. Twin designs of woven knots decorated each of the mallet's cheeks, and three crimson spellstones shone in its handle.

"I'm coming." Briony hefted it across one shoulder. It was heavy, but she didn't care. "I claimed the Relic, didn't I?"

The rain escalated from a drizzle to a downpour as the four of them approached the Monastery. Briony waded through puddles, her trainers sinking into the soggy ground, the Hammer a dull weight against her collarbone. Finley's Guardian's Glow illuminated the building's cracked stone façade, still slightly charred from Gavin, Isobel, and Alistair's attack a few weeks ago. The sight of it stirred up uncomfortable memories. Finley had taken Briony here the first night of the tournament, where she'd managed to talk her way into his alliance with Carbry Darrow and Elionor Payne.

This Landmark wasn't the Crypt, but to Briony, it still felt like a graveyard.

Finley, who'd led the way, slowed to a stop before the wooden gates.

"It . . . it was Elionor's before." His voice faltered for a moment, but he moved closer. "One of us should claim it."

Briony caught his arm with her free hand before he could take another step. "It doesn't have to be you."

Finley turned, his expression resolute in the light of his spell. "I think it should be. I started this tournament at the Monastery. I want to end a piece of it here, too."

With that, he grasped the iron handle of the door and pushed it open. It swung out with a low, heavy groan. Torches lining the gloomy corridor flared to life. Finley dropped his spell, and the four of them hurried inside. Their drenched clothes dripped onto the floor.

"Shit," Reid grumbled, combing wet strands of hair across his forehead. "We should've used a waterproofing spell."

"We can't just waste magick," Isobel said tersely. "We don't know how much power the trial will take."

The Monastery under Elionor's watch had been austere and min-imalistic, no frills, no joy—a fortress, not a home. Now, claimed by Finley, the torchlight was friendly and warm. In a room to their left, Briony caught a glimpse of comfortable-looking couches clustered together beneath a rug the same eggshell blue as the accent wall in Finley's brownstone, a rugby flag pinned up on the wall, before he slammed the door shut.

"The pillar's that way." He jerked his head to the right.

Briony followed, her ankle twinging with pain. Isobel's and Reid's shadows danced up the walls in the torchlight as they trailed behind her. When Briony blinked, she could've sworn she saw two extra shadows at the end of the corridor. She shuddered and looked away.

Finley led them into the rainy courtyard. The pillar jutted from the side of the building, its carvings and cracks glimmering red. The iron table that had once stood in front of it was now tipped against the far wall, as though someone had tossed it there. Briony had sat at that table a dozen times with Carbry, Elionor, and Finley. It was where she'd realized the tournament was a giant septogram, where she'd tried and failed to convince Elionor of her theory. She thought of Elionor's body, split into pieces, and trembled.

"What happens now?" Reid asked.

"Well, last time we tried stabbing the pillar," Briony muttered.

Reid let out a disbelieving chuckle.

"No, seriously," she said. "It was the Sword. It made sense."

"And it worked," Finley added. "The moment the Landmark realizes we're trying to destroy the pillar, it'll start trying to kill us. So keep your guards up. The Cave trial was a puzzle—if two of us could solve it, four of us can definitely handle this one."

Briony surveyed the courtyard, the Hammer digging into her shoulder. She tried to study the stone walls and muddy ground for potential threats once the trial began, but based on the Cave . . . they wouldn't be able to predict whatever came next.

She stepped forward. "Is everyone ready?"

Isobel did *not* look ready, her gaze flitting between each of them too fast to be calculating, too slow to be terrified. Yet she nodded grimly. Reid took a deep breath and did the same.

"Let's get this over with," Finley said.

Briony adjusted her grip on the Hammer, which was now slick with rain. Tonight, they would bury their old alliance at last and solidify a new one.

"What, do you think you're gonna miss?" Reid bit out. "Hurry up. I'm getting soaked."

Briony gritted her teeth and swung. The Relic struck the pillar with an ear-splitting, discordant clang. She pulled it backward, readying a defensive spell.

Isobel and Reid threw up shields. No one spoke. The silence stretched out, unbearably long, as they braced themselves for something to happen.

Finally, Finley murmured, "I don't understand . . . That should've worked. That's exactly what we did last time."

"Last time, it was the Blair Relic and Landmark, wasn't it?" Isobel wiped rainwater out of her eyes. Her shield flickered out, and Reid's followed a moment later. "What if that's the problem? What if it has to be a Darrow champion to destroy the high magick?"

"No, no, that can't be true," Briony said hoarsely. If it was, there was no way they could break the curse. "What if the champion who claimed the Landmark has to do it?"

"The Cave belonged to Alistair when we destroyed it," Finley said.

"Let me try," Reid offered. "I'm a replacement champion, aren't I? Maybe it will work for—"

Crack.

Briony jolted, then lowered the Hammer, relieved. "I think it's finally starting."

A line cut violently across the pillar—not where the Hammer had struck it, but on the side where the champions' names were scratched into the stone.

The ground below them trembled. All four of them tensed, waiting. Isobel cast her shield again; Finley's Lightning Lance gleamed in his hand . . . but there was nothing more.

"This . . . this isn't how it's supposed to happen, is it?" Isobel asked shrilly.

"Don't panic," Finley said, in the excruciatingly calm voice Briony had only ever heard him use when he *was* panicking.

"That's the fifth crack on the wrong side," Isobel countered.

Dread rose in Briony's stomach, hot and thick. The Hammer slid from her grip and clattered onto the ground. "We messed up. We missed something."

Reid cackled with a shrill pitch that bordered on hysteria. He bent over, his hands braced on his knees, as though barely able to hold himself upright. "You think?"

The press conference flashed through Briony's mind again in painstaking detail. She thought of the Darrows handing her that storybook, of Carbry's body sprawled on the moors, arrows protruding from his eyes. "The Darrows gave us that story. So . . . if this didn't work . . ."

". . . then the Darrows lied." Finley's tone stayed dangerously flat.

"Right," Reid sneered. "The family whose son Briony killed. I can't imagine why."

Isobel glared at him so fiercely, he stopped talking. But Briony didn't care about his taunting. She was far too upset about the families lying to them. They'd stood in front of the entire world and claimed their devotion to breaking this curse, only to betray her. Betray all of them.

"There are other unclaimed Landmarks," Briony said desperately. "We could try this again—"

"And risk cracking the pillar a sixth time?" Reid shook his head. "Seven cracks on that side mean it's over. We all die."

"We don't know that for sure," Briony said.

"Are you really willing to test it? Because I'm not."

Everyone fell silent. Although Briony knew logically that the ground below her had stilled, she felt as though the entire world was trembling. She'd thought playing into the persona her family and the press had crafted about her would help them. But they were further from fixing this than ever.

Seven weeks left in the tournament. Five cracks in the pillar. Two stories that they couldn't trust, and two Relics in enemy hands.

They were running out of chances.

"Let's just go." Isobel hefted the Hammer up, winced, then hurried back inside the Monastery, Reid a step behind her. Briony already knew it would be a miserable walk back.

But she didn't follow them. She couldn't. Not when Finley stood before the pillar, frozen, as though he'd become part of its stone.

"Finley?" she whispered. "I know this is bad. But we'll find another way, right? Another strategy?"

He didn't move. The adrenaline of the last few minutes began to fade as she waited beside him. She felt the rain now, unrelenting, soaking through her jacket and puddling into her shoes. Briony wondered if she should cast a spell to shield them, but she didn't see the point. It was too late to keep either of them dry.

When he finally spoke, she had to strain to hear him over the downpour. His words almost made her wish she hadn't.

"We're going to die in here."

Her heart felt heavier than the Hammer had. "You don't know that. The world thinks we have a shot—"

"The world doesn't know about the Cloak." Finley turned to face her. Rain clung to his eyebrows, pooled in the hollows of his throat. She was reminded again of the way they'd sank into the Cave's lake together. He'd saved her from drowning that day—in her guilt, in her memories, in a horrific illusion spell. Now he was the one struggling to stay afloat. "If they knew the truth, no one would bet on us."

"Well, I'm betting on us." She reached for his hand. His fingers were ice.

"Bri . . ." He trailed off, looking pained. Then his free hand wound around her waist and pulled her close. She pressed her forehead into his shoulder and shut her eyes. His jacket was soaked, but she didn't care.

"I'm so tired." He shivered.

"Of the tournament?"

"Of wanting impossible things."

The rhythm of each word reverberated through her, painful, honest.

"Well, we've already done the impossible once," she murmured. "I know we can do it again."

She tipped her head up and met his gaze. His stare bored into her, unguarded, raw. She recognized the desire in it now; wondered if it had been there the whole time, something they'd both tried to lock away. Because it was dangerous. Because they had already hurt each other. Because it was something they couldn't take back.

And yet all of Briony's reservations melted the moment Finley pressed his lips to hers.

The two of them had kissed before, of course, while they were dating. But they'd been younger then, more awkward, more uncertain. This time was different.

His mouth was hot against hers, almost feverish. She reached for the collar of his jacket and drew him closer, while both of his hands braced against the small of her back, lightly brushing the skin where her shirt had ridden up. The warmth of his touch stirred something deep in her, an ache, a need.

The past month of careful words and stolen glances was obliterated in an instant. In their place was something volatile, something that felt both familiar and new.

They stumbled backward until she knocked against the pillar. Briony braced herself against the rough, cool stone and arched her body toward him, heat flooding through her despite the pelting rain. His mouth roamed lower; she gasped as it lingered on a spot above her collarbone that he clearly remembered. But two could play at that game. Her teeth tugged at his earlobe. He let out a muffled sigh in response and met her lips with fresh urgency.

Lightning flashed above them, but she scarcely noticed. All that mattered was each touch, each kiss, each soft, wanting sound that passed between them. He clutched her tightly, as though she might dissolve into the downpour if he ever let go.

Thunder boomed in the clouds, so loud Finley jolted away, then hastily cast a shield spell. He stared anxiously around the courtyard before dropping the enchantment, shuddering.

"No one else is here, Fin," she said gently. "It's just us."

She felt his gaze in her core as she stepped hesitantly forward. Her breathing was ragged, her lips swollen.

"I tried, you know." The rain still drenched them, but he didn't seem to notice. "I tried to stop wanting you."

"I tried, too," she said. "But I never did."

His expression shifted into something somber and careful. "Maybe it was good that we did this, then. One last time."

"What?" Never had her thoughts turned so quickly from desire to dread. "One last time? What were you trying to do, kiss me goodbye?"

His jaw clenched. "That's the only kind of kiss we've ever had."

She understood, then. This kiss had reminded her of a future worth fighting for. But for him, it was a cruel taste of everything they'd never been allowed to want.

She'd been right to warn herself against this back at the press conference. No matter how many times they hurt each other, he was a lesson she couldn't seem to learn.

"I refuse to believe that," Briony snapped. "What are you going to do, give up? You promised me we were in this together. You promised that—"

"I remember what I promised you." He swallowed. "Briony . . . I know this won't be easy for you to hear, but five cracks? I thought we could fix this, that we could save ourselves, but what if we can't?"

"We can end this," Briony said fiercely. "I know we can."

"And succeed where countless other champions have failed? Do we really think we're any different than everyone else who's died here?"

Briony thought uneasily of his confrontation with his mums, of every damning word they'd said.

"So this *is* about your family," she whispered. "You said you didn't agree with them."

"That was before I knew we had the wrong stories. Before we were two cracks away from—from oblivion."

"We can find the right pairings," Briony argued. "There's only so many combinations. I bet if I tell the Thorburns that the Darrows lied to us, they'll figure it out."

"You say I'm doing what *my* family wants? Listen to yourself!" Briony glared at him. "I'm just trying to do what I think is right."

"And I'm trying to be realistic." He sighed. "I don't know how much hope I have left."

"So then what?" Briony hiccupped. "Are—are we even allies anymore?"

"I hope so," Finley said seriously. "I would rather it be us together at the end than anyone else, if that's what it comes down to."

"You're talking about killing the others? Killing Isobel?" Briony asked in disbelief. "If that's the game you want to play . . . you know you'd have to fight me, right? I-I thought you said you couldn't kill me."

"I . . ." His expression twisted with anguish. "I still don't know if I can."

"You just kissed me, and you're *undecided?*"

"What would you rather do?" Finley demanded. "If we really can't finish this—"

"But we *can* finish it." Briony's next words poured from somewhere deep inside her, somewhere she'd never let her mind wander before. "Seven cracks on the wrong side would still end the tournament. Forever."

For a moment, they both fell silent. Rain dribbled over her lips, washing away the taste of him.

"You'd rather all of us die than one of us live?" Finley asked, his voice careful again. Calculated.

"I don't want any of us to d-die, but I'm committed to ending this tournament, no matter what it takes." Briony's voice shook.

"You're . . . you'd . . ." he trailed off, then took another step away from her. "Well. I guess we're still allies."

She sniffled. "Unless you want to leave—"

"I don't."

It felt strange, after all they'd said to each other, that they were still on the same side. And yet when she turned to walk back to the

Tower, he followed. Neither of them protested—neither of them said a single word. Thunder boomed the whole way home, and lightning cut through the sky, a violent pink against the Blood Veil. Briony could still feel every place he'd touched her. The thought of losing him was agony. The thought that both of them had always been lost was unbearable.

But most agonizing of all were her own words: that she would rather every champion die to end the tournament forever than let it continue on. It was a noble choice. A heroic choice.

Surely it was the right one.

GAVIN GRIEVE

"Speculation abounds regarding the validity of Gavin Grieve's claims to access his own life magick. Some say it's a misinterpretation of a curse, or a ploy for attention. I personally have witnessed a renewed—and dangerous—interest in the matter, which has now permeated the public consciousness."

Interview with Dr. Atilio Fernandéz,
SpellBC News: Asking the Experts

Gavin rolled over in the dirt, disoriented. The sight of the Cottage's thatched roof and humble doorway was a massive relief after that battle, where the forest had seemed to shift around him with every step. Fending off Finley's powerful enchantments had tested the limits of his newfound control, and the noxious fumes from Isobel's curse still stung his sinuses. He coughed, eyes watering, trying to rid his mouth of the stench.

"G-Gavin? Gavin?" Hendry's hand clasped his shoulder, feeling only half as solid as a real grip should. "Good. You're awake. I—"

"Yeah, I'm awake. We miscalculated," Gavin snapped, sitting up. "Our plan was—Alistair?"

His ally lay prone, his slack-jawed face pressed into the dirt, his eyes shut. Blood pooled through his sweater and sank into the ground, as though watering the earth. The sight of him sent an unexpected bolt of alarm through Gavin's chest.

"He won't wake up." Hendry's voice hitched. "I've been trying, but my spellstones are drained and I didn't want to leave him alone and—"

"Let's get him inside," Gavin said firmly. "One thing at a time, okay?"

Together, they hoisted Alistair's unconscious form upright. Gavin did most of the heavy lifting; Hendry's movements still betrayed flashes of red as he wrapped an arm around his brother's back. Alistair was surprisingly light. His head lolled onto Gavin's shoulder, dark curls brushing against his neck. A shiver prickled down Gavin's spine.

"The Medallion can heal him, right?" Gavin asked. The drizzle turned to rain as they stumbled through the withered garden.

"If he's lucid enough to use it," Hendry said nervously.

Gavin shoved the door open. They half-carried, half-dragged Alistair to the couch, where he slumped, unmoving. The hearth sparked to life, casting the room in a dim, ominous glow. Yet the Cottage remained freezing cold.

Hendry pulled the Medallion from his pocket. Gavin felt taunted by its proximity. Hendry couldn't claim it, since he wasn't a champion. Gavin could, but because of his mutilated life magick, he couldn't cast its high magick enchantments. Hendry closed Alistair's limp hand around the three spellstones, but they stayed dim.

"Wake up, Al," Hendry croaked. "Please."

But Alistair didn't move. The blood that soaked through the charcoal gray wool of his sweater had turned it almost black.

"We have to heal him ourselves," Gavin said.

"You're right." Hendry squeezed Alistair's hand one more time, then set the grime-smeared Medallion gently on the table. "I'll go get our healing reserves. You take a closer look at that wound. We need to know exactly what they did to him if we're going to fix it."

He rushed off into the bedroom, while Gavin approached Alistair cautiously. The gashes in his back had torn deep, ripping off blood-soaked chunks of his sweater and undershirt. With a pair of kitchen shears, Gavin cut through the fabric and folded it away from Alistair's skin. He recoiled at the sight of the wound. It looked as though claws had shredded into the muscle below the other boy's shoulder blade. Foul-smelling pustules bubbled at the edges of the wound—poison, maybe. If not for the soft rasp of Alistair's breathing, Gavin would have thought him dead.

The Reaper's Embrace twisted across the rest of Alistair's torso, stark white. The physical wound was gruesome, but to Gavin, the cursemark was far more disturbing. It was a death rattle in slow motion, cruel in its inevitability. Because Alistair *would* keep hurting people to save his brother. He would tear the whole world down for Hendry's sake, even if it consumed him.

Maybe that made Alistair monstrous. Or maybe being willing to do anything to protect the people you loved was just . . . human. Gavin wouldn't know. His family had never protected him, not when it mattered.

"Don't die," he muttered to Alistair's limp form. "I'm the one who gets to kill you, okay?" Blood pooled at the edges of the injury, clotting around the pustules. Alistair let out a pained whimper, and Gavin felt a sudden urge to comfort him, followed immediately by confused panic. Alistair was his enemy—but he was *hurt*, and his face looked so soft like this, almost gentle. Gavin reached a tentative hand toward his shoulder, then pulled it back, trembling.

Hendry bolted out of the bedroom, spellstones spilling from his hands. He dumped them on the kitchen table, pushing aside a tray of scones. Then he hurried to Alistair. At the sight of both the wound and the cursemark, he sucked in a horrified breath.

"I need to find the right stone for this." He sounded on the verge of tears. "I know it's in here somewhere, but there's so many—"

"What does it look like?" Gavin asked.

"It's dark green. A class seven Gift of the Forest."

"I'll find it." Gavin inspected spell after spell. He was grateful for his new control—instead of filling each stone automatically, draining his magick and rendering him useless, he could simply sense the enchantment inside and continue on.

"Th-this is my fault," Hendry continued. "I was worthless out there, and if Al didn't have to worry about me, he wouldn't—" He broke off abruptly, and Gavin glanced up. The other boy had completely disappeared.

"Hendry?" Gavin had no idea how Hendry could've left the room so fast, without so much as a flash of magick to signify it. "Where—"

Hendry reappeared in the same spot, flickering crimson. He blinked, looking bewildered, then glanced around the kitchen. Gavin decided this was *not* the time to question him about it.

"Is this what you were looking for?" he asked instead, holding up a spellstone the color of moss, already filled with common magick. Hendry's eyes lit up.

"Yes! Thank you." He took it and leaned forward, resting a hand on Alistair's shoulder. Soft green light shimmered in the air, then misted around Alistair's back like a cloud of fog rising from the forest floor. The air smelled of soil and pine, of growing things, earthy and clean.

The wound began to knit closed, the pustules shriveling, then scabbing over. Alistair stirred, mumbling. Sweat beaded on his forehead; his curls fell halfway across his face, smeared with muck and grime.

"He's stabilizing." Hendry let out a shaky sigh.

"Good." Gavin swallowed. "Alistair says you're a natural at healing spells."

"I've had a lot of practice. Al fell down the stairs about once a month when we were kids."

"So he's always been that clumsy?"

Hendry laughed, then wiped his eyes and nose on the sleeve of his sweater. "If you can believe it, he used to be worse. As a kid, he wore this cape everywhere that was way too long on him. He tripped on it constantly."

"A cape?" Gavin echoed, amused. "Like a superhero thing?"

"Are you . . . making fun of me?" Alistair croaked from the couch. "While I'm on my *deathbed*?"

"You're not dying," Hendry told him, although the relief in his voice told Gavin that his own instincts hadn't been wrong. Hendry clutched his brother's hand as Alistair opened his eyes, his face splitting into a weary smile. Watching them like this was a painful reminder that these brothers shared a bond Gavin had never had with his own siblings. For a moment, he felt horribly alone.

Then Alistair's woozy gaze turned to him. He groaned and sat up, bracing his back against a couch cushion. "I loved that sweater," he muttered, shucking off the remains of it. Gavin noted uneasily that the Reaper's Embrace crept across the front of his chest too, then hastily looked away, not wanting to be accused of staring. "And for the record? It was a super*villain* cape."

"Of course it was," Gavin said dryly. "You were born cackling at the full moon, dedicated to the pursuit of evil. How could I forget?"

The mist around Alistair dissipated as Hendry's spellstone winked out, drained of power.

"The wound isn't all the way healed," Hendry said. "Are you well enough to finish the job?"

Alistair winced. "I can try."

Hendry handed him the Medallion. It was still just as beautiful as it had been in the forest, a finely wrought disc of metal hung on a delicate chain. Three spellstones were embedded in it in a triangular pattern. At Alistair's touch, each of the crystals flared with scarlet light.

Gavin was familiar with the basic properties of the Relics, and he knew that this particular one had separate spells for healing magickal and non-magickal maladies, along with a third spell that allowed champions to void their claim over a Landmark or Relic. Once Alistair was patched up, they could take a shot at the Reaper's Embrace—and at Gavin's transformation into a vessel.

Two of the stones dimmed, while the third brightened. Ruby light shone through the room, almost blinding in its brilliance, far more powerful than Hendry's peaceful green. Alistair exhaled, color returning to his cheeks, and straightened.

"Are you okay?" Gavin asked.

"Never better." Alistair rose from the couch and twisted around. His back was now fully healed, although flecks of dried blood remained crusted around the Reaper's Embrace. "How does it look?"

"I mean, you're still cursed," Gavin said.

"Great. Thanks. I had no idea." Alistair turned around again. "How bad was it?"

"Pretty fucking bad," Gavin answered. Hendry nodded in agreement.

"They claimed they weren't fighting to kill," Alistair muttered.

"They're all a bunch of hypocrites," Gavin said. "We already knew that. Anyway, are you ready to try it on the Reaper's—"

"Hang on. What happened to your face?"

Gavin lifted a hand to his cheek, surprised when it came back red. He could feel a sting in his eyebrow, and another on his neck—casualties from running through the woods, or maybe the trip back. He hadn't even noticed. "It's no big deal."

Alistair gripped the Medallion. Crimson light engulfed Gavin, and a warmth gathered in him, gentle and soothing. The tension perpetually bunched beneath Gavin's skin melted away, and he was filled with a loose, unfamiliar feeling—relaxation. Gavin reached for his cheek again and touched smooth, healed skin. His body was suddenly well-rested and strong, as though he'd just woken up from a good night's sleep.

"Thanks." Gavin's arm throbbed—a reminder that while the physical healing spellstone clearly worked, they'd yet to verify that the magickal one could help them at all. "Are you ready now?"

Alistair swallowed. "As I'll ever be."

Alistair clutched the necklace in his fist. Another spellstone flared. Light pulsed through the room, then wove over Alistair's arm and torso like vines growing across the trunk of a tree. The Reaper's Embrace remained bone-white. Everyone waited for ten seconds, then twenty, until the light faded. The curse lingered, utterly unchanged.

Tension flooded back through Gavin's body. The spellmakers had been wrong.

"Nothing." Alistair's voice trembled. "All that, and . . ." He scowled and gripped the Medallion tighter. Again, crimson light wove around him. This time it faded away in seconds.

"No," he grunted, then shouted, "No!"

The Medallion flared sharply as he cast the spell for the third time. Now the enchantment spread around Hendry, the same color as the lag in his movements. Hendry stiffened with surprise.

"Al," he said softly. "You know this won't fix me."

Alistair glared at him. "I have to try." The light brightened around Hendry . . . then fizzled out. High magick dissipated into the air like tiny fireworks, illuminating Alistair's flushed cheeks. He rounded on Gavin.

Alistair's gaze bored into him, nervous. If the Medallion cured Gavin, he'd have the upper hand in their alliance. And Alistair clearly knew it.

Gavin waited, unsure what to expect. But then Alistair blew out a breath.

"Maybe it'll work for you," he said bitterly. A moment later, Gavin felt that warmth again. He stared at his palms, where red twined around his lifelines and looped through his spellrings. He knew how powerful this magick was, but when the spell was finished, he felt no different.

"Well?" Alistair demanded.

In answer, Gavin shrugged off his thin jacket. The hourglass tattoo remained, the veins around it swollen and distorted. Even though he was used to disappointment, a painful knot still lodged in his chest.

"It didn't work," he said flatly.

Alistair slammed the Medallion down on the table, as though trying to break it. Hendry winced. "So we all almost died for nothing?"

"Not nothing," Gavin said. "We stopped them from getting another Relic."

"Then we're stalling them. Great. We should be *killing* them."

"And we will," Gavin said. "That wasn't our only option. We'll go to the spellmakers again—"

"Oh, so they can help *you*?" Alistair shot back. "Because last time, they did shit for us."

A great, heaving *crack!* broke through their argument, shaking the Cottage floor. As one, the boys turned toward the pillar jutting from the mantel. A rift traced another line across the dead champions' names, obliterating dozens more. Crimson pulsed from the new fissure like a heartbeat.

No one spoke a word until the quaking stopped. Then they turned to each other. Hendry's eyes were wide as coins. Alistair's chest heaved, his nostrils flaring with obvious fury.

"You said that if there's seven cracks on that side, it all ends, right?" Hendry whispered.

"Everyone dies," Alistair snapped.

"All the more reason to get help while we still can," Gavin said.

Alistair grabbed his ruined sweater, then the Medallion. "Whatever. I'm going to bed."

"Al—" Hendry said.

"I'm going. To bed."

He stomped into the bedroom. Hendry started after him, then hesitated.

"Thank you," he told Gavin.

"For what?"

"For helping Al during the battle." Hendry lowered his voice. "In a way that I couldn't."

Gavin remembered Hendry's words from earlier, about feeling worthless. "You were there, too."

"And it wasn't enough. I wasn't—" Hendry swallowed, then looked at him grimly. "At least someone was able to protect him."

"We're allies," Gavin said. "That was kind of the deal."

"Yeah, and I thought it was a bad one. But after what you did for Marianne, after tonight . . . I was wrong about you. I'm glad you're here."

Gavin shifted uncomfortably. "It's okay. I know I'm not the easiest person to trust."

"Neither are we," Hendry said seriously. "Are you going to reach out to the spellmakers?"

"Yeah. I'll send them a message as soon as I can."

"Thanks." Hendry shot him a sad smile and headed to the bedroom.

Left alone, Gavin stared at the freshly cracked pillar.

He felt frustrated that the Medallion hadn't worked. Relieved that all three of them were alive. And guilty, even though it made no sense. Alistair and Hendry had to choose each other, just as Gavin had to choose himself. It was a story that could only end in death. Trying not to make that death his own shouldn't feel shameful. Just necessary.

It took several days to arrange another meeting with Walsh and his friends, and a great deal of effort to make Alistair come along. Gavin didn't know exactly how Hendry had convinced him, but he wasn't foolish enough to question it.

When they finally arrived at Walsh Spellmaking Emporium, the spellmaker's assistant seemed slightly less terrified of the Lowe brothers. She ushered the three of them through the door into the back room, which bustled with activity.

"Oh, excellent." Osmand Walsh waved them over. "You're just in time."

Since Gavin's last visit, someone had pulled an ancient wooden table into the space, shoving some of the spellwork displays aside. It looked like it was about to collapse beneath the collective weight of all the grimoires piled atop it. Liam Calhoun and Diana Aleshire hunched over a spellboard, furiously debating spell ingredients, while Diya Attwater-Sharma coaxed a sprig of common magick off the mantelpiece and into a flask.

"In time for what?" Gavin asked.

"To share our new theories." Diya closed the flask and spun around.

She'd swapped her Ilvernath Prep uniform for a pair of ripped jeans, a flannel, and high-top trainers. Gold bangles adorned her wrists, and that same choker was still fastened around her neck. Gavin could see it more clearly this time—an amber stone set in the center of an engraved flower, petals unfurling around it. He wondered what spell lay inside.

"New theories?" Alistair echoed crankily. "What about the old one? We almost died to get the Medallion, you know."

Gavin shot him a warning look. "We're just curious about why it didn't work," he added diplomatically.

"Well, Mr. Grieve, you're a vessel, not cursed," said Walsh.

"But *I'm* cursed," Alistair said.

"We did think you were the one with the best chance of being cured by the Medallion," said Aleshire, still busy with her spellboard. "But there's no sense dwelling on it. It was one possibility out of many."

Alistair stiffened, but before he could bark out anything else, Hendry put a hand on his shoulder. Gavin glanced between the two of them, then turned to the spellmakers.

"So you have other ideas, then. Let's hear them."

"The Medallion's healing spells are obviously powerful, but they're general," Calhoun said. "We've recently discovered that the Reaper's Embrace is a MacTavish curse, so—"

"We already know it's a MacTavish curse," Alistair interrupted.

"How do *you* know that?" asked Diya.

"He told us," Gavin said. "What about you?"

Aleshire pushed her spellboard aside. "We bugged the Tower. It turned out to be quite fruitful."

"Why did you do that?" Hendry asked uneasily.

"Well, your enemies are our enemies," said Walsh grandly.

"Also, they wanted to see if the other champions were actually onto something," Diya added. The others frowned at her. "What? You did. And it turns out they're totally fucked, so . . ."

"What do you mean, they're fucked?" Alistair's voice was sharp.

"One of their precious Relics is broken," Calhoun said.

"You were correct, Mr. Grieve," Walsh said. "Regardless of whether their theories are accurate or not, they can't end the tournament the way they want to."

So it was true, then. The other champions' quest was doomed.

Gavin's decision to kill them wasn't cruel—it was inevitable, just as it always had been. And it put their fight over the Medallion into an even more brutal perspective. Briony, Finley, and Isobel were struggling against the inevitable instead of embracing it. What a ridiculous endeavor.

"I'm not surprised." But Gavin *was* surprised by the twinge in his chest as he said it.

"Of course the others lied," Alistair mumbled bitterly. "I don't understand why they'd still fight for something impossible."

"It doesn't matter," Gavin said. "It doesn't change what we have to do."

Alistair clenched his jaw. "You're right."

"Did you learn anything else that might help us?" Hendry asked softly. "What about those disappearances in Ilvernath? Are the other champions connected to them somehow?"

"So those rumors have reached you all the way in the Cottage," said Walsh. "I'm afraid we haven't heard them bring it up. I doubt they even know."

Hendry nodded in assent, looking troubled. He hadn't mentioned the letter he'd received again, but clearly it still bothered him. "And did you find anything else that could heal us?"

"We were trying to get to that earlier, before we were interrupted," Diya said dryly, gesturing toward Alistair, who pursed his lips.

Calhoun cleared his throat. "Yes. As I was saying, while the Medallion is powerful, it's general. The Reaper's Embrace was cast under a very specific set of circumstances. So you'll likely need a specific healing spell to counteract it."

Aleshire pulled a grimoire out of the pile and flipped it open to a bookmarked page. "This enchantment is designed to be crafted by someone with a strong connection to the person they're trying to help. Its recipe is deliberately unfinished, as its ingredients are meant to be customized for the spell's intended recipient. If you choose correctly, it could be extraordinarily powerful. We thought perhaps Hendry might want to give it a try. He mentioned during our initial assessment that he has some aptitude for healing spells."

"Yes," Hendry said immediately. "If you think it might help him, of course I'll try it."

"What about blowback?" Alistair asked nervously.

Hendry took the grimoire from Aleshire. "What else could happen to me, Al?" He touched the dog-eared page reverentially, then closed the spellbook. "I also want to talk about my . . . death." He shuddered, red lagging in the air behind him before he continued on. "I've spent weeks trying to understand why I'm here. How I'm here. You told me that my family took my life magick and used it to power a curse, the same way Gavin fills spellstones with his own life magick. But I can't get hurt the way he can, and I can cast with common magick, too. Since we're both life magick anomalies . . . do you think I could help Gavin? Or maybe we could help each other?"

Gavin was stunned speechless. When he'd talked to Walsh about Hendry's usefulness, it had never occurred to him that Hendry might offer up his aid so willingly, without even realizing Gavin had wanted it from the start.

"You want to help me?" he finally croaked.

"Yes," Hendry said earnestly. "If I can."

The word *why* sat on the tip of Gavin's tongue, but he was far too cognizant of their audience to spit it out.

"We've certainly thought about your mutual connection to life magick," Walsh said, his gaze flickering to Gavin. "Hendry, we have a theory that due to the way your life magick interacts with high magick, you regenerate life far faster than an ordinary human."

"Unlike Gavin," added Diya. "Whose life isn't regenerating fast enough."

Hendry looked between the two of them with dawning understanding. "You think I could give him some of mine?"

"No," Alistair said immediately. "You're *not* turning my brother into a vessel."

"We have no intention of doing such a thing," Walsh said hastily. "We believe Hendry could potentially donate life magick to Gavin without hurting himself *or* destroying his ability to cast with common magick. All this would do is strengthen Gavin as we keep trying to find a cure for his condition. And he may not even be strong enough to handle the transfer, depending on how he's responding to the exercises."

"I've been responding pretty well, actually," Gavin said.

Walsh flashed him an oily grin. "Excellent."

"You can't really be considering this," Alistair said to Hendry.

The brothers descended into a muttering argument as Gavin stepped away. He didn't need to hear Hendry trying to convince Alistair, because he'd said it all to him last night. Hendry believed that this would protect his brother. And Gavin, who'd secured an alliance for this exact purpose, should have been thrilled.

Calhoun and Aleshire returned to their spellboard, while Walsh hurried back into the main shop. Gavin hovered uneasily until Diya nudged him with her elbow.

"Got a second, Grieve?"

"I've got about six weeks, actually."

"Why—oh. Until the tournament ends." She cracked a smile. "You've got a fucked-up sense of humor."

"You have to, when your life's a joke."

She snorted again and yanked him to the same velvet chaise longue he'd sat on during his last visit. It was dangerously close to the crackling green fire.

"I've been thinking about your case, a lot," she said, sitting beside him. "I mean, we all have. But I've developed something I want to test on you, while they're all distracted."

"Don't you want them to see?"

Diya shifted uncomfortably. "They kind of told me it was a bad idea."

"Is it dangerous?"

"No . . . or at least, I don't think so."

"Then I don't mind if you try it."

Her entire face brightened. "Good. Now hold still and let me look at your tattoo."

He rolled up his sleeve, and Diya examined him gently, tracing a finger along the bulbous veins that surrounded the hourglass. Gavin caught a glimpse of Alistair over his shoulder, who was staring at them, looking oddly intense.

Hendry tugged on Alistair's arm, and Gavin turned back to Diya, who'd pulled her hand away.

"You said Reid used a syringe and a modified tattoo needle." She reached into her pocket and produced a syringe of her own. Gavin tensed. "I know, I know. But I really think this will help."

"Have you tested this at all?" he asked uneasily.

"Who would I test it on?" she countered. "Look, I know I'm not as old or as fancy as the rest of them. But both my parents are from pretty big-deal spellmaker families, and I've spent my whole life watching them work. I know I can figure this out."

"It sounds like you have something to prove."

Diya sighed. "Maybe a little. Since my grandfather's been in the hospital, everyone's trying to figure out who will take over his responsibilities. It surprised a lot of people when my family nominated me for his spot on the board, but my mum's too busy with this massive grimoire translation contract, Dad's too busy running the shop, and I'm supposed to help both of them when I'm done with university. I want to show Ilvernath's spellmakers that I'm good enough to keep up. That they didn't make a mistake."

"You want them to know what you can do," Gavin said softly. "You want them to take you seriously."

"Exactly." She met his eyes. "So? Are you ready to try this?"

"Diya!" Walsh strode toward them, frowning. "I told you, he's not here to be used as a guinea pig for your theories."

Diya scowled and tucked her syringe away. "I'm trying to help him."

"Then you'll be pleased to know that Mr. Lowe has agreed to see if we can facilitate a transfer of his life magick to Gavin."

"Really?" Gavin asked, rising from his seat.

Walsh nodded. "Indeed."

Back at the table, Aleshire stood above her spellboard and uncorked the flask of raw magick Diya had filled earlier. Clearly, the enchantment she and Calhoun had spent the last few minutes arguing over had been meant for Hendry this whole time. Raw magick winked across the ingredients before swirling into the spellstone.

"You should be able to cast this on yourself," Aleshire said, handing it to Hendry. "It will mark you a bit like Gavin's marked—and allow you to transfer magick to him. Hopefully with *far* less pain."

Hendry nodded and clutched the stone. When he cast it, an awful *crack* cut through the room, and a pattern appeared on his forearm, the same white as the slice across his neck. Gavin soon realized it was shaped like a keyhole—as though Hendry himself were the lock. The spellstone's glow faded, and Hendry dropped it on the table, looking even paler than usual. Crimson light fizzled around him, circled the keyhole, then dissipated into the air.

"Did that hurt?" Alistair demanded.

"Not at all." Hendry locked eyes with Walsh. "How do I use it?"

"Focus on your magick," directed the spellmaker. "You should be able to guide it out of yourself like guiding common magick into a vial, then give it to Gavin."

He held out a glass flask. Hendry took it, then stared intently at his arm. White magick began to shimmer around the keyhole. But instead of swirling neatly into the vial, it floated toward Gavin. He felt the same pull he'd experienced with Walsh, with Elionor, with Carbry.

"Are you sure you want to do this?" he asked Hendry.

"Positive," Hendry said.

Gavin reached out a hand. The magick perched on his fingertips like a moth, then sank into his skin.

His shoulders sagged as the pain in his arm immediately began to ebb. Alistair gasped, and Gavin twisted his head around—just as they had before, the grains of sand in his hourglass were moving back *up*.

He'd been given more time. More life. More power. From the place where he'd least expected it—where he probably didn't deserve it.

"I don't even know how to thank you," he told Hendry hoarsely.

After more promises of answers soon, they left the spellmakers behind and returned to the Cottage. Hendry shut himself in his room with his new grimoire, while Alistair cornered Gavin in the kitchen.

"If what you did to your magick hurts Hendry, if it makes him weaker—"

"I don't want to hurt your brother." Gavin hesitated. "The other champions will eventually have to give up on their plans. Which means they'll come for us again, and they won't hold back. We have to be ready when they do."

"I know. It's the only reason I agreed to this."

"Then we understand each other." Gavin swallowed, hard. "This alliance means something to me, okay? What those other champions did to you and Hendry . . . it was wrong. I don't want them to win."

Alistair paused, as though replaying Gavin's words. His eyes narrowed in suspicion, like the mere idea of Gavin softening was preposterous. "I . . . I don't want that, either."

"Yeah, I figured." Gavin sighed. "I'm going to practice my breathing exercises."

Alistair was still staring at him when he shut his bedroom door. Gavin paced back and forth, heart racing.

He had spent his whole life believing that he needed to fight for himself, because no one else had ever fought for him. And while that had been true for a very long time, it wasn't true anymore.

Gavin didn't want to betray the Lowe brothers. And yet it didn't matter. Because if he wanted to win, he had no choice but to destroy their happy ending.

ISOBEL MACASLAN

"These teenagers have presented their plans to break the tournament as though they are straightforward, but the truth is that the Blood Moon Curse is an extraordinarily intricate work of cursemaking. As far as I'm concerned, anything could happen."
Interview with Dr. Atilio Fernandéz,
SpellBC News: Asking the Experts

Isobel stretched out her back, aching from hours hunched over one of Reid's grimoires. Since proving his loyalty during the battle five days ago, Reid had been given free rein of the Tower, and Isobel had found him researching in the ground floor common area in the early stirrings of the morning, when she'd given up on sleep and crept downstairs for a glass of water. Finley joined them an hour later, then Briony at the first crack of sunrise. Since their failure at the Monastery, tension buzzed between them all like static, but Isobel couldn't be sure she wasn't imagining it. After speaking to Alistair, she couldn't be sure of anything.

"Would you cut that out?" Reid snapped at Briony, who'd been restlessly jiggling her leg. It was, Isobel admitted, annoying, but far preferable to the night before when Briony had been tossing a rubber ball against the wall until they'd begged her to stop.

"Sorry, sorry," she said quickly. "But I've found something promising. This chapter says there's a fable where an old queen created high magick by—"

"It's 'beckoned,' in the original," Reid told her. "Not 'created.' You're reading a translation."

"Oh, all right." Briony swallowed. "I'll keep looking."

And she did, training her gaze on the glossy textbook page. Isobel stared, trying to decipher how Briony could maintain her unshakable optimism, or if it was merely a façade. She'd reached out to her family about the Darrows' lies and heard nothing back, yet still she kept on trying.

But you can't believe in anything, can you?

Isobel had never hated Alistair—not even for turning the world against her. But she did now, bitterly, fervently. Who was he to cast judgment? He'd committed unthinkable deeds, because he could, because he wanted to; she'd only levied cruelty when she'd had no other choice.

Still, his words had cut her lethally deep. If not for them, Isobel might've carried out her treacherous plan that very night, after the Hammer had done nothing but chisel them one crack closer to their destruction. And so she felt wretched, paralyzed. Even now, the cursestone she'd selected to kill her allies lay buried beside the First Kiss and Lovestruck spells in her pocket.

Maybe the Roach's Armor had done nothing but reveal her inner truth: Her heart no longer beat because she'd never had one.

Isobel studied Reid, who'd told her not to give up hope. She didn't like that he'd seen through her so easily, that he pretended to know her.

Noticing her gaze, he glanced up. "Something on your mind, darling?"

Isobel was starting to miss when he'd called her princess.

"Shut up," she muttered, rubbing her eyes and returning to her reading.

Then a startled sound escaped Briony's throat. "There's someone at the wards."

Isobel gripped the edges of the table. Was it possible the other champions had regrouped so quickly, prepared to lay siege? Finley jolted from the couch, reaching into his pocket for more spellstones—no doubt thinking the same thing.

But once Briony hesitantly opened the Tower's door, her shoulders relaxed. "It's Finley's cousin. And some boy."

"What?" Finley stepped behind her to look. "Gracie? What's she doing here?"

Several seconds later, two teenagers strode inside. Isobel dimly recognized one of them from school—Gracie Blair, a year below her. The boy was a stranger.

Gracie flung her arms around Finley. He hugged her back, blinking with surprise, before she pulled away and took in the Tower with awe. Over the past few weeks, the common area had gradually transformed from its original strange Thorburn museum into something far more suited to Isobel's former best friend. The stiff mahogany furniture now stood atop warm shaggy rugs, and a few plushy couches were arranged below the window. Fairy lights dangled above the stairwell. And the enchanted candle they'd received as a gift flickered on the table.

"It's good to see you," Finley told Gracie, leading her to the nearest couch. "But what are you doing here? Did the reporters outside bother you?"

"No—we brought Undetectables. And, well, me and some of the other kids from the tournament families . . . we've been talking, you know? About what you told the papers. About everything. We want to help you."

"You want to help us?" Briony echoed eagerly.

Finley frowned. "Are you sure about this? You know how our family feels about what we're doing."

"I heard your whole conversation with your mums," Gracie said as she sat down. "I don't agree with them. In fact, most of us don't agree with our parents at all. And the city has been a nightmare, recently. The high magick, the tournament, then this serial killer on the loose—"

"Serial killer?" Briony repeated.

"Haven't you heard about all those people going missing?" Gracie asked. "One of them was just found. *Dead*. And like, really messed up. It'll be all over the papers tomorrow."

Finley sat beside her, stiff and agitated. "That's horrible."

"How many people have gone missing?" Isobel asked—not only because she was curious, but to hide the fact that she already knew about the disappearances, from when her father had mentioned them in the café.

"Three," Gracie answered. "Everyone is already gossiping, trying to figure out who the killer is. Half the school is convinced it's Hendry Lowe."

"What?" Isobel asked. "Why?"

"Because of the body. The life magick was sucked out of it or something, and Hendry's, you know, dead."

Isobel hugged her arms to herself, disturbed. She had a hard time suspecting him, from what she knew about Hendry. But neither Briony nor Finley seemed to share her skepticism.

"It makes sense," Briony admitted.

"The Lowe brothers already killed their whole family," added Finley. "At this point, I'd believe anything."

"As fascinating as this all is," Reid said flatly, "I'd like to know who you are." He jerked his head in the direction of the other boy, who hovered beside the staircase, gawking at the pillar.

The boy coughed awkwardly and turned toward them. "Um. I'm Alan. I'm here because my family lied to you."

"Which family?" Isobel examined his crooked bowl cut and pimply face. She didn't recognize him from school.

"I'm a Payne."

Elionor's final moments flashed unbidden through Isobel's mind. The girl's ruthless sneer. Her body, mutilated. Alistair, merciless.

"The Darrows and us swapped our Relics and Landmarks around," he continued. "Our story pairs the Hammer and the Mill—it goes back to our spellmaking roots. I don't know what the Darrow story is, but I overheard my parents say that the Medallion goes with the Monastery."

Isobel scrutinized her allies, trying to discern if they believed him. Briony blinked back hopeful, radiant tears. Reid stroked the stubble on his chin thoughtfully.

Finley's balance seemed to sway as he looked to Gracie. "Are you sure?"

"I cast a truth spell on him earlier," she answered. "He believes it."

"Why would your families lie?" Briony asked sharply. "Do they not want us to break the curse?"

"I—I guess," Alan said. "I don't really know."

"And if that *is* what they want, why would you help us?" demanded Isobel, unable to hide the bite of suspicion in her voice.

"Because pretty much everyone who was eligible for this year's tournament knows it could've been us in here," said Alan. "That's why we're working together—we're forming a resistance. We don't want to send our own kids off to die one day. We want this to stop."

Isobel couldn't picture her cousins Anita and Peter sharing such a notion, with their supposedly booming merchandise business. But he sounded sincere enough, and that sincerity proved enough for Finley.

"Thank you." He wrapped his cousin in a second hug. "Seriously."

"I just want you to come home, Fin," she told him. "I want this nightmare to be over."

Isobel realized not even her father had said such kind, simple words to her. But, she reminded herself, they hadn't been the words she'd needed to hear.

Once Gracie and Alan departed, the four champions regarded one another uneasily.

Reid crossed his arms and leaned against the pillar. "This is what happens when you place more stock in the families than you do in common sense. The Hammer's a bloody *tool*. Of course it goes with the Mill."

"Funny, I don't remember you mentioning that when we went to the Monastery," Isobel said flatly.

"Would any of you have listened to me if I had?"

"What already happened doesn't matter," Briony said hastily. "We have the stories right this time. And we can guess the rest."

"Gavin and Alistair still have the Medallion," Reid reminded her. "And the Mirror."

"We can worry about that later."

"We have a *lot* to worry about later," he muttered.

"Right, but . . ." Briony turned to them, a silent plea in her eyes. "We have the Hammer. We have its story. Which means we can get one step closer to ending this, right now. So let's do this together. Please."

Isobel agreed that the Payne boy had given them a gift, but it wasn't enough to ensure their survival. Not without the Cloak. But if she voiced her misgivings, she risked hinting at the deadly cursestone currently resting in her pocket.

And so, as brightly as she could manage, she said, "All right. Let's do this."

The Mill's huge, imposing structure huddled at the base of the mountains along the edge of the river, with a great immobile wheel on its side, half-submerged in the water. The building had every mark of being deserted. Cobwebs and dirt clung to its stone foundation. Timber was stacked near its entrance, left untouched for so long that the logs were entirely swathed in a green coating of moss.

The four of them approached it, panting from their long walk, shivering from the brutal November cold. If Isobel still needed to breathe, each exhale would've fogged in the chill.

"One of you two has to go first," Finley told Isobel and Reid. "Since I technically have claim to the Monastery, and Briony has the Tower."

Isobel didn't want to lay claim to this place. If this plan, too, failed, then after she'd slain her friends and left the Tower, she'd have to return here, and she already owned too many enchantments to need its spellmaking wares. But she couldn't admit that. And house arrest or not, she knew Briony and Finley would prefer Isobel to volunteer than Reid.

"I'll do it," she said softly, striding toward the entrance.

The moment her hand pressed against the wooden double doors, a vibration hummed beneath her fingertips.

Instantaneously, the waterwheel groaned to life and began to turn. Inside the building, a heavy, rhythmic *thud thud* sounded, like a mechanical heartbeat. One of the mossy logs, half-rotted, was dragged up by the conveyor belt.

Isobel pushed open the doors, and they entered a vast room of antiquated industrial equipment. Per her tastes, the interior shifted. The lanterns emitted a warm glow, and the few benches on the walls lined themselves with baby pink cushions. They looked comically out of place amid all the blades and sawdust.

At the edge of the room, beside the wooden gears powered by the hydroponic wheel, was the Landmark's pillar.

"What do we do now—" Isobel started to ask, but was interrupted when the log from outside reached the Mill's gangsaw. With an ear-splitting screech, the many blades sliced the log into a dozen separate boards.

Briony handed Isobel the Hammer. "We try hitting it again. You want to do the honors?"

Isobel took the Relic by the handle and approached the pillar. As she raised it, she could almost mistake the *thud thud* of the gears for the pounding of her own heart.

She slammed the Hammer down.

The jolt of metal against stone rattled her to her very bones.

"Please tell me it worked," Briony said hoarsely behind her.

At first, Isobel didn't have an answer. Then, all at once, the sanguine light that bled through the cracks of the pillar extinguished.

Around them, the Mill began to change.

The double doors at the entrance slammed closed, and a chain snaked around its handles, glittering crimson with high magick. Various metal contraptions lowered from the ceiling, as though a claw machine reaching toward the ground. The floor shifted, and Isobel lurched out of the way as the boards folded in on themselves into new shapes. Reid wasn't so lucky. A plank of wood caught him beneath his black boots and knocked him off balance, sending him sprawling. Sawdust plumed into the air like a sandstorm.

"What's happening?" Isobel demanded.

Behind her, the pillar crumbled into a heap of spellstones, the coarse, gray rock transforming to shimmering crystals before her eyes. From the other corners of the Mill, barrels of more stones spilled over, sending hundreds scattering across the floor. Each one pulsed red.

"I-I don't understand," Briony stammered.

"Is it just me, or is this place getting smaller?" Finley asked, and he was right. Like the floors, the walls were folding in on themselves, forcing the four champions closer to the room's center. Above, the blades on the ceiling dropped lower and lower, each one a deadly pendulum.

"What do we do?" Isobel asked, barely audible over the grinding of the next log of timber.

"The Relic is a hammer, isn't it?" Reid said. "Smash them!"

Isobel fell to her knees and drove the Hammer onto the closest stone. It split open, and blood oozed out of it like the yolk of an egg. The light inside it faded. "I-It can't mean we have to break all of them, can it?"

"In the Cave, we had to find the right Sword," Finley said. "Maybe the right stone is hidden here?"

"But there's thousands of stones!" Isobel choked, driving the Hammer down on another, then another, then another. Each one broke, but nothing in the Mill changed, other than a puddle of blood pooling beneath her. Her arm was rapidly growing tired, and she clambered to her feet and handed the Hammer to Briony, who was in far better shape than she was. "Here. You—"

She was cut off when Reid threw himself against her, sending both of them tumbling painfully into a pile of crystals.

Above them, a circular blade swung through the air, exactly where Isobel had been standing. If Reid hadn't tackled her, she would've been divided right between the eyes.

"You're welcome, darling," Reid breathed over top of her.

To their left, white shimmered as Finley cast some kind of spell.

"That was the same Blade of Truth I used in the Cave," Finley grunted. "It didn't work this time."

Isobel shoved Reid off her. "You mean we really need to break all of them?"

At that, Reid cast a spell of his own, and a mallet of white magick fell on top of a heap of stones—narrowly missing Isobel's arm. All of the crystals remained intact.

"You could've shattered my hand," she growled at him.

"I was only checking. Common magick won't break the spell-stones. It has to be the Hammer."

Briony huffed as she struck stone after stone. "This is the *worst* game of whack-a-mole I've ever played." Blood oozed around her, coating her left hand as she held herself up.

Isobel stood. Above them, another razor-bladed pendulum detached from its hooks, swinging down in a wide arc. Even if they could dodge the blades now, once all of them fell, there would be nowhere for them *to* dodge.

"There has to be a trick to this," she said desperately.

"The curse doesn't *want* to be broken," Reid pointed out.

"You're not helping." She whipped toward Finley. "You knew Elionor. What would she do?"

Finley gaped. "I don't . . . Elionor never mentioned . . ."

"*Think,*" Isobel snapped. "Did she ever mention a story? Some family tradition?"

"Well, her family are spellmakers, just like Alan said. Maybe— Look out!"

A third blade had dropped from the wall. Briony looked up in time to crawl out of its path.

"I'm getting kind of tired!" she gritted out.

"Okay, Finley, you help her," Isobel told him. Then she turned to Reid, who gazed at her with wild eyes. "Well? You're the spellmaker."

"Cursemaker," he corrected.

"Whatever. What do you think we should do?"

Rather than answering, Reid only gawked as a fourth blade swung down, slicing a path in between him and Isobel, so close that she could see her own reflection in it as it soared past.

Even without the pounding of her heart, fear thrashed her—laden heavy with resentment. When Alistair had asked her why she was the one who'd had to curse him, *this* was why. Because even in a crisis—a crisis she'd wanted no part of—Isobel was the one who kept a level head, who did what needed to be done.

She wracked her brain for what her mother would suggest. If truth spells didn't break this, then it was no illusion, no matter of finding the correct stone hidden among the hoard. But even if Briony and Finley alternated wielding the Hammer, even if they juiced themselves up on speed and strength spells, there was no chance they could break each of these stones before all the pendulums fell.

But there was another way to rid crystals of magick sealed inside them.

Burying stones released magick, no different than burying bodies.

Isobel sifted through her collection of enchantments. She didn't have anything that could— She hadn't thought to bring a spell that—

Then her gaze fell from the dangers on the ceiling to the floor, and an idea struck her. She cast the Bog's Innards, and a wedge of magick drove into the center of the Mill. It spun, peeling back its floorboards and foundation and revealing muddy earth that bubbled hot with poisonous mire.

"What are you doing?" Reid demanded, coughing.

"If we bury the spellstones, the enchantment will disappear. Do you have any spells that can dig?"

"I think so." Then—careful to avoid the sweeping blades—Reid stepped beside her to where the floor dropped off into muck. "This isn't meant for a hole this large."

"Try it anyway," she told him.

Reid cast his spell, and a spear of white magick drilled into the earth. It was no wider than a well, and it dug deep enough to make one.

"Hurry," Isobel said. "We need to bury as many stones as possible."

"I can help," said Briony, who'd given the Hammer to Finley. The three of them ducked to opposite corners of the Mill. Isobel cast a Dying Breath, and a stale gust of wind sent the spellstones around her rolling across the floorboards and spilling into the hole. It felt like cheating, like sweeping dirt beneath a carpet. Twice, she came close to losing an arm—or her head. The metal blades whistled as they zoomed past, never slowing no matter how many arcs they made.

By the time they'd blown every spellstone from the floor, nearly all the blades from the ceiling had been released. There was no place to stand without being in one of their paths, no way to duck low enough to avoid them all. They could only dodge, and the second any of them grew tired or distracted, a pendulum would slice them in two.

Using an Entomb spell, Isobel raked the exposed dirt over the hole, sealing it.

All at once, red light erupted through the earth, so much high magick that it formed a beam of it. The blades tumbled down, clattering to the floor. The double doors fell from their hinges with a heavy crash. The ground rumbled. The *thud thud* of the gears from the waterwheel increased to a rapid pace.

Isobel couldn't take her eyes off the light. Blood bubbled up from the dirt as though the earth boiled with it.

Then a hand clutched hers. "Come on," she heard Reid say, and he tugged her until she was forced to swivel around. The structure of the Mill was collapsing around them, folding in and in until there would be nothing left.

They ran, Finley and Briony already a few paces ahead. The four of them sprinted out the double doors and into the woods. Only seconds later, the Mill caved in. Even the waterwheel disintegrated, until all that remained of the Landmark was a heap of sawdust amid the forest.

For several moments, no one spoke. Briony's chest heaved as her eyes darted between them anxiously. Then Finley's face broke into a true smile.

"We did it," Briony breathed with relief. She and Finley turned toward each other, then stiffened, their smiles faltering. Then Briony glanced back at Isobel, flushed with triumph. "We're going to finish this."

"I—I guess my family came through," Finley said, as if he couldn't quite believe it himself.

Isobel looked away, a sudden pain throbbing in her chest far, far worse than any broken heart. Because, despite such a victory, she couldn't bear their joy. Even after hearing Briony and Finley recount their experience in the Cave, that trial had been far more dangerous than she'd braced herself for. And though they might've survived, barely—what had been the point of it? Without the Cloak, what was she truly risking her life for?

Instinctively, her hand slid to her pocket.

But as she felt the grooves of the cursestone, the visions that plagued her every night forced their way into her mind. Though the Carnivorous Spores was painless, slowly creeping over the sleeping victim until it grew tall and bulbous after feasting on their blood, it left behind a ghastly corpse. Isobel imagined Briony, the closest friend she'd ever had, buried beneath the enchanted fungus, the fuzz on the stalks the same color as her hair, their caps tinted the same as her skin. Next Finley, one side of him rotted, the other bulging and disfigured with growth. And last, Reid, his face fissured with their roots.

Even if she hated Alistair now, it still ached to think of cursing him.

As Isobel banished the images, blinking away tears, she caught Reid staring at her. His expression was stony and knowing, and she averted her gaze before he could guess at her thoughts.

At some point, whether it was weeks from now, or whether it was days, their team would inevitably hit a dead end.

And even if it made her truly despicable, she'd find a way to steel herself before they reached it.

ALISTAIR LOWE

Though the family of the deceased has asked that the photograph of the body not be shared, the victim was reportedly found in a gruesome condition, gray, withered, and not immediately recognizable as human.

Ilvernath Eclipse, "Mysterious Killer
Claims Three Lives"

Alistair and Gavin sauntered through Ilvernath in the early morning.

Neither boy looked like themselves. Alistair had fastened a Whole New Me spell against his face like a mask, filling in the crevices of his cheekbones and narrow nose with softer, rosier skin. Gavin's had darkened his brows and hollowed out his eye sockets. Every time Alistair caught their reflections in a shopfront window, an odd thrill stirred in his stomach. Even when he and Hendry had snuck out for their nighttime excursions, he'd never felt anonymous. Too much of his family's history permeated this city, etched into every crack between the cobblestones, every indentation in the gutters.

Freedom, the feeling was supposedly called.

"Do you know where you're going?" Alistair had rarely visited this section of town before. The stores lacked the gleam of the spellshops on the main strip, with string lights twinkling over their awnings and crystals displayed in rotating tiered stands like macarons.

"Yeah." Gavin jerked his head toward an alley where the glow of the streetlamps didn't quite reach. "This way."

Alistair followed him, passing trampled missing person flyers and discarded, broken spellstones lying on the concrete. A wooden sign dangled above a doorway, creaking ominously despite the lack of wind. On it was nothing more than an arrow, pointing down a stairwell.

"Charming," Alistair said, admiring the garlands of cobwebs along the ceiling.

Gavin rolled his newly brown eyes and descended the steps, Alistair behind him, and they entered an antique shop. Old, tarnished furniture was piled around the room, buried beneath curios that would scare away even the most eclectic home decorators: taxidermied rodents, jewelry boxes brimming with shriveled potpourri and locks of hair, jars of pickled herbs and seaweed, dusty cassette tapes, chipped glassware, the skull of a steer with a crack webbing down its jaw. Above, pipes threaded across its basement ceiling, and exposed insulation painted the walls an unnatural, mold-like chartreuse. The only sound was a mystery dripping.

Alistair sniffed a burning candle on a claw-footed end table. "My favorite. Eau de asbestos." To his right, a music box suddenly groaned out a slow, discordant trill. "I'm pretty sure that if Hendry uses an ingredient from here in his healing spell, I'll sprout a second head."

"As though one of you wasn't enough already," Gavin muttered. "And we're not here for the ingredients—they have a grimoire section in the back."

They wove through makeshift paths of distorted mirrors and oddly sinister portraits. Finally, in the grimiest, dampest section of the cellar, they found bookcases, crammed with as many yellowed, loose papers as tomes. The pair of them had volunteered for this shopping expedition to search for spellbooks related to healing enchantments. Though the spellmakers had provided Hendry with a recipe for a potential cure to the Reaper's Embrace, it was fragmented, so Hendry had asked for more grimoires to round out his research.

Alistair slid one from the shelf and blew off its thick blanket of dust.

"Really?" Gavin coughed as it plumed in his face, and the Whole New Me spell flickered, brown irises interchanging with green.

Alistair scanned the nearby titles and spotted a cookbook that didn't belong. "How do you feel about casserole?"

Gavin crouched to examine the grimoires on the lowest shelf. "You're in a strange mood."

"Strange how?"

"I don't know . . . Good?"

He was right. By all logic, Alistair should be fuming right now.

Even if they'd stopped the other champions from retrieving the Medallion last week, he'd nearly died in the encounter, all for the Relic to prove worthless to them. And yesterday, a new crack had appeared in the Cottage's pillar. Broken Relic or not, the others were seemingly continuing their plan.

But since confronting Isobel, the pieces of him knocked off-kilter had been righted to their proper place. He no longer had reason to hesitate. When it came to her, his conscience was unburdened, free.

"Right, I forget you don't know what a good mood feels like." Alistair returned the dusty book and knelt on the floor to rummage through a pile.

"That isn't true," said Gavin.

"So what does it take then? I'm curious." Alistair showed Gavin a fabric-bound grimoire, its cover a faded illustration of the bones of a human hand. "Skeletons?" He held up a second. "Giant squids?"

Gavin snorted. "No. I'm not *you*."

"Never mind, I found it." Alistair brandished an engineering spellbook featuring a blueprint of a spell-powered locomotive. "You're definitely really into trains."

"Ha, ha," Gavin said flatly. "I like arcade games. And books."

"Phone books? Instruction manuals?"

Gavin's lips cracked into something almost like a smile. "Dictionaries, obviously."

"So what does a typical day look like for you? First you get up at sunrise."

"Of course. Then I go for a run—nowhere interesting, just in circles around my block. After that, breakfast. Bran cereal, unflavored protein powder. Then I go to school."

"Your favorite class?"

"Whichever one assigns the most homework," Gavin answered. "After that, I stare at the wall for a few hours."

"Dinner is assorted boiled foods."

Gavin barked out a laugh, making the haunted music box by the front of the shop resume its impromptu screeching. Alistair jolted, and Gavin laughed harder, throwing his head back and smiling wide enough that the Whole New Me slipped. Alistair stared. As much as he liked the freedom of the camouflage, the spell didn't suit Gavin. He looked wrong, and each time the blond peeked through or his eyes returned to his own, an odd feeling stirred in Alistair—one he recognized and certainly didn't welcome.

"We should get back," he said suddenly. He grabbed the skeleton grimoire and several others from the shelf. "Hendry will be worrying about what's taking so long."

"Oh, um, right." Gavin piled several promising books in his arms, and they paid and left.

Alistair dismissed the feeling—it was an intrusive thought, nothing more.

When they returned to the Cottage, they found Hendry hunched over the kitchen counter, kneading a loaf of bread. A sea of grimoires and notebooks spilled across the living room carpet, temporarily abandoned.

Alistair inspected the flour coating his brother's arms and jeans. "I take it the research isn't going well?"

"Actually, I did find something," Hendry said dourly. "One of the grimoires mentioned that healing spells can be amplified by choosing ingredients tied to the victim, and I have some ideas of what we could use."

A splinter of hope stabbed in Alistair's chest, though he knew it was too soon to let it sink in. "Then why do you sound so miserable?"

Hendry patted his hands clean on his apron, then grabbed that day's copy of the *Eclipse* from the table. "Have you seen this? What they're printing about me?"

Alistair furrowed his brow. "About you?"

"That I'm a murderer!"

Alistair snatched it from him and scanned the front page. "A killer stealing their victims' life magick?" He glanced at Gavin, who was peering over his shoulder. "Anything you'd like to tell us, Grieve?"

"Don't look at me," Gavin muttered.

Hendry slumped into one of the kitchen chairs. "They think I'm some sort of monster, and I don't blame them. I'm surprised the police aren't knocking down our door."

"Hey." Alistair plucked the half-finished tea cup from the table and handed it to him. To his surprise, the old chips in the porcelain were gone, and now that he thought about it, the Cottage's squalid state had improved, if only marginally. Sunlight peeked through clear patches in the windows' grime, and the dust cluttered in bunnies on the floor rather than coating every surface.

Grimly, Hendry accepted the cup and took a sip.

Alistair knelt in front of him. "The world will think what they want to think. Let's focus on the spell instead. Have you ever crafted a class ten enchantment before?" Alistair certainly hadn't.

"No, but what blowback do I have to be afraid of? I'm already dead." Hendry set down the empty cup with a grimace. "And that's something else I wanted to talk about. The ingredients that I'd like to use . . . Getting them won't be pleasant."

Alistair didn't like the nervous edge to Hendry's voice. "How unpleasant?"

"If I'm right about this, well . . ." Hendry swallowed. "I'll need my corpse."

Alistair clambered to his feet, stricken. "No, we can't go back there. We swore we wouldn't."

"I know, but we have to. And it's not just my body. The grimoire suggested familial items—a strand of Mum's hair, something of yours, something of Dad's—"

"Then use different ingredients," Alistair snapped.

"No. Believe me, I don't want to go back there either, but I think this could work. We won't stay long. If we leave now, we'll—"

"*Now?*" Alistair paced across the carpet. He never wanted to step foot in that place again, not for anything. But curing him of the Reaper's Embrace was too important—their very survival hinged on it. And wasn't that how it felt to return last time, to do what needed to be done?

Gavin, who'd been hovering awkwardly by the sink, cleared his throat. "I'll go ready our defensive spells, just in case."

Once Gavin had slipped into his bedroom, Hendry stood and squeezed Alistair's shoulder. "It'll be fine. We'll be quick."

"I know," he said softly. "But you'd do this? You'd look at your body like . . . *that?*" His voice hitched on the last word. He remembered the day they'd buried Hendry all too well, his short, solemn funeral held only hours after their family had told Alistair what they'd done. Alistair hadn't attended. Instead, he'd locked himself in Hendry's bedroom, inconsolable, desperately hoping this was one final, torturous test he had to pass.

"I'll manage," Hendry said. "I'm alive now, aren't I?"

Several minutes later, equipped with enchantments but feeling far from prepared, Alistair followed his brother and Gavin from the Cottage. The reporters camped beyond the wards had swelled in number. As the boys traipsed across the gardens toward the tree line, many journalists scrambled toward them.

"Hendry, would you like to comment on the recent murders?" one shouted.

"Do you have a personal connection to any of the victims?" another yelled.

Hendry's face darkened, and he halted in the grass. Alistair watched uneasily as his brother shrugged off his backpack and rifled through it, muttering to himself.

"What are you doing?" Gavin asked.

"Clearing my name," Hendry answered.

At last, he found the spellstone he was looking for, a shimmering aquamarine, then he squeezed it and marched toward the reporters. As he stepped across the wards, the onlookers careened back but kept their video cameras poised.

"This is a Silvertongue," Hendry declared. Then the crystal flashed as he cast the spell, and a crooked line of white traced across his throat to match his scar. "I didn't kill any of those people. I'm not sucking out anyone's life magick to survive. So just . . . tell the city it's not me, all right? Please." Then he tossed the spellstone in front of them on the dirt. "Verify the truth spell if you want."

He turned back to Alistair and Gavin gaping across the wards, then jerked his head.

"That was *my* spell he just gave them," Gavin said tightly.

"Oh, come off it," Alistair grunted. Then he scooped up the discarded backpack, and the three of them set off through the forest.

Thirty minutes later, the trio walked the length of a long, winding driveway shadowed in weeping trees. A wrought iron gate rose above them, its spokes reaching like claws toward the morning sky. The estate loomed ahead, dark and vacant. Not even a candle burned in the windows, and the lawn had grown unkempt in the family's absence.

Alistair gingerly grazed his fingertips across the gate's padlock, the one engraved with a scythe.

Home, he thought automatically, unable to help himself.

At his touch, the padlock unlatched and clattered to the pavement. The gate creaked open, and the three boys walked the stone path to the front entrance. Already, Alistair's mind traced the route to his bedroom, wondering how much studying awaited him, what training his mother had planned for the night. If not for the yellow CRIME SCENE tape crisscrossing the door, he might've forgotten that time had lapsed at all.

Hendry turned the handle—unlocked.

As the door swung open, the foyer's wall sconces flared to life, illuminating cold hardwood floors and the foot of a massive stairwell with a bannister of iron spokes.

They crept silently inside, and Alistair's gaze immediately locked on the parlor, on the spot beneath the portraits where they'd left their grandmother sprawled. Though her body had been relocated, a brown, bloody splotch still stained the carpet, and faintly, very faintly, he swore a phantom scream clung to the air. He shuddered.

"It's . . . huge," Gavin breathed.

"Huge and haunted," Alistair said. Then, steeling himself, he grasped the rail and began to climb the stairs. The others followed, until they paused at the mouth of the hallway on the second floor. The closest door on their right lay open, exposing the four-poster bed where they'd slain their Uncle Rowan. "So what do we need?"

"A strand of Mum's hair, to start," Hendry answered. "And something of Dad's."

"Those will be in her room," said Alistair, and both brothers glanced at the second door. In the quiet, Alistair could almost hear her voice whispering beyond it, the breathy beginning of *Once upon a time . . .*

Hendry shivered. "I'll go in there. You'll need something sentimental of your own."

"Sentimental how?"

"Something old, from when we were little."

Alistair sighed. "I'll go through my wardrobe."

They split up, Hendry slipping past the second door, Alistair continuing down the hallway. It wasn't until he turned the corner that he realized Gavin trailed after him.

"Sorry you're not getting the grand tour," Alistair said blandly.

"Not sure I'd want one. How many people have seen this place?"

"Upstairs? No one, as far as I'm aware. I guess my dad, but I don't remember him well."

"What happened to him?"

"He died not long after Hendry and I were born. I always figured that once my mum was done with him, she ate him, like a praying mantis."

"You're kidding, right?"

Despite their macabre surroundings, Alistair was more than happy to continue their mocking game from earlier; it was a welcome distraction. So he cast Gavin an amused look. "Of course not. What *else* could my origin story be?"

He paused in front of the glossy black door at the far end. With a turn of the glass knob, he found the room different than he'd left it. Though his usual mess remained—the rumpled bedsheets, the clothing discarded everywhere but the laundry basket—several drawers of his dresser lay open and emptied. And the spellstones on the shelves had been confiscated, probably as possible evidence.

Gavin inspected the sparse decorations and ancient furniture. "But this can't be the *true* lair. Where's the coffin you sleep in?"

"In the tower, obviously. Along with my life-size self-portrait and pipe organ."

"Because of course, your typical day begins at night."

"True." Alistair threw open his wardrobe. "I can't step into sunlight or I'll burst into flames."

On his tiptoes, he rummaged through the heap of clothes shoved in the topmost shelves, yanking out several sweaters he'd outgrown, a wrinkled pair of pajamas, then, at last, a silky fabric, colored to look like scales.

When he turned around, Gavin bent low, studying the notches on his doorframe—marker lines for Alistair's height, measured every year at his birthday.

The image was so bizarre that it caught him off guard. Gavin Grieve, uncovering the ghostly fragments of his childhood. He didn't look like he belonged here, his broad shoulders and golden hair so starkly different than every Lowe who'd prowled these halls.

"So what do you think?" Alistair asked.

Gavin didn't look at him.

A hard lump lodged in Alistair's throat. Gavin's opinion shouldn't matter to him, and not just because they were sworn enemies. Alistair hated this place, with its hideous brocaded wallpaper, the haunting history suspended like dust in the air, choking him a little more with every breath. But a part of him still loved this home, the same way he would always love a monster story—even one he'd grown up in.

"I can see you here," Gavin said finally, a non-answer.

Alistair tried to examine the room the way Gavin might. But as he skimmed the half-finished crossword books piled high atop his nightstand, his sight snagged on the bed, and his thoughts careened into a forbidden direction. Before he could force them to a halt, they were notating every humiliating detail he'd overlooked. The lone action figure atop the shelf. The terrible doodles open in the notebooks on the desk. Then, more alarmingly, the distance between him and Gavin. The silence punctuated only by the ticking of a clock. The tension in the air he knew he was only imagining, just like the heavy, knowing weight of Gavin's stare.

Alistair banished the thoughts, fast and frantic, before they could do irreparable damage. With Isobel, her obvious flirtation had made the notions hard to avoid, hard to stop from forcing their way inside him like a parasite. But this was different. Gavin and he rarely did anything but argue, and any moments otherwise were fleeting. Alistair had never even been certain he liked boys, not beyond the occasional book or television character, figments of fiction.

Then it dawned on him, how the day had begun hopeful yet so thoroughly soured.

This was self-sabotage.

"What's that?" Gavin asked, looking at the item Alistair carried.

Heat rose to Alistair's cheeks. "It's, um, sentimental."

"A blanket? What are those, scales?"

Alistair heaved a sigh and unfurled it. "It's a dragon cape, all right?"

"So Hendry's story about you playing supervillain *was* true." Gavin grinned, and Alistair regretted ever being curious to see his smile. He much preferred his frown.

"Yeah, I know. I'm ridiculous." Alistair stalked toward the door, eager to be anywhere with more space.

"Hey, hold up. You have to at least try it on."

Alistair ignored him and strode down the hall. Hendry waited at the other end, holding their mother's silver hairbrush in his left hand and one of their father's flannel shirts in the other.

"What's wrong?" Hendry asked, seeing his brother's expression.

"Nothing. Ready to go grave robbing?"

"As ready as I'll ever be."

They descended the stairs and wove through the ground floor to the back entrance, Gavin trailing them like a shadow. They rifled through the shed's collection of spellstones, discarding the Green and Grow and PestiShield enchantments in search of one to dig.

"I can't find it," Hendry said. "It should be here. When did someone last use it?"

"When do you think?" Alistair responded.

Hendry shuddered. "Can we not joke about this?"

"Do I sound like I'm joking?" Alistair groaned and shoved the toolbox of spellstones aside. It fell to the floor with a metallic *clunk.* "This is me, having such a great time."

"I'll do it alone if you won't help."

"I didn't say I wouldn't help."

"You don't seem like you want to."

"Of course I don't want to. I didn't want to come here. But we *are* here, so we're gonna do this." He snatched the shovel off its hook on the wall and stormed outside.

The Lowe family graveyard was at the edge of its grounds, encircled by a low stone wall. The tombstones ranged from unreadable, misshapen markers to fresh, gleaming monuments. Their great-great-uncle Kenneth, a past tournament victor, even had a statue, a frightening figure supposedly rendered in his exact likeness, though Alistair doubted even *his* ancestor had hands so much like talons and boar-like tusks jutting from his jaw.

When he looked at Gavin, the other boy's eyes darted from headstone to headstone. All of his levity from earlier had vanished.

"Where is it?" Hendry asked.

"Here." Though the Lowes had used spells to regrow the grass over Hendry's unmarked grave, Alistair would never forget the spot they'd chosen, where Hendry had so often lay to nap.

Gavin hovered behind them, his arms folded across his chest to block out the bitter chill. "We can trade off. It'll probably take a while."

"I think this is something we should do alone, actually," Alistair told him gruffly, though it was only a partial truth. He'd simply breathe easier with Gavin gone.

"All right. If that's what you want." Gavin gave the brothers their space and fled back toward the main house.

With a grunt, Alistair drove the shovel into the earth.

For the first ten minutes, Hendry said nothing. He paced beside the grave of Aunt Alphina while Alistair worked, blisters tearing open on his right palm.

Finally, Hendry blurted, "Why are you *really* mad? You weren't acting like this when we first got here."

Alistair wiped the sweat from his forehead. "Was it a good idea, bringing Gavin?"

"Allies help one another."

"Until one of them murders the other."

Hendry stopped pacing, and he lowered his voice to a hush even though Gavin was far inside. "I can still kill him. But, well . . ."

"Well what?" Alistair asked nervously.

"What does it feel like, to kill someone?"

"You've done it before, Hendry."

"I know. I *know*. But sometimes I feel like I can barely remember it, like I dreamt it. And being back here, it almost feels all the more distant. I know why the house is empty, but it's still strange to see it that way. Being in Mum's room, I felt like I was invading her privacy. Like she'd walk in at any moment and get mad at me."

Alistair understood the feeling. Until he saw them buried in this cemetery, their family wouldn't truly seem gone.

"Do you ever miss them?" Hendry asked quietly.

"What? No."

"Oh."

Hendry didn't say anything for a while after that. Alistair stewed, wondering if he'd upset him, even wondering if he'd lied. He hadn't hated everything about his home. But grieving for Hendry had been the worst experience of his life, and he wouldn't let himself relive even a fraction of that for the rest of his family. He refused to miss people who'd hurt him so much. And most importantly, he refused to miss people he'd killed himself.

"Can we switch? I'm getting tired," Alistair said, simply to have something to say.

"Yeah, that's fine." Hendry took the shovel and stepped into the hole Alistair had already hollowed out.

Alistair sat in the damp grass, leaning back against a tombstone. He closed his eyes and breathed in the scent of the early winter, desperately wishing it would expunge every unwanted thought and feeling from his mind. But they all lurked there. How his mother had held him whenever she told a story. How it'd felt to earn one of Gavin's smiles. How the Payne had looked the moment before he'd blown her apart.

"Killing is easy," Alistair murmured. "It's the afterward that's harder."

"But it's the afterward we're fighting for."

As it had always been, and Alistair wouldn't let *anything* rob them of that. Especially not his own heart.

"When you kill Gavin, how will you do it?" he murmured.

"Not like Mum. I don't hate him. I don't want him to hurt."

Alistair stiffened, disturbed by his own relief. He considered admitting his intrusive thoughts to Hendry. Hendry would set his mind at ease. He always did.

But Hendry was softer than Alistair, and when the time came for him to kill Gavin and claim Alistair's victory, it needed to be without hesitation, otherwise Gavin would claim it for himself.

An hour later, the shovel struck wood with a heavy *thunk*.

Alistair clambered to his feet. Within the hole, Hendry knelt and brushed off the final layer of dirt atop his coffin, then he stood up, staring down at it.

"What will I look like, Al?" he rasped.

"Let me do it," Alistair told him, and Hendry didn't argue as they switched places. While his brother turned away, Alistair bent down and grasped the brass handles on the coffin's side. He heaved open the lid, revealing a sight more ghastly than he ever could've prepared for. Hendry Lowe was unrecognizable, his withered, blistered skin tinted between purple and gray, his face swollen in some parts and sunken in others, all of them wrong. His jaw had opened, the lower half of his mouth a shriveled bowl cradling his fallen teeth. Most of his hair, too, had fallen out. The cut across his throat had opened wider as the skin receded and decomposed, creating a gash so deep his neck only remained sewn together by the barest of threads.

"Shit," Alistair choked, and a sob burst up his throat. The odor brought tears to his eyes, more intense and vile than anything he'd ever smelled, like rancid eggs and cheese and rot. His stomach heaved, and he swallowed down a wave of vomit. "What is it you need? Hurry. *Hurry.*"

"A bone—like a finger or something," Hendry answered, his voice distant. Red light flashed several times above, but Alistair barely noticed.

Shaking, Alistair reached for Hendry's hands, which were crossed over his chest. He grasped his pruned pointer finger and gently lifted it, prepared to cast a spell. But to his horror, the digit snapped off. Liquid oozed from the gaping hole it left behind.

Alistair swayed, and, losing his balance, his gloved hand came down on Hendry's chest. With a sickening *crack*, it collapsed. The ribs sagged downward, and even through the fabric of Hendry's suit, Alistair's glove dampened from the puddle of his decaying insides.

This was what his family had done to him.

What Alistair had done to them.

To the Payne.

To all the champions, if he had his chance.

He wrenched away and vomited onto his shoes. Then, as soon as he was able, he ripped off the soaked glove and slammed the lid closed. Crying, he grasped for a handhold to scramble out, but he couldn't climb.

"Get me out," he gasped. "Get me out!"

A heartbeat later, Hendry knelt over the grave, offering Alistair his hands. Alistair shoved the ruined finger into his pocket and seized them. With a groan, Hendry heaved him out, and Alistair collapsed over him.

For a long time, neither let the other go.

GAVIN GRIEVE

The Grieve family have never once agreed to do an interview regarding their role in the tournament, nor have they provided any comment on their champion's decision to ally with Alistair Lowe. Perhaps they believe their tell-all book makes enough of a statement on its own.

Ilvernath Eclipse, "A Portrait of Each
Blood Moon Family: The Grieves"

Gavin sat across from Alistair in the Cottage kitchen, a steaming cup of tea in his hand. He had brewed a pot for lack of anything better to do, while Hendry shut himself in his room to prepare the healing spell and Alistair went to shower off grave dirt and rot.

He'd heard Hendry and Alistair talk about the Lowe manor enough times to know it would be a painful visit, but none of it had prepared him for their actual homecoming. Gavin had hoped seeing the evidence of the people they'd murdered would make the thought of killing them both easier to stomach, but it hadn't, and he wasn't quite sure why.

"Are you okay?" he asked Alistair, who hadn't been able to wash away his shell-shocked expression. Gavin realized the moment he'd spoken it what a ridiculous question it was. "Never mind. Forget I said anything."

"No—it's fine." Alistair's damp curls hung around his forehead, cracked in the middle by his widow's peak like a broken halo. He scribbled furiously in the crossword book he'd brought back from the bedroom, then swore. "Are you any good at these? It's 'deprived,' six letters . . ."

"I think word puzzles are a bit pointless, actually."

Alistair's lips twitched with amusement. "They're good for you. They sharpen your mind."

Gavin took a sip of tea. "I'll have you know, my mind is—"

"Bereft," Alistair interrupted him triumphantly.

"What?"

"That's the word." He wrote it in, then set the crossword book down. His fingers trembled. Gavin felt a sudden impulse to reach for the other boy's hand, to calm him. He pushed it down, unnerved.

"You can pretend you're not upset if you want, but at least drink your tea."

Alistair huffed but lifted his cup to his lips. When he spoke again, his voice was quieter. Sadder. "There was a reason I never wanted to go back there."

"And you won't. Never again."

"But that's not true," Alistair said grimly. "I go back there every time I close my eyes. Every time I think about what my family did to him, what they did every generation before us, I—I keep telling myself that when this is over, it'll stop haunting me. But after today . . . I don't know if it ever will."

Gavin had heard him tell the reporter what the Lowes had done to Hendry. But Alistair's words had been false then, calculated to incite sympathy. He knew this was different.

"I understand what it's like to feel as though your family will always follow you," Gavin said. "I've spent my whole life trying to prove the world wrong about me. I've done everything I can think of to have a real shot at winning this tournament. But since I saw my sister . . . I've realized that maybe I can fool the world, but even if I come out of this a victor, the Grieves know who I really am. So do I."

"And who is that?"

Gavin had never talked about his family with anyone before. But his visit with Callista had rattled him deeply, kept him up at night. So had the realization that although the spellmakers had helped him, he still felt strangely empty inside. The way Alistair was looking at him, soft and steady, made that emptiness shrink just the slightest bit. And he knew somehow that if he told him the truth, he wouldn't be pitied or judged for it.

"Broken," Gavin whispered. "I must be. Because my family didn't tell me I was champion until after the Blood Moon rose, but

I've known it was coming my whole life. Which means my parents must've seen something wrong with me. Something that made it okay for them to treat my life like it was worthless. I-I'd do anything to fix it. But I don't know if I can."

Alistair's hand, which bore a new leather glove, tightened around his teacup. "I was chosen as champion when I was young, too. My mother had a story to explain it, of course. When I was seven, when winter was just beginning to thaw into spring, she told me specters wandered inside our house, that they were spirits of dead family members. They lurked in the walls, in the pipes, and especially in the darkened corners, terrifying, skeletal creatures draped in shrouds."

Alistair was an excellent storyteller. He seemed to come alive with every carefully crafted word, and although those words were terrible, Gavin could tell how much Alistair loved to get lost in them. It made Gavin want to sink into the story, too. He studied Alistair's face, rapt and attentive, and felt a tendril of unexpected warmth curl in his chest.

"When a Lowe champion was born, the specters always knew," Alistair continued. "Because they could sense nearby death—and death clung to this child, as though they wore a shroud of their own. My mother told me that they were drawn to me. That they lurked behind my shadow when I wasn't looking; floated above my bed when I slept. Even now, every moment I'm not outside, they haunt me. Because they've always known the truth about who I've been, who I've become. I can't escape it. And I can't pretend it isn't true."

Gavin understood, then.

The world told terrible stories about the Lowe family. And Alistair had embraced them. He had done awful things. He had twisted himself into the shape his childhood had asked him to take, and it had led him to desperate, dangerous places. Gavin knew how that felt.

The Grieves had raised Gavin to die. The Lowes had raised Alistair to kill.

Both of them deserved a better story.

"You're not a monster, Al," he whispered.

Whatever Alistair had expected him to say, it clearly wasn't that. At first he inspected him with thinly veiled suspicion, but Gavin didn't avert his gaze, even as he wondered if this whole conversation had been a mistake. Then Alistair turned away, cheeks flushing.

"Well, you're not broken," Alistair grumbled, staring fixedly at the table. "Or worthless. Your family never should've treated you that way."

Alistair's words seared through him, more soothing than a healing spell, more damning than a curse. Because he'd told his enemy his greatest weakness—and instead of using it against him, Alistair had shown him empathy in return.

The emotion that rose in Gavin was terrifying not because it was new, but because it was familiar. He'd felt this way dozens of times—after their battle for the Medallion. While he and Alistair were sorting through fan mail. When they'd gotten drunk at the Castle. But even before that, when Alistair had been nothing to him but a blurry photo and a name. Gavin had spent the past year convinced he wanted to kill Alistair Lowe, or *be* Alistair Lowe, or earn Alistair's respect as a rival, a threat.

Now, the truth he'd tried so hard to hide unspooled within him. He'd never wanted any of those things. What he really wanted was to sit here into the night and listen to Alistair's stories, no matter how terrifying they were. He wanted to know how those dark curls felt twined within his fingers. He wanted—

He *couldn't.*

This desire would only lead to his doom.

"Th-thank you," he choked out, panicked.

Hendry chose that moment to hurry out of the bedroom. Gavin scarcely noticed him until he spoke.

"I'm ready," he said. "I think I can cast the healing spell."

The mood in the room shifted immediately. Alistair shot up, nearly spilling his cup of tea in his haste to clear the table, while Gavin helped Hendry carry everything he needed into the kitchen. He was relieved by the simplicity of the task, by the reminder of where their priorities lay. He set the grimoire down on a nearby counter as Hendry spread the spellboard over the table.

"I need an empty stone." Hendry sounded jittery. "Al, I thought you could choose it?"

As Alistair rooted through the drawers in search of a spare, Hendry laid out the ingredients carefully on each side of the septogram—a swatch of Alistair's cape, a button from their father's flannel, a dark strand of their mother's hair, a sprig of petrified witch hazel, powdered narwhal horn, five grams of pure calendula oil. The last one was

Hendry's own fingerbone. The moment he touched it, red crackled around his silhouette. Then he flickered out of existence. Pain seared through Gavin's bicep. He gasped with surprise, but the burning abated almost instantly—and Hendry reappeared, staggering as he righted himself.

"Hendry?" Gavin asked uneasily.

Hendry coughed. "That was odd. Popped out for a second. Must be the nerves."

"Must be," Gavin echoed, glancing to see if Alistair had noticed. But the other boy was still elbow deep in a drawer.

"Here." Alistair triumphantly brandished an empty piece of yellow quartz. He set it on the spellboard's center, then the three of them sat solemnly at the table.

The only sound was the crackling hearth behind them, robust and warm.

Gavin had thought about what this spell could do, of course, but the possibility of what would happen if it worked suddenly felt real for the first time. With Hendry's life magick as a power source, Alistair at full strength, and the Medallion ready to heal them, the other champions wouldn't stand a chance. The thought sent excitement and nerves fluttering through his chest in equal measure.

He wasn't the only one who was nervous. Alistair's hand shook as he pulled off his glove, revealing the Reaper's Embrace, while Hendry emptied a flask onto the table. White magick hovered over the ingredients, twinkling, before funneling into the stone. Gavin had never seen such a strong healing spell crafted before. Warm light surged through the room, then engulfed the board, blazing brightly, until Gavin had no choice but to look away. When he turned back, the ingredients were gone, Hendry's fingerbone reduced to a gray smear of ash. And the yellow quartz glowed with common magick.

"Well?" Alistair rasped. "Should we try it?"

"Yeah." Hendry's voice cracked. He picked up the stone. Alistair reached out his bleach-white hand, and his brother clasped it, then cast the spell.

Light unspooled from the crystal as gently as a sigh, then disintegrated into hundreds of tiny, dreamlike wisps, so delicate they whirled in the drafty air. Gradually, each one wafted toward Alistair's hand, as though a sparkle of fireflies coated the cursemark.

"Do you feel anything?" Hendry asked.

"I . . ." Alistair hesitated. The spellstone winked out. The magick faded away. And the Reaper's Embrace remained unchanged. "No." Then he bowed his head, shoulders heaving.

Gavin's mind raced. The Medallion wasn't enough. Common magick, class ten, wasn't enough. But maybe . . . "Life magick is stronger than common magick. If I use it to cast this healing spell, do you think it'll work?"

Alistair jerked his head up, eyes wide. "You'd do that for me?"

"It's technically Hendry's life magick, anyway," Gavin said. "And if you're cured, we finally stand a real chance against the others." He tried to say it like it wasn't a big deal, but the truth was, if their final duel came and Alistair was the only one cured, Gavin wouldn't stand a chance.

But the longer he looked at Alistair, the less he cared. With a second rush of panic, he tried to remind himself that this was strategy. That he still needed Hendry's life magick, and their alliance. That he would've done this either way, no matter how he felt about Alistair.

But Gavin knew the truth: He'd let his guard down, and he wasn't sure if he could put it back up again.

"Thank you," Alistair murmured, still sounding stunned.

"I think I'll need more life magick to cast it, though," Gavin said shakily. "Hendry, will you help me?"

"Of course." Hendry rolled up his sleeve, revealing the keyhole on his arm. He furrowed his brow, and a moment later magick crept from the mark, shimmering in the air. Gavin held out his hand. Just as it had back at Walsh's spellshop, the magick sank effortlessly into his skin, sending relief coursing through him.

"I can try it now," he said, and cast the spell.

It was *strong*. Stronger than anything he'd attempted before. If he hadn't spent the last few weeks training, it would've immediately failed. Instead he tried to re-enact one of his breathing exercises and focused on the enchantment, watching with satisfaction as those tiny wisps of magick circled Alistair again. This time they wound around his torso, too, landing on his neck and snaking beneath the sleeves of his sweater.

"Look." Hendry pointed a quivering finger at Alistair's hand.

Alistair let out a small sound of disbelief, while Gavin simply stared, unable to process what he was seeing. Bit by tiny bit, the cursemark was fading.

"It's working," Alistair whispered.

Then an awful pain shot through Gavin's arm, worse than he'd felt in weeks. He groaned and slumped forward, the world around him spinning. Darkness encroached at the edge of his vision, and he gripped the edge of the table, panting. The spellstone fell out of his grasp with a clatter.

"I'm sorry," he gasped, watching helplessly as the Reaper's Embrace crept back over Alistair's fingertips. "I've never cast a class ten . . . I . . . I don't think I can."

All that training, and he *still* wasn't good enough. He couldn't meet Alistair's or Hendry's eyes.

"It wasn't going to work anyway." Alistair's voice hardened. "I could feel it."

"But I was so sure it would," Hendry said, dejected. "Every curse has a cure, and I really thought that spell would do it. There has to be something we're missing . . ."

"What if it's not something—it's some*one*?" Alistair pulled the glove back on his hand. "This curse came from MacTavish. Maybe he's the only one who knows how to break it. Maybe he could even help you, too, Gavin."

The thought that Alistair was considering him the same way Gavin had, despite the risk, gave him a foolish rush of hope.

"Reid told me he didn't know anything that could help me," Gavin said.

"He was probably lying," Alistair pointed out.

Gavin shrugged. "Well, it's not as if he's any more likely to tell me the truth now."

Alistair leaned forward, a menacing glint in his eyes. "Unless we give him no other choice. Unless we bring him *here*."

"You want to kidnap Reid MacTavish?"

"Hey, hey, let's be sensible about this." Hendry frowned. "The other champions are heavily armed. And we can't be sure that Reid knows anything useful."

"You're wrong," Alistair said. "I can verify if he'll be useful or not. I still have two more questions."

It took mere seconds for Alistair to fetch the Mirror. Gavin stayed frozen at the table, unsure of what to think. He found himself shoved beside Hendry as Alistair held the Mirror up. Only two boys stared back—Hendry was invisible to it. Gavin shivered.

"Could Reid MacTavish help me and Gavin?" Alistair asked. The Mirror fogged over, then gave off a scarlet, gleaming light. A sense of calm, of *rightness*, filled the room.

"That's a yes," Alistair said solemnly. "Show me where he is." The Mirror fogged over again, and when it cleared, it revealed Reid, bent over a spellboard in his curseshop. There was a shock of red hair beside him; a hand pulled it back behind one ear, revealing Isobel Macaslan.

Alistair made a noise in the back of his throat. "*She's* there," he said, and then, "If they were in the Tower, they'd be blurry."

"They're in his shop," Gavin said.

"Which means he's not protected by the Landmark's wards. This is our chance."

Gavin gritted his teeth. It didn't matter whether he and Alistair deserved a better story or not, whether they were monsters or villains or anything in between.

This was the story they'd been given. A story where only one of them could live. For a moment, Gavin had forgotten to think like a victor. But he remembered now.

"You're right," he said. "Let's go."

ISOBEL MACASLAN

"Maybe the boy is a competent cursemaker—his clientele seem to think so," Walsh said. "In personal interactions with him within the Ilvernath Spellmaking Society, I've found him to be belligerent and volatile. A very troubled boy indeed."

Ilvernath Eclipse, "Who Is Reid MacTavish
and How Does He Fit into All This?"

For nine nights, Isobel had followed the same pattern. She'd waited restlessly for the others to fall asleep, then she'd slunk into the stairwell, the Carnivorous Spores clutched in her fist. Each night, she alternated which door she visited first—usually Briony, occasionally Finley or Reid—and she'd freeze there, urging herself to twist the knob. Yet her conscience always overruled her, and she retreated to bed, loathing herself for her weakness.

But she refused to let her stalling creep into double digits. Tonight, once and for all, she would correct the tournament's course.

She slowly descended the stairs. Her socks muffled her footsteps, and as she rounded the turn, she spotted a dim light beneath the crack of Reid's door. This wasn't unusual, as he often pored over his research until passing out at his desk, and by half past four, he'd certainly fallen asleep.

After incessant deliberating, Isobel had decided to start with the victim who meant nothing to her.

Still, her hand quivered as she reached for the knob.

Grazed the edges with her fingers.

Finally squeezed it in her grasp.

Without warning, the door was hurled open, yanking Isobel forward. She yelped as she slammed into Reid's chest.

"What the hell?" he cried out, clambering back. "It's the middle of the night. Why are you lurking outside my room?"

"I-I . . ." She couldn't conceive of a single answer.

Reid stared at the crystal in her hand. "Did you . . . Did you come here to murder me?"

"What? Of course not," she hissed, hastily closing the door behind her so as not to wake the others.

When she whipped around, Reid's expression had gone fearful and wild. She realized he looked terrible, his hair stringy with grease and violet rimming his eyes. "Holy fuck, you were, weren't you?" He lunged for his desk and scooped up whichever spellrings he could reach. Then he stumbled back into the corner, shaking as he slid them on his fingers. "I knew I wasn't making it up. You've been shifty for weeks. And . . . *shit*. Are Finley and Briony already dead?"

"Will you shut up? No!" She wracked her brain for what to do. She wore other cursestones, as a precaution, and though she thought she could outmatch Reid, she couldn't afford a racket. However, she couldn't risk him exposing her to Briony and Finley either.

"Oh, so I'm first, then? How flattering."

"You've got it wrong. I came here to . . . to . . ."

He laughed deliriously. "Go on. I want to hear you force yourself to say it, the only other conceivable excuse for sneaking into my bedroom in the middle of the night."

Isobel's cheeks burned, and though she'd spent the past nine harrowing days convincing herself there was nothing she wouldn't do to survive, she hadn't considered she'd need to feign visiting Reid for a booty call.

With a frustrated groan, she stomped her foot and hurled the Carnivorous Spores onto his bed. "*Fine*, all right? But what else am I supposed to do? We both know the Cloak is beyond repair, thanks to you. And now—"

"Not anymore," Reid said quickly. "I figured out how to replace the Cloak."

"Y-you what?"

"It's why I was up all night. I was just about to wake you when you came to *murder me*."

Isobel rested her hand on her forehead, distraught. She knew logically that he was probably lying, that he'd spew anything to protect himself, but truth spells didn't work against him, and his expression remained as grave as ever.

"Just tell me how you'll fix it," she snapped.

He held out his hands as though she were a rabid animal he needed to calm. "All of the Relics hold three enchantments within them, right? If we can craft replacements for each one and bind them to a new object, we can effectively create a fake Relic."

"But we've been over this. We can't just pass common magick off as high magick."

"No, but we could pass life magick off as it."

Chills shot down Isobel's spine. "It's not you, is it? The murderer in the papers?" His bedroom *had* reminded her of a serial killer's. And the flickering candlelight painted a sinister cast over his features, a glare across his glasses that obscured his eyes, the metallic glint of his tongue piercing winking between each breath.

"You honestly think I'm offing people in Ilvernath? With what free time? Just because I'm not in handcuffs doesn't mean I'm not under lock and key."

"Oh *that's* reassuring, that it's just a question of your availability." But even so, she considered his idea. Until the past few weeks, she'd only ever heard of anyone manipulating life magick in movies. "Fine, let's say your plan works. Where are we going to get the life magick, hm?"

"From me."

Isobel barked out a laugh. "You can't be serious."

"Why do you say that?"

"Because you . . . You'd give up your own life? Months of it? Years?"

"Life magick regenerates over time. If I take off, say, a decade, I'll have the rest of my life to replenish it. It's not a pretty process, but it's either that or die in six weeks, so why would I make any other choice?"

Because Briony or Finley would volunteer to donate their life magick—Isobel knew they would. And so would she, if it truly meant saving them all. Even though Reid now bore a champion's ring, Isobel had truly never considered him one of them. Someone who would sacrifice, if called to do so.

"The Cloak's first enchantment is invisibility," Reid continued, lifting three of his fingers to count them off. "The second masks sounds. And the final one is a very powerful defensive spell, one that renders its champion nearly invincible. They're all spells, not curses, but I think if the two of us grab the necessary ingredients from my family's store, we can create something to replicate them. After that, I'll show you how to fill the replacement Cloak with my life magick."

Isobel didn't respond, too focused on parsing through the details of his plan, differentiating between what was truly possible and what she simply wanted. It relied on a lot of luck and improvisation, but it was the only solution they'd come up with in weeks. And it might even be a good one.

So long as he wasn't lying.

"When do we go?" she asked carefully.

He shakily lowered his hands. "Now. And I don't think it should be all of us. The reporters will notice the Tower wards shift if Briony leaves, but I think you and I could sneak past them alone."

Isobel crossed her arms, finally understanding his ploy. One of her spare curserings shone brighter, readied. "Oh, so we'll just sneak off back to all your supplies and not tell Briony or Finley where we're going?"

"Cool it. Obviously we'll tell Briony and Finley where we're going." He studied her warily, from her pajamas to her frizzy hair. "We don't even need to mention your potential little murder spree. Is that good enough for you?"

"I guess." Although her suspicion had far from disappeared.

They found Briony with her mouth open and drooling on her pillow, but by the time Isobel had roused her and explained the plan, her exhaustion vanished, replaced by jittery hope. Isobel had expected her to argue, to voice at least some concern that it was the dead of night, to try to invite herself along, but she accepted Reid's rationale—Reid and Isobel were the ones with spellmaking experience. And, two minutes later, Finley did the same.

Isobel didn't get it. Even if they'd faced death together in the forest and at the Mill, was that all it took for the others to forgive Reid? To *trust* Reid? He wasn't helping them out of the goodness of his heart. He was helping them because they hadn't given him a choice.

Nevertheless, armed with an arsenal of protective cursestones, she snuck off with him toward Ilvernath. Even with the cover of darkness, they left nothing up to chance, concealing themselves beneath a pair of Camouflage spells. And for the first ten minutes, they said nothing. Isobel kept replaying the scene in his bedroom, the terrified way he'd looked at her when he'd realized the truth. She suspected he was dwelling on the same thing.

Finally, Reid said, "For the sound-masking spell, I was thinking a Serene Space."

"Isn't that for soundproofing rooms?"

"If we swap around a few of the ingredients, I think we'll achieve the effect we're after. For the defensive spell, a Warrior's Helm should do the trick. It's an Aleshire spell—I remember her giving it to the Lowes. But I can guess at the recipe."

"And for the invisibility? This Camouflage isn't going to cut it."

"Invisibility spells are tricky—I don't know much about them. But your mum owns a spellshop, doesn't she? What do you think?"

Isobel raised her brows, surprised he'd want her opinion. "Mum specializes in cosmetic spells, not tactical ones. It's not like you need to camouflage your dress to prom."

"I wouldn't know. I didn't go to my prom. Obviously."

"Let me guess. It wasn't your scene?"

"You don't get to judge me. I bet you've had your dress planned out since sixth year. It probably involves a lot of rhinestones." He smirked to himself, as though his insipid jokes were anything to be proud of.

"I didn't plan for prom," she said flatly. "By the time it almost made sense to, I didn't think I'd live to see it."

Reid's smirk fell, and he shoved his hands into his coat pockets. "I *was* supposed to go to prom. But it was the week my dad died. He'd wanted me to go—he'd been sick for a long time. But I . . . I couldn't."

Isobel had already known that both of Reid's parents were dead. Not just from his empty house, but because he'd told her as much when they'd first met. The Macaslans had attended his father's funeral.

"Is that when you wrote the book?" she asked tightly. No matter how tragic Reid's life story, this was the detail she couldn't move past.

"After I graduated, yeah. I had a real plan for about a month. I was going to go to school and temporarily close the shop for a few years. But then I remembered the Blood Moon was coming, that the Mac-Tavishes had been part of it for so long that I'd be expected to play along as well. Then I wrote it that summer."

Isobel had spent the past weeks hating Reid for what he'd done, but she now begrudgingly understood what the power of high magick meant to him, if it could've saved his father. What it felt like to carry the burden of a story that only played out every twenty years, to grow up with the weight of something that your parents and family knew firsthand but that felt so removed from you.

Isobel grimaced as though she'd swallowed a worm. She didn't *want* to sympathize with Reid, who, barely an hour ago, she'd been prepared to slay without remorse. Who she might still need to slay, if his plan failed.

"And at what point did you decide to murder all the champions for high magick?" she asked.

"At what point did you decide to murder all of your allies in their sleep?" he countered.

Rather than respond, Isobel glowered at the red stars twinkling in the night sky.

"You and Briony, you've been best friends since, what, forever? And just like that"—he snapped his fingers—"you're stalking up to her bedroom to kill her? Even I think that's sick. But you've probably been planning her death for years. Barely three weeks after my book came out, you *leapt* at the chance to declare yourself champion."

"That's not even remotely close to how it happened," she growled.

"Oh really? Enlighten me then. Tell me how you became a killer."

As far Isobel was concerned, she didn't owe Reid MacTavish anything. But she hated his smug tone, like he'd dragged her down to his level. She hadn't *wanted* to betray Briony, and if they did manage to recreate the Cloak, she would remain her ally, gladly. Contrary to what the world thought of her, she was no monster.

And so she bit out, "The *Ilvernath Eclipse* named me champion, and believe me, no one was more shocked than I was."

"What do you mean?"

Isobel decided to omit Briony's part in it, not wanting him to think her vengeful when she wasn't. "It was a publicity stunt. I barely knew my dad's family before then—I only visited for holidays and events. I never, ever thought that I'd be champion. But after I became famous overnight, the Macaslans told me they liked the idea. That I could make them proud. I kept saying no, of course, but all my friends left, and well, my family was there for me. And then I did want to make them proud." She laughed softly. "I probably *would've* bought my prom dress by now."

"So you could say that it's my fault that you're champion," Reid said, his voice oddly subdued. "If I hadn't published the book, there'd be no story to sell. And the Macaslan champion would've been some cousin of yours."

"Yeah, probably," she said blandly.

Though Reid never apologized, he didn't provoke her again either. He didn't say anything until they approached the front door of the MacTavish curseshop.

"The coast looks clear," he whispered, and the two of them slipped inside. As Isobel reached for the spellstone light switch, he caught her hand. "Careful, darling. I wouldn't put it past the vultures to circle if they know we're inside."

He was right, annoyingly. The last thing she needed was another manufactured scandal smeared across the headlines.

"I'll gather the ingredients for the Warrior's Helm and Serene Space," he told her. "You check my office for a camouflage spell. My dad had about a hundred grimoires. I'm sure you'll find something."

While Reid ducked off to his storerooms, Isobel nervously entered his office. Last time she'd been here, she'd been his prisoner.

She scanned the titles of the books on the shelves. *The Forbidden Arts. Cursemaking in the Modern Age. The Ingredients of Death.* She flipped to their indexes, searching for a spell that sounded suitable. After several minutes, she found one called In Plain Sight, used by hunters stalking deer or foxes, who'd wanted their clothes to blend into their surroundings. It was class six, which wasn't as strong as she would've liked, but she could think of a few ways to modify the ingredients.

When Reid reappeared, he had a shoebox of ingredient vials clutched in his hands, a spellboard tucked beneath his arm, and a black hoodie thrown over his shoulder.

Isobel snatched the hoodie off him. "You're replacing my family's ancestral Relic with *that*?"

"It was this or my dad's old beige parka."

"Fine," she muttered, because it didn't matter, and because Reid had already used a spell to sew three stones into the fabric along the zipper. "I found a camouflage spell."

"I keep all my ingredients in the pantry down the hallway."

Isobel left, retracing steps hauntingly familiar to her. She paused at the foot of the stairwell, examining the same family photos she'd noticed before. She found them strangely endearing. Neither of her parents decorated with photos. Her dad didn't decorate with much of anything, and her mom found them tacky and preferred to cover the walls in tapestries and art instead.

She lingered in the storeroom for a while, combing through hundreds of different vials organized in alphabetical order. By the time she returned to the office, the bloodshot sunrise seared through the windows, and the sounds of traffic trumpeted outside.

"I thought the chameleon tail would make a stronger ingredient than the moth wings," she said. "And rainwater is just outdated. Filtered or bottled water would work better."

"Good. I've already finished the first two stones. Let's get this one ready, then we'll fill it." Isobel watched Reid sift through the recipe's ingredients and match them up with hers, nodding as he read. Even without his ridiculous eyeliner, he looked more like himself than he had in weeks. He seemed to breathe easier, as though the odor of the pickled botanicals and old parchment was a comfort to him. And he moved in an effortless dance, snatching a grimoire from the shelf, adjusting vials on the desk, licking his lips before he turned to a fresh page. "Yeah, I agree with all the switches you made. This should produce something class nine, at least. And I wouldn't have thought to use corydalis. That's clever."

Isobel was flattered, but rather than show that, she nodded at the black velvet box clutched in Reid's hand. It looked expensive, as though for a piece of jewelry far more luxurious than anything sold in this shop. "What's that?"

Reid opened the box, revealing a dark metal dappled in clear, olive green mineral deposits. "It's pallasite, a type of meteorite fragment. It's hellishly rare—and hellishly expensive. My family owns the only one in Ilvernath."

"Which spell is it for?"

"The Warrior's Helm. I hate to use it, but I can't think of anything else that could take an invincibility spell to class ten."

The next four hours crawled past. Several of their ingredients required complicated preparation, from rehydrating the dried corydalis petals to twice boiling the filtered water to siphoning the preserved blood from the chameleon tail and emulsifying the scales into a thick, gritty paste. Only after they'd finished arranging each substance on the spellboard did Isobel ask, "So how does extracting life magick work?"

"Ah, that," Reid said hoarsely. "Normally, I'd knock the person out—it's extremely painful. But I need to walk you through the steps."

"How many times have you done this?"

"Um, once. Sort of, with Grieve. This won't be the same. In that case, I bound his power to his life magick. All you'll be doing is taking life magick from me." Reid reached into the bottom drawer of his desk and pulled out a leather pouch. He unrolled it, revealing a series of syringes and surgical instruments.

"Ah, yes," she said sarcastically. "Exactly the sort of thing a normal person has lying about."

Ignoring her, he rummaged through his collection of pointy objects. "The first step will be hurting me. My life magick will automatically be drawn to the location of the wound, as my body will naturally channel it to begin the healing process. After that, you'll need this."

He handed her a black spellstone.

"An Everlasting Ink. It puts a mark on my skin, representing a seal—trapping the life magick in that spot, at least temporarily. It'll be a septogram, like a spellboard. And then last, the syringe."

"How should I hurt you?"

"What, looking forward to it?" he asked, and she rolled her eyes. She was starting to. "What curses do you have on you?"

"A Bog's Innards. Entomb. Dragon's Breath. Shatter and Break. Poisonous Pincers—"

"The Shatter and Break should work."

Isobel grimaced. "It's class eight."

"So? We both know you can cast it."

She'd mentioned the class for *his* sake, not hers. But the irritating clip in his voice reminded her that she didn't care. "Fine. Whatever."

Reid pushed aside the paperwork on his desk and sat atop it. He rolled up the short sleeve of his shirt to his shoulder. "This is my nondominant arm. You have the healing spellstones?"

Isobel glanced at the tray resting on one of the bookshelves, where each stone glimmered white, already filled. "Yeah."

"Then I'm ready." He turned his head from her and squeezed his eyes shut. When she hesitated for a few moments, he snapped, "Well?"

"You're not the only one who has to brace yourself."

"Just get it over with."

Isobel placed a hand on his other shoulder. It was meant to support him in case he fell, and he must've known that, but he stiffened at her touch anyway.

"Sorry," he muttered. "Your hand is cold."

She bit her lip, but she didn't let that interrupt her concentration. She focused on his arm, specifically where his upper brachium met his shoulder. Then she cast the Shatter and Break.

Instantly, a loud *crack* split through the room, as though she'd struck a mallet directly on his bone. Reid screamed, and his entire body wrenched back, his foot automatically kicking her in the shin. She stepped closer to him and tightened her grip, knowing the curse was far from finished.

His elbow broke next, then his forearm, his wrist. Each bone from shoulder to fingertip fractured until the only thing holding the shape of his arm together was his skin. Sweat broke out across his forehead, and though he'd stopped shrieking, he whimpered between every heaving breath.

"*Faster,*" he rasped, and Isobel shook as she let go of him and grabbed the Everlasting Ink cursestone. It was so jagged that its edges dug painfully into her palm.

While Reid slumped over, panting, she cast it on his arm, and a blue septogram bloomed across his swollen skin, as though painted by his own veins.

He writhed as she inserted the syringe, his head jerking back, his mouth open and gasping for air. To her shock, the liquid that pooled out wasn't blood—it was foggy and translucent. It shimmered, too faint to resemble common magick, but like magick all the same. As soon as she removed the needle, she reached for the healing spellstones. It took five uses to right each of his bones, and when she finished, he rested back against the wall, his eyes still closed, his arm hanging limply, as though he didn't dare move it.

"The Cloak," he said weakly.

Isobel unscrewed the back of the syringe and dumped its contents over the spellboard. The liquid pooled across the septogram, unlike any magick she'd ever seen. But even so, the stones beckoned it, and it crept toward the crystals and seeped inside. One by one, each of them glowed white.

Isobel stared at the stones, at the ridiculous hoodie bought from a shopping mall. It didn't look anything like the Cloak.

"I hope this was worth it," she told him, but her voice had lost its sharp edge. If she hadn't witnessed what Reid had submitted himself to, if she hadn't cast the curses herself, she wouldn't have believed he'd volunteer for such an agonizing procedure.

Maybe she'd judged him too harshly.

Then Reid jumped to his feet, his balance teetering. "I'm gonna throw up." He raced out of the office toward the bathroom, and Isobel doubted he wanted her to follow.

Instead, she grabbed the sweatshirt. No power stirred at her touch, as it would when claiming a Relic or a Landmark. It felt no different than any article of clothing embedded with enchantments. Not ancient, not special.

Nevertheless, she slipped it on. It was too big on her, with Reid being so tall and gangly, even by her own tall and gangly standards. She wanted to test its spells, but because she couldn't claim it, she couldn't use it. Could this paltry replica really compare to the actual Cloak? If it didn't fool her, could it fool an eight-hundred-year-old tournament?

After ten minutes, Isobel decided it was past time to see if Reid was all right or if he'd collapsed beside the toilet. She knocked awkwardly on the bathroom door.

"Are you dead?" she asked.

When no one answered, Isobel braced herself for a possibly unpleasant sight and swung open the door. The bathroom was empty.

"Reid?" she called loudly. "Reid?"

No one answered.

Her throat seized up. There was no way Reid had fled. Not only did she doubt he could in his current condition, but for once, she trusted him. He'd sacrificed ten years of his life for the sake of recreating the Cloak. He wouldn't abandon them now.

She walked around the back hallway, where the door she'd once tried to escape through hung ajar. On the wall beside it, a MacTavish family portrait had fallen to the welcome mat, its glass cracked over nine-year-old Reid's face.

"Shit," Isobel breathed, and she bolted into the narrow back alley.

Reid hadn't run—he'd been taken.

BRIONY THORBURN

There has been much speculation about the nature of these "trials" the champions of Ilvernath undergo to break pieces of the curse. Examples of defensive magick can be found in places as ordinary as your home security system, but the defenses of this high magick curse manifest in a way that seems connected to the sacrifices it has been given over the years, fascinating folklore experts around the world. Here I will provide examples of similar ancestral death curses, some crafted with high magick, some without, to demonstrate that high magick has a "memory" in a way that common magick does not.

Kendalle University Quarterly, "Generations of Agony"

Briony lay on the couch on the Tower's ground floor, tossing a rubber ball from hand to hand. Before the tournament, this had steadied her restless mind, but her problems had felt a lot less dire back then. Briony groaned and pitched it at the stone wall. It gave a satisfying *smack!* before careening past the candle on the table and banging against a kitchen cabinet.

"Can you stop that? Please?" Finley bit out. "I'm trying to prep our cursework."

Briony swung her legs over the couch and sat up. The two of them locked eyes for a terse moment before he ducked behind a stack of grimoires on the kitchen table.

"Sorry." She sighed. "Maybe I'll go on a raw magick run or something."

"That's a good idea. We're running a little low. And we don't know when Isobel and Reid will be back."

"Uh-huh."

Since the kiss, things had been unbearably awkward between

them. Briony was grateful that Finley was still here—but even now, after pairing the Hammer and the Mill, their argument lingered painfully in her thoughts. Neither of them could take back what they'd said. Neither of them had even tried. And yet at night she replayed the taste of his mouth, the touch of his hands, tormenting herself.

Briony laced up her trainers and got to her feet, but as she approached the front door, Isobel stumbled inside, gasping. Her face was slick with sweat, and she carried a rumpled black hoodie in her arms.

"They took him." Her face was nearly paper-white. "He was in the bathroom, and when I went to check on him—"

"Reid?" Briony asked, trying to catch up.

"Yes, Reid!"

"Are you sure he didn't just escape?" Finley yanked back his chair and rose to his feet. "He's technically still our prisoner."

"No. Definitely not." Isobel held up the hoodie, revealing three glowing spellstones. It was ratty and worn, the kind of thing Briony would throw on after volleyball practice. "We just made a replacement Cloak. If he'd tried to escape, he would've taken it with him."

Briony's entire body went hot, then freezing cold. She staggered toward Isobel and touched the scratchy fabric, her vision blurred with tears.

After all this time, after all she'd lost, here it was. A replacement Relic.

"Are you sure?" Finley asked, sounding unconvinced.

"I know it doesn't look like much, but it's real," Isobel said. "I promise."

Briony sniffled and pulled her hand back, then wiped her eyes. "I believe you."

Wonder flashed momentarily in Isobel's gaze—replaced quickly by worry. "Reid sacrificed a lot to make this. We need to get him back."

"If Alistair and the others *do* have him, they must want him for something," said Finley sharply. He gestured toward the pillar. "His name isn't crossed out."

"Exactly," Isobel said. "All three of those boys have told every newspaper in town how badly they want their curses broken. The Reaper's Embrace is a MacTavish curse."

Finley nodded, concern creeping into his voice. "And Reid is the one who warped Gavin's magick. They'd have real motive to kidnap him if they think he can break their curses."

"He doesn't actually know how to break their curses, though, does he?" Briony asked.

Isobel looked grim. "We just made a replacement Relic. If anyone's capable of it, it's Reid."

Briony remembered how dangerous the fight for the Medallion had been. "If Alistair and Gavin are cured . . ." She didn't need to finish the sentence. She could tell Finley and Isobel were both aware what a threat Alistair and Gavin would pose. But it wasn't just about that.

Reid was part of their team now. They couldn't lose him—not when they'd just figured out that saving everyone really *was* possible.

"We have to go," she said.

"That's what I've been saying," Isobel snapped. "Come on! Grab your strongest curserings."

Finley hurried to his room to fetch some, while Briony turned to Isobel.

"Will the Cloak help us? Maybe we can use it to sneak in."

"I don't think any champion can claim it, which makes it useless to us," Isobel said, frowning. "We'll keep it here." She draped the makeshift Cloak delicately across a chair, then paused. "Do you see that?"

Briony followed her pointed finger and saw that the bottom of the sleeve had come loose. A thread twisted and tugged, unraveling a centimeter of fabric in seconds.

"Yeah, I do. What's happening?"

Isobel touched the sleeve, which began to come apart in her hand. The two of them watched together as the light in the spellstones dimmed ever so slightly.

"Shit." Isobel wrenched away from it.

"The Relic's not going to last, is it?" Briony whispered.

"I don't know."

"We need to check if those stones still work," Briony said gravely. "*Now.*"

"What's going on?" asked Finley, who'd returned from his room with a handful of curserings.

"The Relic's falling apart," Isobel croaked. "Do you have anything on you to test if a spellstone's still properly enchanted?"

"I think I do, actually." Briony fumbled through her pockets before pulling out an Enchant-Me-Not, which she'd been using to check on the spellstones embedded in the Tower walls. "Here. If there's a functioning spell inside a stone, they'll light up."

As she cast it, Finley's rings lit up immediately, flaring neon yellow; Isobel's arsenal did, too, along with what appeared to be a dozen more stones tucked into her jacket pockets. Neon blazed around the room, illuminating crystals scattered around grimoires and lost within the couch cushions. The three champions looked anxiously at the Cloak's spellstones. Light circled the first, then the second, then the third.

"They still work." Briony exhaled with relief. "Okay, if we head to the Crypt right now—"

"Why is the candle shining like that?" Isobel asked warily. Briony whipped from the makeshift Relic to the candle perched on the table. The stone set into the glass glowed yellow—but the glow was far brighter than any other enchantment. Briony's eyes watered as she squinted into the glare.

"We don't have time to worry about that," Finley said.

But Briony had a horrible guess. "I think there's another spellstone inside it." She tipped the candle over, shook out the block of soy wax, and clawed into it with her fingernails until she pulled out a crimson stone, winking like a ruby.

Her dread deepened swiftly into horror as she sensed the enchantment inside.

"It's some kind of Listen In," she croaked. "A really strong one. We—we've been bugged."

Finley went very still, while Isobel looked as though she might vomit. Briony wondered, panicked, if this had come from the other champions, and if so, what awful things they'd learned. She bolted for the potted plant and pushed the stone into the dirt, hastily covering it with soil. Magick leaked into the air.

"This is bad, but we can't lose focus," Isobel said firmly. "Reid could be dying."

"And the Relic's still falling apart," Finley countered.

Briony grimaced as she watched another thread come loose from the Cloak's sleeve. She couldn't bear the thought of their one chance at victory—at survival—slipping away. But she didn't want to condemn Reid, either.

"Do you think you can make another one?" she asked anxiously.

Isobel wrung out her hands. "I . . ."

"Isobel," Briony pressed. "Can you?"

"I-I don't know. We used an ingredient that was so rare, it was the only one of its kind in Ilvernath. I'd like to think we could find a substitute . . ."

"But you can't guarantee it?" Finley asked sharply.

Dismay washed across Isobel's face, but finally, she shook her head.

And Briony felt the agony of a choice none of them wanted to make descend upon them. If they decided to try and destroy part of the curse right now, Reid could die. Briony knew how dangerous the other champions were—they'd almost killed her, after all. Could she leave him to suffer at their hands after she'd been the one who bound him to the tournament? After he'd given up his own life magick to craft this Relic?

Maybe it made her terrible—but Briony decided that she could.

"We need to take the Cloak to the Crypt," she said firmly. "This could be our only shot at a replacement Relic, and it's breaking. If we don't pair it with a Landmark, we'll be just as screwed as we were before."

"You think we should just abandon him?" Isobel rasped.

"Reid would make the same choice," Finley said somberly.

"It's him or all of us," added Briony. "I'm sorry, but we have to do this. Otherwise—"

"No. You're right." Isobel hugged her arms to herself, her features hardening with cold resolve. "Of course you're right."

Briony grabbed the Relic off the chair and clutched it as if it were made of gold. "Let's go, then. We've got no time to waste."

Because of the Relic's time limit, they elected to use several precious Here to There spells. The three of them arrived on a grassy knoll at the forest's end, at the very edge of the tournament grounds. Behind them rose the external Blood Veil, revealing an empty field through the thick red wall of magick. Briony spared a second to gaze longingly at the world beyond the tournament.

"The Crypt must be somewhere underneath here." Isobel looked dispassionately at the grass.

Briony sent out a Seek and Find spell, and sure enough, there was a massive structure directly beneath them.

"Stand back," she told the others. After her distress at Reid's kidnapping *and* the way they'd been manipulated by fan mail yet again, it felt good to cast a powerful spell. Her Avalanche ring flared, and the ground quaked, clumps of earth crumbling away until they revealed a smooth slab of stone. An etching peeked beneath its crust of dirt, but even after Isobel strode toward it and brushed the filth away with her trainers, the design remained indecipherable, entirely eroded from what it had once been.

"I guess it has to be me again to claim the Landmark." Isobel crinkled her nose, then squatted and grasped the stone's edges. With a groan, she slid it aside, exposing a grimy stairwell.

Briony tried not to gag. Even from several steps away, the air wafting from it smelled like damp mold.

As Isobel descended the stairs, Briony and Finley at her heels, the Landmark responded to her. A mint green carpet unfurled at the bottom, disappearing into the darkness of an eerie hallway, its edges soiling from the puddles on the ground. White chandeliers dropped from the coarse ceiling, their crystals clattering, and mounted vases of delicate, dried flowers lined the walls on either side.

Isobel shuddered, then stood at the landing, eyeing the decor. Behind her, Briony looked around nervously. Claiming the Tower had felt a bit like coming home, a warm, friendly flame kindling in her chest. But each step into the Crypt gave her the sensation of an insect squirming lower down her spine. These touches of Isobel only made it more bizarre. Even as a floral scent drifted through the musty air, it wasn't enough to drown out the underlying stench.

She turned to Finley, who was tugging on a few extra spellrings. "Any idea where the pillar is?"

"Probably at the back of this hallway." Isobel clutched her arms to her sides.

"Are you—" Briony ventured.

"I'm fine."

Briony decided not to push it. Instead, she strode forward, Finley a step behind. But after a few seconds of walking, she heard a frantic patter of footsteps, slightly muffled by the carpet. She whirled around just in time to see Isobel disappear up the flight of stairs.

"Hey!" she called. "What the hell are you doing?"

Briony started after her, determined to drag Isobel back, but Finley caught her arm before she'd even taken a step. "She's made her choice pretty clear, Bri."

"She abandoned us!" Briony yanked her arm away from him.

"She went after Reid. She must've. We can be angry with her later." Finley sounded deathly calm.

"Isobel knows there's nothing more important than breaking the curse. We've sacrificed so much to get here—"

"You've made it very clear what you're willing to sacrifice."

Briony glared at him. "That's *not* what this is about. And besides, you made the same choice I did. So let's just handle this, the same way we handled the Cave."

She stalked ahead of him into the gloom. Cool air brushed against her forearm, and she realized unhappily that this hoodie was turning into a very unfortunate fashion statement.

The chic decorations persisted as they walked deeper into the Crypt, but the smell of decay increased, dampening their glamour. The carpet grew muddy and moldy, the mint green washed out in the chandelier light. Briony spotted an antechamber with a stone replica of Isobel's vanity table from her bedroom at her mum's house. Perhaps the sight should've been comforting, conjuring up memories of slumber parties and Isobel doing her makeup, but it had the opposite effect. Maybe all she and Isobel had ever done together was play pretend.

Finley was the first to notice the coffins slotted into the walls, plain and unadorned. Beneath each of them was a tiny plaque engraved with a name. They all ended in Macaslan.

"Creepy." Briony fiddled with one of her spellrings. Their footsteps echoed through the empty space as they kept walking. The silence between them stretched and stretched until Briony thought she might snap. It had been so easy for them to talk to each other before this—but now she had no idea what to say to him.

After what felt like an eternity, the chamber's ending loomed ahead, a slightly raised dais. The pillar was set into the back wall, a statue hunched above it: a beautifully carved but cracked figure with tattered wings, arms extended toward the coarse stone. Several fingers were missing from its outstretched hands. Briony climbed the few stairs and studied it closely.

"The Hammer and the Sword were easy," she said. "How do you attack a pillar with a hoodie?"

Finley let out a surprised chuckle, then coughed, as though trying to stifle his amusement. "I don't know."

Shadows danced across the statue in the chandelier light, and Briony eyed one of its hands again. There was something expectant about the way it reached toward them, beckoning.

"Hang on." She pulled off the Cloak, which was now missing an arm, and turned to Finley. "I think I know what to do. Are you ready?"

"I'm ready."

Briony hung the hoodie from the statue's hand.

She pulled her fingers back—and immediately, all of the lights extinguished.

Finley swore, while Briony tried to cast a Flicker and Flare. But the Crypt's enchantment was so strong, she couldn't even see the shine of her spellrings.

"I guess it's started," she said, voice hushed. "Whatever it is."

She tried to brace herself for battle and collided with Finley instead, his hands brushing her waist, her forehead knocking against his chin.

"Shit!" she gasped. "Sorry."

"I thought you were . . ." He trailed off.

"An enemy?"

"Something like that." His grip loosened, and he stepped away. In the all-encompassing darkness, it was harder for Briony to lie to herself about how much she wanted him to kiss her again.

For a few heartbeats, the only sound was their breaths, quick and shallow. Then a series of tiny patters rang out across the Crypt, dozens and dozens, overlapping like a rainfall. Finley turned, pressing his back against hers, while Briony shuddered and tried to cast another Flicker and Flare. Nothing. And when the red light of the pillar returned at last, each chandelier flaring crimson where they had once glimmered a soft gold, Briony almost wished they were still in the dark.

Hundreds—no, *thousands*—of maggots squirmed out of the Crypt's walls. They fell in a steady stream on top of one another, crawling slowly but surely toward them.

"Oh, *gross*," she said, suppressing a gag.

Beside her, Finley sent out a Blaze Barrage in a neat ring, frying the first row of maggots to a crisp. But they kept coming, their brethren creeping across the scorch marks. His cursering glowed again, while Briony pushed back another row with an Overcharge that electrocuted hundreds more. But a grotesque ocean of maggots flooded down the hall, as far as she could see. The smell of all those fried and burned corpses made her eyes water.

"I don't like this," Finley mumbled. "This doesn't feel like enough of a threat."

"Oh, I'm sorry, are you daring this place to hurt us more?"

"It's just that right now, we could easily escape—"

One of the coffins along the walls creaked open, then another. Bony hands emerged, tinted crimson in the light.

"Happy now?" Briony cried. "Skeletons!"

They stomped onto the maggots, crushing some into goo. One of the skeletons wore the rags of a dress; the other's skull bore wisps of hair. Finley cast the Blade of Truth, but no illusion dissipated. This wasn't like the blood lake they'd faced in the Cave—this was real.

The skeletons advanced far faster than the maggots, arms outstretched. Finley's Lightning Lance fired a crackling blue bolt toward one, while Briony flung an Arachnid's Anger at the other. A massive net slammed into it and pinned it to the ground, leaving the corpse to the maggots. But to her dismay, scattered bits of bone tore through the net. A hand crawled determinedly through the insects; a leg tried desperately to stand.

While Briony and Finley had both focused on the undead, the maggots had drawn closer to their fiery perimeter. One slid through the flames and latched onto Briony's trainer, then burrowed through the leather with a surprisingly strong bite. Briony howled and kicked it away, gasping at the chunk of missing shoe *and* missing flesh it took with it.

"So they want to devour us," Finley said pragmatically. "Makes sense."

At which point three leapt onto his pant leg. Now it was his turn to yelp with pain. He shook them off while Briony covered for him.

"We can't hold them back forever," she said.

"I know," Finley said, as yet more skeletons clambered from their coffins. "There's a trick to every trial. We just need to figure this one out. Can you take over for a second?"

Briony barely had time to nod before he turned around. Without his added enchantments, the pressure of their predicament bore down on her. But she refused to crack. She kicked flesh-eating maggots from her shoes and shattered two more skeletons with her Ten of Daggers. She could do this. She *would* do this. She wouldn't let the tournament—

"Briony. Look at this."

A shape had opened in the pillar, a shape that looked an awful lot like a coffin. What remained of the makeshift Cloak hovered in the center.

Briony stepped toward it, away from the squirming maggots. "Are we supposed to put a body in there?"

"I think so." Finley swallowed. "Got any spare skeletons?"

"Um. I think they're all blown up." She moved closer to the Cloak. "But if someone needs to go in there to finish the trial . . . I'll do it."

"What?" Finley's fingers closed around her wrist. "Absolutely not. Landmarks collapse at the end of these trials—it could kill you."

"Or we could break part of the curse," Briony snapped. Maggots writhed and oozed from the walls around them, crackling and popping against their firebreak. Finley's forehead beaded with sweat. "The Cloak's unraveling fast. We don't have time to put a whole skeleton back together. And I made my choice, and I—I can't take it back, so it *has* to be the right one, okay?"

"Bri. I can't lose you." Finley's voice broke, his calm façade vanishing in an instant. "Not like this."

At first, the words soothed her. But that comfort melted in moments, washed away by a wave of anguish.

"Not like this?" Briony choked out. "You told me we were always a lost cause. I can't even say you gave up on us, because you never thought we had a chance at all, did you?"

"That's not fair," Finley whispered. "I've chosen you every time I could. I only entered the tournament because I thought you wouldn't be here."

"You told me you were trying to figure out if you could kill me!"

"And I can't. You know I can't, I just . . ." Finley's grip slid away from her wrist. Around them, hundreds more maggots fell from the walls and died in the semicircle of flame around the dais. Bits of smoldering bone crept through the fire—hands, feet, a chattering skull. "I'm not willing to throw my life away for this the way you are, or to let *you* throw your life away, either. Maybe that's not particularly noble of me, but it's true."

Briony remembered what she'd told herself, after he kissed her. That the thought of all six champions dying so the tournament could end for good was the right choice. The noble choice. It was no different than what she'd said while condemning Reid.

While forsaking Alistair. While hurting Innes.

Was it worth all of this, to end the curse? Was she really just throwing other peoples' lives away until, at last, she threw away her own?

"You think what I said was *noble?*" she rasped.

"I think that's how you justified it to yourself, sure," he shot back. "But if it's not that, then what is it?"

"I . . . I want what we're doing to actually mean something. To *change* something. I'm willing to give anything for that, but . . . but I think I've been making choices for other people who might not feel the same." She hiccupped. "I guess Innes was right about me. I'm still trying to play the hero. I still believe in fighting for a better future, no matter what I have to sacrifice."

"So, what, you want to die down here?" Finley demanded.

"Of course not." A skeletal hand closed around Briony's ankle. She kicked it away, then cast a half-hearted Overcharge at another wave of maggots. "I'm not saying that my way is right. But I *do* think it's messed up that you were ready to throw away everything we promised each other. I don't understand how you could ever go back to the way the tournament was before if you knew there was even the tiniest chance we could change it."

"I was raised for this the same way you were," Finley said quietly. "I've done my best to break all my rules, to change my mind. But there are chances I'm not willing to take. Maybe I was wrong about our odds, but . . . I wanted to protect myself."

"Well, maybe you should've thought that through before you kissed me."

"That was a mistake."

Briony glared at him. "You've made that pretty clear. Don't worry. If we survive this nightmare, I promise never to talk about it again—"

"That's not what I want." Finley sighed. "If we *do* get out of this, then we'll have a real chance at surviving. And then maybe we can . . . talk about us. About if we want to try again. I just—I said that was a mistake because I thought we had no real shot. But maybe we do."

Again, his words sank deep into her, words she'd so desperately wanted to hear—that he felt the same way she did. That he wanted her, too. But after all the ways they'd hurt each other, that didn't feel like enough anymore.

"You said you wanted to protect yourself," she said. "But there's always going to be something that might break us up. More Relics, more danger. I don't know if I can be with you if I'm always scared you're going to cut your losses and leave. If I'm just another strategy for you—some weird calculation. Can you actually believe in ending this tournament? In . . . in *us?*"

A row of maggots swept through their flame perimeter, and it snuffed out entirely. They squirmed toward Briony and Finley, a horde of decay. Finley cast another Blaze Barrage, but it was too late—he stumbled, then fell, the insects swarming over his body.

Briony cried out in horror. There was no time to think, to breathe— all she knew was that she couldn't let him die. Two of her spellrings flared. Then a third. Then a fourth. When she exhaled, she cast them all at once.

Briony was no exceptional spellmaker, no researcher, no master tactician. But when it came to raw casting potential, she was utterly unmatched.

The Prismatic Protector twined outward, enclosing her and Finley in a great translucent dome made of tiny diamond-shaped bits of light. Her Overcharge crackled across the maggots on Finley's clothes, disintegrating them. And the tunnel shook as her Avalanche sent rocks raining from the ceiling, crushing the maggots outside their shield into dust. Briony rushed to Finley and grabbed his shoulder, panting, as her Healing Hand stitched up the chunks of flesh the maggots had managed to take away.

The drain of the enchantments thrummed through her—it felt like holding something that was both massive and fragile, all on a knife's edge of concentration that could break at any moment.

"Fin," she gasped. "Fin, are you okay?"

He looked up at her, dazed—then broke into a grin.

"You still make it look easy," he whispered.

"I'll do five next time," she whispered back. She smelled iron and felt something dribble beneath her nostrils—blood. But she ignored it.

One of Finley's spellrings shone, too, and another Blaze Barrage burned at the bottom of the shield. Maggots burst against it, splattering into pulp, and skeletal fists pounded against the wall of light.

"I do believe in this, Bri," he murmured, as she helped him to his feet. "I won't pretend it's easy for me. But if you can change, I can, too."

Briony gripped him tighter, her spellrings radiating a kaleidoscopic array of colors. "Good," she said. "So, what do you say? Want to make the world's most disgusting jigsaw puzzle?"

ALISTAIR LOWE

"There's a reason that the Lowes raise their children separate from society, and I know I can't be the only one asking myself—if this curse really breaks, where does this young man go? I don't want him in class with my kids."

SpellBC News: Wake Up Ilvernath!

Alistair had yet to meet the infamous Reid MacTavish other than in passing, but he didn't look so impressive now, unconscious and tied to a chair in front of their fireplace.

Reid stirred, his head lolling onto his shoulder.

"Wakey, wakey," Alistair said, earning him a scoff from Gavin. "What? What would you rather I say?"

"You're making a joke out of this," Gavin muttered.

"No. I'm getting into character." Alistair dragged one of the wooden kitchen chairs before Reid, letting its legs screech across the floorboards. He sat and leaned forward, close enough for Reid to feel his breath on his face. "Wake up," he said, sharper this time.

Reid's eyes fluttered open. Then he jolted, and his chair teetered back. Hendry lunged to catch him before he tumbled into the fire.

"Careful," Alistair warned. "You could've burned yourself."

He watched with satisfaction as Reid's gaze ricocheted fearfully around the Cottage, from the fresh currant scones resting on the counter, to Alistair's crooked smile, to Hendry readjusting the laundry drying over the hearth, to Gavin looming behind Alistair like his comically bulky henchman.

He tugged at his restraints. "What is this? Where's Isobel?"

"It's just you and us," Alistair told him. "We've got some questions we'd like to ask you. Gav?"

On cue, Gavin cast the Truth or Treachery, and a ghostly line of white traced across Reid's throat, as though to match Hendry. Reid thrashed trying to rise from the chair, but his magical restraints didn't give—and they wouldn't. Alistair was all too familiar with the class four Straitjacket after a childhood subjected to his mother's maniacal training methods.

"Why don't we start with this?" Alistair slid off his glove, revealing the bleach-white skin of his cursemark. "The Reaper's Embrace comes from one of your family's grimoires, does it not?"

Reid's chest heaved as he took it in. Despite his half hour of forced slumber, he looked no better than when Gavin's Iron Fist had struck him, hunched over the toilet in the MacTavish curseshop. His greasy hair dangled limply over his forehead, and the only color in his face was the violet spilled beneath his eyes.

"It's one of our curses," he finally bit out. "An old one."

"How do I cure it?"

"You can't."

Beside the fireplace, Hendry's breath hitched, and Alistair struggled to hide his panic. They'd faced their empty home. They'd disturbed Hendry's remains. That couldn't all have been for nothing.

"Why not?" Alistair croaked. "There has to be something that—"

"It's class ten, which means it's designed to be unbreakable. The sacrifice required to craft—"

"I'm aware of the sacrifice," he snapped. "It was my own damn blood that made it."

Something strange flitted through Reid's expression, almost imperceptible. Then he turned away, fixing his gaze resolutely on the floor. "It's impossible."

Alistair scrutinized the cursemaker, suspicion gnawing at him. The mark of the Truth or Treachery hadn't faded from his neck, which meant, more than likely, Alistair was only seeing deception because he wanted to.

Nevertheless, he clasped Reid's hand.

Reid tried to lurch away, but Alistair held firm. "Wh-what are you doing?"

"There's nothing wrong with my spell," Gavin said stiffly, but Alistair ignored him and cast the Divining Kiss.

Several seconds passed, yet Reid's thoughts never poured into Alistair's mind. Alistair closed his eyes and squeezed Reid's hand tighter, trying to tune out the crackles of the fire, the creaks of the floorboards from Hendry shifting side to side. Still, nothing happened, and when he examined the cursemaker once more, white stained the side of his wrist, in the shape of Alistair's lips.

"What is this?" Alistair demanded. "The Iron Fist worked on you. Why won't these?"

A sheen of sweat glistened on Reid's forehead, and his gaze never wavered from the floor. He'd been lying to them, then, pretending to be compelled by the Truth or Treachery.

Alistair growled in frustration and lurched to his feet. Behind him, Hendry and Gavin looked equally stunned. The three of them backed into the living room.

"My curses worked on him that night in the forest," Hendry whispered. "I know they did."

"So, what, it's some kind of mental ward?" Alistair asked. "That doesn't make sense. We took off all his spellrings."

"Unless he's done something to himself," said Gavin darkly. "I wouldn't put it past him, after what he did to me."

"I helped you," Reid grunted, still glaring at his shoes.

"Helped me?" Gavin growled. "You nearly broke my magick. I'm lucky to be alive."

"I told you the consequences up front."

"No, you took advantage of me to make me your experiment."

"As if you would've survived this long if I hadn't."

Alistair didn't have patience for their bickering. "*Damn it*," he shouted, making everyone jolt. He paced across the Cottage. As he passed, the grime clinging to the windows edged farther up the glass, smothering the daylight. "What are we supposed to do now? We wasted a whole set of Here to Theres to get him, and soon the others will swoop in to rescue him, won't they? We . . ."

His gaze snagged on the pair of garden shears resting on the counter.

An awful idea occurred to him.

Without pausing to reconsider, he snatched them, then wrenched open the kitchen's junk drawer. His hands trembled as he grabbed a hammer, a knife, a set of matches, a pincushion full of needles, a spackle—whatever horrid or creative instrument caught his eye. He tossed them across the table with a clatter.

"What are you doing?" Gavin asked.

"What does it look like I'm doing?" Alistair couldn't cast curses—not without risking the spread of the Reaper's Embrace. But he had other methods to obtain answers. And though he'd never done this before, he could—he knew he could.

Hendry squeezed Alistair's shoulder. "Al . . . You don't have to—"

"Don't I?" he asked, his voice steady and grave.

Across the room, Gavin stood rigid, his arms crossed, his expression calculating. Heat simmered in Alistair's stomach as he waited for the other champion to protest.

Then, stone-faced, Gavin nodded.

"Winning was never going to be easy," Alistair told his brother. "Is this any more despicable than what we've already done?"

Hendry gaped at him, at the white of his hand, at the resolve hardened on his face. Nothing about Hendry resembled the boy who'd washed his mother's blood off his hands in the Cottage sink, and despite all that the brothers had endured together, Alistair suddenly, acutely, felt the weight of all that he'd lived through alone.

The years of training.

Hendry's death.

The beginning of the tournament.

Hendry had promised that they would claim their victory together, but maybe it was better this way. Because once Alistair did this, once he knew how to cure himself, he could spare Hendry any more suffering, even if it meant he suffered alone.

"Why don't you give us some privacy?" Alistair asked softly.

"I . . ." Hendry looked between Alistair, Gavin, and Reid, his expression queasy.

"Please," Alistair added.

After several heartbeats, his brother swallowed and slipped into the bedroom. The door closed with a quiet *click*.

Alistair white-knuckled the closest chair. He could do this. He'd already done worse.

He plucked up one of the needles and held it at eye level. He flicked it, for effect. Then he returned to his seat in front of Reid. "Tell me how to break the Reaper's Embrace."

Reid glared, his chin raised. It seemed the cursemaker hoped to play it brave. "I told you—it's supposed to be unbreakable."

"Then you better start thinking hard." Alistair grasped Reid's right hand and slid the needle beneath the nail of his pinky. Reid sucked in his breath and arched in his chair, but he didn't reward Alistair with a whimper. "What good is it to lie to us? Or do you get off on playing noble?"

Gavin scoffed. "There's nothing noble about him."

"Then why not just tell us what we want to know? Wouldn't you rather it be quick?" Alistair extracted the needle and wiped its bloody tip on Reid's jeans. "Even if the others try to save you, these wards are impenetrable."

When Reid still didn't answer, Alistair jabbed the needle beneath his fourth finger. Reid writhed and squeezed his eyes shut. Purple spots bled beneath the remaining flecks of his black polish.

"I'll ask again," Alistair said. "How do I break the Reaper's Embrace?"

Reid never responded, not even as Alistair went through the rest of his fingers. He slouched, his chest heaving.

Alistair cupped him by the jaw. "We can play this game all night. You're only making it harder for yourself. You know that, don't you?"

Reid seethed, craning his neck away from him even though Alistair never loosened his grasp. "Isobel was right to cast it on you. You're a monster."

Those words once would've wounded him, but they didn't anymore—and not because Gavin had refuted them. Because they were true. If Alistair could face his childhood home, if he could disturb his brother's rotting remains, then there was *nothing* he wasn't capable of.

"Have it your way," Alistair said softly, then he stood and seized the iron poker from the fire, its tip molten orange. He bent, grasping Reid's shoulder with one hand and resting his chin against the other. He traced the poker up his arm, letting it hover over his skin.

Before Alistair could press it against his forearm, Reid spit out, "It was me, you know. I wrote *A Tradition of Tragedy*. It was me, all this time."

Gavin sucked in a breath, and he took an unsteady step forward. "What did you say?"

"I pinned it on your family because I knew everyone would believe it," Reid snarled. "Only a Grieve would stoop so low, right? Eight hundred years of tournament history, and all the Grieves have ever been is pathetic."

Gavin lunged at him, and Alistair only had a second to duck away before Gavin landed a punch squarely on Reid's nose. Alistair stumbled, his head smacking against the pillar. The poker clattered to the ground. By the time he'd gathered himself enough to look up, Gavin had grabbed a fistful of Reid's shirt. Blood poured from the cursemaker's nostrils.

"You're. Lying," Gavin growled.

"I'm not," Reid gasped out.

One of Gavin's rings flashed, but before he could curse him, Alistair seized Gavin by the shoulders and steered him across the room.

"He's goading you," Alistair said. "He knows he has information we need, and he's baiting you so you kill him before he breaks."

Gavin moved to attack again, but Alistair held him back, struggling against Gavin's strength. His head still throbbed where he'd knocked it.

"Are you listening to me?" Alistair demanded. "You can't kill him."

"I-It all makes sense now. When my sister said it wasn't her . . . There was no one else . . ." He fixed Reid with a venomous glare. "Do you know what you did to my family? What the world put us through?"

But there was no hint of remorse on Reid's face, only satisfaction. He grinned and licked his lips, snakelike, his silver tongue piercing flashing orange in the firelight. "It's not like I made anything up for shock value. The tournament is shocking enough. You all chose this."

"I didn't choose *anything*." Gavin practically trembled in Alistair's grip, and Alistair didn't recognize the look on his face, not even when they'd fought each other in the forest. His head hanging down, blond hair fallen over his eyes. His teeth, bared.

After all their weeks of arguments, of battles, Alistair couldn't understand how it had only taken a few words for Gavin to come undone.

"You can leave, too, if you want," Alistair told him. His voice sounded strangely gentle, even to his own ears. Gavin must've thought so, too, because surprise flitted across his face, and he locked eyes with him.

"No," Gavin said firmly. "You're not doing this alone."

Maybe words would be both of their undoings. Alistair's heart clenched, and he was suddenly aware of how close they were—dangerously so—and he lurched back as though burned.

Seeing that his plan was failing, Reid added, "That's why I experimented with your magick—I knew there was no cost to it, if it killed you. It wasn't like you were going to survive the tournament anyway."

Alistair held his breath, expecting Gavin to strike him, to curse him, anything. Instead, Gavin strode toward the assortment of weapons on the table. Alistair joined him, frantically trying to regain his composure.

When he went to grab the shears, however, Gavin reached for them as well. Their hands brushed. Alistair's pulse quickened, and he counted five erratic, anxious beats before he had the wits to yank his hand away. He glanced at Gavin, wondering if he'd noted it, if he cared. But Gavin had seized the hammer and stormed over to Reid.

"Do you have a favorite finger?" His voice had gone sinister, lethal—Gavin made as good a villain as he did. Then, as Alistair raised the garden shears, pretending hard to examine them, Gavin added, "How about a favorite ear?"

Reid swallowed, but before he could answer, Gavin slammed the hammer on his right hand. His middle finger broke with a decisive *crack*. Finally, Reid let out a scream.

"Go ahead," Gavin said, "tell me again how pathetic I am."

A moment later, another fall, another crack.

"Or better yet, tell us how to fix him. Or me."

When he'd finished squirming, when the tears had stopped leaking from his eyes, Reid choked out, "I d-don't know how to cure either of you."

Swiftly, Gavin brought the hammer down, crushing his pointer. Reid shrieked, and Gavin stroked his swollen knuckles. "See that?" He nodded at the Medallion resting by the sink, and Alistair grabbed it and strung it around his neck. "We have infinite healing power. We really can do this all night."

"I-I'm not . . ." Reid shuddered, then dry heaved.

Alistair snatched the pail from the sink and thrust it into Reid's lap. He was a moment too late. His vomit spilled down the bucket's edge, seeping onto his jeans. He hunched over it for several seconds before Alistair grabbed him by the hair and wrenched his face up. Sick dribbled down his chin.

"I-I'm not . . . I'm not lying," Reid said hoarsely. "I don't know how to reverse what I did to your life magick. I barely knew how to do it in the first place."

With a frustrated howl, Gavin jumped up from his seat and paced across the floor. "I don't believe you. There has to be a way."

"Maybe, but a wrong attempt could kill you."

"What about Alistair?"

"I don't . . ."

"You're *lying*."

Reid hung his head back, panting. "Doesn't it matter to you at all that we could break the tournament? Do you both really want to win that badly?"

Gavin scowled. "You're bloody hypocrites—all of you."

"And it's never been about winning," Alistair said hotly. "It's about saving my brother."

"Your brother, who half the city thinks is a serial killer? Did he really think a truth spell—"

Alistair snatched the hammer from Gavin and swung it. This time, he cracked a fingernail along with the finger.

Reid's scream broke into a sob, and Alistair dragged the hammer's claws over his swollen knuckles in an agonizing glissando.

"Careful what you say," Alistair warned him. "I might not like it."

Reid had to fight to catch his breath. "Is one life . . . really worth the lives . . . of everyone else? Isobel? Briony? Finley? *Him?*"

Reid jutted his chin in Gavin's direction, and, to Alistair's surprise, Gavin had grabbed the pitchfork from where it rested beside the mantel. He leaned against it, his head tilted to the side. Shadows licked across his face and clothes from the firelight, catching on the sharp edge of his nose and the hollows of his throat. He gnawed at his lower lip, and as his grip tightened against the iron, the muscles tensed across his arms and chest.

Whatever Alistair had been thinking before careened off course, like a train plunging off a cliffside.

Self-sabotage or not, Alistair was starting to realize he *did* like boys.

"Don't you have anything to say for yourself?" Reid strained to sit up straighter even as cries still wracked his chest. When Alistair couldn't summon a response, Reid spat on his lap. "You're no different than your grandmother."

Fury shot through Alistair like a bolt of lightning, but before he could bring the hammer down once more, Gavin caught his wrist midair. "The cursemark. It's growing," Gavin rasped, and Alistair stiffened, dread drenching him like an ice bath. He hadn't realized the Reaper's Embrace would spread even through magickless wrongs.

Ignoring the horrified look in Gavin's eyes, Alistair wrenched the pitchfork from his grasp and pressed its points against Reid's throat.

"What will it take?" he demanded. "What will it take to break my curse?"

Reid craned his neck up, but Alistair only dug the points in harder. Finally, Reid choked, "Was your sacrifice freely given?"

"Yes."

"Then another sacrifice might be able to undo it. Something powerful. Something good." He paused. "I don't think your brother would work. He doesn't even bleed."

"And I wouldn't ask him. What would be the point when I'm making sure we both walk out of this alive?"

"Or, better yet, you could not kill anyone. The curse only makes you look like a monster if you are one."

The spellstone on Gavin's thumb glowed, and a white light flashed in Reid's eyes. An instant later, his head lolled to the side, asleep.

Alistair swiveled around. "You knocked him out? What if he had more to say?" Gavin swallowed, and Alistair's irritation burned brighter. "Don't tell me you don't have the stomach for it. You played the part as well as I did."

"You saw what was happening. He was trying to goad you until the Reaper's Embrace finished the job. It almost worked."

Alistair seethed, because he knew Gavin was right. He set the pitchfork against the table and glanced at the Mirror resting on the counter. He couldn't bring himself to grab it.

"How bad is it?" he asked quietly.

Gavin treaded closer to him, his eyes roaming over Alistair's features. "It's spread higher. Some of your hair is white."

The curse only makes you look like a monster if you are one.

As his adrenaline faded, Alistair stared at his hands, at his cursemark, at the speckles of Reid's blood staining his fingertips. He clenched his fists.

"Cut if off," he said suddenly. When Gavin didn't respond, he added, "*Please.*"

Gavin nodded and scooped the garden shears up off the floor. Alistair slumped into one of the chairs at the kitchen table, his back to Reid MacTavish and their gory handywork. He tensed as he felt the cold kiss of the blades against the side of his neck, wielded in his enemy's hands.

"The white has spread up to here," Gavin said softly, his fingers threading through the bottom corner of Alistair's curls. "If I cut it, it'll make your hair asymmetrical."

"I don't care."

At the first quiet slice, Alistair closed his eyes, replaying Reid's words in his mind.

A powerful sacrifice. A good sacrifice.

Maybe he really was beyond saving.

"There," Gavin said finally, and when Alistair looked, tufts of white hair littered the floor around him like snow.

Shakily, he lifted the bottom of his sweater. Just as he'd feared, the cursemark had engulfed all of his stomach, likely even some of his legs. The white scar that had once traced up his abdomen was invisible now.

He sighed and leaned his head back against the chair, staring up at Gavin. When their eyes met, Alistair caught his cringe, even though he tried to hide it.

"It's on my face, isn't it?" Alistair asked grimly.

"Yes."

"Where?"

With a quivering finger, Gavin traced a line from the top of Alistair's left ear in a slant across his profile, slipping down the slope of his cheekbone, grazing the corners of his lips, trailing down the curve of his throat.

To the right, the grime receded on the windows, and the room, just barely, brightened.

Alistair shuddered with self-loathing. Because even after the last person he cared about had damned him, he'd seemingly learned nothing from it. He'd insulted Gavin. Fought him. Hated him. And yet, he realized he wanted him, a moth drawn to a lantern even knowing it would burn.

Alistair might've tolerated that—even welcomed it—with Isobel, but he couldn't now. He was no longer fighting for himself. And he didn't mind. He'd give more to Hendry, if he could.

But he couldn't resist asking, "In a different story, would we still have been enemies?"

"Does it matter?"

It shouldn't—didn't. And as much as Alistair wanted to press him for an answer, he couldn't risk betraying the truth and arming Gavin with a weapon to one day use against him.

"What do we do with him now?" Gavin asked quietly.

Alistair had nearly forgotten about the cursemaker. "We'll have to kill him eventually."

A grave silence fell, increasingly frustrating by the second. Because Alistair couldn't be the one to dispose of Reid, and he had no wish to ask that of Hendry. But he could tell from the look on Gavin's face that he wouldn't volunteer. Because despite how well Gavin played the part, it turned out the only person who Gavin had ever wanted to kill was him.

Alistair wondered if *he* could still watch Gavin die, when the time came.

He hoped so.

"Leave him there," Alistair muttered. "We'll figure something out in the morning."

He stood, and Gavin's voice trailed after him as he grasped the knob of the front door.

"You're not going to sleep?"

"I need to clear my head." Yet even as Alistair strode outside, he tossed several glances at his shoulder, hoping—recklessly—that Gavin would follow.

He didn't.

ISOBEL MACASLAN

When asked about the history behind the Macaslans' Landmark
and Relic: the Crypt and the Cloak, Cormac Macaslan offered
this: "We're a family who holds our traditions and the past in high
esteem. Death is about contemplation and respect. I can't think of
any descriptors that better embody who we are."

Ilvernath Eclipse, "A Portrait of Each
Blood Moon Family: The Macaslans"

Isobel staggered to regain her balance as her Here to There spell deposited her in the thick of the forest. A breeze raked through her
hair, carrying the scent of campfire and the echoes of laughter, and
she whipped around and scanned the tents nestled amid the trees in
the distance—tabloid reporters, hungry to capture a picture of Ilvernath's favorite bad boy.

Frantically, Isobel cast a Shrouded from Sight, shuddering to
imagine what stories they would spin if they spotted her. She wasn't
supposed to be here. She was supposed to be with Briony and Finley,
facing her family's ghastly trial, breaking another crucial piece of the
tournament. But after nearly killing Reid this morning, after everything he'd sacrificed to craft the Cloak, she couldn't bring herself to
abandon him. It wasn't even about whether Reid was as terrible as
she'd originally believed. It was about whether *she* was.

She didn't want to be.

Isobel approached the wards, a wall of red haze that surrounded
the Cottage's plot of land. She'd have to be clever about this. The
last thing she wanted was to alert the other champions that she was
coming, Alistair especially. Just because he hadn't attacked her at the
MacTavish curseshop didn't mean he'd hold back now.

She sifted through her collection of enchantments until she found the one she was looking for—a Without a Trace. Alistair's wards were too strong to break, but maybe she could slip through them.

Steeling her concentration, she summoned the spell, then, gingerly, stepped forward. Though the dried leaves crunched beneath her trainers, they made no sound, and even when she forced a breath in and out, her exhale didn't fog in the air. It'd worked, but it was hard to maintain it at the same time as the Shrouded from Sight. If she dropped her focus for a single moment, the spells could break.

Bracing herself, she touched the gleaming barrier. To her satisfaction, her hand passed through as though there was nothing there.

She slipped forward behind a tree. Warm light spilled from the Cottage's windows. It was a tiny Landmark; the Beauty Sleep she'd packed this morning would more than cover the space. But she'd have to get closer to cast it.

Crouching low, Isobel dashed across the grass and through the garden. She knelt beneath the window box of dead plants, then peeked in through the mucky glass.

She spotted Reid immediately. He was tied to a chair, and his head drooped down, his black hair obscuring any view of his face. Judging from his stillness, he was unconscious.

Gavin sat in the seat in front of him, staring at Reid with his arms crossed.

"Creepy," she muttered.

She lifted a little higher, searching for Alistair or Hendry. They must've been in the other rooms.

Gathering her nerve, Isobel dropped her cloaking spells and cast the Beauty Sleep. A glimmer of magick sprang out from the crystal ring on her right thumb, then flew upward. She stood, her back pressed against the front door, and watched the enchantment trickle over the Cottage like fairy dust.

She counted to ten under her breath, her spirits rising at the sound of a low *thud* from inside. She peeked in the window again. Gavin had slumped over and fallen to the floor. Reid hadn't changed position at all.

She eased open the door. Like the Cave, the inside of the Cottage was a hideous place. Cobwebs hung from the ceiling as thick as curtains, and a mouse—also asleep—lay at the foot of the counter.

Isobel snuck forward and grabbed the knife conveniently resting on the kitchen table. She stood behind Reid and pressed her hand over his mouth. Then she cast a Smelling Salts.

His eyes flew open, but his gasp was muffled by her palm. She tipped his head back, letting him see her, but she froze before she could raise a finger to her lips. He looked terrible. His left eye swelled an ugly violet. Small cuts oozed from his neck. And when her gaze roamed lower, she saw that all the fingers of his right hand were crushed. Her stomach heaved, but she quickly swallowed that down.

Realizing she was here to rescue him, his shoulders relaxed, and Isobel let go of his mouth and went to work on the restraints. It occurred to her that the last time she'd cut through such knots, they'd been around *her* wrists, and she'd been Reid's prisoner. The thought made an unwelcome, delirious laugh burst from her, and both she and Reid froze, waiting for Gavin to wake.

He didn't.

"Some spell," Reid croaked.

"Well, you can thank my mum for it," she said.

After she'd cut through all the ropes, their enchantment dissipating with a white shimmer, she helped Reid up. He swayed for a moment; then he straightened and peered around the Cottage.

"Let's go before they wake up," Isobel hissed. They didn't have time to stall.

"Wait." Reid crept over Gavin's body to the couch, then grabbed something she hadn't realized was there. The Medallion.

Her eyes widened. It hadn't even occurred to her that she could steal their Relics on this mission, too.

"And the Mirror?" she asked.

Reid looked around the room and shook his head. "It's not here."

"Whatever. We'll figure something out later."

The two of them tiptoed back to the front door, then Isobel grabbed Reid by his left hand and tugged him through the garden path. They raced to the trees, where she skidded to a stop.

"What?" he breathed.

"My Without a Trace only works on one person at a time." She glanced behind her at the Cottage. "Do you think Alistair will wake if—"

Crack! A twig snapped somewhere through the thickets. Isobel grabbed Reid and shoved him against a tree, and he collided with it with a low "oof." Weakly, he clutched at his abdomen.

"Gav?" Alistair's voice rasped through the dark. She hadn't realized that he and Gavin were on a nickname basis.

Neither Isobel nor Reid moved.

"Do we run?" he whispered, his breath warm against her cheek, his heartbeat rapping against her chest.

Once they made it past the wards, they could use Here to There spells. The crimson mist was only a few paces away.

But so was Alistair.

"Hendry?" Alistair asked, noticeably closer. He was on the other side of their tree.

It occurred to Isobel that she could curse him now, and he probably wouldn't have the reflexes to deflect it. She'd already killed him when she cast the Reaper's Embrace—what was one more to speed up the process, to eliminate their greatest threat once and for all?

"There's no monster, you fuck," Alistair said, presumably to himself. Then there was the sound of his sweater scraping against the trunk. He'd slumped to the ground. He sighed loudly, almost pathetically.

It would be so simple.

Isobel felt Reid's gaze on her, and she saw her own thoughts reflected in his eyes. It would be ruthless, but Reid's expression never wavered. He was every bit as ruthless as she was.

Yet when she glanced at her hand—pressed against Reid's chest—her heart clenched. Her heart, which she hadn't felt truly beat since the day Alistair had almost killed her. Because she remembered how he'd held her afterward. How she'd once been in a similar position with him against a tree. She would've kissed him, if they hadn't been interrupted. She wondered how much would be different if she had. Maybe everything would be.

Isobel looked up at Reid and shook her head, then she handed him her spare Here to There stone and nodded toward the wards.

Reid grimaced, but he nodded too.

She raised her fingers and counted down.

Three.

Two.

The pair took off running through the grass.

"What the—" Alistair clambered to his feet, only to stumble on a root. A white curse tore through the forest, whizzing over Isobel's shoulders. The tree it struck immediately turned to stone. "Isobel?"

But he wasn't fast enough. Isobel and Reid sprinted through the wards, and all at once, the barrier flared a violent orange, and an alarm screeched through the night—no doubt waking Gavin and alerting all the journalists nearby.

Isobel grabbed Reid by the arm and the two of them cast their Here to There spells.

For a moment, it felt like freefalling.

Then they landed on a different tuft of grass. The new slope of the ground made them lose their balance, and they fell. Reid let out a low, pained groan while Isobel rolled onto her back and spit out a mouthful of brittle, fragmented leaves.

"Why did you save me?" Reid asked. He was panting, and even after all this time, it unnerved her that she was not. Her heart should be pounding. She should have a stitch in her side.

"Because it was the right thing to do," she said. "Look—What almost happened this morning, I never wanted—"

"You don't have to explain yourself to me. I get it."

"But I—"

"I mean it. If anything, I respect you for it. It's what I would've done, and I can't be the only one around here with any sense."

Reid's words did little to comfort her. She didn't want to be the same as him, the boy who'd imprisoned her, condemned her, mocked her. But the fragile, barely audible whisper of her conscience warned that she was no better. If anything, she was worse.

He pushed himself to his knees. "Where are we?"

"The Crypt," she answered.

Shakily, she stood and peered at the slab of stone amid the grass, returned to its original place. She heaved it back once more, then frowned. She'd thought the Landmark would be no more than rubble now, yet the stairs remained as intact as ever. And the chandeliers that dangled from the tunnel's ceiling blazed an ominous red.

Which meant Briony and Finley were still inside.

"Something's wrong," she croaked. "Wh-what if the Cloak didn't work? What if they didn't—"

"Not to put a pause on your panic," Reid said, "but I'm in a lot of fucking pain."

Isobel spun around to him, still lying on the forest floor, clutching his crushed hand to his chest. "Right. Here." She rummaged through her pockets and handed him half of the stones she carried on her. While he went to work healing his fingers and broken nose, she descended toward the Crypt's mouth.

A rancid draft escaped from it, like rot, like death.

"Briony! Finley!" she called.

No response.

"We have to go in," she said hoarsely.

Reid swore. "This day just keeps getting better." Nevertheless, he rose to his feet, then he licked his fingers and smeared away the blood crusted in the stubble above his lips. He might've been healed, but the sacrifice of his life magick had rendered his skin sallow and the whites of his eyes almost gray. "Lead the way, darling."

They wove through the winding, red-cast tunnel, their steps sinking into the damp, mint-green carpet. Wet shuffling noises were all that broke through the quiet.

"Briony?" Isobel called again. Still, no one answered.

As they twisted around the corridor, Reid grasped her sleeve.

"What?" She shrugged away from him. "Briony and Finley have to be—"

"*Look.*" He nodded at the floor, and a scream burst from her throat, reverberating across the marble walls.

Maggots covered the ground below them. White, yellow, black. Glistening. Writhing.

"Isobel?" a voice called out.

"Briony?" Isobel shrieked back.

"Come help us!" Finley shouted.

But Isobel froze, unable to tear her eyes from the squirming sea of insects. On some level, she knew that their presence and the scarlet chandeliers meant that the replica Cloak must've worked—Briony and Finley had triggered the trial. But any relief she might've felt was dampened by the bile spewing up her throat, and she seized Reid's arm as she forced it down.

She didn't understand. The Landmarks and Relics were supposed to harken back to each of their family's stories, and though the

Macaslans might've not been pure or heroic, they prided themselves on their resourcefulness, their cunning. Yet all Isobel saw around her was filth.

"Shit." Reid lurched back, and before Isobel could ask what had happened, a searing pain stabbed into her calf. She wrenched up her pant leg in horror. Maggots had crawled up her on both sides, eating at her skin.

With a cry, she smacked at them, until her shins were caked in blood and larvae pulp. Reid stepped ahead of her and cast a Dragon's Breath, and flames shot out from each of his hands at the floor. Putrid smoke wafted into the air, fluttering with scorched skin.

"Come on." He linked his arm with hers and pulled her forward.

The end of the corridor opened into the central room of the Crypt, lofty and cavernous, the plaques marking each tomb blanketed in a thick film of dust. Much like the soiled carpet at the entrance, every decoration the Crypt had tailored to Isobel's taste had been ruined. Yellow pus dribbled down the canvases on the walls, and insects wriggled over a nearby vanity, its mirror cracked, a rotten, broken rib cage hooked around the legs of the stool.

At the opposite end, Finley and Briony stood within a dome of iridescent light. A circle of decrepit, broken bones littered around it.

"Reid?" Finley called. "What happened? How did you escape?"

"Never mind that now!" Briony shouted. "Just get over here!"

By the time Isobel and Reid reached their sides, both their clothes were smothered in soot, and charred maggots clung to their shoes.

Isobel stared at the dismantled skeletons, a hair's breadth from hurling. "Are those . . . ?"

Briony coughed uncomfortably. "Yeah, they're your dearly departed. Uh, the ones we didn't blow up, anyway."

"It was that or die," Finley said. Both of their hands were smeared in an ashy brown layer of grime. Below them lay a single corpse, its parts mismatched—the scapula of a man, the pelvis of a woman, the skull of a child. "We're almost done. We just need a foot."

While Reid helped look, Isobel took in the scene around her with revulsion. A few treasures caught her eye—the gold of an urn cased in the wall; the sheen of an ancient, silken shroud; a gemstone the size of a cicada. Yet their beauty was lost amid the rot.

As she nervously approached the urn, wanting so badly to understand, her reflection bored back at her. Her cosmetic spells had long since worn off, exposing her unnaturally pale complexion, the dark veins lacing her forehead and cheeks. Isobel might've always resented her family for forcing her into the role of champion, but she certainly looked like she belonged here.

"Are you going to help?" Reid snapped as he scrabbled across the floor for the proper bones.

"Sorry," Isobel said hastily, then she squatted and pinched a splintered ulna between two fingers. Disturbed, she tossed it aside.

"Here," Reid said at last, handing Briony a skeletal foot.

"That's a left foot. I need a right foot."

"Does it really matter? Just get it up already."

Briony rested the withered limb on the ground, then straightened. She spread her hands out over the skeleton and cast a Mending Helper. Threads wove around each of the bones, then drew them together as though magickal ligaments. Briony leaned down, grabbed the skeleton by the spinal column, and hoisted it up. Its many bones clacked and clattered together.

Briony grinned. "I see the family resemblance, Isobel."

Beside her, Finley looked like he couldn't decide whether to laugh or gawk. Isobel had to stifle her cringe. The two of them, cheerful even amid the chaos, so completely unaware that Isobel had been ready to murder them only six hours before.

Trembling, she stared at the hoodie-Cloak, floating mystically in the upright coffin behind them. It was working, truly working. Which meant that if Isobel had made up her mind even a single night earlier, she would've committed the most despicable mistake of her life.

"Just finish it," Isobel shot back.

Briony rested the skeleton in the coffin, awkwardly shoving its head into the hoodie-Cloak, now little more than a tattered vest.

"There," she breathed. Then she stepped back, and the four of them stared at it, waiting.

"Why—why isn't anything happening?" Finley stammered.

The triumph drained from Briony's face. "Is it the Cloak?"

"The replacement should work." Reid's hand automatically touched his shoulder where it'd fractured this morning. Then, his voice lowered, "We better hope it does."

Their eyes all swiveled to Isobel, and she stiffened. "Why are you looking at me?"

"It's your family," Finley croaked.

Yes, but Isobel didn't know what to make of this place. Maybe it was because she'd been raised distant from the other Macaslans. She might've grown closer with them this past year, attended funerals by their side, reluctantly befriended her cousins, but she didn't feel like she was one of them—not really. She couldn't describe a single Macaslan story. On the morning the tournament began, her father had told her that the Macaslans once claimed a special connection to death. But he'd said it in passing, which made it practically meaningless. The only phrase he'd ever repeated with any emphasis was that "she was a survivor."

The words, as always, soothed her. She'd come too far and sacrificed too much to die in this horrid place. No matter what it took, she'd walk out of here alive.

Then the realization dawned on her. This trial wasn't the culmination of some family story; it was their legacy, reinforced every time the tournament played out. Because the Macaslans *were* disgusting, conniving, greedy. They spun whatever tales suited them; they took advantage of every contemptible opportunity that fell at their feet. And the only way to finish their *true* story was to stoop to the vilest low possible to survive.

"Oh," she uttered softly, clutching her stomach.

"What?" Reid asked.

"I think . . . I think I know what's left."

She considered telling them, letting someone else finish the repulsive task for her. But even this disgusting deed paled in comparison to murdering her three allies in their sleep.

There was no denying it—no matter how much perfume she spritzed on to cover her stench, Isobel was a true Macaslan champion.

Wordlessly, she leaned into the coffin and kissed the skull of the skeleton, her lips pressed directly against its dusty, half-rotted teeth.

A crack split across the stone floor, growing longer and longer. Then the ground shook beneath them, so strong that Isobel nearly lost her balance.

"It worked." Briony's voice breaking into a sob. "It worked. We did—"

"*Run!*" Finley shouted, pushing her forward. "Go! Go!"

The four of them sprinted over the discarded bones and squirming maggots through the tomb. As they wove through the snaking hallways, the floor tipped violently, as though the Crypt had tilted its head back and planned to swallow the champions whole. Isobel stumbled and fell to her knees, but Briony grabbed her, and with arms linked, shoulders crammed side by side, the four of them threw themselves into the light streaming through the exit. They clambered up the stairs and collapsed in a heap on the grass outside.

A moment later, the Crypt shuddered and collapsed. Nothing remained but a small slab of stone peeking up from a sliver within the earth.

Briony untangled herself and sat up. Splintered rays of sunshine beamed from the forest canopy onto her face as it broke out into an incredulous, victorious smile. "We did it! The Cloak worked!"

It took all of Isobel's self-control not to weep at those words. For the first time in weeks, hope blossomed in her like a single daisy sprouting atop a grave.

"You're welcome," Reid said snidely, earning a friendly shove from Briony. But he grinned as he reached into his pocket. "Oh, and you're welcome for this, too."

Around two hooked fingers, he lifted out the Medallion.

Finley slung his arms around their shoulders and let out a triumphant, whooping holler. And the whole team—even Isobel—joined him.

BRIONY THORBURN

"Perhaps we came down too hard on the families of Ilvernath. After all, none of them chose to be part of this curse, either. But some of them *are* choosing to play a part in ending it, and for that, I commend them."

Champion Confidential, WKL Radio

For the first time since the Blood Veil had fallen, Briony and her allies celebrated. The four of them sprawled across the Tower's top floor, recounting the wild twists and turns of their evening over endless snacks and energy drinks. There was a euphoria that came with not just triumphing in the face of mortal peril, but in finally knowing they could make it out.

"They took a hammer to my hands. And a *pitchfork* to my throat." Reid fidgeted restlessly on a beanbag that he'd pulled up from the ground floor. Empty snack packets were littered around him. "They're both absolutely unhinged."

Isobel rolled her eyes. "Well, you would know, wouldn't you?" The room had changed over the past few weeks, the elegant high-backed seats gaining cozy cushions, the scattered grimoires now stacked neatly on shelves. Isobel was curled up on one of the chairs. She tossed a crisp at the cursemaker, who batted it away.

"That's a weird way to say thank you for stealing the Medallion."

"That's a weird way to say thank you for saving your life."

They both sounded flippant, but Briony could tell the two of them were shaken. Reid kept flexing his fingers, as though reassuring himself that they were still intact. And Isobel hugged her arms to her chest, glancing at him nervously. Before they'd congregated here, everyone had disappeared to wash off grime and skeleton residue. But when Briony blinked, she still saw flashes of squirming maggots.

"About, uh, saving lives," she said. "I'm sorry we chose the Cloak over you, but . . ."

"Don't be," Reid said, without hesitation. "It's the decision I would've made."

"Oh. Okay." Briony wasn't sure what that said about her moral compass, that she'd been on the same wavelength as Reid.

"Did you learn anything interesting about the other champions, while you were there?" Finley asked, leaning forward. He'd sat beside Briony, and although neither of them had talked about what had happened in the Crypt, each time their gazes met it felt like an electric shock.

"I was the one being interrogated, so . . . no," Reid said flatly.

"What about the bug?" Isobel asked. "Did they mention listening to us at all?"

"Bug?" Reid echoed, perturbed. In the aftermath of the Crypt, they'd forgotten to tell him. The three of them explained their discovery, and Briony held up the offending spellstone. Even drained of magick, the heft of it turned her stomach.

"I don't think it was them," Reid said gravely. "Honestly, if they'd been listening in, they would've known a lot more."

"Then who *did* spy on us?" Briony asked worriedly.

"The press might've cared about getting a better story," Isobel said.

"But then they would've broken the news about the Cloak weeks ago," Finley said. "Or any petty gossip they could get out of our conversations."

"Let me see that stone," Reid said. "Maybe I'll recognize the cut."

Briony tossed it to him. He caught it—barely.

"Hmm . . . it's not that distinctive. Could come from any major spellmaking shop."

"So, anyone could've bought it," Isobel said flatly. "Great. How helpful."

"Including any of the families," Reid muttered uneasily.

Briony recoiled, while Finley and Isobel went still. Briony's gaze crept to the three massive windows, where night had fallen hours ago. From here Ilvernath looked like the sleepy city it had once pretended to be, lights twinkling gently from below. No serial killers, no paparazzi, no families with terrible secrets.

"We'll figure it out," Briony said. "Right now, let's just focus on the next thing we know we can do." She scooped up the Medallion, which lay next to the map of Ilvernath. But the spellstones embedded in it stayed dim at her touch. Either Gavin or Alistair had claimed it, so its healing magick still belonged to them.

"We know this goes with the Monastery now," she said. "And we also know that these trials are sort of . . . playing out the old family stories, right?"

Finley hesitated. "What happened in the Cave wasn't exactly the legend I grew up with."

"The Crypt didn't match any legend either," Isobel added. "I thought the trial would resemble whatever my family's story was, but it only matched who they are now."

"That makes sense," Reid said. "Even if the tournament's curse was built on legends, it's been reinforced with real history. Every time a champion was sacrificed, it cemented a pattern. And if *that's* what holds the curse together now, of course the trials have more to do with reality than lore."

"So you think these trials are the curse trying to keep that pattern going, one last time?" Briony asked.

"Sounds like it," Finley said.

Briony had been bracing herself for how it would feel to relive her family's story. But at least it was a story she'd heard hundreds of times before. The idea that this trial would draw on something new—the family she'd actually known instead of the glorified tales she'd been raised on—unnerved her, because sometimes Briony still struggled to differentiate between the two.

"So we should think about what we know about the Darrows," she said, trying to focus.

"And we should pair the Medallion and the Monastery as soon as possible," Finley added. "Once we're fully recovered. Tomorrow morning?"

"Tomorrow morning," Isobel agreed.

"I'll set an alarm," Briony said. She doubted she'd be able to sleep at all.

"So, what now?" Reid asked. "Should we play never have I ever? Truth spell or dare? Spin the bottle?"

"Truth spells don't even work on you," Briony grumbled.

Isobel got to her feet. "We should all get some rest."

Reid muttered something about all of them being boring, but he followed Isobel down the steps.

Which left Briony and Finley. Together. Alone. In the absence of a deadly trial and celebrating friends, the silence in the room felt loaded. Briony turned her chair toward him and realized he'd already risen from his seat. The torchlight dancing down the bridge of his nose and cheekbones did unfair things to his already unfairly handsome face. His gaze fixed on her with a nervous expression.

She stood, hands clammy. Their alliance had recreated a Relic. Destroyed part of the tournament. Proven that there *was* a way forward where all of them finished this alive. And yet the thought of what to say to Finley right now felt more daunting than any of that.

Thankfully, he spoke first.

"Do you remember when you asked me to kill you?"

Of all the conversation starters that had flitted through Briony's mind, this was the last one she would've expected.

"Um. Yes." It had been an abysmal low. Fresh off the heels of being locked in the Castle dungeon and betrayed by Isobel, wracked with guilt over slaying Carbry, she'd knelt before Finley and begged him to grant her a quick death.

Instead, he'd given her a second chance.

"You said you didn't belong in this story anymore," he said seriously. "And I . . . I wanted to start a new one then, with you, but the truth is that I wasn't as ready as I thought. Part of being the perfect Blair meant believing the tournament was the most important thing. And I never questioned that, until you. When we broke up, I figured it was for the best. You've always made me hope for a different story—and I've always been terrified of it."

"You made me feel that way, too," Briony whispered. Around them, the torches flared, then dimmed, the magickal flames flickering in time with her ratcheting heartbeat.

"I tried to believe we could do it, but when everything seemed hopeless . . . I got scared again," Finley continued. "I pushed you away."

Briony swallowed. "I mean. I didn't exactly handle things perfectly, either."

"But you wanted to fight for this, for *us*, and I didn't."

He sank to the ground, kneeling, a perfect mirror image of a month ago when she'd knelt before *him*. "I know it's easy for me to say it now, when the Relic's fixed. I understand if it's too late for us. If you can't believe that I'll stick it out this time. But I promise you, I will. No matter what else happens . . . I'm here, Briony. I want this. I want you."

She took him in, head tipped toward hers, expression unguarded and anguished. Then she cupped his cheek. Briony knew they might still end in tragedy. She'd been terrified to lose her heart, then her life. But she hadn't lost her heart at all—she'd found it. And this time, she wouldn't be foolish enough to let it go.

"I want you, too," she murmured, drawing him to his feet.

He shuddered, as though in disbelief. His fingertips brushed her waist, hesitant. She put her hands on his shoulders, and he pressed his forehead against hers, his grip tightening.

At the Monastery, they had both been so eager. Now he was achingly, teasingly slow. Briony closed her eyes and felt the barest brush of lips against her cheek, her nose, her earlobe, until she thought she would collapse beneath the weight of her wanting.

"Oh, come on," she muttered, after yet another kiss ended as swiftly as it had begun. Finley chuckled, his breath warm against her skin.

"As I recall, you enjoy a certain degree of frustration."

"I've been *frustrated* for over a year."

"Hmm." His mouth trailed to the slopes of her throat. "I'll take that under advisement."

"Fin—"

His lips caught hers again, sending heat crackling through her. The way he'd kissed her before had felt almost desperate; this was decisive, firm, but no less passionate. She collided with a chair, gasping out a laugh as it toppled over. Finley pulled her back to him, grinning, then steered her to the table. She wrapped her arms around his neck as he lifted her easily onto the map of Ilvernath.

Books and miniature champions clattered to the floor, but she paid them no mind as he slid his knuckles down her spine, his spell-rings tugging at the thin fabric of her T-shirt. She sank into his touch with an involuntary gasp. The world melted away until there was no Blood Veil, no Tower, no tournament at all. Until the story they were telling belonged only to the two of them.

Until something twinged in the center of Briony's chest, painful and insistent.

"The wards," she gasped, breaking away from Finley. "Someone's trying to get into the Tower."

It was too dark outside to tell who their intruder was. Briony rushed downstairs, nearly tripping over a pile of grimy shoes they'd left on the ground floor, then peered through the window.

The face staring back cut Briony to her core.

"Please," Innes begged. "Please let me in."

The Warden's Shackles hung on her sister's skinny wrists, the glowing manacles an ugly reminder of her last visit to the Tower. But Innes didn't protest when Briony insisted on the precautionary enchantment. She let Briony and Finley confiscate her spellstones and her backpack, then sat trembling on the couch.

"Are you sure about this?" Finley murmured to Briony. "You promised not to let her in again."

"I-I know," Briony stammered. "But there's four of us watching her this time. It's different."

"I hope it is, for your sake." He squeezed her shoulder, then bolted upstairs to fetch the other champions.

Briony wasn't entirely sure it *was* different. But Innes looked wretched—tears streaked down her cheeks, purple sagging under her eyes, a breakout inflamed on her chin. And she wouldn't stop shaking. Again, Briony felt the urge to comfort her, but after what had happened the last time she'd tried, she didn't dare. Instead, she pulled a kitchen chair close to the couch and lowered herself into it, watching Innes carefully all the while.

The sisters didn't speak until the others joined them, Isobel in pajamas, Reid barefoot and yawning.

"What's going on?" Isobel asked anxiously.

"She says she has something important to tell us," Briony said.

"And you believed her?" Reid demanded. "After the shit we've been through today?"

"She's my sister, even after . . . everything," Briony choked. "Let's hear her out."

She met Innes's eyes, then cast a Truth or Treachery. Silver streaked across her sister's throat. "Are you here to hurt us?"

"I don't want to hurt any of you," Innes said gravely. "I'm here because I—I think the life magick murders have something to do with the government. And our family."

"What?" Briony swayed in her chair, suddenly woozy. "Wh-what are you talking about?"

"I noticed that something strange was going on weeks ago," Innes said miserably. "After your interview was published, government agents started hanging around the Thorburn estate. The one we met, Agent Yoo, and this other one who's always with Elder Malvina—tall, scary-looking?"

"Agent Ashworth?" Briony asked, her stomach churning.

"Yes. Him." She sniffled. "After you took my spot as champion, I thought they wouldn't care about our family anymore. And they didn't, for a while. But suddenly they were *everywhere*."

"Wait. You thought they wouldn't care about your family anymore—does that mean the government worked with the Thorburns *before*?" Finley asked, turning to Briony.

Briony swallowed, the answer snagging on her vocal cords.

Reid circled the two sisters, inspecting them with narrowed eyes. Briony remembered with a rush that he knew what had happened to her and Innes—he'd deduced it from their conversation back in the Thorburn gardens, during the champion-crowning ceremony.

"They can't talk about it," Reid volunteered. "It's an oath spell, isn't it? The government meddled with their family and chose Innes as champion over Briony. Why do you think she was so pissed off about it?"

Briony glanced nervously at the other champions. Isobel shifted back and forth, looking pensive, while Finley's brow furrowed.

"That explains a lot," Isobel said neutrally.

Finley, meanwhile, leaned closer to Innes. "So they've always wanted something from your family. What?"

"High magick," Innes croaked. "That must be it. I just . . . I can't figure out why they're killing other people to get it."

"How do you know they're connected to the murders at all?" Isobel asked.

"I got suspicious after you told our family about the Darrows and the Paynes switching their stories," Innes said quietly. "They were *so* furious—everyone was gossiping about it. And then, a few days later, a Payne had an accident in their workshop. It wasn't fatal, but their mind was completely destroyed. As soon as I wondered if it was retaliatory, I found . . . patterns."

"Patterns?" Briony and Finley echoed at the same time.

The truth spell faded from Innes's throat. Reid cast another one immediately, and Innes gagged for a second, then kept speaking. Briony felt a rush of concern; any more and they'd risk causing Innes permanent damage.

"The victims are all tied to our family somehow," her sister explained. "It took some digging, but . . . the first two, some of the elders owed them money. The third one—the body they found—was a bookseller who'd heavily promoted *A Tradition of Tragedy*. And I think they're getting bolder, or sloppier, because the latest person who's disappeared is a reporter for the *Glamour Inquirer*. Barbara Scott—she's the one who wrote the interview with the other champions. The one that made them look really good."

Briony's stomach curdled. She felt as though the Tower were constricting around her, the stones about to collapse atop her head. One of the tapestries on the walls tipped from its hook, then tumbled to the ground in a heap.

"That's concerning, but it's circumstantial," Isobel said. "Do you have anything *else?*"

Innes nodded emphatically. "I broke into Elder Malvina's study, and I . . . I found something. Check my backpack. But make sure you wear gloves first."

"Ah, that's a request you love to hear," muttered Reid.

Briony rose unsteadily from her chair before the others could touch anything. "I'll do it." She went to the coat tree, fetched a pair of winter gloves, and opened Innes's backpack. A sheath of papers was wedged inside—her sister's research—and a flask of magick.

Briony drew the flask out carefully. It felt oddly heavy.

"It was in a safe inside her desk," Innes said. "I think it's full of life magick. I know it looks really similar to raw common magick, but I'm pretty sure it's different."

"Could you verify that?" Briony asked Reid.

"Probably, yeah. But why don't you want us to touch it?"

"I cast a forensic spell on it," Innes said proudly. "There's at least one fingerprint on there. It's evidence."

"Wait—why didn't you just go to the police?" Briony asked, handing the flask to Reid after he pulled on the gloves.

"Our family's powerful," Innes answered. "The government is even more powerful. I don't trust the Ilvernath PD not to just bend to what they say."

The second truth spell faded away, and she shuddered, bunching her leggings beneath her fingers. The Warden's Shackles gleamed ominously in the dim light.

Everyone fell silent as Reid uncorked the flask of magick. A wisp of white curled into the air. It was almost identical to raw common magick—*almost*.

"See how it glitters?" Reid murmured. "How it's got this sort of . . . weight to it?" He carefully coaxed it back into the flask, then sealed it. "Maybe some scientist could tell you whose—I don't have that kind of training. But that's definitely life magick."

Briony thought of every time she'd followed her family, even once she'd sworn to change their legacy. How she'd claimed their Landmark. How she'd willingly become a pawn and a mouthpiece, all the while believing that it was for the greater good.

She wondered if this was still some kind of trick. But in her bones, she knew it wasn't. She'd been hopelessly naive and now innocent people were dead—and she didn't even know why. She was no hero, not even a pretend one.

Her spellring flared, and the Warden's Shackles dissipated. Innes rubbed at her wrists gratefully.

"I'm sorry, everyone," Briony said hoarsely. "I let them use me—use all of us."

The room fell into a tense silence. Briony shuddered, trying not to cry. And then a hand clasped hers—a hand that was shockingly cold. Isobel didn't say a word, just squeezed. Briony squeezed back.

"It was my idea to do that interview," Finley said.

"We all agreed to it," Isobel added.

"Also, how the hell could any of us have known your family was this fucked up?" Reid demanded. "I mean . . . even for a tournament family, this is dark. At least the Lowes just kill each *other*."

"We can't let them get away with it any longer," Briony said firmly. "I have to make this right."

"I have an idea about that, actually," Innes said. "It's part of why I came here. Our family and the government are powerful. But all of you are really, really famous. If you talk to the media again . . ."

"I don't know." Briony bit her lip. "If we go public about this, we'll all be in even more trouble than we already are. Pissing off the Curse-breaking Division is a huge risk."

"We could become targets," Reid said anxiously.

"We already *are* targets," Finley said. "The Thorburns and the government have shown that they'll kill people to get what they want. And we're directly in between them and high magick. As soon as they realize they can't use us anymore, we'll be in danger."

"I think Briony and I can take our family down without endangering anyone else," Innes said shakily. "If we do it right."

"Well then," Briony said. "How do you feel about throwing another press conference?"

Briony showed up to the Thorburn estate the next morning, dressed in crimson. Autumn had fully swept through her family's gardens, leaving the flowerbeds wilted and the fountains dormant until next spring. The evergreen hedges and some trampled leaves were the only bits of color to contrast the cloudy pink sky above. Although she'd told the rest of her alliance that it was important she attend this press conference by herself—Finley was off briefing Gracie and the rest of the resistance on what they'd learned, while Isobel and Reid had hung back to prep for their next Relic pairing—she still felt uncomfortably alone as the eyes of the media and family members raked over her.

"Briony!" cried the nearest reporter, brandishing a notepad, while the photographer beside him began eagerly snapping pictures. "Are you here to talk about the new cracks in the pillar?"

"Is it true you were behind the collapse of both the Mill and the Crypt?" added Ed Caulfield.

"What about Hendry Lowe's claims of innocence?" called out another journalist.

"Don't worry, I'll answer all your questions," Briony said. Just as they'd done before, the Thorburns had arranged a few rows of chairs in the grandest part of their garden, neatly tucked between the hedges. Facing them all was a bigger, grander chair Briony recognized from the dining room, with a spellstone-studded microphone already waiting on the seat. She took it and sat down.

The audience was crammed with reporters, some other tournament families, and various Thorburns, all looking at her curiously. Innes sat in the front row, her teeth worrying her bottom lip. She hadn't wanted to go back to the Thorburn estate, but Briony had been concerned about her arousing suspicion otherwise. She was grateful that their ploy seemed to have worked.

Agent Yoo and Agent Ashworth lurked at the back of the garden, along with several other unfamiliar people. Innes had warned her that plainclothes government agents were a distinct possibility.

"But first," Briony said, "I have an announcement to make."

Nerves knotted in her stomach—once she did this, there would be no taking it back. But her alliance had talked it all through the night before. If they presented their evidence privately, it could easily be covered up *and* they'd be targets anyway. Weaponizing the press guaranteed that their story would get out there, even if they had no idea how it would be interpreted.

"I'd like to start off by saying that, yes, my allies and I are now two steps closer to breaking Ilvernath's curse," Briony announced. "We've destroyed three Relics and Landmarks so far—soon, we'll have destroyed four. And I have full confidence that when all seven trials are complete, this tournament *will* end. Forever."

The audience burst into raucous applause. Shutters snapped as photographers leaned forward, jostling for the best angle. Briony took a deep breath and braced herself for what she was about to do. All her life, her family had held themselves up as paragons of morality in Ilvernath—trusted confidantes, balanced mediators, powerful, respected spellcasters.

Briony had come here ready to tell the truth about them. But the truth was messy and complicated, and she knew the press wouldn't care about that. They wanted a splashy headline, a brutal story. Victim or victor. Hero or villain.

Today, Briony Thorburn would show the world just how villainous her family really was.

"But that's not why I'm here," Briony continued. "Instead, I'd like to call your attention to the string of murders that have taken place around Ilvernath these past few weeks. I believe I've identified the culprit."

The applause trailed off uneasily. Whispers trickled through the crowd. The Thorburns stirred in their seats, some murmuring eagerly amongst themselves, others looking bewildered. Briony caught a sharp, flinty stare from Elder Malvina.

"Is it Hendry Lowe?" called a reporter.

"No, not him," Briony said. "A brave witness has reached out to me with documentation linking these murders to the Thorburn family— who, as we all know, have close ties to the Cursebreaking Division. I believe my family and these agents, working together, are behind the four deaths and disappearances."

The whispers grew into a roar. Photographers whipped around, their cameras flashing not just at Briony, but at the Thorburns. In the back of the garden, Agents Yoo and Ashworth went completely still.

"What is the meaning of this?" Elder Malvina stood. The crowd around her fell silent, temporarily cowed. "I'm not sure where our champion has received this information, or why she's chosen *now* to discuss it. But I assure you, these are baseless accusations."

"Then you won't mind me talking them through," Briony shot back. She searched for Innes's gaze and found it fixed on her, steady. Her sister nodded, and Briony felt a rush of confidence. She explained Innes's theory to the reporters, even passing a list of the victims and their connections to the Thorburn family to the nearest journalist.

"Do you have any harder evidence?" called Ed Caulfield.

"I'm glad you asked." Briony pulled the vial from her pocket. "This flask of life magick was found in a Thorburn elder's study."

"There's no possible way to prove that!" cried out one of the elders.

"There is, actually." Innes rose nervously from her seat. "I'm the witness. I'm the one who found it. And I have a spell that can prove one of the Elders touched it."

Innes walked to Briony's side, reporters parting in her wake, and held up a spellstone.

Briony looked toward the Cursebreaking Division for a reaction, but they'd vanished from the back of the gardens. The Thorburns, meanwhile, were still crowded by reporters, glancing wildly at each other.

The stone blazed, and bright green fingerprints appeared on the flask. Across the garden, someone gasped.

Elder Malvina's hand glowed that same green.

"We'll be turning this over to the Ilvernath PD," Briony said. "They can verify that it's life magick—and, hopefully, establish whose. Our family's been getting away with murder while working alongside our government to carry it out. The world needs to know."

"And you expect us to believe you had no idea about this?" called out one of the reporters. "Aren't you your family's champion? The hero of Ilvernath?"

"All of this could be a hoax!" cried another reporter.

"I assure you, it is," snapped Elder Malvina. "I don't know what kind of trick this spell is, but the pressure of the tournament has clearly—"

"Trust me," Briony growled. "This is the only time in my life I've seen *beyond* the pressure of the tournament."

A chair crashed to the ground, followed by a shout; Thorburns attempted to flee as reporters swarmed them. Ed Caulfield shoved through the crowd, brandishing his microphone like a weapon as he called out more questions toward Briony and Innes.

"We should go," her sister murmured. "It's only going to get worse."

"I know," Briony breathed. They'd already planned their exits—Innes's Here to There would take her to the resistance, who knew she was coming, thanks to Finley. Briony's would return her to the Tower. But instead of casting it, Briony grabbed Innes's arm and tugged her toward the nearest hedge. Then she cast her Undetectable. Eyes skidded over them; reporters looked momentarily confused before turning their focus elsewhere.

"Before we leave," Briony said. "I—I wanted to tell you that I'm glad you're safe. And that we're all so grateful you warned us."

"Thanks," Innes muttered. "Um. I'm sorry for attacking you."

"It's okay," Briony said ruefully. "You're the only real family I've got. I'm sorry I let myself forget that."

Innes gave her a cautious smile. "I'm still not completely ready to forgive you. But I believe what you said. That you're different now."

Briony thought of two girls, whispering bedtime stories under the cover of night, one brash, one cautious. Two lost little girls who had only ever had each other—until she'd thrown it all away.

Until she'd been given a chance to put things back together. Briony wouldn't waste it.

"I love you, you know that?" she said to Innes.

Her sister sniffled and swiped at her eyes. "Yeah. I know."

Then she disappeared.

Briony took one last look at the Thorburn gardens, at the grand manor house that stood behind them, at the perfectly manicured hedges surrounded by yelling family members and reporters.

She could never come home again. But it had never been home at all, not really.

Maybe someday, she would find a better one.

ISOBEL MACASLAN

"I mean, come on. We all can tell the curse is going down. The Champions Pillar is practically falling apart. Which is why it's important to support your champions now more than ever. Fifteen percent of all official Macaslan merchandise goes to food and supplies for our favorite heroes."

Interview with Cormac Macaslan,
SpellBC News: Wake Up Ilvernath!

Isobel swore under her breath—her winged liner wasn't even on both sides.

"Going somewhere, darling?" Reid asked from where he lay on the couch. His eyes were shut, his own arms folded over his chest. Like a corpse.

"Nope." Carefully, Isobel cast a Cat Eye and redrew the right flick, then, having extended it too far, lengthened the left. She was sorely out of practice.

"So it's for me then? And they say romance is dead."

Isobel snorted and swapped the enchantment for her First Kiss lip gloss, swiping it on while holding up a tiny compact mirror. After weeks of only applying enough to conceal the Roach's Armor, she needed this, the comfort of routine, of feeling good about herself. She'd remove it before Briony and Finley returned.

She smacked her lips together, relishing the strawberry flavor. But in the compact's reflection, Reid stared at her, his neck craned, one eye peeled open.

"Is that all you're going to do? Pretend to nap?" Isobel asked him. "After yesterday, aren't you—"

"I'd prefer not to discuss yesterday," he replied flatly, then he resumed his feigned slumber. Even wiggled a bit, making himself more comfortable in the cushions.

She twisted in her seat toward him. "Are you serious? You almost died." And he looked it. Whether it was from the stress of being tortured, donating life magick, or both, his skin had lost nearly all its color, and it looked thinner, like a pale film clinging to his muscles and bones.

"Yet I didn't. It's done. It's over."

"If you really felt that way, you would've slept fine last night."

"Who said I didn't?"

"You pace. I can hear you even through the floor." But that wasn't all that had kept her up. No matter how hard she tried, she couldn't stop dwelling on the maggots, the skeleton, the kiss. She'd thrown off her quilt multiple times to check the bed for bugs.

"How could I not, when I'm wondering if I'll get another night-time visitor?" Reid asked.

Isobel swallowed and hastily slid her cosmetic spellstones back in their pouch. "That's also over now, so I'd rather not discuss it, either."

"Really? You go from planning to kill us all to lipstick, just like that?"

No, definitely not. The thought of how close she'd come to need-lessly murdering them made her ill enough to vomit. But dwelling on it would do her no good, not while Briony and Finley were exposing the Thorburns for their crimes, while Alistair and Gavin were still at large, while they had four remaining Relics and Landmarks to destroy.

"I'm just trying to move on," Isobel said tightly.

"Whatever you have to tell your . . . Do you smell that?"

"I only breathe to speak, Reid."

"It smells like . . ." Reid leapt to his feet, then dashed toward the pillar. "Oh shit."

"What?" Isobel lurched up and caught sight of the answer. Blood seeped through the pillar's cracks, dribbling down in crimson veins and puddling on the floor. She sucked in a deep breath, and sure enough, an unmistakable reek permeated the air, leaving a tinny taste on her tongue.

Reid crouched and dipped two fingers in it. As he spread them apart, the blood dripped, viscous and *real*.

"What's happening?" Isobel croaked. No new fissures severed through the pillar. No new names were crossed out.

"We're running out of time." Reid pressed his palm flat against the stone, and, to Isobel's horror, a small piece of rock crumbled away and plunked to the floor. He wrenched away, leaving behind a scarlet handprint. "The curse is beginning to collapse."

"But . . ." Her voice hitched. She couldn't lose hope only hours after getting it back. "We're so close. It can't break like this. A-And we told Briony and Finley that we'd pair the Medallion with the Monastery today, after the press conference. That only leaves—"

"The Mirror, which is currently in Alistair's possession. And the Crown and Shoes, neither of which have fallen yet." Reid seized her by the shoulders, smearing blood on her sleeve. "This is bad, Isobel. This is really, really bad."

Isobel didn't need him to tell her that. She already felt a moment away from tears, and the tight way he grasped her wasn't helping. "What are we supposed to do? Briony and Finley are still—"

"We should unite the Medallion with the Monastery. *Now.*"

"The two of us? Won't that just make the tournament break faster?"

"The curse is destabilized. We need to keep pushing it in the right direction, and we can't afford to wait." He tore away from her and bolted toward the door.

Isobel stumbled after him, panicked. "Are you even well enough to fight? You haven't slept in—"

"I'll have you, won't I?"

She swore under her breath, because he was right—as much as it frightened her, they had no choice but to act without Briony or Finley. She charged after Reid, who'd scooped the Medallion from where it rested on the table and strung it around his neck. Together, they grabbed as many enchantments as they could carry from the Tower's arsenal.

Then Reid reached his hand out to Isobel. In his other, he clutched a green Here to There spell. "Are you with me?" His voice was urgent, but not impatient.

Isobel hesitated, trying to steel herself. Twice, she'd nearly died pairing a Relic to a Landmark. But she hadn't survived so much to perish now, when hope was nearly within their grasp.

She slipped on a Here to There spellstone of her own and squeezed his hand.

Reid offered her a slight smile. "There you are."

Their Here to Theres spit them across Ilvernath. They staggered as they appeared in the shade of the Monastery, the lone structure amid the desolate, wintertime moors. It was hauntingly quiet, the only sound the brushing of the heather blown flat from the wind. With views of the hills extending out in all directions, she felt as though they stood on the edge of the world.

The two of them didn't stall. They raced inside, retracing familiar steps to the courtyard. Like in the Tower, the pillar oozed with blood, pooling down until the earth was sodden with it.

Reid slipped off the Medallion. "I guess I'll just put it here." He set the necklace on a groove in the stone, the only place where it would balance. Then he stepped back. When nothing happened, he grumbled, "What else am I supposed to do? Smash it against the rock?"

"I don't think you should try to break it."

"I'm not seeing a lot of alternatives."

Isobel circled the pillar, scrutinizing every irregularity in the stone. Unlike the last time they'd visited, they had the right Relic. She was sure of it.

"There." She pointed at the base, where a circular depression nestled into the rock, nearly obscured by the brittle grass around it. She grabbed the Medallion and pressed its amulet into the indentation. It was a perfect fit.

A bell tolled from somewhere in the Monastery, low and resonant.

"That's not ominous at all," Reid muttered.

The two of them followed the sound to a set of double doors already open, as though waiting for their arrival.

Inside was a library.

Like the other Landmarks, the high magick of the Monastery had restored it to its original glory; however, the library appeared untouched. A quilt of dust shrouded the scrolls and books piled on the shelves, and grime coated the stained glass windows, rendering the light splintered and murky. Writing desks were arranged throughout the room, parchment scattered across their surfaces, so old and delicate that Isobel guessed they would dissolve beneath a single drop of ink.

As soon as they crossed the threshold, the doors slammed shut, making both of them jump. The windows closed next, one by one, plunging the library further and further into darkness. Until a lone beam remained, shining like a spotlight onto a lectern in the room's center.

For several seconds, they froze, the only noises the diminishing chimes of the bell and Reid's nervous breathing beside her. Then the pair cautiously approached the lectern, where there lay an open book, with three words scrawled across the page.

Record your name.

"You should do it," Reid whispered, as though they might disturb the silence of the library.

"Why?"

"Because you're a real champion."

Knowing he was probably right, Isobel swallowed and lifted the quill resting between its pages, its feather large and black, as though plucked from a raven. She dipped it into the wooden inkwell on the lectern's corner, then scratched her name.

As she finished, more ink bled into the page.

What do you seek?

Isobel wrote, reading aloud as she did so. "To break the tournament's curse."

Record your story.

"All of it?" she asked.

"I think it means your story as champion," Reid said. "The Darrows are the tournament's historians. They've recorded as much about the past tournaments as possible—both the victors *and* the fallen champions. They're the ones who gave me the research I needed for the book."

"So it wants to record our history as well? That's not much of a trial."

"No, it isn't. So be prepared for anything, I guess."

Isobel stared at the page. She wasn't the sort who kept a diary, and she hardly wanted to explain every ugly choice she'd been forced to make in the tournament. The only way she'd learned to survive was to bury what was already behind her.

"Do I have to?" she asked hoarsely.

"Would you rather there be maggots all over the floor? Or pendulums swinging from the ceiling?"

Reid was right—of all the trials they could've encountered, this was far from the worst-case scenario. And in the year since she'd been thrust into the public spotlight, Isobel had never had the chance to tell her side of the story, with no one to willfully misrepresent her meaning or to take her words out of context. It would be painful to detail the events of the past, but maybe it would also feel good.

She began on the day she was named champion.

It took a long time, so long that standing still made her lower back begin to ache. Bored, Reid sat cross-legged on the floor. The spotlight from the belltower overhead cast a fiery radiance across the ridges of his brow and nose.

"Do I get to read this when you're done?" he asked.

"I'd rather you didn't."

"Embarrassed about your two weeks cozying up to Alistair?"

Isobel had already passed that part, and she'd refrained from overly descriptive details. This eight-hundred-year-old book didn't need to know that she'd once fallen asleep with her head on Alistair's chest, that she'd liked his monster stories, that the words he'd said to her in the forest still haunted her.

She didn't lie. She recounted how Alistair had gifted her the Cloak, how he'd used his own blood to fuel the sacrifice of the Reaper's Embrace so that she could get her sense for magick back. She only omitted the details that wove between the facts—that she'd cared for him as much as he had her.

Because if she didn't, she knew how it would look to anyone who read her story. That she was cruel. That she'd chosen her head over her heart. That she hadn't had a heart at all, even before it'd stopped beating.

When Isobel didn't answer, Reid continued, "I'd love to hear about it, you know. What does one *do* for two straight weeks, alone in a cave together? Other than the obvious."

"You're breaking my concentration," she grumbled.

"It was hard not to think about it while I was with them. Every time Alistair asked me something, the thought kept prickling in the back of my mind, like, huh, the two of you must've really put the *lust* in *bloodlust*."

"*That's* what you were thinking about?"

"Well, that and my imminent death. I thought about that a lot." Reid quieted for a minute, which Isobel was grateful for, as it was difficult to write while speaking. But then he went on, his words hushed, "I spent most of it thinking that I deserved it."

Isobel's quill paused mid-word. "Deserved it? They crushed your fingers. You looked—"

"I mutilated Gavin's magick. He's stronger now, sure, but his power is definitely more trouble than it's worth. And I'm the one who wrote the book in the first place. After my dad died, I just thought . . . I thought it wasn't fair, that your seven families hoarded all that power, power that could help a lot of people. In my head, the champions were barely more than chess pieces, and it was all your sick game, not mine." Reid held his head in his hands.

"Are you saying you regret writing it?"

"No. I do think the world deserved to know. I just don't think any of you deserved it either." Seeming to realize he'd said something sincere, he added, "Are you done yet? I'm starving, honestly. The book asked for a historical account, not your entire memoir."

His voice was awfully nonchalant for what they were doing, but then again, they hadn't encountered any danger. Maybe she really could relax. "I'm almost done."

"Can I ask you something?"

"Not if it's about Alistair."

"It's not." After a moment's pause, he blurted, "Why did you save me? We'd made the Cloak. I didn't have any other worth to you."

Isobel shouldn't have been surprised that Reid thought her heartless, after what she'd nearly done to them—to all of them. He hadn't told Briony or Finley, which was a relief, but still, their truce felt strange and hollow.

"And miss seeing you as the damsel in distress?" she asked lightly.

Reid snorted. "You missed most of the show. Have you ever felt like a third wheel at your own torture scene?"

Isobel didn't respond to that, as she'd just finished writing her passage. The account stretched across two pages, but it was complete, ending with where they were now. She set the quill on the book and stepped back, waiting.

Above them, the bell pealed once more—as thunderous and ominous as a death knell.

"What's going on?" Reid clambered to his feet, but Isobel shushed him. New words bled onto the page.

You lied.

"You lied?" Reid demanded. "To the creepy, eight-hundred-year-old book?"

"I-I didn't!" She hadn't altered any of the events of the past two months.

"Well, clearly you did, otherwise it wouldn't say that." Before she could react, he snatched the book from the podium and scanned its pages. Isobel watched his eyes dart from line to line, feeling utterly, wretchedly exposed. "'We reached a mutually beneficial agreement. I provided him spellmaking expertise while he helped me to restore my magick,'" Reid read, his tone falsely nasal and tight. "Wow. I'm practically sweating, darling. Should everything you write be rated M for mature?"

"It's the truth," she hissed.

"And what about this part? 'After a month of research and deliberation, we used improvisational spellmaking to successfully craft an artificial replica of the Cloak.' Funny how you never mentioned that you also spent this past month deciding whether or not you were going to off and murder all of us. An innocent little Plan B you had tucked in your pocket."

"I didn't—I wasn't . . ." she stammered, but it was useless to lie to him. "I didn't include any of that because I didn't think it mattered. It didn't actually happen!"

"It didn't want a textbook recounting of the tournament. It wanted *your* story of it."

"How was I supposed to know—"

She was cut off as a gust tore through the library. Several books on the shelves tumbled to the floor. Loose, yellowed pages and paper scraps were picked up and scattered throughout the room like autumn leaves. And they didn't stop. The wind blew Isobel's hair into her mouth, made Reid flatten down the book on the lectern so its pages wouldn't be added to the mess of parchment around them.

"What's happening?" Isobel choked.

"I don't know, but we need to fix this. *Fast.*"

He thrust the book against her chest, but she swatted it away. "What was I supposed to say? That Alistair didn't nearly kill me—twice? That I'm some kind of heartless, manipulative bitch, just like all my hate mail says? I'm not—"

"It's just a test! Who the hell is going to read this, anyway? Once we're done here, there will be nothing left of this place but . . ." He trailed off, his head whipping toward the door. Dark smoke wafted from beneath it. In the room's corner, several pieces of paper had ignited, and the flames grew as they ate through the brittle parchment.

Now Isobel understood what this was.

A pyre.

"Fine. You know what?" Reid shoved Isobel aside and slammed the book atop the lectern. He dunked the quill in the ink bottle and began scribbling across a fresh page.

"What are you doing?" she demanded.

"Playing champion after all. I just . . . *Fuck.*"

He doubled over, one hand braced against his stomach. Isobel watched in horror as his name faded from the paper, like he'd never written it at all. Desperately, she stole the quill and started her story over, and though her words remained, they smeared, illegible.

"I-I don't understand," she stuttered. "What's happening?"

"You've lost your chance," Reid choked out.

"Then what do we do? You can't write—you're not from the families."

"*That* isn't why my words disappear. *This* is." With a pained expression, he straightened and lifted the bottom of his T-shirt, exposing a grotesque bulge on the side of his abdomen, the size of an apricot. The skin over it was thin, and a dull, white light shone through it.

Isobel gaped in horror. "Is that—is that a *spellstone?*"

"After Briony and Finley brought you to my shop when you were injured, and you cast the Divining Kiss on me, I realized how easily my whole plan could be exposed. It's why truth spells don't work on me, and it's why the Landmark won't listen to me." He winced and pressed his palm against it. "As soon as I tried to write, it started throbbing—"

"What the hell is *wrong* with you?" Isobel pushed him backward. He tripped over the base of the lectern and crashed onto the floor. Behind him, the flames scaled up the bookshelves, and smoke had begun to gather like storm clouds on the ceiling. "You implanted a spellstone *inside* yourself? Do you hear how deranged that sounds?"

"It was the only way to cast the wards on myself permanently."

"I don't know why I'm surprised. You were willing to kill us to break the tournament, so this is hardly . . . *What are you doing?*"

Panting, Reid lay back and lifted his shirt, biting it to hold it up. One of his curserings glowed.

"What does it look like I'm doing?" he gritted. "I'm cutting it out." Then he jerked his head toward the flames. "Do something about that, would you?"

Isobel bit back a retort, hating that she'd messed up, that her survival now rested on the shoulders of someone so spiteful and sadistic and *frustrating*. While he wheezed in pain behind her, she fished through her pockets for the spells she'd grabbed when they'd left the Tower, and she found a basic Firehose. By the time she clutched it, the flames had crawled up one of the walls of bookcases. The heat of it smothered her like a blanket pressed over her skin. She shed her cardigan and aimed the spell.

Water blasted out of her crystal with so much force that she nearly fell backward. She widened her stance and clenched her jaw, but no matter how much she doused the fire, the flames climbed ever higher. There was no sliver of this room that wasn't kindling, and with every door and window shut tight, it would only be a matter of minutes before the library was consumed.

"To the left!" Reid shouted, and Isobel swiveled around. Another fire had started across the room, sweeping over the paper-strewn floor.

"The water isn't working!" she yelled.

"Just keep going." Behind her, Reid staggered to his feet, a gray spellstone clutched in his bloody hand. He pocketed it and lunged toward the lectern. "I'll make this quick—honest, but quick."

He better, otherwise they were about to be burned alive.

Isobel sprinted until she stood in front of the wall of shuttered windows. She grabbed another curse from her pocket—a Siege Mortar.

As though a cannon firing, a blast tore across the wall, adding *more* smoke to the already suffocating room.

Reid screamed. "What the hell are you—"

"I'm trying to save us!" Isobel called back. But when the haze dissipated, her stomach sank. The wall remained perfectly intact. They had nowhere to go.

She returned to Reid's side, peering down at his writing. His hand quivered as he scribbled his story, so hurried that she could barely decipher any of the words. But they remained on the page.

"What happens if this doesn't work either?" she asked.

"Do you want me to answer that?" Reid's voice cracked, and sweat dribbled down his temples and above his lips. With his left hand, he gripped his stomach, and his wound—though shallow—bled profusely. He looked a second away from tears, and Isobel didn't know what she would do if he broke down. Every time she'd faced her death before, she'd done it bravely—the way her family would've wanted. But she didn't have any bravery left.

Trembling, Isobel took Reid's hand. His skin was bloodslick, making his fingers slip easily in between hers. She thought he'd pull away, but he didn't.

As two more minutes ticked by, the smoke was so dense that Reid had succumbed to coughs, hacking and shaking even as he wrote on. She could've read the truth he was telling, but she didn't bother. From the few words she did catch, Reid's story was no different than what he'd already shared with her.

"That's it," he rasped, dropping the quill. "I'm done."

Nothing happened for several moments, and Isobel's thoughts plummeted into the darkest of places. Alistair had claimed she couldn't believe in anything, but all along, she'd been *right* not to believe in a happy ending. And now she regretted every terrible choice she hadn't made, every glimmer of hope, every fragment of friendship. They were all worthless if she died here.

And when Reid fell unconscious from the smoke, she would burn alone.

Then above them, the bell tolled once more.

"Look," Reid breathed, and Isobel glanced down. In the darkness, she could only make out the faintest outline of the writing on the page.

Truth can be buried, but it is never destroyed.

How ironic from the family whose lies had nearly doomed them.

The windows and doors behind them blasted open, and light streamed into the library.

"Come on," Isobel said, and the two of them raced through the corridors of the Monastery, hand in hand. The fire behind them only seemed to gain speed as it followed at their heels.

At last, they burst through the final doors into the garden. The ground quaked, making them each lose their footing and tumble into the mulch. While Reid hacked out more coughs, Isobel rolled onto her back, staring as the Monastery was engulfed in flames.

They'd done it.

She should've felt victorious. Instead, a sob shuddered through her. It felt wrong and awkward without the need to breathe, but she couldn't stop. She buried her face beneath her arms, hating how broken her body was, how broken her heart was. She'd steeled it so many times that maybe it had finally shattered.

"What was that for, Reid?" she choked out, too humiliated to remove her arms and look at him.

"What are you talking about?" He sounded as though his throat was lined with sandpaper.

"The pillars are *bleeding*. The tournament is unraveling faster than we might be able to break it, and then we'll all die, and all this will have been for nothing." The sobs wracked her chest, violent and uncontrollable. "I can't keep risking my life, getting my hopes up. I know I'm supposed to say that I c-couldn't kill you or Briony or Finley, but when the two of us were in there, I was so scared that all I kept thinking was that I wish I had. And—"

"Hey. It's all right—"

"It's *not*. We almost died because I couldn't admit the truth. That I'm a monster."

"Isobel. Isobel, *look at me*." He grabbed her arms and tugged them away from her face. His eyes were bloodshot and his forehead coated in soot, much of it streaked from trails of sweat. She must've looked the same way. "You don't have to punish yourself for what you did to survive."

"But betraying you all isn't what Alistair would've done. It's not what Briony or Finley—"

"It's what I would've done. Cast a truth spell now, if you don't believe me." Reid's expression was gravely serious. He meant every word he said. "And maybe that makes you feel worse. But for whatever it does matter to you, I would've fought, too. I would've been ruthless. I've made my own mistakes, but yours? I don't judge you for any of them. And if they came to you naturally, they wouldn't have taken this toll on you."

Isobel stared at him, trying to determine what his words were worth. Who was Reid MacTavish to her? An enemy? An ally? A friend?

"But what if we never get the Mirror back?" she asked softly. "What if the Crown and the Shoes don't fall in time?"

He sighed and let go of her forearms. Then he collapsed beside her, shoulder to shoulder, and when he spoke, he did so more softly than she'd ever heard him. "If you're ashamed of what you were willing to kill for, then maybe it's time to ask yourself what you're willing to die for."

She stilled.

As much as she loathed to admit it, Reid was right. Even if they'd regained their chance of survival, that survival hinged on so much danger.

She needed to choose now, once and for all: her life or her heart?

Above them, a tower of smoke plumed into the morning sky.

After Reid finished healing the wound on his stomach, he sat up and studied her calmly. "If you leave, I won't chase you."

"I'm not leaving," she said firmly, wiping her eyes. "I never had a choice in becoming champion, becoming famous, becoming *this*." She gestured to her body, so lifeless and cold. "And maybe freedom isn't a good reason—maybe I should care more about doing what's right. But there's still this voice inside me that isn't sure we'll pull this off, and I think it's too much of a part of me to ever go away, not until this is over. So if I die, I die. But I want it to be something I chose." She stared at him. "Is that enough?"

He let out a low, amused breath. "What are you asking me for?"

Isobel had an answer, another truth she wasn't ready to speak. But he didn't make her tell him. Instead, he held out his bloodied hand, and she grabbed it.

GAVIN GRIEVE

"Disturbing new phenomena have been reported this morning on the Champions Pillar. Despite immediate reports of panic in the area, the enchantment has been proven to be illusory in nature, although attempts to dispel it have thus far been unsuccessful."

WKL Radio

The pillar in the kitchen was bleeding. Gavin watched with trepidation as red welled up from the cracks and seeped across the stone. The overwhelming smell of rust wafted through the small room, making nausea roil in his gut.

"What do you think it means?" Hendry asked from beside him, voice hushed.

"That the tournament's close to breaking." Gavin traced a fresh crack on the pillar's side—it had shaken the Cottage floor the previous afternoon, shortly after Isobel and Reid fled with the Medallion in tow. They'd made short work of destroying it.

He'd been tormented all night by images of Reid's bloodied face and broken fingers, of the cursemaker's confession that *he* was the one who'd written *A Tradition of Tragedy*. And yet Gavin still hadn't been able to end Reid's life.

If he couldn't kill the cursemaker, he couldn't kill *anyone*.

Which meant he was as good as dead.

Gavin shuddered and yanked his hand away. It was stained crimson.

"I thought we still had a month and a half." Hendry reached for the stone, too, but his silhouette flickered as he approached it, crimson lagging through the air. Gavin felt a twinge of pain in his arm before Hendry solidified again.

It was the same sensation he'd experienced when Hendry had

vanished while making the healing spell. Gavin knew the other boy's life magick was tied to the tournament. But as the curse weakened . . . it was clear that Hendry was growing weaker, too.

"Yeah, well, looks like the other champions are overachievers." Gavin hesitated. "Hendry . . . about how you keep, um, disappearing . . ."

But before he could say anything further, Alistair threw open the bedroom door. "What's going on?"

The sight of Alistair reminded Gavin of the other reason he hadn't been able to sleep—the way Alistair's cheek had felt beneath his hand, his skin warm and soft despite the brutal creep of the Reaper's Embrace. When he'd brushed his fingertips against the curve of Alistair's throat, he'd thought of how many times he'd dreamed of closing his hands around the other boy's windpipe. The image had warped in Gavin's mind until it was his lips there instead, and he'd pulled away, his breathing ragged.

"Something's wrong with the pillar," Hendry said soberly. "Gavin thinks that means everything's close to breaking."

"But they can't end it," Alistair protested. "They have a broken Relic."

"They can't end it peacefully, no," Gavin said. "But this must mean the tournament's close to ending the other way. The one where everyone dies."

"Why would they want that?" Alistair demanded.

"I doubt they did it on purpose."

Hendry shifted back and forth. "Or . . . they want to be martyrs?"

Gavin considered it. Briony and her friends *had* made a lot of grandiose claims to the media about their plans to finish things for good. "Maybe they think it's noble."

Alistair's face contorted with frustration. "Well, it isn't. We're running out of time. We need to finish this. Now."

"Your curse," Gavin argued, but Alistair waved him off.

"You heard Reid. It can't be broken by anything but a . . . a powerful sacrifice. A good one. That's not happening."

"Reid's resistant to truth spells," Gavin said. "He could've been lying."

"Then the whole thing was a waste of time, and we still need to fight them. Kill them." Alistair said the last words pointedly. Gavin thought of their conversation the night before and swallowed hard.

All Gavin's wants and wishes felt hopelessly tangled together. He knew exactly how he felt about Alistair, and after all the time they'd spent together he'd thought—maybe foolishly—that Alistair might feel the same way. But he didn't even know if Alistair liked boys. And if he *did* like Gavin . . . the thought was too painful for him to linger on for more than a heartbeat.

"Let's strategize, then," Gavin said bitterly. "How exactly do you plan on doing this?"

"We'll need to distract them, split them up." Alistair's cadence shifted, his tone slow and deliberate. His expression was now the same cruel, vacant one he'd worn while torturing Reid. "The way the reporters talk about it, Briony and Finley are always together. If we take one of them out in front of the other, they'll lose focus."

"Or they'll get more dangerous," Hendry murmured. "They'll want revenge."

"More dangerous, sure—but sloppier," Gavin said, his stomach churning. He'd been preparing for this moment for years, but try as he might, he could not steel himself for the slaughter.

Alistair, however, leaned forward eagerly. "Which leaves Isobel and Reid. Both of them are strong, but I can distract them . . . before you finish them off. Will you need more of Hendry's life magick for that?"

Right. Hendry's magick. Gavin stared at the sleeve of his sweater and pictured the hourglass underneath it. He felt so distant from the person who'd come to the Cottage determined to claim this power.

"I've got plenty," he muttered. "I can handle it."

Gavin didn't know who he thought he was kidding. Just like the first Grieve, he'd become the architect of his own destruction. He'd fought for better spellwork, better allies, better casting abilities. Yet he was still too weak to do what needed to be done.

Maybe that weakness was what his family had seen, all those years ago.

"If we're going to give ourselves our best chance of winning, I should head back to the Castle," he blurted.

Alistair's brow furrowed. "Why?"

"To collect any supplies there. A-Anything that could help us."

"And you didn't think to do that when we nearly died trying to claim the Medallion?"

"I didn't know how badly they'd hurt us," Gavin shot back.

"I think it's a good idea," ventured Hendry. "If we're going to fight them, we should be armed with everything we have."

"Fair enough." Alistair reached for his coat, slung over a chair. "We'll go now, then."

"No!" Gavin realized he'd said it too loud, too fast. He coughed, then croaked out, "No, you should get ready here. Divide and conquer, right?"

"Right," Alistair echoed, looking at him suspiciously.

"I'll see you both soon."

Gavin stood and hurried out the door before either of them could protest. He realized as he left that he had no idea if he was about to clear his head, or flee.

Gavin didn't go to the Castle. Instead, he cast Alistair's Whole New Me on himself and headed into town. He'd barely breached the city limits when he realized that something had gone very, very wrong in Ilvernath. Sirens rang out in the distance, blaring and insistent. Wards descended over storefronts and flat windows. The people around him rushed past, heads down, murmuring worriedly to each other. Unease settled in the pit of Gavin's stomach, but he continued on.

He soon found himself on a dead-end street where the sirens were barely audible, in front of a townhouse that looked identical to the others flanking it in a semi-circle. It was plain and unremarkable in every conceivable way—well-kept enough that the neighbors had no cause for concern, but with an utter lack of character or flair. Maintained, but not loved.

There was a plaque on the heavy wooden door, above the mail slot. GRIEVE, it said, in a way Gavin had always thought of as more of an instruction than a name.

The bell rang, and rang, and rang. Gavin sighed, then realized the door was cracked. It let out a mournful, drawn-out screech as he pushed it open.

"Hello?" he called, stepping inside. "It's me."

There was no response. He treaded into the foyer, which was flooded with the sickly sweet floral scent of a stale air freshening charm. The Lowe manor had been devastating and lurid, like something from a gothic novel or a frightening fairy tale. But the Grieve townhouse was neat and bland, with the half-hearted, soulless feeling of a model home.

When Gavin flipped on the light switch, he caught sight of his disguised face in the hallway mirror—his blond hair long enough to partially cover his eyes, his jawline round instead of square. He sighed and dropped the spell. For better or for worse, there was no hiding who he was. Not here.

"Anyone home?" he tried again. It would be just his luck to show up while his entire family was gone. But then, he'd spent most of his life at the Grieve house alone. Locked in his room, plotting, planning.

He climbed the stairs, reflexively stepping more softly on the fourth one, which creaked. Several frames with insipid platitudes hung in the stairwell, interspersed with his parents' wedding photo and a few shots of Fergus and Callista. Gavin had never quite gotten out of the habit of looking for himself in the pictures—or of feeling a pang of disappointment when he wasn't there.

He gritted his teeth and walked down the upstairs hallway, wallpapered in beige.

When Gavin pushed open the door to his old bedroom, he froze.

His neatly made bed—gone. His free weights and used book collection—gone. His beloved wooden desk, crammed with files on the other champions—gone, gone, all of it gone.

The world around him swayed. Gavin shuddered and rested his hands on his knees, his breaths coming in short, tight bursts. He stared at the champion's ring on his pinky, the red stone glimmering, taunting him, and thought he might pass out.

This was what awaited him if he won the tournament. He'd return to a life that had never been meant to extend past seventeen. To a family who had erased him so thoroughly, it was as though he'd never existed at all.

"Why did it have to be me?" he whimpered, each word feeling as though it had been ripped painfully from his throat. "D-did you know I wouldn't be able to kill the others? Did you just decide I was the easiest kid to stop loving? No, fuck that—you never loved me at all."

But words weren't enough. He straightened up, gazing at the blank walls appraisingly. His Iron Fist cursering glowed, and a moment later, a massive hand appeared in his childhood bedroom. It slammed into the wall with a horrible *crash*, ripping the beige wallpaper aside and leaving a crack the size of his torso in the plaster.

The enchantment dissipated, and Gavin rubbed at his eyes, his shoulders heaving.

He knew why he'd come here now. He'd wanted to remind himself of who he'd been before the tournament, a boy who'd studied and trained and promised himself that he would find a way to live. Instead, Gavin was reminded of the family who'd taught that boy to hate himself before he died.

Maybe there was a twisted sort of relief in finally accepting the truth the Grieves had spent his whole life trying to tell him. Maybe knowing that he had always been meant to die in the tournament would make that death less painful.

"Gavin?"

He whirled around. His younger brother, Fergus, stood in the doorway, slack-jawed. He was thirteen and terrible, with unkempt blond hair and a once-gangly frame that was starting to fill out the same way Gavin's had. The week before the tournament, he'd been suspended from school for starting yet another fistfight. His mother had claimed Fergus was acting out because of Gavin, but Gavin was pretty sure his brother had only wanted an excuse to get some payback on his bullies.

"I was just going," Gavin muttered, starting toward the doorway. But Fergus blocked his path before Gavin could push past him.

"You punched the wall," he said.

"Yeah, and?"

"And also I heard you. Um. Talking to yourself."

Gavin groaned internally. How utterly humiliating. "I thought I was the only one here."

"I was watching TV," Fergus mumbled. Gavin could hear the tinny, distant drone of it now, emitting from his brother's bedroom. "There's some weird stuff happening in Ilvernath. The Pillar's bleeding, and Briony Thorburn told everyone that her family took all those peoples' life magick, and now everyone's freaking out—"

"The Thorburns were behind the murders?" Gavin tried to wrap his head around the perfect poster children for heroism supporting something so horrible. Maybe Alistair really *was* the only noble champion in all of this, fighting for his brother's life. His brother, who was fading.

Gavin thought of the times Hendry had blinked in and out of existence. Of the pain on the other boy's face as Gavin tried to ask him about it.

Maybe it was too late for the brothers to have their happy ending, even if Alistair won.

"I dunno. That's what people are saying." Fergus scratched his head, then blurted, "You don't think we love you?"

Gavin couldn't handle another twist of the knife. "Our parents don't love me. That's just the fucking truth."

"B-but I do." Fergus flushed, clearly mortified. "I cried after you left, you know. Every night. Until Mum told me to cut it out."

Gavin's chest clenched. He and Fergus had always been antagonistic. But he didn't know why his brother would be lying—not when he could've stayed hidden in his room.

"Can I show you something?" Fergus continued shyly.

"Sure," Gavin mumbled. It wasn't as though he was in a rush to get back to his death. He let Fergus lead him into his own bedroom—full of actual furniture, and a large TV, and—"You stole my desk?"

"They were going to throw it out," Fergus said, his voice high and nasally in a way that told Gavin he was close to tears. "Anyway. Look."

He shoved something at Gavin, and Gavin took it. It was a folder just like the dossiers he'd made on the other six champions, before the tournament. But instead of their names . . . this one bore his own.

Gavin paged through the quotes from his and Alistair's interview. The pictures they'd pulled. Some random fan who'd called Gavin the "ultimate underdog." He'd known the media was covering him, of course. But the fact that Fergus had paid attention to it felt different. He knew firsthand how it felt to be taught that everything the Grieves did was shameful. And yet Fergus had overcome that, at least a little bit.

"I wanted to see how you were doing," Fergus said. "And then I just . . . sort of wound up paying attention to how people talked about the tournament, or whatever. So I started talking to some of the other kids from the tournament families who also think it's all wrong. I dunno if they'll change anything. But they're trying to."

Gavin had no idea how to feel. Grateful, that someone in his family seemed to give a shit whether he lived or died. Furious that he felt grateful for that, when it was something *everyone* deserved. And heartbroken, because it wasn't as though any of it mattered.

The next time Fergus saw him it would be in a coffin, and that was assuming there'd be enough of him left to bury.

"There are some things you just can't change." Gavin shoved the folder back at Fergus. "No matter how much you want to."

Fergus blinked at him, then his face locked up into a defensive expression Gavin knew well. "You think I don't know that?"

"Not the way I do."

Fergus glared. There was a beat of tense silence . . . and then the floor below them began to shake. The folder toppled from Fergus's hands as he grabbed at the desk chair for purchase, sending newspaper clippings flying. Gavin braced himself against the bed frame.

"What's going on?" Fergus demanded, panicked. "An earthquake?"

"I don't know," Gavin gasped. The rumbling stopped after a few moments, and the boys looked at each other, shaken.

Then Gavin saw it—a grainy, silent image on the TV screen behind Fergus's head. The Champions Pillar.

"Give me the remote," he said hastily. Fergus fumbled for it and handed it to Gavin, who cranked the volume up.

". . . breaking news," said a reporter on the screen. "We'd like to report another crack in the Champions Pillar." The camera zoomed in, and sure enough, there it was—on the side with seven stars, just above the one that had appeared the night before.

The oh-so-heroic champions had broken another piece of the curse.

Gavin ran through the active Relics in his mind: the Cloak, the Sword, the Medallion, the Mirror, and the Hammer. Four gone. One at the Cottage. Two others yet to fall.

It didn't add up.

The spellmakers had told him there was a broken Relic.

The spellmakers had lied.

Which meant the tournament really *could* be ended with the remaining champions still alive.

It was as though the world had shifted on its axis. Everything he'd believed about himself, about his future, about one narrow, bloody path forward—all of it was wiped away.

In its place was a blank slate. An empty room.

Gavin took a deep breath, feeling as though it were his first, and turned to Fergus.

"I have to go. I . . . I guess I'll try to change something, too."

Alistair had asked him who they'd be, in a different story. He wondered for the first time if they could have one. If they could truly acknowledge what was happening to the tournament. To Hendry. Between each other.

He didn't know what kind of story that would be, exactly. But he knew it was one worth fighting for.

ALISTAIR LOWE

Several times, the final body recovered after the tournament's end has been found prepared for burial, as though the victor has tried to give their last opponent dignity after their death.
Collecting the Dead: Essays of a Would-be Champion,
Darrow Family Archives

Alistair stared at the blood pooled across the mantel, dripping in a slow, steady rhythm onto the floorboards. A new crack severed through the side with the stars, but Alistair couldn't dwell on what that meant, couldn't dwell on anything other than his dizzying, building rage.

"How long?" he uttered gravely.

"What?" his brother asked behind him.

"How long does it take to gather supplies from the Castle?" According to his watch, over forty minutes had passed since Gavin's departure—ample time for Alistair to prepare his own arsenal. His hoard of cursestones lay piled atop the kitchen table, freshly filled and sorted. "How long until we decide Gavin isn't coming back?"

"What? Of course he'll be back," said Hendry behind him. "He wouldn't—"

"You heard how he sounded." Alistair swiveled around, and above him, fresh cobwebs drooped from the ceiling. In the sitting room, the couch's fabric faded to a sallow gray. "He was jittery, anxious. He didn't even sound like that the day you nearly killed him."

Hendry furrowed his brow and leaned back against the kitchen counter. "You think he, what, joined the others? Or that he wants to go it alone?"

"I don't *know*." Alistair slammed his fist on the table, making several of the crystals clatter to the floor. Although there might be a reasonable explanation for Gavin's absence, dread had seized him in a chokehold. Last time he'd been betrayed, it'd happened at this exact moment, when it would hurt the most. "What if this has been his strategy all along—waiting for the Reaper's Embrace to claim more of me while *he* got stronger?"

"No. Th-that can't be what this is," Hendry stammered, even as doubt drained the color from his skin. "It's okay to be nervous—we're all nervous. But don't you think you're being paranoid?"

"*Paranoid?* Look at the pillar! The tournament is collapsing around us, and he just leaves?" Alistair frantically replayed the events of last night, Gavin's gentleness as he'd cupped his cheek, the way his eyes had bored into him. Of course it'd all been a trick. Gavin was clever—brilliant, even. Gavin would've realized he didn't need to employ Isobel's obvious, over-the-top tactics. Instead, he'd opted for a subtler strategy, targeting Alistair's greatest weakness: his heart.

"We need to be ready." Alistair's voice was strangled. "The only reason he has to come back now is to kill me."

He lunged for the kitchen table and rifled through his cursestones.

"You can't be serious," Hendry choked.

Alistair ignored him. With trembling hands, he slid the Demon's Pyre onto his fourth finger.

"Al—*Al!*" Hendry seized his wrist and spun him around. "Do you hear yourself right now? Gavin doesn't want to kill you. If anything, he—"

"Gavin has *always* wanted to kill me, from the first day I met him. This alliance was nothing but a ploy to him." Alistair wrenched out of his brother's grasp, his shoulders heaving. "And I can prove it."

He snatched the Mirror from the table.

Hendry's eyes widened. "B-but that's your last question."

Alistair didn't care, because, duplicitous or not, Gavin was the final doubt in his mind, the last thing standing between him and their ultimate, remorseless slaughter. And so he held the Relic in front of him, cringing at the panic in his eyes, at how far the Reaper's Embrace had expanded across his face.

"Why did Gavin ally with me?" Alistair asked.

On the handle, the already dim light of the topmost spellstone extinguished.

The glass rippled as its image shifted, but even once it stilled, the changes were slight. Alistair's curls, lopsided from his impromptu trim, lengthened. Freckles popped across the bridge of his nose and summits of his cheeks. His cursemark retreated down his jaw until the only white that remained was the thin horizontal line etched across his throat.

Hendry.

Alistair's balance swayed. "Th-that doesn't make sense. Why would . . ."

Then the answer struck him in stark, agonizing clarity. Clutching the edge of the table to steady himself, he met Hendry's eyes. His brother's shock perfectly reflected his own.

Automatically, Hendry's hand raised to his neck.

"My life magick," he rasped.

In a rage, Alistair grabbed the nearest chair and shoved it to the ground, and the room darkened as grime crusted over the windows. He'd sworn to win the tournament to protect Hendry, yet Gavin had used his brother—no different than their family had.

And Alistair—pining, pathetic, foolish—had let him.

"I'm going to kill him!" he shouted. "I'm going to . . ."

He trailed off, looking up and realizing Hendry was gone.

"Hendry?" He crept toward the bedroom, wondering if Hendry had slipped away without his notice. "Hendry?"

Suddenly, his brother reappeared in the Cottage's sitting room. High magick flickered in and out around him as though he were a faulty light bulb.

"What the hell happened?" Alistair demanded. "Are you all right?"

"I'm fine." Hendry squeezed his hand into a fist, making high magick wink across his knuckles. "It's nothing. It'll go away."

"It's happened before?"

"Once or twice."

Alistair narrowed his eyes. Hendry's tone was clipped, the way he always spoke when he lied. But of course he was fading. Hendry was connected to the tournament, and the tournament was falling apart. If Alistair didn't win it before it collapsed, then Hendry would be gone forever.

They were done stalling. The two of them would end this tournament just as they'd originally planned—together.

And they would end Gavin first.

"Come on," Alistair snapped. "We're leaving. *Now.*"

Still gripping the Mirror, he stalked to the front door and threw it open, letting cold blast into the Cottage.

Hendry scrambled after him. "Al, wait! Are you sure this is still what you want?"

Alistair spun around on the threshold, his hair whipping in the wind, his nostrils flaring. "What is that supposed to mean? You think I've changed my mind about saving you?"

Anguish crossed Hendry's face. "I just don't want to see you get hurt."

"It's a little late for that."

"I mean it," Hendry said hoarsely. "This wasn't supposed to be about saving me. This was supposed to be about saving both of us."

"It still is. After this is over, you and I are leaving Ilvernath forever. Maggot, too."

"And what happens to *our* children? The curse will only—"

Hendry vanished.

Alistair's heart seized in panic. "Hendry?" he croaked, but no one answered except the howls of the wind behind him. The fire in the hearth, the last comfort the Cottage offered, snuffed out.

His knees wobbled, and he braced himself against the doorframe, but he didn't let himself break. Instead, he steeled his fear into rage, into desperation, into resolve. Because even if the Reaper's Embrace consumed him, Alistair would fight until his dying breath to save his brother.

And he would fight alone—just as it was always supposed to be.

But when he turned to leave, a figure passed through the Cottage's wards. In the short time of his absence, Alistair hadn't thought to lock him out.

In his clenched fist, Alistair readied a curse.

"There you are," Alistair called, and he stormed across the lawn toward Gavin, seething. "Is this it, then? Will we finally have our duel?" The words bore twice as much malice as when he'd spoken them to Isobel.

"What are you talking about?" Gavin asked, and Alistair had to hand it to him—he made a flawless liar. "I just want an honest conversation. You, me, and—"

Alistair cast a Giant's Wrath, and as though an ocean's wave, the ground in front of him buckled and swept forward. Gavin had no time to react before he was thrown into the air, and he groaned as he slammed down and rolled across the grass.

"What the fuck?" Gavin pushed himself to his knees. "Have you completely lost—"

"This whole time, y-you've been using me," Alistair growled, not even caring how his voice quivered. "You used me to get to Hendry's life magick."

Gavin stiffened, and his expression—normally so controlled, so careful—betrayed true fear. "That's not—I didn't—"

"Don't bother pretending otherwise. I asked the Mirror, and the Mirror never lies." Alistair advanced toward him. "All this time, you must've been so *proud* of yourself, thinking you'd wormed your way in here, that you had me beat. So let's have at it. Get up, and we'll see which of us is really stronger."

Gavin leaned back on his heels and shakily raised his arms in the air, as though in surrender. "Y-you're right about part of it. When I told Walsh about Hendry the day after Hendry came back, he thought his magick could help me. But I—"

"And Hendry gave it to you," Alistair said hotly. "He *trusted* you—"

"I know, and I'm sorry. I'm so sorry. But you have to believe me—I didn't come here to fight you." Slowly, Gavin clambered to standing, his arms still held high. "Like I said, I came here to talk."

"And why the hell should we listen?"

"Because it's important. It's about the tournament breaking, and about Hendry, and about you."

Alistair scoffed. "Don't tell me you've had a change of heart and want to play hero, not after everything you've done."

Gavin only hiked up his chin in response.

Alistair barked out a deranged laugh. Of all the deceits he'd braced himself for, he hadn't considered this—that Gavin, who'd mutilated himself, who'd held a man hostage, who'd taken advantage of a murdered boy, could suddenly flee to the other side. "Oh, that's rich. So you're just going to stroll into the Tower now and beg forgiveness? You think Briony will take you back? *Reid?*"

Gavin winced, then stared at the Cottage. "Where's Hendry?"

"I told him I wanted to deal with you myself."

The other boy stared at him intensely, and from his bloodshot eyes, Alistair realized he'd been crying. But he didn't let that perturb him. He prowled closer, slow and predatory.

"Hendry disappeared again, didn't he?" asked Gavin.

Alistair recoiled. "You knew?"

"It's happened before, and it's only going to get worse." Gavin took a cautious step forward. "The Relic that was broken? The other champions must've fixed it. Now there's only three left, and even if there weren't, you've seen what's happening. The whole city is in chaos. The pillars are *bleeding*. One way or another, this tournament is going to break."

"Not if I win it first."

As Gavin once again walked closer, Alistair moved to the side. He didn't want Gavin near him, and so they circled each other, waiting for the other to strike.

"How can you win, Al? How—"

"Don't call me that," Alistair snapped, squeezing the Mirror's handle tighter.

"I'm done fighting, and with Hendry gone, you have no one to kill for you. So even if you did slay one of the other champions or . . ." He cleared his throat. "Or me, the Reaper's Embrace would kill you."

"You don't know that."

"I'm looking at you, aren't I?"

Alistair resisted the urge to turn his head to the side, to hide the cursemark. "What would you have me do? I just got Hendry back. You want me to abandon him? To help the other champions doom him? I'd rather give him a chance, any chance, and if I die, so be it."

"You'd throw your life away? Hendry wouldn't want—"

"Don't talk about what Hendry would want, not after you used him," Alistair fumed. "You think you can still trick me. But I won't fall for it. You've been obsessed with killing me from the start."

"I'll cast a truth spell on myself, if that's what you want," Gavin said. "I know you must hate me, and I know how hard this must be to hear, but you can't win the tournament. Even if you cured the Reaper's Embrace, this curse is unraveling, and it's going to take Hendry with it."

"*You can't know that.*" Alistair's voice cracked, and no matter how hard he tried, he couldn't take a full breath. But he refused to break. Not now. Not in front of *him*.

"I know it, and I think you do, too. Even if you won't admit it to yourself."

It was true that without Gavin, without Hendry, Alistair didn't know how he'd kill the other champions. But that didn't mean he'd give up. Even if he could survive the tournament's downfall, he wanted no future without his brother in it.

Alistair halted and regarded Gavin with a lethal glare. "You have no idea what I'm capable of."

Gavin froze, too, and he flexed his fingers—fingers studded in curserings. For someone claiming he didn't want to fight, he'd certainly come prepared.

"Don't do this," he choked. "Don't make me stop you."

"Don't worry. You won't."

Before Gavin could respond, Alistair cast the Conjurer's Nightmare.

The red sun overhead faded, and dusk swallowed their surroundings as though a shroud had draped over the world.

The grove around them began to change. The stalks in the garden rose, entire trees sprouting and rearing toward the sky. Roots broke from the earth and coiled across the ground. The stone gargoyles enlarged over ten times their original size. Their wings writhed and unfurled. Their claws lengthened and raked across the dirt.

"I know this isn't real," Gavin called to him.

"Isn't it?" Alistair asked, ducking behind a nearby tree.

One of the five gargoyles whipped toward Gavin, mere meters away. It crawled forward hungrily, each of its steps heavy thuds of stone. Gavin cast his Spikeshield moments before the creature's fists slammed overtop him. Though the monster was little more than illusion, Gavin still staggered out of the path of its next blow.

Alistair smiled. He didn't even need to summon another curse to strike Gavin down. If Gavin cast enough spells, then his life magick would drain on its own—the very life magick he'd stolen from his brother.

Another gargoyle flew overhead, and Alistair crouched low to avoid its notice. The downside of the Conjurer's Nightmare was that it also affected the caster. The monsters would target him as readily as they did Gavin, even if they were born of Alistair's own imagination.

Alistair craned his neck to peer around the tree. Two gargoyles now flanked Gavin, grasping at his armor from either side.

Gavin switched tactics. "You can't want this!"

Alistair's wrath burned so hot he swore his blood curdled. How like Gavin to patronize him even while being overpowered. But he didn't respond, unwilling to betray his position.

"I came here to *save* you!" Gavin called.

Doubt crept into Alistair's mind—exactly, he expected, as Gavin wanted it to. But he couldn't help but consider his words. Why would Gavin Grieve, who was every bit as ruthless as he was, risk his life all to offer Alistair a chance at redemption? A chance he must've known Alistair would never take?

Alistair could only think of one reason, but it was far too painful to fathom.

This was not the time for weakness.

And so, no matter how unwise, he couldn't resist shouting back. "That was your mistake!"

At that, Gavin cast a flurry of curses. A blast erupted around him, flinging the gargoyles away and pulverizing them into a heap of stone. Then a large metallic hand materialized at Alistair's right. Alistair rushed to throw up an Exoskeleton just as the Iron Fist seized him in its grasp. It squeezed, making him gasp for air. With no other choice, Alistair cast the Vampire's Stake, and the curse plunged straight through the hand, narrowly missing Alistair, as though he were a magician in a sword box. The Iron Fist dissipated, dropping Alistair to the ground.

Panting, he sprinted through the vegetable patch and ducked behind the cover of the garden bench. Thankfully, the Mirror hadn't cracked—it would take far more power than Gavin's curse to break the Relic.

A gargoyle crept over the Cottage's roof, and Alistair froze. It'd sighted him.

The gargoyle swooped down, slamming against the soil with such force that the ground trembled. Alistair crabbed backward, ignoring the fear knotting in his stomach. Because the only way to master the Conjurer's Nightmare was to never once waver in your conviction. The only true monster in the enchantment was him.

He raised his hand and cast a Revenge of the Forsaken. The gargoyle exploded, and Alistair shielded his face with his arms as crumbled stone flew in every direction.

He clambered to his feet. Gavin must've wisened to the curse's trick, because he ignored the remaining gargoyle charging toward him. But even he couldn't stop himself from flinching as the monster tried to strike him, and he stumbled over the broken body of another defeated gargoyle at his feet.

Alistair stalked toward him. As it noticed him, the gargoyle lurched forward, but with a flick of his wrist, it met the same, quick fate as its companion.

Same as their original duel, Alistair cast the Strangling Vines.

Gavin's eyes widened as tree roots snaked across the underbrush and coiled around his ankles, and even as he tore at them, they wound further, tighter. Another shot from the earth and grasped his wrist. He grunted as it yanked him down, tethering him to the dirt.

Alistair's breath hitched as he took in his enemy, writhing in the grass. An image so akin to his fantasies that, if not for the cool kiss of the wind against his cheek or the frantic pounding of his heart, he wouldn't believe it real.

Gavin stilled when he caught sight of Alistair advancing closer. Alistair drank in the fear in his enemy's eyes as Gavin realized he was about to meet his end.

"You don't have to do this," Gavin choked.

"Ah, so we've reached the part where you plead."

Apparently Gavin hadn't abandoned his pride, not yet. A curse flared from one of his rings, and Alistair lazily deflected it with the Mirror. It ricocheted off the glass and struck the ground. The fallen leaves sizzled, and smoke wisped into the air.

"I wouldn't bother, if I were you," Alistair told him. Then he knelt beside Gavin. Gavin might not have been crying, as he had in his fantasies, but Alistair realized he actually preferred this version, his chest heaving, the fury contorting his features. Gavin hating him had always been better than the alternative.

"Is this how you pictured it?" Gavin spat.

"No, it's better."

"You won't break me."

"I know." Gavin Grieve might be killed, but he'd never be beaten. No champion worthy of being Alistair's true rival ever could.

"Do you have any last words?" Alistair asked.

Gavin hesitated, seeming to mull over his choice, only to repeat the same uninspired phrase from before. "You don't have to do this."

"The time for pleading is over. Your last words are supposed to mean something."

"*Fine.*" Gavin seethed. "You make a terrible villain, and one day, you're going to regret this. Because you're not like your family. You're good, no matter how hard you try not to be. And . . ."

He trailed off, his anger seemingly dried up. Alistair was almost disappointed. In his fantasies, Gavin's scorn had far more bite.

Alistair tugged off his glove, exposing the white of his skin and the only two rings he wore on his left hand: his champion's ring, and the Demon's Pyre. He'd been reserving it for just this moment.

But before he could ready himself to cast it, Gavin rasped, "I don't want to be another thing that haunts you, Al."

Alistair froze, imagining himself seeing Gavin every time he looked to the forest, every time the full moon rose. If Gavin's memory truly wanted to torment him, then it wouldn't be this fantasy that he tortured him with—it would be the others, the ones that he'd pondered at night yet spent the morning trying desperately to forget. A phantom touch tracing down his spine. The ghostly press of lips against his wrist, his neck, his mouth. A voice, comforting and tender, whispering stories to him as he tried to sleep, each one ending, not with "happily ever after," but the tantalizing phrase of "what if."

His wretched heart clenched, with rage, with longing. Even without casting a curse, Gavin had laced poison into his words, and if Alistair didn't expunge this despicable feeling now, it could prove fatal.

With his cursed hand, Alistair leaned forward and cupped Gavin's cheek, and Gavin didn't lean away, not even as the glow of the Demon's Pyre seeped over him, catching in the blond of his eyelashes—like the very image of him that had first caught Alistair so off guard.

"You're wrong," Alistair said softly, his face hovering over Gavin's. "I will never regret what I've done for my family, not even this."

A soft, shuddering breath tore from Gavin, warm and pleasant against Alistair's cheek. He'd finally realized he was going to die.

Seconds ticked past, and the Demon's Pyre burned on his fourth finger, waiting for release. Yet Alistair couldn't bring himself to move, as though time itself had caught him in a snare. So much time that hopeful uncertainty crept across Gavin's face, and Alistair warred with himself. He couldn't hesitate. This wasn't how the fantasy was supposed to go.

Then Gavin lifted his chin higher, and in such a small, simple move, rendered Alistair defenseless. Barely an inch separated their lips, and even though Alistair knew this ploy well, he couldn't stop his body from betraying him. His breath hitched. Heat flared deep in his stomach, flushing across his cheeks. It didn't matter if Alistair loathed him or not—Gavin had him entirely at his mercy.

Then a twig snapped behind them, and Alistair wrenched himself back. He shuddered, regaining himself, despising himself.

But before he could finish casting the Demon's Pyre, a cool voice cut through the trees.

"I'm sorry, Al," Hendry said. "But I'm doing this for family, too."

Alistair turned just as his brother cast a curse of his own.

The world brightened as the effects of the Conjurer's Nightmare winked out, and Alistair squinted into the glare of the red-tinged sky.

A heartbeat later, his vision went black.

GAVIN GRIEVE

"There was immense pressure to offer sponsorships to Ilvernath's families," explains Liam Calhoun, a board member of the Ilvernath Spellmaking Society. "We had no real choice in the matter—what power did we have in the face of high magick?"

Glamour Inquirer, "Ilvernath's Insiders"

The Castle had changed in Gavin's absence. His Landmark's decor was faded, tapestries shredded, knights tarnished and rusty. He peered miserably into the throne room where he'd once played drinking games with Alistair. He did a half-hearted chin-up in the home gym. He stared at his regal four-poster bed and decided that he almost—*almost*—missed the Cottage's broom cupboard.

Gavin's arm throbbed horribly from the battle with Alistair, but he wasn't brave enough to check his hourglass tattoo. Instead, he sat on the edge of the Castle's parapet, between two battlements, and tried not to cry as his legs dangled over the moat. He couldn't stop thinking about Alistair's hand on his cheek. The rage on his face. He'd wanted Alistair to touch him like that for so long that it had hardly mattered to him if it was the last thing he ever felt.

"He's still asleep." Hendry appeared out of nowhere, and Gavin startled and nearly fell.

"H-how long until he wakes up?" Gavin stammered, rattled.

"A few hours, I think. The spell I cast on him should let him rest for a while." Hendry clambered onto the wall beside Gavin, then sat, gazing up at the afternoon sky. The moors stretched out beyond them, the filtered light drenching the heather in pink and violet. "I don't think we should talk to him right away. He needs time to calm down."

"I don't think so, either." Gavin eyed the other boy's pained expression carefully. The red lag in his image had worsened, making him look blurred at the edges.

Gavin had thought Hendry would do anything to protect his brother . . . right up until he'd cursed him. Now, everything felt upside down.

"You attacked Al to help me," Gavin said. "Even though I used your life magick. Why?"

There hadn't been time to ask over the last hurried half hour, between transporting an unconscious Alistair to the Castle, stripping him of his curserings, and dragging him to a cell. The irony was not lost on Gavin that the moment he stopped claiming he wanted to lock Alistair Lowe in a dungeon was the moment he'd been forced to do so. Hendry had blinked out again while Gavin inspected the Castle, hoping grimly that the other boy would come back.

"Because I believe that you don't want to hurt him," Hendry said. "And because I really need to talk to you about something. Something important."

"So do I," Gavin said quietly. "I'm sorry for not telling you the truth about Walsh and then taking your magick anyway." Gavin's arm throbbed again, and he winced. "That was a fucked-up thing to do."

"I appreciate your apology," Hendry said. "And obviously I'm not thrilled about what you did, but I understand why."

Gavin thought of who he'd been when he'd arrived at the Cottage. Only a few weeks had passed, but it felt like a lifetime ago.

"I still feel like I need to explain myself," he said. "When I first showed up, I was desperate to win the tournament. But I—I don't want that anymore."

"I know." Hendry looked at him wryly. "You can't kill my brother. You like him too much."

Gavin flushed. "I don't—I—he just tried to kill *me*!"

"But you're still here," Hendry countered. "And he's still alive, and you don't seem interested in changing that."

"I'm not," Gavin muttered. The fantasy of Alistair Lowe, dead at his hands, had once felt like a prize all its own. Gavin now knew those thoughts had been poorly disguised attraction for far longer than he wanted to consider.

"I know he doesn't want you dead, either," Hendry said. "Or you already would be."

"Reassuring." Gavin's heart twisted painfully. "Is *this* what you wanted to talk to me about?"

"Sort of." Hendry hesitated. "I wanted to talk about ending the tournament. That . . . that's what you want now, isn't it?"

Hendry's voice quivered. He didn't sound defensive or angry, like Alistair had, but Gavin still knew he was treading somewhere extremely fragile.

"That's a complicated question," he answered carefully. "I chose to keep fighting because I thought the tournament couldn't be broken without killing all of us. I don't think that's true anymore. It's just . . ."

"It's just that it would kill me," Hendry murmured.

The two of them fell silent. The moat lapped at the edges of the Castle; a breeze rustled through the air. Eventually, Gavin heard the soft, unmistakable sounds of sniffling. He turned and saw tears glimmering in Hendry's eyes.

The first time Gavin had seen Hendry and Alistair, across a crowded pub, he'd thought of Hendry as a sun and Alistair as his shadow. But they were both shadows now, Alistair nearly consumed by his cursemark, Hendry fading like a drawing, half-erased. His freckles stood out starkly against his nearly translucent skin, and his curls wisped into smoky smudges at the ends.

"I don't want you to die," Gavin said fiercely. "Maybe you don't believe me. Maybe it doesn't matter. But it's true."

"It's all right," Hendry said bitterly. He turned away from Gavin and stared fixedly at the horizon, where the city skyline was etched in the cloudy haze. "Dying is the only thing I was ever supposed to do."

Gavin wondered if Hendry, too, had spent countless nights trying to understand why his life had been made forfeit. Trying to find some way, any way, to change the inevitable. He knew exactly how that felt. He knew exactly how it hurt.

"All the more reason you shouldn't fucking have to," Gavin said. "None of the other champions even treated you like a *person*. Neither did your family. Even Ilvernath thought you were a serial killer. It— it's not fair."

"No, it's not." Hendry shuddered. "I thought I would feel better after we killed our family, but I didn't. Because even though it was about revenge for Alistair, for me, I just wanted to prove to them that I wasn't weak. That *I* could be feared, could be worth just as much as him." His expression twisted with momentary anguish. "It feels awful to say that, as if they didn't hurt Al, too. They decided who both of us would be before we ever got the chance to figure it out on our own. I thought without them, we'd be free, but . . ." Hendry trailed off. Gavin remembered what Alistair had said, about the other Lowes haunting him. He could tell that Hendry felt the same.

"You *are* more than who they wanted you to be," he murmured. "Both of you."

Hendry wiped his eyes with his sleeve. A breeze danced across the moat, rippling Gavin's distant reflection—but since Hendry didn't have one, it looked as though Gavin sat alone. "Thank you. You know, I really thought Alistair and I might get another chance at a happy ending, at least at first. But after I died, Alistair had almost found one on his own. It's hard to wonder what might've happened to him if I hadn't come back at all. If he'd still be cursed. If he'd still be a killer. I never *wanted* him to kill anyone, especially not you."

It was true that Hendry coming back had changed everything. But Gavin didn't think it was as simple as the other boy had made it sound. Isobel and Briony had also chosen not to listen when Alistair had asked them to—maybe they would've turned on Alistair regardless. Maybe without Hendry, Gavin would've slid down a far darker path than the one he'd walked this past month. And while each of the champions had made those decisions on their own, Hendry had never had any choice in his resurrection. Just as he'd had no choice in his slaughter.

"I don't want Alistair to kill anyone else, either. But if he doesn't win . . ." Gavin scowled. "You deserve a better ending than the one your family gave you."

Hendry closed his hand into a fist, and even the slightest movements now made the red light follow him. He looked far more magick than boy. "I think something's wrong with me. I-I'm fading."

The final word came out in a cracked, rasping whisper. Gavin watched in agony as Hendry's shoulders began to shake.

"I'm sorry." Gavin was close to tears. "I'm so, so sorry."

"You saw it happen," Hendry croaked. "This morning . . ."

"Yeah, I wanted to talk to you both about it, but Al didn't want to listen."

"I'm not Al." Hendry met Gavin's gaze, and although his face was wet with tears, his stare was steady. "I've always known that if the tournament breaks, I go with it. But the tournament's going to shatter, s-soon. And even if Al wins, I don't think that'll be enough anymore."

"You don't know that for sure." Gavin wondered if he was advocating for his own death—but Alistair and Hendry had both fought so hard for their future. He hated that after everything they'd been through, there was still no way out for all three of them.

"I don't," Hendry agreed miserably. "And it hurts to think that this is how my story ends. That this is all I'll ever be, all I'll ever get." He traced a trembling hand across the scar on his own throat. "I know it's cliché, but there's still so much I want to do."

"Like what?" Gavin asked gently. "You don't have to get into it if you don't want to, but . . ." *Maybe it would help to talk about it.* Gavin had thought for so long that it was better to push such things down, but all that had done was leave each of his wants and wishes lodged painfully in his chest, tangled into bitter, aching knots.

"I wanted to go to school," Hendry admitted. "I know other kids complain about it, but it always felt so normal, and I've never gotten . . . normal." He tilted his head back, blinking furiously. "I wanted to travel. I wanted friends. I wanted to have a pet one day, a dog. I wanted to host a party, like a sleepover or a costume party or something. And I wanted to fall in love, the kind from the sort of stories my family never told."

Gavin was struck by how simple these desires were. The families claimed that the tournament gave them all some kind of grand destiny, but when it came down to it, Gavin's truest wish was to just be ordinary. No high magick, no fight to the death, a world where he'd never even heard of Ilvernath at all.

Only this morning, Gavin had been ready to accept the end of his own short life. Now he had hope that his story might not be over. But the thought of Hendry's drawing to a close with so many roads not taken, so much left unfinished, made him want to weep.

He reached for Hendry's hand and squeezed it. When Hendry squeezed back, his grip felt weak.

"You should've had all of that," Gavin said. "You never should've died for this."

"The thing is, I've died before. So I shouldn't be this upset, or this scared. Because I know that when it's over, I won't hurt. I won't want these things anymore, because I won't want anything. I won't *be* anything. So maybe the way it hurts right now doesn't matter. But I really want it to matter. I—I don't want to die knowing that everything I've suffered through meant nothing."

"Of course what happened to you matters," Gavin said, through blurred tears. "Because it matters to *you*. Because you feel something, right now. That's enough, isn't it? Doesn't that make it mean something?"

Hendry let out a harsh gasp, then descended into sobs. They cried together, as the sun sank toward the horizon, as the clouds above the city skyline dissipated into a clear sky. The clumps of heather out on the moors rustled, and Gavin heard the distant call of a bird, surprised to remember that there was anything living beneath the Blood Veil that had no idea of what was at stake.

Eventually, Hendry straightened, then clambered off the wall and onto the walkway. He looked wretched, but when he spoke, his words were no longer choked with tears. He opened his palm, revealing a familiar yellow spellstone.

"I've been trying to figure out what went wrong with this healing spell. At first, it felt like my only shot at survival—if I could cure Al, he'd be strong enough to win. But now I just want him to get better, for *his* sake." He swallowed. "I know the spellmakers used me. But I'd like to ask them for help, one last time."

Diya showed up much faster than Gavin had expected, wearing a leather jacket and a giant backpack slung over one shoulder. He dropped the wards for her, and she strolled confidently down the drawbridge.

"Thank you for coming," Gavin said, as they walked to the throne room where Hendry waited.

"Of course! I've always wanted to know what it was like inside a Landmark." Her enthusiasm echoed off the stone walls. "It's all made of high magick, right?"

"I mean, that and some ancient rubble," Gavin said dully.

Diya knocked on the nearest rusty helmet, then touched a tapestry, her hands lingering on the torn fabric. "Is it true that they change based on what kind of decorations you like?"

"I can promise you that this kind of thing is *not* my taste." Or at least it wasn't anymore.

"Hmm. Sounds like a convenient excuse so that I can't judge you."

"You said you could help," Gavin said, frustration creeping into his voice. He'd had more patience before nearly dying at Alistair's hand, before watching Hendry break down. He was long past finding awe in the tournament. "This isn't a game, Diya. Things have changed since the last time we saw each other. I don't . . ." He wasn't sure if he could trust her. But it felt unfair to ask for her help without her knowing what that really meant. "I guess I should start by saying I'm not planning on killing anybody anymore." He gave her the quickest possible version of how the fixed Relic had led to his change of heart, leaving out every embarrassing detail he could think of. As it turned out, there were plenty of embarrassing details.

"So Hendry and Alistair know you were using them," she said nervously. "And I'm not walking into an ambush?"

"No, you're not. Cast a truth spell on me if you want."

She waved a hand in the air, two of her bangles clinking together. "Don't need to. I'm pretty good at reading people. And for the record, I don't have direct access to that bug in the Tower, so I had no idea the Relic was repaired. But I'm glad to hear this can actually be finished peacefully, because . . . because things are getting scary out in Ilvernath."

"Scary how?" Gavin asked, remembering how tense things had been in town.

She raked her fingers anxiously through her pixie cut. "Everyone knows the tournament's close to breaking, but no one knows what that means. People are losing their minds over the murders, the Thorburns, the government. Not to mention high magick. And Walsh and the others . . ." She trailed off, then bit her lip. "Whatever."

"What about Walsh and the others, exactly?"

"They're being weird. Cagey. There's something they won't tell me, probably because they never wanted me to be part of this in the first place. I don't think you can trust them."

"Of course I can't trust them. But Walsh swore an oath spell to me."

Diya shrugged. Her hand tightened around one of her backpack straps, and Gavin realized it was quivering. "I'd still be careful, if I were you. Especially now that you've gone rogue. I didn't tell them I was coming here for a reason."

"Thanks for the warning," Gavin said uneasily, wondering if he should've cast a truth spell on her. Although if Reid MacTavish could ward himself against those, for all he knew, every spellmaker was walking around with some kind of immunity to compulsion spells. The thought left him deeply unsettled. "Here's your new workshop."

Diya surveyed the throne room, then wrinkled her nose. "The bloody pillar really adds to the ambiance. You're sure this isn't the dungeon?"

"The dungeon probably smells better than this." Now that Gavin could tell Diya was shaken up and probably using humor to cope, he was more willing to play along. He was grateful she'd come at all. And the blood oozing from the pillar, illusory or not, had left a metallic, coppery stench in the air.

Hendry cleared his throat and rose to his feet. He'd been sitting on a slab of rock in the corner, fiddling with the spellstone. "You came." He sounded relieved.

"It's no trouble." Diya cast him an assessing look. "Where's your brother?"

"Um. He's busy."

"Uh-huh." Diya raised a brow. "I heard you made the healing spell. Can I take a look?"

Diya set up shop at a slightly crumbled table in the corner of the room, beneath a halo of light that she conjured with a quick flash of a spellring. Gavin sat on one side of her, Hendry on the other, as she pulled a spellboard from her backpack and unfolded it on the table.

"Do you have the recipe you used?" she asked Hendry. "The filled-in version, I mean? I need to know what ingredients you chose." He handed her a folded piece of paper from his pocket.

Diya examined it thoughtfully, her expression shifting to the exact midpoint between horrified and impressed. "Holy shit, your own *finger bone*?" Hendry squirmed in his seat. "Well . . . this should've worked, if you crafted it right. Do you have the stone?"

Hendry passed it to her. She lifted the yellow quartz up to the light, frowning.

"Interesting." She set it in the center of the septogram, where it sat, dull and opaque. "Let me try something."

The amber spellstone on her choker blazed, sending a warm light dancing across the gold necklace. The spell above her flickered out—clearly, she was focusing intently—and slowly, the corners of the septogram began to glow. First one, then three, then all seven. Then, all at once, like a breath exhaling, the lights shot down the septogram and into the center of the spellboard, engulfing the healing spellstone.

"I invented this spell myself." Diya picked up the stone again, then turned it over in her palm. "It should tell me everything I need to know about this enchantment. Including . . . oh, shit."

The spellboard faded as the light within the crystal extinguished. Diya grimly set it on the table.

"What happened?" Hendry asked anxiously. "What's wrong with it?"

"Technically, nothing. The spell will work fine if you can cast it. The problem is how much power that'll take. I've examined several ancient spellstones that were crafted as class ten spells meant to be cast with high magick—so, basically, class twenty. For this spell to fully work . . . it needs *more* than that."

"What about life magick?" Gavin asked.

Diya shook her head. "Life magick's not as strong as high magick."

Hendry reached for the crystal, his expression solemn. "But I'm made of both."

Diya paused, brow furrowing. Then her eyes went wide. "What are you saying, exactly?"

But before Hendry spoke again, Gavin already knew.

"When my family killed me, they put my life magick into an enchantment," he said. "Could I do that again? Would that be enough to make it work?"

"I . . . I don't know." Diya swallowed. "If, theoretically, you *did* fill this stone with the life magick and high magick that makes you . . . exist . . . it would be extraordinarily powerful. *But* it would need to be cast by someone who can wield high magick. And right now, there's no one in Ilvernath who can do that."

"What about when the tournament ends?" Gavin asked.

"When high magick comes back, you mean?" Diya shrugged. "Then, yeah. I guess anyone could cast it."

"Not anyone," Gavin said quietly. "Not me."

"Right. About that." Diya unzipped her backpack again and rummaged around until she'd procured a syringe. "Walsh wouldn't let me attempt this at his spellshop, but I really do think I might be able to heal you. If you're willing to let me try, of course."

Gavin's heart leapt with foolish hope. That hope felt twisted when Hendry had just suggested sacrificing himself to protect Alistair, but when he turned to face Hendry, the other boy was already watching him, his gaze resolute.

"Of course I want you to try," Gavin said hoarsely.

Hendry's lips raised into a small, sad smile. But some of the tension seemed to ease from his shoulders. "I hope it—" Then he flickered out of existence, and Gavin's arm twinged with pain.

Diya yelped and jolted to the side. "What the fuck?"

"He does that sometimes," Gavin said, with a calmness he did not feel.

"How do you get him back?"

"You wait." Gavin hesitated. "There's not much else we can do."

"Well . . . do you still want me to try and cure you?"

"Yeah, I do."

Diya sent him to change into a T-shirt. When Gavin returned, she was studying a strange diagram in a well-worn notebook. Several loose flasks of raw magick were scattered across the table, and her light spell glittered above it once more.

"You said Reid basically knocked you unconscious for the procedure." She gestured for him to sit beside her. "I'd really prefer not to do that."

"I would also prefer it if you didn't do that."

"I *will* try to numb your arm, though. It'll probably still hurt, but not as badly as you described. Here's how this should theoretically work: I'll cut off your body's ability to use its own life magick as a power source. Then I'll try and restore your connection to common magick. I think Reid used a syringe because he injected a spell into you, so I'm going to do the same. But hopefully with way better results, because I am in fact a *far* superior spellmaker to MacTavish."

"Did you two know each other?"

"A little bit. Honestly, I think he's kind of full of himself."

"He's not exactly a friend of mine, either."

Diya snorted. "So I've read." She snatched up a spellstone, and white light gleamed around Gavin's bicep, rendering it pleasantly numb. A buzzy, tingling sensation spread from his wrist to his shoulder. Then she set it down, grasped his arm, and reached for the syringe.

"Just don't watch," she said. Gavin looked away obediently, but not before he saw the needle sink into the top of the hourglass tattoo.

It still hurt. A lot. So much so that, despite Diya's claims to the contrary, his vision began to darken around the edges. He swayed, woozy, then collapsed.

When Gavin came to, he was propped against the wall of the throne room. Hendry crouched in front of him, his brow furrowed anxiously.

"You're okay," he breathed.

Gavin groaned and straightened. "You're back. I—I'm glad."

"Yeah. When I showed up, you were . . . kind of unconscious."

"We stabilized you," Diya said, hurrying over. She shoved a water bottle at him; he drank deeply, greedily. "You should eat something, too. Get your blood sugar up."

"My magick," Gavin croaked, setting the water aside. "Did it work?"

"See for yourself," Diya said.

As Gavin examined his left bicep, the first thing he noticed was the hourglass tattoo. His heart sank. But then he realized that the sand inside it was gone, the interior blank. And the veins surrounding it that had once been engorged and glowing, green and purple, were now fully receded. In their place was unblemished skin.

"Is it . . . am I . . . ?"

"Cured? I think so." Diya grinned at him. "The tattoo seems to be permanent—I mean, tattoos kind of are, I guess. But your life magick shouldn't be accessible to you anymore. Which means it can regenerate naturally, over time, the way it's supposed to."

"What about common magick?" Gavin asked. "Can I cast again?"

"There's only one way to find out." She sat cross-legged on the floor beside him and tugged off one of her spellrings. "It's already filled. Class three. Pick something to move."

Gavin started to reach for it, then hesitated. He turned to Hendry, who now hovered stiffly behind Diya. But as he met the other boy's eyes, his expression softened into a smile, and for a moment he looked like the sun again, warm and hopeful.

"I didn't get to say it before, but I'm glad you're getting what you deserve," Hendry said.

"Thank you," Gavin rasped. He took the spellring and clutched it in his hand. The second the stone touched bare skin, he felt the power in it. Something he'd once taken for granted now made him shudder. A sob rose in the back of his throat.

The ring flared to life, common magick radiant. And for the first time since before the tournament had begun, Gavin Grieve cast a spell—and felt no pain at all.

BRIONY THORBURN

In this story of murder, mayhem, and madness, all of us were tempted by the thought that one of Ilvernath's Slaughter Seven could rise above their bloody destiny. That was our mistake.

Ilvernath Eclipse, "From Hero to Hated:
How Briony Thorburn Fooled Us All"

Briony paced back and forth before the massive windows on the Tower's top floor, a mock-up edition of tomorrow's *Ilvernath Eclipse* clutched in her trembling hands.

"Your family moved fast." Finley hovered in the doorway, looking perturbed. He was the one who'd brought her the mock-up. After the events of that morning, he'd checked in with the resistance to make sure everyone was safe. The good news: Innes, Gracie, and the others were fine, if a bit shaken.

The bad news: Briony and Innes's press conference had thrown Ilvernath into chaos. Panicked people had shut themselves in their homes, while emboldened protestors gathered at the Thorburn estate, demanding justice. And the flock of reporters that had hovered outside the Tower for weeks had fled, leaving only litter behind. In the midst of all this, the resistance had gotten their hands on the next day's scoop.

Briony had successfully exposed the Thorburns, but they'd done everything they could to drag her down with them. Since Briony was the one who'd thrown the press conference, she was the sole champion who'd drawn their ire—and as it turned out, her family's rage was a powerful, nasty thing.

"It's everything I've ever done wrong, but ... twisted," Briony said shakily, scanning the article. "How I hurt Innes, how I killed Carbry ... they're using it as evidence that I was ruthless, and greedy, and decided that high magick wasn't a big enough prize. They're claiming I was the one who gave our family the idea to kill people, because I wanted life magick, too."

"That doesn't even make sense," Finley protested. "You never would've told the world what they were doing if you were in on it."

"Apparently I'm 'erratic' and 'hysterical' and that's why I've imploded. Apparently I *never* could've been so close with my family and not known what they were doing. And there's no real mention of the government. Just some quote from a random representative who insists the Kendalle Parliament wasn't involved at all."

Briony slammed the paper down onto the table. Her chest heaved, and her breaths came faster and faster. A wall sconce loosened on the wall, squealing. The Tower's walls creaked, and mortar loosened, sending defensive spellstones clattering onto the floor. Briony hated the Landmark. She *hated* it. Every moment spent here was another torturous reminder of her family's treachery. She wished with all her might that she'd never claimed it in the first place.

"Hey, it's not all bad." Finley wrapped his arms around her, and she curled against him, sniffling. "The article also says that the Ilvernath PD took some of your family in for questioning. And that they verified the flask had life magick in it."

"I-I'm glad." She hiccupped. "And I doubt they'll hurt anyone else, so that's good. But everyone's going to think I was part of this. They might decide you and Isobel and Reid were in on it, too. Even if we make it out of the tournament . . . it'll still be horrible."

Briony had believed she could change her family's story. And she had—for the worse. She didn't regret what she'd done, and she felt grateful that she and Innes had found some way to do it together. But it was devastating to consider that her reward for surviving the trials to come, and the tournament's impending collapse, would be returning to a world that hated her.

"You don't know that," Finley said gently, stroking her back. "And even if they do, they don't have proof."

"Proof isn't the point," Briony said miserably. "It's all about whatever makes the best story. Your family was right—my family's *always* treated me trying to break the curse like another tournament. If they can't win, they want everyone to lose."

"I think it's a bit of a stretch to call my family *right* when they wanted me to murder you."

"I mean, Gracie said your mums joined the resistance. I think they've had a change of heart."

"Maybe." Finley's hands stilled on her back. She could tell he was deep in thought. "Why don't we rest for a little while? I know you're supposed to be working right now, but I'm sure Isobel will understand."

The tournament was breaking too fast to risk waiting for the Shoes and the Crown to fall—so Isobel and Reid had committed to making new ones. With so little time to waste, they'd decided to rotate sleep schedules while they researched potential replacement spells for the remaining Relics. Briony had been about to take her first shift when Finley arrived with the resistance update.

It was tempting to lose herself in him instead of sinking into the painful abyss of her own mind. But Briony knew that try as she might, she wouldn't be able to relax.

"No, it's okay," she said. "I want to focus on ending this. It's the only thing that matters anymore."

"It's the most important thing, yes." Finley pressed a soft kiss against her forehead. "But it is *not* the only thing that matters. Promise me you'll remember that the next time our lives are on the line."

"I promise," Briony murmured. The room, dank and dim, brightened just a little bit.

Downstairs, Isobel had taken a quilt from her bedroom and draped it around her shoulders, then pulled the couch over to the kitchen table and loaded it with an overflow of grimoires. All evidence of the ground floor's classic Thorburn decor was gone—the tapestries removed from the walls, more blankets and pillows heaped atop the couches.

But the cozy effect was dampened by the blood that wept from the pulsing crimson cracks in the pillar, as if they were open sores. Briony knew it was only magick, but it was still disgusting. The metallic, rusty reek of it hung permanently in the room, no matter what spells they cast to flush it out.

"There you are." Isobel glanced up from an ancient tome that looked as though no one had touched it in centuries. "Here—take this."

She handed Briony a notebook filled with loose, yellowed pages. Briony sat on the couch, the leather creaking beneath her leggings, and flipped it open. Dust plumed out. When she'd finished coughing, she saw lines upon lines of faint, scrawling scribbles.

"What *is* this?" she asked.

"MacTavish family notes on spatial enhancement spells." Isobel turned a page in her grimoire. "We need a speed spell for the Shoes."

"Like a Pick up the Pace, but better?"

"Exactly." Isobel hesitated. "Are you . . . are you crying?"

"No." Briony sniffled. "Maybe."

"I know about the article," Isobel said quietly. "Finley told me on his way upstairs."

"Oh." Briony bit her lip. She didn't want to talk to Isobel about bad press.

"You'll survive, you know. It'll feel like hell at first. And it might never stop hurting, not completely. But it *will* hurt less."

"Thank you," Briony mumbled. "I just feel so naive. They killed people and used me as a cover for it, and I still don't even know why."

"Our families all use us. We're raised to think it's normal. An honor, even. Falling into that pattern . . . maybe it is naive, but it's understandable. I mean, my family is selling *merchandise* about me."

"Really?" Briony asked, picturing an Isobel Macaslan–branded blood-red lipstick. "At least tell me a cut of that goes into your college fund or something."

Isobel snorted. "If we make it out of here, I'll take it up with my dad."

They lapsed into a silence that, if not comfortable, was at least companionable. Briony squinted at the text, then cast a Flicker and Flare above the page, attempting to read it better. She squirmed and fidgeted and pored over the notes for what felt like hours but was probably about thirty minutes, until at last, she blurted, "I wish I could just skip to the part where the spells are finished, and I donate life magick."

"No, you don't," Isobel said sharply. "What Reid went through to give his life magick . . . it was agony."

"It's still way less of a sacrifice than the one most champions have given this tournament."

"That's fair." Isobel sighed, then added carefully, "You and Finley offered it so willingly. I suppose you're wondering why I haven't volunteered."

Briony *had* noticed during their earlier conversation that while she and Finley had been quick to promise some of their life magick, Isobel had stayed silent. Thinking about it now struck a strange chord in her brain, knitting together an idea that she'd been too preoccupied to consider before.

"There's something wrong with you, isn't there?" she asked. "I thought it was just the stress of the tournament, or maybe the way the press was treating you, but . . . I don't know. After that battle where we got the Hammer, your breath didn't fog in the air. And you're *cold.*"

Isobel tugged her quilt tighter around herself. "Before the tournament, my family gave me a curse—an heirloom curse, so they claimed. It saved my life when Alistair nearly killed me, that day at the Champions Pillar."

After her visit to the Crypt, Briony couldn't help but have disturbing suspicions of what the Macaslans considered family magick. "What kind of curse?"

"They never told me how it worked—or, I guess, I never asked. All Dad said was that it would protect me. And it did, but there's a price to casting it. A sacrifice." Isobel swallowed and extended her hand. "Go on, check for a pulse."

Briony inhaled sharply, nearly choking on the odor wafting from the pillar, and pressed her fingers to her friend's wrist. Just as she'd noticed before, it was far too cold.

And try as Briony might, she found no heartbeat there.

"Oh," Briony whispered. "Oh, shit, Isobel, I'm so sorry. Do you have any idea how to cure it?"

"No, not yet." Isobel pulled her wrist away. "It's why I can't donate life magick. Reid isn't sure I have any to give."

Briony thought of Isobel, who'd always been so practical, so put together, choosing to conceal such a dreadful secret. It made sense that she'd want to hide it from the world. But it sent a painful twinge through Briony's chest to think of how Isobel had chosen to confide in Reid, who'd once kidnapped her, instead of her old friend.

"Your name's not crossed out on the pillar," Briony ventured. "So you're not . . ."

"No. I might look it without cosmetic spells, but I'm not dead. Something to thank my family for, I guess."

She sounded resigned, but not bitter, not exactly. Like she'd accepted the Macaslans for who they were. Briony wondered if she would ever feel that way. It was hard to wrap her head around the reality of what her own family had been willing to do for power. Harder still to think of herself as a casualty in that fight.

"I should've told you a while ago, probably—you and Finley," said Isobel.

"Then . . . why didn't you?"

"Because I was embarrassed, which is ridiculous, I know." Isobel chuckled mirthlessly. "It's such a little trade-off considering the curse saved my life, and if I had to do it over again, knowing what would happen, of course I'd still make the same choice. I used to think it was silly when all the papers called me Murderous Miss Perfect, because it's not like I don't own sweatpants or that I get top marks on every test or am not—I don't know—normal. But I was embarrassed because, deep down, I realized it did matter to me. That I really was shallow and vain. Why should I care if my body doesn't feel like my own if I'm still lucky enough to have one?"

"I don't think it's shallow to want to feel like you're in charge of your own body," Briony said firmly. "You said so yourself, our families use us. Between them and the tournament, we don't get a lot of choices. So having even more control taken away from you . . . I understand why that would make you upset."

Briony thought of how she'd insisted that ending the tournament was the only thing that mattered, even in her own mind. But Finley had been right to remind her otherwise. The toll it had taken on her *did* matter, just as the toll it had taken on Isobel did. Pushing away how badly all of this had hurt her wouldn't make breaking the curse any easier. It would just make her miserable.

Isobel smiled warmly, more warmly than she had smiled at Briony in a long time. "Thanks. I'm glad I told you. Reid only knew because my dad commissioned the curse from him, and Reid didn't know me before, not like you did."

"I'm glad you told me, too." Briony grinned back at her. "If there's any way I can help . . ."

Crimson flashed in Briony's peripheral vision.

"Look," she breathed, pointing. Isobel whipped around.

One of the two remaining stars on the pillar had begun to fall. A rivulet of blood dripped down the stone in its wake.

"The Shoes," Isobel gasped, and then, "We can't let them get another Relic."

"We can't and we won't."

Waking the boys was a trial in and of itself. Reid actively attempted to burrow under his pillow, while Finley jolted up, clearly disoriented from a nightmare. But both were quick to run for spellrings and warm clothes, and within minutes the four of them had bolted out the Tower's back door, chasing the line of red across the sky.

Briony's Pick up the Pace spell propelled her up the mountain, while Isobel and the others followed a hair behind. The rocky terrain made for a tricky climb in her trainers, but she didn't stop, didn't slow. Instead, she followed that crimson streak of light as though her life depended on it—because it did.

As it turned out, the Relic had fallen relatively close, right in front of the ruins of the Cave. Isobel and Finley cut in front of Briony before she could rush to the crater, both with a finger at their lips.

"Stay on your guard," Finley murmured, casting the Cavalier's Shield. A disc of silver metal materialized in front of his arm, carved with intricate knots. He slid his hand into the strap and raised it high. Isobel nodded in agreement and cast her Exoskeleton, while Reid's Camouflage turned him nearly invisible, and he slinked against a tree. Briony sent out a Seek and Find into the surrounding forest.

"I don't feel any other magick," she said.

"Me neither," Reid added.

"That doesn't mean there isn't any," Finley pointed out. "Let's scout the area. Fan out. Be careful."

"Someone should claim the Relic," Briony said nervously.

"It was a trap last time," Isobel countered. "Finley's right—we need to be sure we're alone."

As they crept through the wilderness, Briony wound up next to Reid—a strange echo of the time they'd retrieved the Hammer. They were both so tense, every snapped twig made them jump. When Briony fired a wild blast of cursefire at what turned out to be a bird, Reid grasped her shoulder in warning.

"Easy, Thorburn," he said. "Or you'll hit one of us next."

Briony shrugged his grip away, then sighed, her posture sagging. "I'd just like this one thing to go how we planned it."

"Believe me, I don't want Ilvernath's favorite bad boys to be here any more than you do. I've had my fucking fill of them, thanks."

"You don't want a rematch?"

"I'm good," Reid said darkly. "All of you were taught to fight a whole lot better than I was."

Briony maneuvered around a tree and pressed her back to the trunk, heart racing as she peered over the edge of the crater. The Shoes floated in the center, a simple leather pair of boots. Crimson light swirled around them in enticing whorls, sending an eerie gleam across the crater's walls.

"We weren't taught to fight," she said. "We were taught to kill."

"Yeah, I'm well aware." Reid surveyed their surroundings, then sighed, running a hand through his hair. "Before I became a champion, I thought all of you were bloodthirsty assholes."

"I mean, I definitely was an asshole. But I didn't have, like, a grand evil plan to murder everyone or anything." As Briony said it, she realized that actually was technically true. "I mean . . . ugh, you know what I mean. Yours was different."

Reid huffed. "Well, I changed. Just like you."

Reid *had* changed. She knew he'd allied with them by force, but now it really felt as though he was fighting for something more than saving his own skin. It was a surprise, but definitely not an unwelcome one.

"I've wanted to ask you something for a while now," she said, as they approached the former mouth of the Cave, treading on mossy rocks.

Reid shrugged. "Go for it."

"Why was I the one you pushed toward breaking the curse? When you talked to me about dismantling the tournament that day at Innes's party, when I read your book, it changed *everything*."

Reid had been Briony's first step down a long, winding path that had led her here, with the tournament so tantalizingly close to ending, with her own life twisted beyond recognition.

"Honestly? I tried pushing Grieve, too," Reid said. "The two of you . . . I mean, no offense, but you were both desperate."

Briony thought of herself back then, grasping at any possible excuse to be a champion. Desperate might not have been the most flattering word, but it was certainly accurate.

"None taken," she said dryly. "Do you regret it?"

"No." He spoke without the slightest hesitation.

"But I would never have bound you to the tournament if you hadn't messed with me."

"I know. Honestly, I don't really care what choices landed me here anymore. I'm . . . glad I'm here now." He sounded surprised, then nodded to himself. "Yeah. I'm glad. Whether or not I wanted to, you gave me the opportunity to fix my mistakes."

"I think we're alone!" Finley called. Briony turned and spotted her allies across the crater, shield spells dropped.

"So do I!" Briony called back.

"Briony basically told the whole forest where we are," Reid added. "So I think we'd have been attacked by now if we had company."

Briony rolled her eyes. "I was *defending us.*"

"From some random bird, yeah."

"I'll claim the Relic, then," Isobel said. Briony gave a thumbs-up as Isobel slid into the crater and headed toward the Shoes. The moment she touched them, they shrank to what looked like her size. A spellstone winked at the toe of each shoe; a third was studded at the top of the left boot.

"They really match your tracksuit," Reid said. Isobel frowned at him.

As they trekked back to the Tower, Briony thought of her family again. All her life, she'd dreamed of being remembered as the ultimate Thorburn. Now she dreaded it.

She'd spent so much time agonizing over whether she was good or bad, heroic or villainous, selfish or selfless. Now, it seemed the rest of the world had made up their mind. Even though she *had* changed, the story she told herself would leave a much smaller impact than the story the media told about her.

A story she couldn't control.

A story she didn't want.

A story that wasn't even *true.*

Briony had initially focused so hard on the tournament ending because she'd wanted to believe that it would fix all her other problems. And now that the outside world was hostile, she'd slid back into that mindset, her tunnel vision mixing with panic.

But she couldn't control what happened outside the tournament anymore. Instead, she remembered that she was defined just as much by her victories as her losses, whether the rest of the world deemed them important or not. A sister who didn't hate her anymore. An alliance that felt forged in friendship, not just necessity. Her rekindled relationship with Finley.

And a family that couldn't hurt anyone anymore, even if they'd taken her down with them.

Briony took a deep breath and focused on the next thing she could change.

The Shoes paired with the Cottage, and Alistair, Gavin, and Hendry still had the Mirror.

Soon the two sides would face each other again. And this time, Briony vowed, they would win.

ALISTAIR LOWE

"Life magick is a fascinating topic, one that science certainly has only grazed the surface in understanding. It is an intrinsic part of us. Just as our cells are made from the earth and will eventually return to it, so does our life magick. It allows us to see magick, to cast enchantments. Our species would be fundamentally different without it."

Interview with Dr. Hanife Erdogan,
SpellBC News: Asking the Experts

Alistair had always been fond of dungeons, their dankness, their darkness, but he'd never realized how dull it was to be held prisoner in one. How the days bled together. How he'd grown accustomed to his own reek. How the only anchor to his drifting sanity was his voice, muttering his name into the silence, careful not to forget it.

With a sharp stone he'd found on the grimy floor, he carved a fresh tally into the wall. Where he sat was distant from the lone torch, burning dimly near the stairwell, and so he used his fingers to trace the total number of notches, counting them by touch. "Forty-seven," he said. Logic reminded him that such a duration couldn't have passed, otherwise the tournament would be over by now, but he'd stopped paying attention to logic long ago. It made for an unpleasant cellmate, always pointing out Alistair's mistakes.

It wasn't his fault he was in here, wasting away.

"I let him distract me," he spat. "He made me hesitate. He made me think . . ."

But even alone, he couldn't bring himself to speak those words. As he scraped his stone against the wall over and over, he considered how humiliation was its own death by a thousand cuts. Even uttering his enemy's name made Alistair's already rotten heart shrivel with shame.

"When I escape, I'll kill him. I'll make his blood boil in his veins. I'll skewer him upon a stake and leave him for the crows to feast on. I'll fashion myself a crown out of his bones."

Logic also reminded him that it hadn't been his enemy who'd cursed him, but his brother. But the more times Alistair replayed their confrontation in his mind, the easier it was to rewrite it. He'd held his enemy in his arms with an army of gargoyles flanking him. His enemy had pleaded and wept, and Alistair, moved to uncharacteristic compassion, had hesitated. And then his enemy had plunged a knife into his back.

Footsteps thudded down the stairs, and the flickering figure of Hendry Lowe appeared outside Alistair's prison bars.

"You're too late," Alistair told him. "I've long descended into madness."

"It's been fourteen hours."

When Alistair refused to respond, Hendry sighed, then he sat cross-legged on the floor outside the cell. He lit a Flashlight spellring, and Alistair cringed—both from the brightness and the grave expression on Hendry's face.

"You and I need to talk," Hendry started.

"Don't do that."

"Do what?"

"Play older brother. You're about to lecture me, aren't you? Was cursing me and throwing me in a dungeon not punishment enough?"

Hendry winced. "I'm sorry. I-I had to do something."

"No, you didn't." Alistair seethed, squeezing the stone so tightly that it bit into his palm. "Would you believe what Gavin told me when he bothered to show up again? That he *switched sides*. That he suddenly realized the curse can be broken—"

"I know. I've talked to Gavin, too."

"Then you already know what a shit he is." Alistair stood up and paced around his cell. His legs were stiff from weeks and weeks of disuse, and he stroked his chin, surprised he hadn't grown a full beard by now. "It doesn't matter. Things will be harder going forward, but not impossible. If we corner him, I'll find a way to distract him, while you—"

"I don't want to fight Gavin." Hendry sighed and knit his hands together in his lap. "I never really did."

"What do you mean?" Alistair snapped. "What did he say to you? Because if he claimed he found a way to save you *and* break the tournament, he's lying. He just wants you to think—"

"Listen to me, Al," Hendry said, and Alistair halted, staring at Hendry's unusually somber expression, so very like the ones their family had worn that day Alistair would give anything to forget. "When I came back, I was so angry. I—"

"You had a right to be angry," Alistair told him fiercely.

"I know. I wanted a second chance, and I thought I had to fight for it. Mum and Grandma . . . they clearly believed I was worth more to the family dead than alive, and I thought that I could prove them wrong."

"They've *always* been wrong."

"I know. I *know*. But you're not hearing me. I don't want to be like them. I don't want anyone to die for me, or kill for me. Least of all you. So I've made up my mind."

Alistair's dread pulsed through him, stronger than his own heartbeat. A darkened room. A hushed voice, urging him to listen. He'd lived through enough of his family's horror stories to know how one began.

"What are you saying?" he rasped.

"You wanted to break the tournament, before. I don't want to be what stands in your way."

Alistair didn't trust himself to speak—not to shout, not even to whisper. His composure was fracturing, each of Hendry's words a fresh crack. If he let out even a single breath, he would shatter.

Again.

"Before you ask if Gavin convinced me, he didn't. This was my decision. But there is something else that you should know," Hendry continued. "I met with Diya, and we think we found a way to fix my healing spell. If I put all my life magick into the stone, when the tournament is over, you—"

"No," Alistair gritted out between clenched teeth. "I don't care about being cured—I'm not losing you again. How could you—"

"I was already lost."

"So? You're here now. You're alive. You really want to—"

"Yes, I *do* want to. The tournament is collapsing, one way or the other. And if I-I'm . . ." Hendry's voice trembled. "If I'm going to die either way, I'd rather be a casualty in a good story than a terrible one. And that's what I want for you, too. A good story. Isn't that what you want, Al?"

Alistair's imagination, always overactive and overeager, slipped out of his grasp. His entire life, he'd wanted a future with him and his brother, happy, free. And though he'd always known that freedom would only last until Ilvernath's curse called to their family once more, he'd never considered an alternative. That future meant everything to him, the furthest limits of what he could want.

But now he imagined a new future. He imagined the Lowe name being rendered meaningless. He imagined growing old without his brother. He imagined quiet nights spent alone, homework and crosswords, takeout dinners and evening news and places far, far away from Ilvernath. He imagined nights that were neither quiet nor alone. How it would feel to have someone and know they could have each other always, without counting down the days until the moon shone red. Alistair would always look like a monster from the Reaper's Embrace, but if he begged forgiveness, if he learned how to be good, maybe he wouldn't be miserable.

It was the guilt that made him come apart. He couldn't control every twist and turn of his thoughts, but he *could* control what he wanted. And he was not allowed to want this.

"You think I'd rather you were gone?" Alistair growled.

"Of course not," Hendry said softly. "But do you *want* to kill the others? To be what they say you are?"

Alistair's shoulders shook. "I just want us both to live."

"So do I, and it's not fair, but we can't. And I've already made up my mind."

"So that's it? I don't get a say? You're just abandoning me?"

"I am *not* leaving you alone."

"Oh, how could I forget? I have Maggot. I have a fan club who draws me with fangs and a six-pack. And I have five other champions who hate me. A world that hates me." Alistair was so distraught that each word came out blubbered, loud, furious. His balance veered, and so he sank into a crouch, his arms hugged around his knees, his back pressing into his forty-seven tallies. The memories he'd tried so desperately to lock away prickled at him like thorns. The last words his mother had spoken to him. The forest outside his family's home. How he'd run there afterward, Maggot's hand crushed in his, Hendry only paces behind them. How he'd kept looking over his shoulder, feeling like he was in a dream, or a monster story. But in those stories, the monsters always won.

With a spell, the metal padlock on the dungeon cell unlatched and fell with a *clank* to the ground. Hendry knelt beside Alistair and wrapped him in a hug. Alistair buried his face in his brother's chest, and there was so little substance to Hendry now, he could barely feel him. But he could smell him—like pastries and grass, like home.

"What about Gavin?" Hendry asked quietly.

"What about him?" Alistair said scathingly. "He's probably with the others now, playing hero."

"He's still here. He's upstairs."

Alistair's breath hitched, but he didn't let go of Hendry. "What do you mean?"

"He's waiting to see if you're all right, if you'll go with him."

Even though Alistair had heard him perfectly, his words didn't make sense. Alistair had replayed their next encounter over and over in his mind, and in no scenario did Gavin forgive him. It had to be deception.

"That doesn't make sense." His voice quivered. "He's lying, somehow."

"He's not, but I think you are. I heard you the other night, talking to Gavin. You asked him what the two of you would be, in a different story."

Hendry's accusation bore no malice, yet it buried like a dagger into his gut. Alistair wrenched back, furiously wiping his eyes. "Wh-what? That wasn't . . . You don't understand—"

"I'm not angry. I'm relieved. I want you to want something else, after I—"

"No, I mean, you don't understand—I always do this to myself. I get these . . . twisted thoughts about whoever is close to me." Alistair dug his nails into his legs. "It's not real. It's just a way to hurt myself or trick myself into believing that things are different. Because I'm too weak to be champion, just like Grandma always knew I'd be. I wasn't terrible enough for her, and I'm too terrible for anyone else."

"That isn't true," Hendry said. "That's never been true."

"Then what about Isobel? I'm just repeating the same pattern, aren't I? And when Gavin and I fought . . ." Alistair stared at his hands, both of them bone white. "He must hate me."

"He doesn't. I promise you, he doesn't."

Alistair didn't know if he believed that. He wanted to, but that made it dangerous.

"But even if that's true . . ." Alistair struggled to get the words out. "What must I look like, now?"

Hendry cupped his brother's cheek. "You've never not looked like you, not to me."

"*Don't*," Alistair warned, because he realized he didn't want to hear it. He didn't want to hear one good thing ever again.

Several minutes later, when Alistair had stopped crying, Hendry said, "I know you'll be okay, but I need you to tell me."

Alistair wasn't so sure. For all he knew, when the tournament broke, it could take all the champions down with it. If he was going to lose Hendry, more than anything, he didn't want it to be for nothing.

"Please," Hendry said hoarsely.

"I'll be okay," Alistair choked, but he did not want to be.

Hendry squeezed his hand and stood, pulling him up. "Then come on. Let's go."

"Now? Right now?" Alistair asked, alarmed.

"I don't want to wait any longer. The tournament is crumbling, and if I disappear again, I might never get another chance."

"But how will I convince the others I'll help them? I don't think I can—" He swallowed. "I don't know how to be good without you."

"I know you can, because you already have been."

Alistair let himself be led out of his dungeon and up the stairs. He squinted into the daylight filtering through the windows of the Castle. It felt as though barely any time had passed since he was last here, and he hadn't realized such recent memories could cut him so deep. How he'd set Briony free, the one thing he'd *known* was good, that he'd been sure of through and through. How Isobel had disappointed him. How Gavin had goaded him until he'd buried Hendry's ring, with neither of them understanding what consequences that tiny action would cause.

The brothers strode down the corridor until they reached the entrance to the courtyard.

Gavin stood there, over a small mound in the dirt. But instead of looking down, his gaze was fixed skyward. He turned at their approach, and Alistair realized that the tattoo on his bicep, normally swollen and bruised, resembled an ordinary one. And there was a strength to his stature, a color to his face that he'd never seen before.

He'd done it. He was cured.

Alistair stiffened then quickly wiped his face with the sleeve of his sweater. "Leave," he said, relieved that his voice was level. "*Leave*."

"All right," Gavin said softly.

Before Gavin could disappear beneath an archway, Hendry asked, "Could you get the chalk powder?"

Gavin's brow furrowed. "Now?"

"Now," he murmured. After Gavin left, Hendry added, "I don't know if it will work, but it's the best chance we've got."

Alistair nodded numbly, struggling to pay attention. He glanced over his shoulder, but there were no monsters there. His mother's scream had never sounded so loud, so close.

"Take care of Marianne, if you can," Hendry told him.

"Sure."

"Sell the house. Burn it. Just don't go back there again."

"All right."

"Even if this doesn't work, don't give up on your curse. You'll cure it one day, I'm sure of it."

Alistair didn't know how Hendry could speak with such certainty about a future after the tournament. Alistair could just as easily end up in the ground with him.

Gavin returned carrying a jar of chalk powder. Wordlessly, he handed it to Hendry, who tipped it and drew a seven-sided star over the same mound of dirt where Alistair had once buried the Lamb's Sacrifice.

Then he stepped into the center of it.

Alistair's breath caught in his chest, and as Gavin hurriedly started to leave, Alistair seized him by the wrist. Gavin jolted, immediately bracing himself in the defensive, as though Alistair was going to attack him.

"Stay," Alistair whispered. "Please."

Immediately, he regretted it. He was leaving the door open all over again, hurting himself for the sake of it.

But then Gavin nodded, and he moved to stand at Alistair's side. Alistair's breath burst out, shaky, and he was unsure whether or not he should feel relieved.

Below his feet, Hendry placed the empty spellstone.

"I've decided to call my spell the Wishing Flower," Hendry said. And then, impossibly, he smiled one of his true sunlight smiles. "It feels good to do the right thing. It feels better to know how much they would've hated it."

Alistair wanted to say something. He was normally good with words, good with stories. Yet, even if unintentional, Hendry's choice of name had tainted some of Alistair's most precious memories, of broken leaves and dandelion spores, of wishes he now knew would never be fulfilled. But the name was still beautiful, still undeniably Hendry, and Alistair would never forgive himself for spoiling the moment.

And so, wordlessly, he lurched forward—nearly tripping over himself—and threw his arms around his brother. Of all things that were right and good, the two of them had always felt like the one right and good thing he had. It'd always been them and no one else.

"I love you," Alistair said.

"I love you, too."

"I'll be okay."

"I know."

Alistair still didn't, but it was a comfort to hear Hendry say that. He could believe anything if his older brother told him to.

After what could've been a few seconds or forty-seven days, Alistair stepped back toward Gavin.

"All right." Hendry's voice trembled, but only a little.

He slid the ring onto his finger.

His body, already flickering with magick, began to glow red, first faint and then brighter, until he was radiant. Gradually, his solid form faded, growing transparent until all that remained of Hendry Lowe was a sheer reflection, a trick of the light.

Alistair became dimly aware of Gavin beside him.

"I—" the other boy said, then coughed uncomfortably. A second later, he grabbed Alistair's hand and interlaced their fingers.

A ruse, Alistair's instincts warned. But for this one brief, horrible moment, he ignored them. He squeezed tight.

When his brother disappeared entirely, the ring fell and plunked onto the grass. Its inside pulsed scarlet with high magick.

Alistair let go of Gavin's hand so he could pick it up. He slid it onto his pointer and turned, wiping away tears even as more continued to fall.

"I'm sorry," Alistair said. His first good thing, and he was terrified of it. Terrified that Gavin would reject it—or worse, twist it. Whatever Alistair felt for Gavin, whether it was genuine or a symptom of self-sabotage, he didn't need Gavin to return it. But Alistair didn't know how he'd go forward if he didn't have someone to believe in him. And he wanted that someone to be Gavin.

"Me, too." Gavin's voice was distant and unsure. The way they'd used to speak to each other.

"Why did you stay? After what I did, you had the Mirror, you were cured . . . You could've left."

"No, I couldn't have," Gavin answered seriously. "I'm not going without you."

In a bout of weakness, of confusion, of whatever he wanted to call it, Alistair embraced Gavin, his arms locked around his enemy's shoulders. Gavin froze for a moment, but then his hands folded around Alistair's back. Alistair felt strangely small within them, and he didn't mind it. He grasped at Gavin tighter—his fingers intertwining with the cotton of his T-shirt—and pressed his face into his chest. Gavin couldn't let go now even if he tried.

"Hendry wanted me to help you," Alistair said.

"Is that what you want?" Gavin asked warily.

Alistair's imagination leapt, painful and guilt-ridden and yearning. "Yes."

ISOBEL MACASLAN

"Put me in a death tournament with my ex? Nope. He's not lasting till morning."

Glamour Inquirer, "Your Opinions,
an Alistair and Isobel Reunion"

Where are they?" Reid asked as the four of them waited at the
ruins of the Monastery, its charred rubble a dark blight on
the moors. Dense storm clouds roiled overhead, and while
the first raindrops had yet to fall, the air felt charged, as though moments before a lightning strike.

Isobel spit a strand of hair out of her mouth as the wind battered
against her back. According to her watch, it was precisely noon, the
time that she and Gavin had arranged to meet.

For a truce, so Gavin claimed, and his message had sounded sincere enough. But even if Isobel had chosen to stake her life on a happy
ending, she hadn't relinquished her logic. Every one of her instincts
warned that this was a trap.

"Maybe they're a no-show," said Finley warily.

"We could go back," Reid suggested.

"Gavin offered us the Mirror," Isobel reminded him. Dubious
or not, it was an opportunity they couldn't turn down. They'd even
brought the Shoes at his request, and she hugged their leather soles
tightly to her stomach.

Reid clenched and unclenched his fist, each finger stacked with
several cursestones. "Whatever. Just don't let your guard down."

"Do I *look* like I'm letting my guard down?" Briony held her arms
outstretched, maintaining the Prismatic Protector that surrounded
their hill at all sides. She quivered from effort as much as from the
force of the wind.

Muttering under his breath, Reid slunk away to the highest point on the hill—a boulder swathed in moss and a rippled crust of lichen. A lookout. He climbed atop it and glowered at the ruddy horizon.

Isobel followed and sat at his feet, trying to decide what comfort to offer someone before a rendezvous with the people who'd tortured them two days ago. After *her* last confrontation with Alistair, she could use some comfort herself.

Thankfully, Reid saved her from speaking first. "I've felt better, if you're wondering."

"I don't blame you."

"They slid *needles* under my *fingernails*."

She cringed, remembering the state she'd found him in at the Cottage—the swollen mess of his crushed hand, the vomit caked down his shirt. "So you think it's a trap?"

"I don't know. It would make for a poor one, warning us ahead of time." He paused. "You seem nervous."

"Do I?" she bit out sarcastically, fiddling with the Shoes' laces on her lap.

"No one relishes a reunion with their ex."

Isobel didn't know how he could manage to tease her right now, in that matter-of-fact, arrogant tone she'd always loathed. "He's not my . . ." But when she glared up at him, she realized he was smiling, and she couldn't bring herself to snap at him. She no longer loathed anything about Reid MacTavish.

"Last time Alistair and I spoke," Isobel told him gravely, "he said I didn't know how to believe in anything."

"Interesting. Was this before or after he tried to kill you?"

"Before, and I'm not trying to defend him. But if this isn't all some ploy, if he's really coming here to help us, then I was wrong about him. He's not beyond saving."

"It was never your responsibility to save him."

"Not even after he saved me?" After Alistair had sacrificed himself for Isobel to fix her magick, she'd repaid him by betraying him. "What if I made a mistake?"

"You know you're asking the wrong person," Reid said.

"Maybe you're the only right person to ask."

He lowered himself beside her. Their thighs touched, and even through their clothes, he was warm. No doubt he must've found her cold, but he didn't move away.

"If you tallied every wrong you did to each other, would it really matter if they were even or not?" he asked. "If Alistair hurt you one more time than you hurt him, would you feel better?"

"Probably not," she answered bitterly.

"Then why dwell on it?" Reid's voice shrunk to a throaty whisper. "Is it because you miss him?"

"I did, for a little while. But we weren't good for each other. The whole time we were together, his mind was somewhere else, chasing some fairy tale." Just because Isobel had liked his monster stories didn't mean she wanted to live in one. "So no, that's not why I dwell on it. I dwell on it because no matter how much we've hurt each other, ultimately, he will die, and that will be my fault."

"You've never forced him to kill or torture anyone," Reid pointed out. "The Reaper's Embrace is only deadly if the victim is—"

"We're in a death tournament," she snapped. "You know it's not that simple."

"Sorry. You're right, you're right." He drummed his fingers against the rock. "I want you to feel better, but the truth is, I do kind of hope you forgive him."

"What? Why?"

"Because it makes me hope you could forgive me."

Isobel couldn't pinpoint the exact moment when Reid had earned her forgiveness, but he had. Even so, she couldn't muster up the nerve to look him in the eyes, to burn under the heat of his stare. Because he might've been wrong about her when they'd first met, but now, he knew her. He saw *through* her. And after a year of assumptions and accusations and judgment, she'd almost forgotten what that felt like.

It felt good. But it also put her on edge.

"I'm pretty sure I forgave you a while ago," she said.

"Pretty sure?"

"Ah, there's that mocking tone again."

"Sorry—I'm still thinking about the fingernails. Have you considered that you have the most intimidating ex-boyfriend in the world?"

She snorted. "Once *again*, he's not my—"

Her words died when two figures appeared at the edge of the Monastery's wreckage.

Gavin and Alistair.

As the pair sighted the group and started toward them, Isobel and Reid leapt off the boulder and rushed down the hill to Briony and Finley. The boys halted at the edge of the shield, and the spell's light rippled over them like rays of sunshine on a lakebed. Gavin looked freshly showered, while Alistair was oddly filthy, as though he'd slept on the forest floor. Isobel didn't put it past him that he had.

But more shocking than Alistair's hygiene was his cursemark. It now engulfed more than half his face, rendering one of his irises and most of his hair an unnatural, colorless white. He looked like the sort of monster that the children of Ilvernath whispered about.

Automatically, Isobel clenched her fist, readying her enchantments in case of attack.

But neither the boys' stances nor their expressions bore any indication of battle. Gavin seemed hopeful. Alistair, shaken.

He did not look at her.

One of Gavin's spellrings flashed, and Isobel and the others scrambled back.

"What are you—" Briony gasped out, but before she finished, matching lines of white traced across both boys' throats, glimmering even against the pallor of Alistair's skin. A truth spell.

"Thank you for agreeing to this," Gavin told them. "As you can see, we've brought the Mirror, and we're ready to help in any way we can."

Isobel narrowed her eyes. Though she doubted that Gavin knew how to utilize the same extremes as Reid to thwart the power of truth spells, the image starkly reminded her of Hendry Lowe, who was notably absent.

"Where's your brother?" she asked, unable to hide the accusation in her tone.

Alistair tensed, as though he hadn't been expecting this question, as simple and obvious it was. When his two-toned gaze at last found hers, he rasped, "He's gone. It was his own choice. He wants the curse broken."

Guilt stabbed through Isobel like the point of a stake. Even if he'd lost Hendry before, she knew Alistair well enough to imagine how agonizing that goodbye must've been.

"So . . ." Gavin said awkwardly. "Where do we begin?"

No silence on the moors was truly silent, with the wind free to howl across the open skies and the mountains to echo in response. But as the seconds ticked past and no one spoke, gradually, the champions inside the shield relaxed their defensive stances. With a sigh of relief, Briony lowered her arms, and the Prismatic Protector faded until no divide remained between them.

"The Shoes and the Cottage are part of the Grieve story," Gavin said. "But I think you already guessed that."

"Yeah," Briony admitted. "And the Mirror and Tower belong to the Thorburns."

"I thought we could trade. I-I know it doesn't matter, but I want to be there to unite my family's Relic and Landmark. I want to be there when they break." His eyes fell on the Shoes in Isobel's hands, and, casting the last of her suspicion aside, she handed them to him. Expressionless, he inspected the spellstones in their toes, the sagging, peeling leather.

Wordlessly, Alistair held out the Mirror. Isobel numbly took it. When she peered into the glass, Alistair's own reflection stared back at her.

Just as he did now.

She swallowed. The last time she and Alistair had stood so close together, he'd been trying to kill her. And though she knew she had nothing to fear, countless other emotions hovered in the space between them, oppressively heavy. It seemed she *could* suffocate without needing to breathe.

"Are you sure you want to face the Cottage alone?" Finley asked. "The trials force you to play out the truth of each family's legacy, which I swear is more dangerous than it sounds. And if there's six of us now, we could split in half."

Alistair flashed his familiar sneer of a smile. "And which of you would like to volunteer to join us?" When they tensed, he continued, leveling a glare at each of them, "Briony? Isobel? Reid? *You?*"

Finley shifted. "I . . ."

"No," Gavin cut in. "Al and I will handle it alone. And when we all finish, that only leaves—"

"The Castle and the Crown," Alistair murmured. "The Lowe story."

"But the Crown hasn't fallen," said Gavin. "Do we wait for it?"

Reid cleared his throat, yet he still choked out his words. "W-we don't have time for that." Though he obviously spoke at the two boys, his gaze was fixed firmly on the swaying grass. "This curse is unraveling around us, which means we need to craft a replacement Crown, and I think we can pull it off. Isobel and I managed it for the Cloak."

Alistair cocked his head to the side. "I guess it's lucky we didn't kill you then, huh?"

"Cool it, would you?" Finley snapped.

"Oh, I'm sorry," said Alistair. "I missed the part where we agreed we have to be friends just because we're on the same side."

"Believe me, none of us are pretending to be friends," Reid growled.

"*Enough.*" Briony stepped between them, her shoulders heaving. "We can all hate each other when this is over. But until then, we have to work together."

"When this is over," Gavin repeated softly.

They quieted, and Isobel studied each of them. Even though it'd taken so much heartbreak to reach this point—some of it demanded, some it needless—if they succeeded, they wouldn't simply be the six surviving champions of the tournament.

They would be the last ones.

Clinging to that notion and whatever courage it offered, she blurted, "Alistair, can I speak to you for a moment? Just over there?" She nodded at the same boulder where she and Reid had sat minutes before.

Alistair stiffened. Then, his voice losing the edge it'd once had, he murmured, "All right."

The pair of them trekked up the hill, and even once they were out of earshot, Isobel could feel the others staring at them, rubbernecking. She tried hard to ignore them and focus on Alistair, who watched her intently with his eerie, mismatched eyes.

"I'm sorry," she forced out. "What you told me in the woods—you were right. After everything we'd been through together, I should've trusted you. Instead I . . ."

"Cursed me?" he finished for her flatly.

Isobel almost wished the sky would storm now, that a bolt of lightning would strike her down on this very spot. "Yeah."

She waited, yet Alistair's countenance remained as stoic as ever. She'd thought her apology would have an effect on him. Maybe not forgiveness, but anger, sadness. Instead he merely looked empty.

"You shouldn't be sorry," he told her. "If I'd joined your alliance, eventually I'd have realized Hendry couldn't be saved. Which means, one way or another, I would've betrayed you."

"You're here now."

"Am I? Because I feel . . ." He peered down at his hands, both now consumed by the cursemark. And despite how much his face had changed, Isobel realized she knew that expression—he was somewhere else, lost. When he finally returned, if only slightly, he asked, "Why doesn't your breath fog in the air?"

Isobel hugged her arms to herself, both surprised and self-conscious that he'd noticed such a small detail. "When your death curse struck me, that day at the Champions Pillars, I paid a price to survive."

He let out a noise that could've been a sigh or could've been a laugh. "The two of us really made monsters of each other, didn't we?"

She flinched, but she couldn't deny the truth of his words. "I'm sorry. I know you said I shouldn't be, but I am."

Alistair twisted a cursering around his finger. "You know, I kept a lot of the enchantments you helped me make. They saved my life a few times."

Isobel knew that Alistair had offered her consolation, not redemption, yet a small fragment of her burden lifted from her shoulders with the relief of a sigh.

"And same for yours," she told him. The Dragon's Breath had burned away the maggots in the Crypt.

Alistair smiled at her weakly, then, without a goodbye, he stalked down the hill. Isobel let several seconds pass before she mustered up the nerve to rejoin the others.

"So you're saying we shouldn't trust the spellmakers?" Briony asked Gavin.

"If you can help it, don't trust anyone," Gavin told her. "But yeah, they bugged you, and they've been helping us. I don't think they did it for the right reasons, and I don't plan on telling them that I've changed our deal." He turned to Alistair. "Ready?"

"As I'll ever be," Alistair muttered. Then, to Briony and Finley, he nodded. "Good luck."

"You, too," Finley told him.

While the others finished their goodbyes, Reid watched from higher up the hillside, as though still determined to keep a reasonable distance between him and Gavin and Alistair. He was wound so taut that he jolted as Isobel stepped beside him, then he leaned down and whispered in her ear, "How'd it go?"

"It went . . . all right."

He grunted noncommittally.

Though she'd avoided it before, Isobel finally met his gaze, and she shivered despite the heat of it. A question burned in her throat, one she'd been working herself up to asking for a long time, but had been too scared to hear his answer.

"Do you think there's a way I can heal myself?"

Something flitted across his expression, and Isobel guessed that he was also thinking of the day they met, when he'd crafted the Roach's Armor on her father's commission.

A smile crept over his face, even as he bit it down. "I guess you really have forgiven me, if you're finally asking me that."

Isobel shoved him with her shoulder. "Don't push your luck."

His grin faded, and he buried his hands in his pockets. "I'll admit it—I've thought about it, a lot. And I wish I had something better to tell you. Even though I crafted the curse, it's a Macaslan recipe, and it's unusual, with the sacrifice paid by the caster."

"Oh," she said softly.

"But I'm going to try—I promise. As a cursemaker, I know I'm in the business of harm, and I think . . . that's always bothered me. I can't pretend that's why I wanted to break the tournament, but it was a piece of it. When this is all over, I want to use what I know for something good, and I can't think of anything better to start with than you."

A promise to try was not a guarantee, but Isobel didn't let her disappointment show, unwilling to tarnish the hope that brimmed so obviously in his eyes. After every monstrous thing the two of them had done to each other, she hadn't realized that Reid cared so much about her. Warmth kindled in her stomach, and, flustered, she tore her gaze away, out to the horizon.

Still, she dwelled on his words. He spoke about after the tournament with *when*, not if—something she'd never yet dared to do. But for the first time, she imagined what that after might look like. Late-night sleepovers with Briony. Returning to school with Finley. Even weekend visits to Reid's curseshop.

She wanted that—normalcy. She wanted it so badly she could almost feel her heart ache with it.

"Thank you," she told him, while at the same time, Briony waved them down from the bottom of the hill.

It was time to depart.

BRIONY THORBURN

Neither Briony nor Innes Thorburn can be reached for comment regarding the allegations of assault revealed by their family. However, leaked medical records do provide evidence of a severed finger, and Briony Thorburn's last-minute entry into the tournament cannot be denied. If she's capable of maiming her own sister, what else could Briony Thorburn have condoned?

Glamour Inquirer, "Betrayal Beneath the Blood Veil"

Rain splattered against Briony's shoulders, and the wind whipped her braid behind her head. Above her, clouds descended on the horizon, dark and heavy with the promise of a burgeoning storm. Her allies were inside the Tower, waiting, ready. But Briony found herself frozen outside the door, clutching the Mirror, filled with dread.

Gavin Grieve had told her that he and Alistair had been allied with a group of spellmakers. Spellmakers who'd bugged them. Spellmakers who'd been experimenting with his life magick. Spellmakers who couldn't be trusted.

She'd put her allies and Innes in danger, destroyed her family, had her reputation annihilated by the press. She'd thought her actions were worth it to stop whatever the Thorburns and the government were planning. But it couldn't be a coincidence that spellmakers were *also* experimenting with life magick. And if they were working with the government just like the Thorburns . . . if their plans still weren't finished . . .

Then everything she'd sacrificed had been for nothing.

"Briony?" Finley emerged from inside, frowning. "Are you coming?"

"I . . ." Briony swallowed. "I can't put it all together, Fin. We still don't know what final plan the government was working toward—we just know they want high magick. What if breaking this curse is playing right into their hands?"

Once, she'd thought the government regulating high magick would be a good thing. But seeing what they were willing to do to obtain it made her doubt they'd use it well.

"I've been thinking about that, too," Finley said gravely. "But the curse is close to breaking, no matter what. We need to end it our way before it's too late."

Inside the Landmark, the fairy lights popped and burned out, crumpling to the ground. Some of the pillows and cushions had split, spilling foam and feathers like entrails onto the floor. In the midst of all this, Reid and Isobel were collecting their strongest enchantments. Once the Tower was destroyed, anything they left behind would be destroyed with it.

"It's like someone threw a rager in here," Reid complained, cramming spellrings onto his fingers.

"It's about to collapse," Isobel said, casting Briony a cautious glance. "Who cares what it looks like?"

"Does everyone have their essentials?" Finley asked. Briony hurried to her bedroom and grabbed all her favorite spells. The rest didn't matter anymore.

Attaching the Mirror to the pillar was virtually impossible. Blood welled from the cracks, too slippery for her to lodge the handle into. She shoved it into a fissure at the top, where it teetered before slumping sadly out of the rock. When Reid snorted and even Finley chuckled at how absurd it looked, Briony felt ridiculous.

"I'm *trying*," she grumbled. "You said there was some special slot for the Medallion? We hung the Cloak on that creepy statue . . ."

"You could show the pillar its own reflection," Finley suggested.

But that didn't work, either. Briony groaned. Alistair and Gavin were probably halfway through destroying their Landmark by now.

"Think about the truth of your family," Isobel said. "What would they do?"

"I don't know," Briony snapped. "We spied on people! We used their weaknesses against them! We were two-faced and horrible, and . . . and . . ."

Briony grasped the Mirror tightly, her hands shaking.

"Briony?" Finley sounded concerned.

"And I destroyed it," Briony whispered. "I destroyed everything."

She lifted the Mirror above her head, just like she'd lifted the Hammer. Then she slammed it against the rock. It shattered immediately, not just the glass, but the empty frame. The three spellstones flew across the room. One hit Reid in the shoulder.

"Some warning would've been nice," he muttered.

But there was no time to respond.

The trial had begun.

The shards of glass on the floor shuddered, then rose one by one, spinning like vicious little tops. They whirled around the room as the ground shook, doors slamming shut while the Tower walls closed in. The plant on the windowsill crashed onto a rug; furniture skidded toward them, chair legs screeching. The kitchen table toppled, sending grimoires tumbling everywhere.

A single path remained unobstructed—the staircase.

Briony knew a trap when she saw one. But it didn't matter.

"The stairs!" she called out, bolting onto the first step. The others followed. The moment Reid's feet touched the bottom stair—he was the last of them—they began to *move*, hurtling them up through the Tower like an escalator, whiplash-fast. They collided with the door on the upper landing. Briony staggered forward, dizzy, and threw it open.

All four of them rushed in and fanned out as the room changed, walls and floor widening in an impossible feat of architecture. The door to Briony's bedroom had vanished, as had their way out, replaced by solid stone. The books and junk they'd left behind blew everywhere, clearing the table at the center of the room. Soon, all that remained on the map of Ilvernath were the crimson miniatures of each champion. They stood in a neat row, each one pulsing with a menacing red light.

"Oh, shit," Reid said. "Are they *growing?*"

Finley frowned. "That can't be good."

Sure enough, each tiny champion shot up in size, doubling again and again in the span of a few breaths. They grew until the table collapsed beneath them, until there was not one, not two, but seven figures staring back at the four of them, each a terrifyingly detailed, life-size statue made of crimson marble.

Finley looked disturbed. Reid clenched his hand, curserings glowing, while Isobel readied herself into a defensive stance.

They were the champions as the tournament had originally intended: Carbry Darrow. Elionor Payne. Gavin Grieve. Alistair Lowe. Isobel Macaslan. Finley Blair.

And Innes Thorburn.

The statues gazed at the four flesh-and-blood champions with murder in their scarlet eyes. The two who were dead bore the wounds that had killed them—Elionor's intestines dangled from her abdomen, while arrows protruded from Carbry's eyes and throat.

Briony thought she might be sick. The Thorburns had a penchant for reflections, for knowing one's enemy, for psychological damage. But she had never imagined the truth of their story would produce a trial like *this*.

She had only a heartbeat to take in the scene before the false champions attacked.

The crimson Alistair lunged for Isobel. Finley bolted toward his own double, who was already drawing a Sword identical to the one he and Briony had destroyed. Briony cast an Avalanche on the ceiling above their opponents, temporarily burying the false Isobel and Innes in a pile of stone. The statue of Gavin flung himself at Reid, and that was all Briony had time to see before Carbry Darrow's overgrown miniature slammed her into the nearest wall.

He was much stronger in death than he'd been in life. The arrow in his throat dug into her shoulder, and she gasped, kicking at his knee. Her trainer collided painfully with solid stone, and he stumbled back. She seized that opportunity to cast a Guillotine's Gift. The curse struck him, but instead of severing his head from his body, it left a mere fracture on his neck. His blank, lifeless expression didn't change as he attacked her again. Briony ducked beneath his outstretched arms and cast an Arachnid's Anger. It pinned Carbry against the wall in a sticky net, where he wriggled like a trapped insect—then slowly but surely began to pull the strands of magick away. It wouldn't hold for long.

Someone's back brushed hers, and she whirled. But it was only Finley, who'd conjured his Lightning Lance to defend against the Sword his false opponent wielded. Elionor shambled toward him, too, her intestines dragging on the floor like worms.

"Magick barely works on them," he called out.

"I've noticed," Reid yelled from his battle with Gavin. "I think it's because they're made of high magick."

Beside him, Isobel fired curse after curse Alistair's way. Carbry yanked another section of webbing free. Briony glanced across the room, where the statues of Isobel and Innes had shaken off most of the rubble, their forms bathed in the light that poured through the hole now gaping in the roof. They moved at half the pace she'd expected.

"They're slower than us," Briony said, turning back to Carbry. Something glinted on his face, something that wasn't stone, but she only had a second to squint at it before he broke free of his restraints. She clambered away from him, mind racing.

"And they don't use magick," Isobel added. She'd managed to stun the false Alistair, but her own double was only a step behind him. Her hand reached for the real Isobel's chest, as though trying to rip her heart out.

Finley ducked beneath his double's blade. "Anyone have ideas for how to stop them?"

"Working on it!" Briony shouted. Innes lurched toward her, arms outstretched. But thanks to Briony's Hold in Place, her statue froze, fingers grasping at empty air.

"They could've at least given me a better outfit," Isobel grumbled. "Or better hair." Then she cast a curse on her fake self. A pair of phantasmal pincers clamped around the waist, crushing her.

"I'm sorry she's not up to your standards, darling—"

"Shut up, Reid."

Briony eyed Carbry, panting, and caught another glimpse of his cheek. She recognized the glittering object now—a shard from the broken Mirror.

It was embedded in the false champion just as the first Thorburn champion had embedded spellstones in the walls, protecting herself. What would happen if Briony destroyed that protection?

She shoved Carbry's shoulder against the wall, then clawed at his face. Her fingers scrabbled against the high magick he was made of; it was viscous and smooth and cold. The moment she touched the shard of glass, he let out the first sound any of them had made besides footsteps—a harsh, piercing wail.

Briony remembered how the real Carbry had died beside her, hand clutched in her own, blond ringlets smeared with blood. But this boy wasn't that one, and she had stopped punishing herself for his death.

The press had used it as evidence of her monstrosity, but . . . they were wrong about her.

She knew that. She knew it where it mattered: in her core, in her heart.

Briony yanked the glass shard out of his cheek. The wailing stopped immediately. He began to shrink again, then clattered to the floor, his tiny crimson form disintegrating into dust.

Briony stared at the shard, wondering if it would hurt her, but instead it winked out into bits of high magick.

"I figured out the trick!" she cried.

After that, their battle changed into something far closer to a fist-fight than a magick duel. Finley stabbed his Lightning Lance straight through his double's shoulder, pushing out the glass that glimmered there. Then he rounded on Elionor, another curserse flaring.

Across the room, the false Gavin did his best to strangle Reid. Isobel dispatched herself swiftly, using the pincers to gouge out the shard embedded in her frozen locks of hair. Then she turned to Alistair, eyes narrowing.

Which left Innes, still frozen in the center of the room.

It's not her, Briony told herself as she stepped forward, the rubble of the map of Ilvernath crunching beneath her feet. But this felt far different than facing Carbry had. It was like stepping back in time to a month ago, when she and the real Innes had fought in this very room.

Her sister had nearly killed her that day. Now, Briony felt as though she were gazing at a version of her that *would* have been champion—another choice, another life, another world that she would never know.

But this version of Innes as the star of a Thorburn story was no more real than the version of Briony currently being slandered in the press. These trials were supposed to show the truth, but there was no truth to her family's legacy—because they'd lied to everyone, but they'd lied to themselves most of all.

As Briony drew closer to Innes, she saw no sign of any glass. Instead, the three spellstones from the Mirror glimmered on her sister's hands, like spellrings.

One of them was on her still-attached pinky.

The false Innes broke free of Briony's Hold in Place, then swung. Briony dodged a second too late.

The blow hit her in the jaw, *hard*, whipping her head to the side and sending her reeling. She tried to counter with another punch, but Innes grabbed her wrist before it could connect and yanked it painfully behind her back, pulling Briony against her. Before Briony could even suck in a breath, the statue's other hand closed around her throat.

She choked, eyes watering as she pried frantically at Innes's grip. The spellstones dug into her neck, hard enough to bruise. Her vision began to darken around the edges. And then, with a rush, she remembered how the real Innes had beaten her before.

Her gaze locked on the three massive windows. They were unobstructed. Perfect.

She kicked and flailed until Innes's grip loosened just the slightest bit, but that was all Briony needed. She ripped herself away from her sister and bolted toward the windows. As she'd expected, Innes chased after her.

When Innes reached her, she lunged for Briony's throat again. Briony ducked beneath her—then *lifted* with all her might, grasping Innes's armpits and pushing her sister's statue over her shoulder. The strain of it shuddered through her whole body, but it worked. The statue toppled over her back . . . and then smashed through the window, head over heels. Briony tumbled over, too, rolling across the floor. She caught herself against the window ledge, gasping, and peered through the shattered glass.

She'd expected to see Innes's form crumpled on the rocks. Instead, a crimson hand clung to the Tower stone nearest to the windowsill. Briony jolted backward—but not before Innes's other, spellstone-studded hand reached up and closed around her wrist.

Briony shrieked as the weight yanked her forward, struggling to brace herself against the windowsill. From her precarious perch, she saw Innes hanging in midair. The arm that wasn't clutching Briony scrabbled for purchase. But the Tower's exterior was crumbling. The floor shook beneath Briony's feet, and Innes shook, too. Cracks fissured across her forearm. She gazed up at Briony, impassive, uncaring. Briony's vision blurred with tears.

Maybe her family really *would* drag her down with them, after all. But no. *No.*

Even if all of it was for nothing, Briony had given this quest everything she had. Whether the world loved her or hated her for it, whether she was remembered or forgotten, she was determined to do what she knew was right.

This trial was her family's truth, not hers.

Briony blinked her tears away and wrenched back as hard as she could. The statue's forearm snapped at last, and Innes fell, shrinking. A pair of hands grabbed Briony's waist and yanked her away from the window. She shuddered with relief against the familiar warmth of Finley's chest.

"Hey," he murmured into her hair. "Did you—*holy shit.*"

The false Innes's hand was still locked in a death grip around Briony's wrist.

"Hang on," Briony gasped, and he released her. She clawed at the scarlet marble, prying out the spellstones. It was only once she'd yanked the third one out that the hand disintegrated into crimson dust. The crystals winked out a moment later, dead. She dropped them on the floor. Blood dribbled from the cuts the window had left on her arm, but other than that, she was unharmed.

When she looked up, Finley stood where the door had once been. The other champions were gone, along with the statues they'd been fighting. The floor below them quaked furiously.

"We need to hurry," he called out as she reached him. "It's about to—"

And then the Tower collapsed.

Briony was always at her best under pressure, but even *she* surprised herself with how quickly she cast the Prismatic Protector. She and Finley hurtled toward the ground in a rain of rock, clutching each other. But the debris didn't touch them. When the dust settled, they were intertwined beneath a pile of stone, a few centimeters of shining, refracted light all that stood between them and a crushing death.

"I wouldn't mind this normally," Briony mumbled into Finley's neck. Their bodies were curled gently around each other, his arms braced as if to shield her from a blow. "But I'm not sure if I can get us out of here in this position. You have some Here to Theres, right?"

He chuckled in a way that Briony had started to notice was unique to *her* bad jokes, and then mumbled something about how he shouldn't be laughing right now.

"Hang on," he said, then, "I think some of my spellstones cracked in the fall."

Briony groaned. "Seriously?"

They were talking through the best ways to free themselves when daylight streamed through her shield. Briony had never been more relieved to see Isobel and Reid as they peered through the rubble.

"You two look pretty cozy in there," Reid said. "You sure you want us to help you out?"

Isobel elbowed him. "Stop being an ass. What he's *trying* to say is that he's glad you're both alive."

"So are we," Finley said quietly. They clambered to their feet and away from the ruins that had once been the Tower. Briony looked at her wrist and shuddered at the swollen marks there.

Then she turned away from the remnants of her family's broken, twisted story, toward the people who'd helped her start a new one.

"One Relic left," she said. "How fast do you think you can craft it?"

GAVIN GRIEVE

"Shouldn't it be easy for them to figure out their families' stories?
It seems as though telling them is all these champions have ever
done."

Call-in, *Champion Confidential*, WKL Radio

Gavin stood before his family's Landmark, gripping the Shoes. A light rain misted on the Cottage's roof, and the garden was gilded with frost. It was hard not to feel as though he was at the start of a story—not the new one he was fighting for, but the old one that he'd sworn never to speak of again. Hard not to look at the wreckage of the garden and think of the fight he'd endured only the previous day.

He turned from the broken vines on the ground to the boy at his side. White crept across Alistair's cheek and blotted out his iris, curling across his face like a crescent moon.

"Well, they didn't attack us," Gavin said. "And we got out of there without some bullshit babysitter. So that's . . . good."

"We don't need to talk about it," Alistair muttered. "We have the Relic. Let's just finish this." He strode ahead, then flung the door open so violently it slammed against the wall. The hearth sparked to life at its champion's approach, its small, pathetic flame revealing the mess Alistair had left behind. Spellstones were strewn across the counters, chairs toppled on the floor, a broken glass left lying in the sink. The pillar now looked as though it were more cracks than stone; blood had clotted and congealed across most of the dead champions' names, obscuring them. Alistair brushed past all of it, while Gavin set the Shoes down on the table and began shoving crystals into his pockets.

"Do you want this one?" Gavin held up the Gift of the Forest Hendry had used to heal his brother after their fight for the Medallion.

Alistair blinked at it, recognition dawning across his face. "Y-yes."

He snatched the mossy green quartz from Gavin's outstretched palm and slid it onto his finger.

It was sobering to know that although Hendry's things were still scattered throughout the Cottage, the boy who'd made a home there was gone. All that remained of him was the Wishing Flower spellring on Alistair's pointer. Gavin missed Hendry, although he knew the sorrow he felt was a mere fraction of Alistair's grief. It was why he didn't begrudge Alistair his agitation—he was impressed the other boy was still standing, after the day he'd had.

Gavin remembered how Alistair had crumpled into his arms in the courtyard; how he'd felt so fragile there, as though all the villainous armor he'd so carefully constructed had fallen away. Gavin had known at that moment it no longer mattered to him what they'd done to each other. He still wanted this. Wanted Al. But after a lifetime of Gavin pushing his desires aside, he had no idea how to approach something so important. And he knew that right now, when Alistair had just suffered a tremendous loss, was probably the worst possible time to broach the subject. Maybe if this tournament really did have an *after*, he'd be brave enough to confess his feelings.

"Are you ready?" he asked.

"Almost." Alistair gestured toward the Shoes, then looked at him expectantly. "Tell me your story."

Gavin should've been expecting this, based on what the other champions had told them about these trials. But he'd told Alistair the Grieves didn't have a story.

"My family's not like yours. We've been over this. And they said it's about the truth of our families, anyway, not an exact replay of the fairy tale."

Alistair rolled his eyes. "Come on. You must know *something* that could help us."

Gavin gritted his teeth. His pride wasn't worth more than their potential deaths. Probably.

"Fine. But I don't even know if this *is* the actual Grieve story."

He recounted the tale Callista had told him, resentful of every word. But an odd thing happened as he talked about the first Grieve, who'd spent his short, miserable life bitter and hiding. Gavin thought of Fergus and his newspaper clippings, Callista and her misplaced condolences. And instead of rage, he just felt sorrow.

"As long as the Grieve champion kept his fire burning in the Cottage's hearth, he was safe," Gavin said. "But maybe he got too comfortable, or maybe he wanted to try and match up to the other champions, for once. I don't know. He made a mistake, and the Shoes—his own Relic—tore him in half."

Alistair deadpanned, "Well, now I'm twice as excited to get started."

Gavin wasn't sure what kind of reaction he'd wanted from Alistair. At least it wasn't pity. He sighed, hefted the Shoes off the table, and headed to the pillar. "Hey—how are we supposed to attach these to a giant rock?"

They examined the stone jutting out of the mantel, both of them at a loss.

"The others said they attacked the pillar in the Cave," Alistair ventured.

Gavin eyed the Shoes suspiciously, his family's story still painfully fresh in his mind. "That seems dangerous. Also, what are we going to do, kick it? It's all the way up there."

Alistair let out a petulant grunt in response. Gavin's patience with him was beginning to fray. He turned, scanning the Cottage for a solution. When his gaze found the crackling hearth, he understood.

Grieves were uniquely gifted at sabotaging themselves. For a moment, Gavin felt that familiar self-loathing curdle in his chest. But then he stared at the spellrings on his hands, glowing white with common magick at last. He was the strongest he'd been in his entire life. He was ready for whatever horrors this trial would bring.

"Get ready," he warned. Then he tossed the Shoes into the fire.

Immediately, the flames in the hearth roared, transforming from orange to a violent, vicious scarlet. They reared higher, fiery arms reaching toward the boys. Gavin began to cast a Spikeshield, but before he could, Alistair lurched back in surprise, tripping over a fallen chair and tumbling into Gavin. They fell together into the wreckage of the kitchen until Gavin hit the ground, hard, Alistair crashing on top of him. They both scrambled hastily away from each other as the scarlet light from the pillar brightened. The fire loomed closer.

It flared so tall, it nearly touched the ceiling—and then, inexplicably, it snuffed out.

In an instant, the Cottage plunged into cold.

"What the hell?" Gavin's breath fogged in the air. He braced his hands on the suddenly freezing floor and turned to Alistair, who looked equally as bewildered.

"I d-don't know." The other boy's teeth chattered. A spell brightened above his palm, then extinguished. "M-my magick. It's not working." He yanked one of his rings off, swore at it, then chucked it across the room.

Gavin tried to cast a Gleamspark to warm them up. But nothing happened.

"You can't be serious," he said in disbelief, rising to his feet. "I . . . I just got it back. What if Diya was wrong? What if I'm not cured, and it's disappearing—"

"If it's both of us, it can't be that," Alistair said firmly, his breath releasing a cloud of fog. "This has to be part of the trial."

A stench wafted through the air, putrid and rank, so thick it felt like a noxious puff of smoke. Gavin clamped his sleeve over his mouth, but even muffled, the smell seeped through, coating his tongue like wax. He tried to cast the Gleamspark again, but it sputtered in the air for the briefest of moments before winking out.

Gavin's stomach sank with despair. Each time he believed he'd broken free of his family's indignities, they found a new way to get inside his head.

Something gray landed on his pant leg. Gavin flinched and scrambled back—but it wasn't an enemy. It was dust, clumps of it, fluttering through the air like gnats.

"What *is* this?" Alistair mumbled, coughing, as it coated his brown and white curls and smeared across his nose. Then he snorted at Gavin. "You look absurd."

"So do you," Gavin said through coughs of his own. "Honestly, I'm surprised you don't like the Cottage better this way."

"Ha ha," Alistair grumbled.

Cobwebs dropped from the ceiling like streamers. Sludge leaked from between the wooden panels on the walls, as thick and sticky as sap. Muck spread across the windows, smothering the daylight, turning Alistair into nothing but a silhouette.

"I'm trying the door," Alistair growled.

"I think we're trapped in here."

Alistair ignored him. He collided with yet another piece of furniture on his way, cursed, then tugged uselessly at the handle. "What is this place trying to do, drown us in dirt?"

"The others said there was a trick to these. Maybe if we could actually see something . . ." Gavin stepped toward the window, his trainer sticking in the muck. He scowled and dislodged it, then snatched up a rag off the dusty counter, reached up to the grimy pane of glass, and scrubbed at it. A sliver of daylight burst through.

"Hey!" Alistair called out. "Look at this."

Gavin whipped around. A tiny flame flickered in the hearth.

"What did you do?" Alistair asked.

"I'm not sure." Gavin scrubbed at the window again. Another beam of light joined the first. "Did that change anything?"

"Yeah. The fire looks . . . brighter."

The realization dawned on Gavin in a humiliating rush. His family's story about keeping the hearth lit, about conserving power, about maintaining shelter above all else . . . the number of competitors who had probably huddled before that fire until some Lowe hunted them down . . .

"I think we're supposed to clean the Cottage, without any magick." He struggled to keep the fury from his voice. "What an absolute joke."

"Clean?" Alistair said, aghast. "Without spells?"

"Why doesn't it surprise me that you've never done it?" Gavin sighed. He and Hendry had always been the ones to tidy up.

"But this will take *forever*! Where do we even start?"

"I have some ideas." Gavin stomped to his former bedroom and threw the door open. Cleaning supplies were packed inside the cupboard, the only part of the entire Cottage that wasn't covered in filth. Two mops and a pail leaned against one corner, along with a broom and dustpan. Gavin rifled through and found some scrubbing brushes, dozens of rags and bars of soap, and a feather duster.

"Go see if the tap in the sink still works." Gavin handed the pail to Alistair. "We'll start with the walls, then the cabinets, then deal with the . . . everything else."

"You're being very calm about this."

"Oh, trust me, it's taking everything I have not to set this whole place on fire."

"Do you think that would work?" Alistair asked eagerly, glowering down at the pail.

"I'm pretty sure it would just trap us in a filthy, burning house."

Alistair let out a wordless grumble, and the two of them got to work.

As it turned out, the tap still ran, and the water it produced was clean and clear. Gavin mixed it with the soap until it produced suds, and then the boys set to work washing the windows, with the hope that giving the rooms more light would make them easier to clean. It did, but it also illuminated the full breadth of the task ahead of them.

They cleaned in silence for a while, although it didn't feel quite as tense as it had when Alistair had first stalked into the Cottage. Gavin tried not to think about how *this* was the collective truth of his family's legacy, but his anger was impossible to avoid. It grew inside him as he dusted the cabinets, then moved to the counters, the hearth still little more than a tiny flame. And then, out of nowhere, the ground began to shake.

He grabbed the nearest countertop, heart seizing in alarm. He locked eyes with Alistair across the room, who'd clung to the table like a life raft. Plates clattered and fell from their cabinets. Spellstones—now useless—rattled like dice.

"The pillar," Alistair managed.

Gavin, who was closer, turned to check its dusty surface.

Crack! A fifth strike shot down the side with the stars.

"They did it," Gavin breathed. "They destroyed the Tower."

Across the room, Alistair let out a triumphant holler, and Gavin couldn't help but join him with a loose, relieved laugh.

When the quaking had quieted, Alistair asked, "What do you think their trial was like?"

"Well, it was probably *actually* dangerous." The others had warned them of skeletons and saw blades; currently, their biggest life-threatening obstacle was arguably mold poisoning. "I'm sure they all got to play the hero to their hearts' content."

Based on what Diya had said, the Thorburns were being called anything but heroic right now. But Gavin doubted it really mattered. When the tournament was done with, the champions who'd fought for this from the beginning would still be the ones people gushed about.

"Do you want to be a hero?" Alistair asked him.

"Fuck no. Heroes are just villains with worse survival instincts and moral superiority complexes. All I care about anymore is surviving this." Gavin paused. "Why, do you?"

Alistair stared at his ungloved hands. "I don't think I'm the hero type."

"I'm not so sure that's true," Gavin said quietly. "I mean . . . your fan club would disagree."

"My fan club also thinks I drink blood and sleep in a coffin."

"Don't you?" Gavin gestured at the filthy walls.

"Speaking of drinking blood." Alistair cocked a brow. "I'm starving. That food you gave me in the dungeon was practically gruel."

"It's called a protein shake," Gavin said dryly. "But I'm hungry, too." They checked the pantry. Everything in it was either rotten or moldy.

The daylight streaming through the window faded to sunset, then darkness. The pair of them leaned against the kitchen counter, side by side. Their work was a little more than halfway done, and the fire in the hearth had grown enough to light the room—barely. Gavin felt slightly delirious from the combination of hard work, lack of food, and cleaning chemicals. His magick might be cured, but he was pretty sure scrubbing the bathroom had taken years off his life.

"First spell you ever cast," Alistair said, yawning. They'd resorted to games to stay awake. Gavin had offered to let Alistair rest while he kept working, but the other boy had protested so vehemently that he hadn't asked again.

"I don't really remember. I . . . I think it was a silencing charm. For my bedroom."

"What were you doing at night?"

"It wasn't what I was doing. My parents yelled a lot."

Alistair's earlier ire had worn off gradually, and for the first time since Hendry's sacrifice, the pain that flitted across his face didn't seem to be his own. "I'm sorry."

"It's not a big deal," Gavin muttered, even though the flare of warmth in his chest told him otherwise. "What about you?"

"Uh . . . I think I was trying to fly."

"In your supervillain cape?"

Alistair glared at him lethally.

Gavin chuckled. "Did it work?"

"Oh, absolutely not. I have the scars to prove it." He tapped his knee, looking rueful. "I was a dragon, shot down by a knight. And then I burnt him to a crisp."

"Another monster story," Gavin said.

"Yeah." Alistair hesitated. "I know you hate your family's stories, but . . . I don't hate mine. Even though I hate how they used them. What does that make me?"

If Gavin had learned anything over these past few months, it was that it was impossible to fully disentangle yourself from the stories that had built you. He'd tried to ignore the Grieves' tale, but instead, he'd let it swallow him whole.

"I think maybe people need stories to survive, but they can also use them to hurt each other. Or themselves," Gavin said. "If you've found a way for your family's stories to feed you without feeding *on* you . . . that seems worth holding on to."

Alistair's gaze bored into him. Gavin had no idea if he'd soothed him or tormented him, until finally, the other boy joked, "I didn't realize you were so insightful."

"It's all the bran cereal. It builds character."

Alistair smirked. "Your turn."

The hearth set Alistair's face aglow the same way it had dozens of nights before, sending orange licking across his cheekbones and accentuating his widow's peak. He looked at Gavin as though studying him, and while Gavin had once considered that stare conniving, now he welcomed it.

The thought flared in him, risky but impossible to ignore. Perhaps a less exhausted Gavin would've succeeded in dousing it. But he didn't.

"First kiss," he said hoarsely. Maybe it was his imagination, or the aforementioned exhaustion, but the dust specks in the air seemed to still, the dripping faucet quieted. As though the entire room was holding its breath.

He expected Alistair to blow the question off, but instead he coughed, and his eyes darted to the floor. "You, uh. You've seen it in the papers."

"Holy shit," Gavin said. "The first time you kissed someone, they cast a death curse on you?"

The part of Alistair's face that wasn't covered in his cursemark flushed pink. "It sounds bad when you say it like that."

Gavin knew he'd strayed into dangerous territory. He wasn't sure he cared. He leaned to the side; his arm brushed Alistair's. Alistair did not move away.

"So that's the *only* time you've ever kissed someone?" Gavin asked.

Alistair raised his brows. "Well, that was a month ago. Who exactly do you think I've been kissing since then?" He licked his lips, then chuckled softly to himself. "Despite my *many* offers . . ."

Gavin regretted bringing up the fan club earlier, if only because he now suspected he'd accidentally become its president.

"I've read a lot of those offers," he said, trying not to sound jealous. "I think most people would be disappointed to find out that your maniacal laughter leaves a lot to be desired."

Alistair heaved out a dramatic sigh. "And after all those years I've spent perfecting it . . ."

They both burst into not-quite-maniacal laughter, but when the sound faded, neither of them spoke. Gavin stared at him, remembering how it'd felt to run his hand along the Reaper's Embrace, when it had first spread to Alistair's cheek. How Alistair's expression had quivered as he loomed above him in the garden, readying himself to cast that final curse. Gavin had once agonized over whether the real Alistair Lowe was more boy or monster, but now he understood that Alistair was both. And even though neither canceled the other out, he didn't think that made Alistair beyond redemption.

"I'm sorry you had the world's worst first kiss," he said. "You deserved something better."

"I think you could argue I deserved exactly what I got," Alistair murmured.

"We both know that's not true."

Gavin had half a thought—about kisses, about curse conditions. About the specificity of the Reaper's Embrace. But the idea of voicing it felt fanciful at best, delusional at worst.

"What about your first kiss?" Alistair challenged.

"Lara Marsden," Gavin said. "We went to middle school together. And then I think we dated for about two weeks afterward."

"How normal," Alistair grunted. Then he seized the mop handle from where it rested at the edge of the counter. "Anyway. We should probably get back to work."

Gavin could only watch, bewildered. Maybe Alistair *would* be the death of him, after all.

Again, the hours slipped by, and once daybreak arrived the two of them were nearly finished. Gavin felt as though he'd completed the most grueling workout of his entire life. But although he'd despised this trial at the beginning, he now found himself oddly proud of the work he and Alistair had done together. The Cottage looked cleaner than it ever had, its windows polished, its counters spotless. The hearth roared merrily in the fireplace.

"I think this is the last of it." Alistair pointed at a lingering clump of dirt in the corner. "It's your family's trial—do you want to do the honors?"

"Sure." Gavin picked up the broom and stared around the Cottage, knowing it would be the last time he'd ever stand inside its walls.

His whole life, he'd believed there was something fundamentally wrong with him. But the truth was, his entrance into the tournament was nothing more than a cruel trick of fate. The truth was that his family had failed him, just as they'd failed every other Grieve champion who'd been taught they were destined for the slaughter. Who'd never had the chance to learn otherwise.

Gavin vowed not to waste his chance.

He swept the last of the dust into the pan.

Crack!

A fresh sliver of light spread across the pillar, and blood poured from it, immediately soiling the clean floorboards. The ground shook. The walls heaved. The boys bolted toward the door. This time, it was unlocked.

They rushed into the garden, a Here to There already blazing on Gavin's finger. He felt a rush of relief as magick stirred in his spellstones once again. Behind them, the Cottage's roof collapsed, rendering their night of work completely moot.

Then a noise burst above them, so loud and terrifying that Gavin instinctively dropped to the ground, Alistair a hair behind him. His chest pressed against the garden path as he gaped upward. Bright veins threaded across the Blood Veil, more and more of them, bulging and expanding, far too many cracks to count. They reached higher and higher before finally meeting at the dome's apex.

Then, in an explosion of sound, the Blood Veil shattered.

ISOBEL MACASLAN

Cursemaking is a delicate art, one that balances danger with significant amounts of legal red tape. Few independent cursemakers remain as their licenses become harder and harder to secure, and since their oldest grimoires were confiscated during the cursemaking paranoia at the turn of the last century.

Ilvernath Eclipse, "Cursemaking vs. Spellmaking:
What You Might Not Know"

The four champions left the ruins of the Tower in delirious, exhausted triumph.

Finley slung his arm around Briony's shoulder. "That was brilliant. *You* were brilliant."

Briony grinned as she leaned into him, stumbling on the uneven forest floor. "You know what I want, after all this is over?"

"What?" Isobel asked. Between the slivers of the canopy, the Ilvernath skyline edged closer and closer. Though it seemed dangerous to admit it with so many challenges still ahead of them, each step felt almost—*almost*—like going home.

"Chips," Briony answered longingly. "The greasiest chips in the world, drenched in ketchup and vinegar—"

"Don't," Reid said with a groan. "After a month of eating nothing but pretzels and cheese puffs, I—"

A light winked in the corner of Isobel's vision. She'd barely had time to turn her head when an explosion blasted in front of them, drilling a hole straight through the thick trunk of an ash tree. The four champions screamed as bark exploded into the air like shrapnel.

As Isobel staggered to regain her balance, cursefire shot at them in all directions, so bright it was impossible to tell who was firing. Briony reacted first, throwing up a Prismatic Protector. But by then, one enchantment had grazed Isobel's leg, burning through denim and skin with a painful hiss. Her vision darkened around the edges, and she swayed, grasping Briony to keep from falling. Beside them, Finley was struck in the stomach. His body crumpled to the dirt.

"Finley?" Briony choked. She made to take a step toward him, but her shield flickered under the barrage pounding against it. She gritted her teeth and dug her heels into the ground, holding it. "Are you okay?"

Finley didn't respond.

Reid squinted at the figures in the distance, stalking them through the woods. "Is that . . . Is that Calhoun? Who's the man next to him in uniform?" A curse whizzed toward them like a firework and struck Briony's shield, hissing out a shower of sparks. Reid staggered back, colliding with a splayed wall of pine needles. "Never mind. We need to leave—now! How many Here to Theres can we cast?"

"Two," Briony answered.

"Good—you take Finley. Isobel?" He swiveled around, then his eyes widened as he took her in, her balance teetering. "What's wrong? Did you—?" Briony's Prismatic Protector shattered with a powerful gust of wind, making Isobel tumble beside Finley. Reid ducked beneath a curse a split second before it could hit his head. It skidded across the ground, leaving scorch marks in its path. "Shield! We need more—"

"I'm casting them as fast as I can!" Briony shouted.

While she summoned a new Prismatic Protector, a voice hollered through the trees. "We have you surrounded and are prepared for pursuit. Remove any curserings and we'll—"

"Isobel," Reid said urgently, gripping her shoulder. "Can you cast a Here to There?"

She placed her hand on her forehead. The world teetered like a top. "I . . ."

Reid swore and straightened. "She can't, and I can only cast one."

"Then I'll cast three," Briony said firmly. "Give me some of yours."

"That's risky even for—"

"I said I'll do it!" she snapped. Reid scowled, but handed her several spellstones. With one arm outstretched, still maintaining her barrier, she stepped back until she stood directly over Isobel and Finley. "Three . . . Two . . . One!"

Briony seized Finley and Isobel, and with a *pop*, the forest disappeared, replaced by the brick and concrete of the alley behind the MacTavish curseshop.

However, the chaos had far from vanished. Car horns blared, mingling with the shrill screeching of security alarms. When Isobel rolled over on the damp pavement, she spotted several columns of smoke drifting into the sky. The parking lot to their right, normally full, was almost completely vacated.

"Seriously?" Reid bit out, taking in the red graffiti smeared across his back door, even his rubbish bins. Several crude words. A slapdash mural of a zombie-like creature, threads of magick tangled around it. A crescent moon dripping blood. He scooped up one of many spellstones scattered across the curb—Stinkbombs, judging by the crinkle of his nose.

"Forget that," Briony breathed, dropping beside Finley and placing a hand on his shoulder. A line of crimson trickled from her left nostril, but she didn't seem to notice. "He's hurt. Let's just get—"

"Halt!" someone called from down the alley. Isobel pushed herself to her knees. Some kind of uniformed officer advanced on them, wearing a shimmering armored vest.

A bright stun spell shot toward them, forcing Briony to cast yet another shield.

Reid, meanwhile, lunged for the back door. The moment he touched the handle, white shone from within the keyhole, and the shop's locking spell released. He wrenched the door open, then hoisted Finley over his shoulder with a groan. Isobel desperately crawled for safety inside, nearly collapsing over the stray shoes and wrinkled welcome mat. Reid and Briony bolted in after her, and the door slammed closed. The sound of shattering glass rang out from the front of the shop, making all of them startle.

"Wards," Reid grunted as he lowered Finley. "We need more wards."

"I'm casting them as fast as I can," Briony said frantically. "Isobel, can you—? What's wrong?"

Isobel braced one hand against the wood-paneled wall. "I got grazed. A knockout curse." The shop around her blurred in and out of focus.

"Give us your defensive spellrings," Reid said. "We'll finish this."

Shakily, she ripped them off her fingers and thrust them into Reid's hands. Then she slumped to the ground beside Finley. Voices clamored outside, but she couldn't make them out.

While Reid reinforced the enchantments on the back door, Isobel shook Finley's shoulder.

"Fin, Fin, wake up." Neither of them could afford to sit this out. They needed to help.

"There's a Smelling Salts upstairs in the medicine cabinet," Reid said.

"No, I have . . ." Isobel fought to rein in her concentration and fished a small spellstone out of her jacket pocket. A class one Wake-Up Call, far, far easier to cast than a Here to There.

A spout of water poured onto Finley's face, and he sputtered, eyes flying open. "Wh-what the . . . I feel really woozy."

"We can't hold them off, not forever," Briony called from the front of the shop. "Who are they? They didn't look like police—"

"I definitely saw a spellmaker I recognized in the forest," Reid said.

"What? Why?" Briony appeared beside the stairs at the end of the hallway, clutching the banister as she panted.

"I have no idea. I'm not exactly on friendly terms with the Spellmaking Society."

"What if they really are working with the government? You heard what Gavin said. And who else would wear uniforms other than agents?"

"If that's true, then this is bad—real bad." Reid peeked out the blinds on the door, then grimaced and turned back to Briony. "I'd say we should take the ingredients and run, but I don't think we can leave. It's going to take time to craft the Crown."

"What's the fastest you can do it?"

"I don't know—a day?"

"A *day*? I'll give this everything I've got, but you'd better have some incredible wards—"

"I'll help you," Finley said, still sounding woozy.

"And you're in a renowned curseshop," Reid added. "I have excellent wards."

With that, Reid grabbed Isobel by her arm and hoisted her up. She teetered, dizzy, but he pressed her tightly to his side.

"Come on. We've got a deadline, apparently." He guided her into the back room, where he pulled out the desk chair and ushered her into it. "Wait here." A moment later, his footsteps thudded up the stairs, and when he returned, he carried the same first aid kit she'd used to heal him after she'd bludgeoned him to free herself. He brandished a topaz spellring.

An unpleasant stench burned a path down Isobel's nostrils. She shook her head, her vision clearing. "Ugh. That smells like cat piss."

"Well, do you still feel like swooning?"

She rolled her eyes. "You make it hard to want to thank you."

"Since when do you ever thank me, darling?" Though his old joke had long since gone stale, it didn't bother Isobel as much as it once had. The thought of *that*, of him, now intrusively prodded at her mind. She banished it—she needed to focus. "Right now, we have to figure out how to craft the Crown. What progress did we make yesterday?"

"Not much." If given the choice, she would've picked any other Relic to craft. Its enchantments all centered on power augmentation, which was tricky even for the most experienced of spellmakers. "We know the Crown strengthens your enchantments. That's the first spell. The second makes it harder for other champions to attack you."

"It's a play on fealty. Willpower. It'll be a nightmare."

"And it weakens the other champions' Landmarks."

"It pays to wear the Crown, doesn't it?" Reid yanked a desk drawer open and snatched three empty spellstones. He scattered them atop the surface. "We'll also need a replacement Crown. There's a cupboard near the back—well, you already know that." She did, as she'd once tried to hide from him in it. "You'll probably find a beanie or something in the basket. And don't go saying—"

"A beanie," Isobel repeated flatly, unable to help herself.

Reid let out an exasperated sigh. "Just get it, would you?"

She raced around the corner and rifled through the wicker basket within the hall cupboard. Buried beneath several umbrellas was a black beanie that smelled strongly of cigarette smoke and unwashed hair.

In the office, Reid awkwardly deposited an armful of ingredient containers on the desk, wincing as several clattered to the floor. He'd already stacked a tower of huge leather trunks in the room's corner. The top one lay open, exposing dozens of tiny compartments filled with flasks. Isobel shuddered as she considered how truly daunting an undertaking they had ahead of them.

"How should we do this?" he asked. "Divide and conquer?"

"Works for me."

The next few hours passed in a frenetic blur. Hurriedly uncapping vials and dumping out ingredients. Tearing through the pages of countless grimoires and spellmaking textbooks. Scarfing down an unappetizing dinner of Reid's collection of freezer-burned entrées.

By eight, they finished the first enchantment—the magick amplification spell, which Reid had modeled after a class nine Mythic Augmentation he'd uncovered in what was almost certainly an illegal grimoire. Afterward, Reid helped her put the finishing touches on the Landmark spell, using a scrap of rubble he'd salvaged from the Tower as a key ingredient.

All that remained was the final spell of fealty, and by then, night had long since fallen.

Reid sipped his mug of instant coffee, unperturbed by the thick steam wafting from it and fogging his glasses. "Obviously these are Lowe spells. When you crafted spells with Alistair did you notice any pattern? Ingredients they favored? Anything that—"

"No," Isobel answered tightly. "I was too preoccupied with convincing him not to kill me to take notes on his process."

"It'll need defensive ingredients. I'd say calcified nautilus shell and liquid platinum. They cost a fortune for a reason—they'll help increase the class, and it has to be class ten. Then there's the willpower components. A lock of hair is always a good choice. But it's not about fealty over anyone—it's fealty specifically over the other champions. It'll take something of ourselves."

"Blood?" Isobel suggested. It was always a good guess.

"Maybe. But I hope it's enough. It's not like we have the blood of all the champions to offer."

"We could include lotus seeds. They increase resistance—"

"No," he said dismissively. "They're too weak."

She crossed her arms. "Well, what do *you* suggest then?"

He set down the mug and grabbed yet another grimoire from the shelf, then traced his finger down the faded table of contents. "I don't know. Willpower curses have been illegal for centuries."

And for good reason. Using magick to warp someone's desires

was despicable enough, but it also risked lasting effects on the victim: a loss of memory, change in personality, and depression-like symptoms.

However, the thought gave Isobel an idea. "What if we modeled it after a love spell?" They were history's most famous form of willpower enchantment, after all.

"The Lowes hardly crafted any of their spells based on love."

"We wouldn't use the same ingredients. If we changed infatuation to admiration. If we played with loyalty, respect. Definitely fear—"

"Fear?" Reid cocked a brow. "I'm not sure I'm familiar with that seduction technique."

For the first time, Isobel was thankful for the effects of the Roach's Armor, otherwise she'd flush. "Don't be purposefully obtuse. I'm not in the mood."

He snorted and sat at the desk. "Should I write down ridicule, too?" He yanked the cap off a pen with his teeth and spit it onto his notebook.

"Should I write down disgust?"

"You assume I'm flirting with you." Reid scribbled down their list in his chicken scratch handwriting.

Isobel knew he was only joking, but her insides needled with embarrassment, as though she'd swallowed a wasp. "You assume *I'm* flirting with *you.*"

Instead of answering, he smiled to himself, head bent down over his notebook. Isobel spent far too long dissecting that smile—focus she should be devoting to the Crown, not to Reid, with his ridiculous greasy hair and tacky beanie and infuriating way of pretending to be better than everyone, because he was just *so* smart and *so* good-looking. It'd been easier when she'd hated him.

But even if they *were* friends, Isobel refused to give him the satisfaction of knowing he flustered her. No, she would not give Reid MacTavish an *inch.*

She plucked a suspicious grimoire from their discarded pile, and as suspected, the book lacked a publication page, an author, or identifying information of any kind. Considering its list of vile, murderous curses and unspeakable tricks, she was unsurprised to find a romance spell amid its contents. She grabbed the spare chair in the room's corner and slid it beside Reid, then set the book in front of them.

"Look at these ingredients. A first bloom of spring. A freshwater oyster shell . . . We can modify these. It'll just take some clever theory."

"'Some clever theory.' You're talking about the sort of cursemaking that people write doctoral theses about. We can't afford to fuck this up."

"Do you have a better idea?"

He sighed. "No."

"Instead of the first bloom, we can try dried veronica. I've seen that used in allegiance spells."

"*Allegiance spells,*" Reid mocked. "This isn't a Pinky Promise, like we're on the playground in primary school. I say we use a petrified heart valve."

Isobel kicked his chair. "Forgive me for not realizing you had a collection of illegal ingredients at your disposal. What else do you have?"

"Preserved nightshade, which could work."

"For the veronica, we could try fermented pomegranate essence."

"That's not . . . No, actually, that's brilliant."

They gathered their ingredients and supplies. Several needed prep, including chopping, measuring, and distilling. The two of them stood over the electronic boiler, watching the petals of nightshade gradually regain their vibrant violet color. The room smelled overpoweringly of syrup, and the bubbling water had made it humid and warm.

Reid yawned, his head resting on his hand. "What time is it?"

Isobel checked her watch. "It's one."

"Great. Only six more hours until the flowers rehydrate and the essence ferments." He straightened and glanced up at her, looking excessively tired. Since donating his life magick, the color had yet to return to his skin. Isobel wondered how long it would take until he recuperated his sacrifice—days? Months? Years? "If we're going right to the Castle from here, we should try to get some sleep. You're already acquainted with my guest room."

Isobel was too tired to meet that with a snide retort. "Someone needs to watch over this. Maybe Briony or Finley—"

"They're holding the wards. And it's fine. I'll stay."

"You wouldn't fall asleep if I left you in here alone, watching water boil?"

He pursed his lips. "Fair point."

Isobel rubbed her temples. She was no stranger to all-nighters, but the past eight weeks had taken a toll on her sleeping habits. "At the very least, we can take a break for more coffee, hm?"

Reid nodded, and the two of them climbed to the flat upstairs. In the living room, Briony and Finley jolted on the couch, *SpellBC News* playing on the television.

"Oh," Briony squeaked, while Finley hastily snatched the clicker. "You're upstairs."

"What, are we interrupting something?" Reid asked.

"No, no," Finley answered tightly.

Isobel glanced at the broadcast, which played footage of stalled traffic on both the major highways exiting the city. Updates slid across the bottom of the screen in a reel.

PROTESTORS GATHER OUTSIDE CITY BANQUET HALL— THOUSANDS ATTEMPT TO FLEE ILVERNATH AS CURSE NEARS COLLAPSE—THORBURN STILL WANTED FOR QUESTIONING

"People are scared, and I think they're right to be," the voiceover said. "Hundreds of people are camped outside the Blood Veil, hoping to seize high magick if the curse breaks—"

"We're getting more coffee," Reid told them. "Want some?"

"Sure," Finley said, while Briony declined.

Isobel and Reid shuffled wearily into the kitchen, and even with the volume low, the voices of the news anchors still sounded from the living room.

"Well, what are people supposed to think? First the news about Thorburn and now MacTavish. It's been a shocking few hours—"

"What?" Reid gasped out, dashing back toward the television. Isobel followed, and to her horror, an image of Reid was superimposed on the screen, of him flipping off the photographer. Beneath it read the headline REID MACTAVISH CONFIRMED *TRADITION OF TRAGEDY* AUTHOR.

"Oh shit," Isobel murmured, her gaze swiveling between the broadcast and him.

For several seconds, Reid stood frozen, then, without a word, he bolted down the stairs.

"We're sorry!" Briony called. "It's been playing all day. We didn't want to interrupt—"

Isobel ignored her, hurrying after Reid. He paced across the curse-shop, his face contorted in dread.

"I-I don't understand," he stammered. "I had a non-disclosure. I told myself I was being careful. No wonder this place is covered in graffiti. Fuck, if my dad saw how it looked outside, he'd be so upset—"

"It's all right," Isobel told him. "You'll figure this out—"

"What is there to figure out? Even if we survive the tournament ending, what do I have to go back to? I've ruined my life, all because I got so . . . so . . ." With an unintelligible groan, he stormed past her into the back room, where he yanked several grimoires off the shelf. It was the first time Isobel had ever seen him handle books with anything other than care. Several delicate pages tore from their binding as he frantically flipped through them. "M-maybe I could change my face. If I disappeared—"

"You can't be serious," Isobel said from the doorway.

"Do you know how this looks? Like I'm some kind of freak mastermind, manipulating everyone behind the scenes."

"But isn't that kind of the truth?"

"*No.* I mean, yes, I don't know. I barely remember writing the manuscript. When I think about that summer, all I remember is that my dad was gone, my friends were gone, and I was *here*, surrounded by these books. Books that could teach you to make vile things. Books that should've been burned centuries ago. And the people who came into this shop? The things they'd ask me to make? I thought writing *Tradition* was the right thing to do, but then it became about breaking the curse, and breaking the curse became manipulating all of you, which became killing all of you, locking you in my guest room, implanting a dangerous spellstone into my stomach. I—"

Isobel ripped the grimoire from his hands and snapped it closed. "Reid, this was going to come out eventually. Didn't you realize that?"

"I know how ludicrous it sounds, but really, no, I didn't." He reached out to snatch the book, but Isobel backed away.

He hitched his breath, and for a wild moment, Isobel actually thought he would lunge to pry it from her grasp. And as they locked eyes, she realized that, just as Reid had been able to see through her, she could see through him. And although she didn't see someone good, she did see someone worth saving.

"I know how scary it is, to realize there's nothing you're not capable of," she said. "But you stopped me once, before I did something terrible. So before you stay up all night reading these horrible books trying to bend nature so you can run from your mistakes, just . . . let me talk you out of it. Or we don't have to talk. We can just sit here, making sure the beakers don't bubble over."

Carefully, she placed the grimoire on the desk and slid out the two chairs. Reid's chest heaved, anguish still plain on his face. Then, wordlessly, he collapsed into one of the seats, and she sat beside him. Their thighs touched, and she thought he'd move away, grumbling under his breath, but he never did.

Isobel wasn't sure how much time passed after that—perhaps thirty minutes, perhaps an hour. Reid slumped with his arms crossed atop the table, his cheek pressed against them, glaring at the titration set. And though he might've preferred the silence, she did not. Her fear whirred as though gnats were trapped inside her ears.

Finally, she couldn't stop herself from choking out, "If the spellmakers and those agents are working against us, they'll be waiting at the Castle." Reid didn't respond, only continued glowering at their ingredients. "Every time we've faced a Landmark's trial, we've barely escaped with our lives. How are we supposed to fight them *and* destroy the Crown?"

"Assuming our Crown works." Then, glancing up and catching the grimace on her face, he added, "Sorry. Not helping, I know."

"I'm serious. I'm scared. We keep surviving on luck, but what if we don't get lucky tomorrow? We're going to be exhausted. Who knows how Alistair and Gavin fared at the Cottage. We haven't felt the ground shake, which can't be a good sign."

"They're smart. They'll figure something out."

"Do you honestly believe that?"

Reid straightened and met her stare, and, as always, Isobel could tell that he *knew* what she was asking, even if she was too terrified to voice it.

"I'd give us a fifty-fifty shot," he said softly. "Less than that, if Alistair and Gavin are already dead."

Dread hammered in her chest, harder and more painful than any heartbeat could've managed. Already, her mind was conjuring escape routes. She'd promised herself that she'd never return to her old plan, and she was still committed to that vow. But that didn't stop her from imagining it. It didn't make the urge to fight or flee disappear.

She felt more awake than ever now—awake and restless.

"So this is my last night of living," she said with a shrill laugh. In all her time spent with Reid, she must've picked up his habit of joking in the face of utter doom. "Not exactly how I pictured spending it."

"In the dusty back office of my family's curseshop? Can't fathom why." There was an edge to his voice that Isobel didn't think she was imagining. "How *did* you picture spending it?"

Quickly, almost imperceptibly, Reid's gaze flickered to her lips.

Now Isobel knew she wasn't imagining it, and her mouth went dry as she fought for the words to answer. Every intrusive thought she'd buried today rose to the surface, adding weight to the already loaded question. A question she wouldn't normally consider, not with stress clouding both their judgments. But of all the reckless, dangerous choices she'd made since the Blood Moon first rose, this was so ordinary, so inconsequential.

A muscle in Reid's jaw clenched, and Isobel knew she was taking too long to answer. And if she'd had her heartbeat to dissuade her, if it weren't the middle of the night, she might not have been so bold as to take her time. Her eyes drifted across the slope where his neck met his shoulders. At the skin exposed above his oversized T-shirt. At the smudges of pomegranate juice on his fingertips.

Apparently the suspense was too much for Reid, who blurted, "Screw being subtle, I'm asking you if you want—"

Isobel grabbed him by his collar and pulled him toward her. When his mouth met hers, his breath was warm with every word he'd meant to say, replaced by a small, wanting gasp. His hands snaked around her waist, crushing her against him, and for the first time in far, far too long, heat kindled inside her. It ignited more with every touch against her skin, every kiss they let melt into another, then another. Her fears, so loud and all-consuming mere moments ago, snuffed out.

All except one, reduced to the faintest whisper. A reminder that Reid was pretentious, spiteful, manipulative. But he'd seen her own worst qualities and never judged her for them, because if he was terrible, then so was she. And if she could press her lips to the same spot she'd once cursed him, if he could make her shudder with want when he'd once made her shudder with fear, then she would gladly rewrite every wrong they'd done to each other, however many times it took for their redemption to sink in.

But not even an hour ago, he had confessed all his mistakes to her. And however agonizingly she now burned, she refused to be one of them.

She broke away, then pressed her forehead against his. "Are you sure you want this?"

"Want this?" he repeated incredulously. "I've spent so much time thinking about you, and what you think of me. I've wanted this so much I've obsessed over it."

Then he pushed his chair from the desk, and Isobel straddled him. His arms felt warm and steady around her. His lips tasted like coffee. And more than anything, she liked the way that he touched her, as though she were more dangerous and valuable than any book in his collection. His one hand traced a slow, sedulous curve down her spine, as though memorizing its every groove. With the other, he intertwined his fingers with her hair, gently tugging her head back until she opened her neck to him. Every kiss was deliberate, every graze and tease carefully considered, betraying exactly how truthful his words had been, how thoroughly he'd dwelled on this moment. It didn't matter that a clock ticked down until their probable demise; he would make a study of her, as though she had any more secrets or desires to lay bare to him.

Finally, when her impatience edged toward torture, she pulled off his shirt and then her own. It was a relief. With the door closed, the room was hot from each boiling concoction, making condensation drip down each of the vials and sweat slicken across their chests. But still she clung to him tightly. His heartbeat drummed against her, quickening as her own touches became rougher and more urgent, as she kissed without needing to pause for air. Yet even as he pulled away, flushed and panting, his mouth returned to her in an instant, and she shivered as the heat of his tongue piercing met the cold of her skin.

Time slipped away from them, and when light bled through the crack beneath the door, it felt too fast, like a trick. Reluctantly, Isobel lifted her head from Reid's shoulder and reached up toward the stop-watch on the desk.

Reid caught her wrist in midair. "Don't."

But it was too late—she'd already seen the time. "It's nearly done. We should go talk to Briony and Finley." This was the part of the process she'd been dreading the most—one of them would have to donate life magick.

Reid closed his eyes for a moment, then sighed, kissed her one final time on the temple, and stood up. He grabbed his discarded shirt with one hand and the spellboard with his other. "You're right. Go get one of them."

Isobel dressed and slipped through the shop. She found Briony and Finley upstairs in the living room—Finley was awake, while Briony was passed out, her head in his lap. Gently, Finley shook her arm.

"It's ready," Isobel told them.

"I'll go," Finley said, but as he moved to stand, Briony shot up.

"No. If it's only going to be one of us, it should be me," she said.

Finley sighed. "How did I know you would try to argue with me?"

"I chose to join this tournament. The rest of you didn't. So please, Fin, don't fight me for choosing this."

Finley glanced at Isobel, as though hoping she'd take his side. But Isobel didn't say anything. She might've put everything she had into crafting the replacement Crown, but this was one sacrifice she couldn't give. It didn't feel right to weigh in on a decision that was ultimately between them.

"I can tell you won't back down," Finley said at last, begrudgingly. He sank into the couch, fiddling nervously with his curserings. "Fine. I won't fight you."

When Isobel returned to the office with Briony, Reid had finished setting up the spellboard, the seven ingredients arranged on each point of the septogram.

"You mentioned this is going to hurt," Briony said. "What should I brace myself for?"

"We're going to break several of your bones," Reid answered in the flat, matter-of-fact tone of a physician.

Briony made a startled noise in the back of her throat.

"It needs to be a serious enough injury to siphon out life magick, but as soon as I'm finished, Isobel will heal you. The process will only last a few minutes."

"A few minutes," she repeated to herself. Then she shook out her arms and jumped in place a few times, as though psyching herself up for a volleyball match. "Yeah. I can handle that."

Still, she gratefully accepted Isobel's offered hand as she lowered herself into the seat.

Isobel squeezed it, bracing herself as well. It'd been hard enough to hear Reid scream in agony when she'd still despised him.

However, Briony seemed determined not to scream—not after the first crack, or the second, or the third. Instead, she clenched Isobel's hand so tightly that Isobel thought her own bones might shatter. But she didn't pull away. Not until Reid plunged the syringe into the greenish-purple septogram that had appeared on Briony's bicep, and a glowing, foggy liquid spilled into the glass.

While he siphoned the life magick into the Crown, Isobel cast three spellstones' worth of the Healer's Touch. Briony's bones reset into place, and the swelling in her arm gradually diminished. She panted, her forehead slick with sweat, her skin ashen.

"Huh," she breathed. "I thought that'd be worse."

Isobel snorted. "Liar—"

Boom!

An explosion thundered outside, and the floor below them heaved, making books and vials tumble onto the floor.

"What's happening?" Briony cried out.

At first, Isobel wanted to say that it was the Cottage—that Alistair and Gavin had destroyed it after all—but that didn't explain the noise. Even from inside, she made out the wailing of car alarms and indistinct, panicked voices shouting from down the street.

She raced out of the office into the curseshop, where Finley already stood, gawking at the sight through the front windows. The red that normally painted the morning sky was gone, replaced by clear, brilliant blue.

ALISTAIR LOWE

"We're interrupting our program with a breaking news update:
The Blood Veil surrounding Ilvernath has fallen."

SpellBC News

Sound roared around them, so thunderous Alistair swore the very seams of the world were splitting apart. The pressure blasted through his ears and into his core, and he dropped, too overwhelmed to cast a shield spell, to do anything but cradle his head in his arms as the force threatened to explode inside him.

After what could've been seconds or could've been minutes, the world stilled of anything but the breeze against his neck. He lifted his head, deafened, disoriented. Shards of the Blood Veil drifted from the sky like scarlet snow, disintegrating before meeting the grass, and Alistair gaped as he took in the unfiltered sunlight.

As he clambered to his feet, for a brief, delirious moment, he thought the curse had broken. He laughed even as his skull pounded, as his balance swayed. Then, with a heart-wrenching stab of disappointment, he saw the champion's ring still glinting on his pinky.

The tournament wasn't finished with them yet.

Several meters away, Gavin sat up, his gaze fixed skyward, marveling at what the two of them had done. Slowly, his eyes lowered to Alistair, but instead of joy or relief, his expression was plastered with panic.

He shouted something, but Alistair couldn't hear it—he couldn't hear anything.

Then a flare of light whizzed toward him, and Alistair didn't have time to react before it struck the ground and ice burst in all directions, a glacier conjured from nothing. It seized him by his right leg, encasing him from his trainer all the way to his thigh. He swore at the cold's bite, then twisted around as more cursefire rained over them.

Gavin leapt in front of him, his Spikeshield deflecting the oncoming blows.

Several figures advanced from the tree line, no longer inhibited by the Cottage's wards. Two faces Alistair recognized instantly—Osmand Walsh and Diana Aleshire. The others were strangers, each of them clothed in a matching unobtrusive black uniform, with thick leather boots and a shimmering enchanted vest.

"Who are they?" Alistair demanded. Even his own voice sounded muffled, drowned out by the whirring in his ears. "And what the hell happened to Walsh's oath spell?"

"I don't know," Gavin grunted.

One of the uniformed agents called something out, his words faint and indistinct. But clearly he hadn't offered them a truce, as a heartbeat later, two more curses pummeled against Gavin's armor. The spell quivered before snuffing out.

Alistair swore under his breath, yanking his leg as hard as he could. The ice seared his skin even through the fabric of his jeans, and he frantically inventoried his spells. The Reaper's Embrace had progressed too much to risk even a single, trivial curse.

Behind him, Gavin backpedaled into Alistair's side. Then he cast the Dragon's Breath.

Alistair had only seen Gavin attempt such a powerful enchantment on a handful of occasions—as a vessel, his magick had been too strong to ever need to. Gavin staggered, one hand clutching his abdomen, as he opened his mouth and fire spewed from his throat. Their assailants cried out as the curse scorched through the clearing, and they scattered to avoid the violent path of the flames.

Finally, thanks to the added heat, Alistair freed his leg, pulling so hard he lost his balance and toppled to the grass. Gavin's hands were on him an instant later, hoisting him up even as his shoulders heaved. Then, as Alistair righted himself, Gavin stared at the embers.

"I did it," he said breathlessly. The sheen of sweat on his face glistened orange and gold.

But they didn't have time for congratulations. "Great, now come on." Alistair grabbed Gavin's hand and cast two Here to Theres.

The heat of the Dragon's Breath vanished, replaced by the brutal, frigid wind that blustered across the moors. The Castle loomed over them, and, at its champion's arrival, the drawbridge lowered with a mechanical groan. The ground rumbled as it struck down, seemingly the only sound for kilometers.

"Where are the others?" Alistair squinted across the lifeless landscape. "They destroyed the Tower yesterday. Shouldn't they—"

"They said it would take time to craft the Crown," Gavin reminded him.

"*This* much time?" Alistair shook his head. "If we were attacked, they could've been, too."

"We can contact them once we're inside. Then we—"

Suddenly, Gavin shouted and collapsed to the grass. Restraints like rope tethers materialized over his back, pinning his arms to his sides and sizzling with static. He screamed, writhing at Alistair's feet.

Horror grasped a choking hand around Alistair's throat, but before he could make any move to help him, a familiar, patronizing voice called across the desolate landscape behind them.

"It's over, boys."

Alistair hitched his breath and whipped around. Walsh strode toward them, his expensive clothes singed and marred with soot, his expression lethal.

"I-I don't understand," Alistair stammered. "Your oath spell. You shouldn't be able to hurt him."

A sinister grin crept across Walsh's toadlike face. "Ah, I'll admit it was a pleasant surprise. You see, when the Grieve was cured, so was I." He drank in Gavin's pained grimace as Gavin gritted his teeth, seemingly determined not to reward the spellmaker with another scream. "Putting both of you back in your place feels even more satisfying than I imagined."

A curse sprang from one of Walsh's spellrings and burrowed into the soil. The earth where it struck began to shift, then bulge, as though a creature had tunneled beneath it, and the heather overtop it drooped and grayed. The enchantment crawled toward Alistair and Gavin, serpentine, leaving a trail of decay in its wake. Heart hammering, Alistair cast an Exoskeleton a mere moment before the creature leapt toward him. Its stone jaw gaped open, mulch spilling from its gaps, and its all-white eyes bored at them, cloudy and empty. But as it hit the barrier, it disintegrated, and Alistair shielded his face with his hand as dirt sprayed into the air.

Then, as Walsh strolled closer, Alistair asked, hoping to stall him. "Where did all your other goons go?"

Walsh scoffed. "They're hardly goons. The Cursebreaking Division has been observing your actions during the tournament, and they've now decided that none of you or your deranged families are fit to wield high magick. And practically all the spellmakers of Ilvernath agree with them, as did the Thorburn family. So our three parties came to a far more sensible arrangement."

"That you'd help them break it," Alistair realized with a dark tone, "in the way that leaves all of us dead."

"Exactly," Walsh said smugly.

"But what are you getting in return? I overheard their agents speaking to my grandmother—you know the government has only ever wanted high magick for itself, right?"

"They're willing to share. You see, they need us, as we've designed them a new curse to contain Ilvernath's high magick, and it'll bind four of them, and three of our own. And I promise, whatever lives go into making it, it'll be far more honorable than the curse you've all reveled in." Walsh's grin widened with a cruel sort of pleasure. "In fact, we have you to thank for making this happen. Without studying your brother and Mr. Grieve's life magick, we couldn't have crafted something so powerful."

Alistair stiffened. He'd never trusted the spellmakers after they'd meddled with his enchantments, but he hadn't realized the extent to which they'd manipulated his brother. Rage rose in his stomach, but he clenched his fist. He couldn't risk a curse.

"You and the Thorburns . . . *You're* the serial killers, stealing people's life magick," Alistair growled at him. "You've been using them to fuel your curse."

"How can you have the audacity to judge me after everything you've done?" Walsh asked viciously. "We've shed far less blood than your family."

Then a flurry of new curses hurled toward him, forcing Alistair to pour more and more magick into the shield. Before long, the Exoskeleton's spellstone emptied entirely, and he switched to his next one—a lower class Shark's Skin. While it trembled under the barrage of cursefire, Alistair knelt beside Gavin and grabbed his restraints.

Then he shouted and wrenched away. White sparks of magick sizzled over the bindings. Only Alistair's curserings could cut them, and so, painful or not, he had no alternative but to pry the ropes off by force.

Alistair pressed his palm against Gavin's chest. "Hold still. I have to—"

"Whatever it is, just do it," Gavin grunted, writhing all the same.

Alistair clasped the tethers. The sparks pulsed, and every muscle in his arms begged to recoil. He bit down on his tongue as he tried to wrench them apart. But he wasn't strong enough, and finally he pulled back, panting. Beside them, his shield spell had dissolved, and when he tried to summon it again, he realized that spellstone, too, had run out.

He swore under his breath. Casting any curse was a gamble, but Walsh might give him no choice. "This is bad. I don't have many more shields—"

Boom!

An explosion blasted in front them, sweeping both the boys from the hillside. Alistair tumbled down the steep slope, and icy shock greeted him as he plunged into the moat. He thrashed for several seconds, grasping in every direction for the surface or a foothold. Then his head broke to the frigid kiss of air. He coughed then sighted Gavin weakly shuffling up the bank, still trapped in the tethers' clutches.

"G-Gav!" Alistair sputtered, rushing toward him. His feet barely scraped the moat's slimy bottom, and every nerve in his body tensed from the cold.

But before he could reach him, a current yanked him from behind. He cried out as the ground slipped from beneath his shoes, and the water dragged him backward—faster and faster, until he couldn't even keep his head above the surface. He cast a haphazard string of spells: a Come Hither, a Trick of the Light, a Purify—each of them illogical, useless. Then a wave flung him against the Castle, and the back of his skull struck stone. He gasped as his vision erupted with stars, then squirmed against the water's grip. It clutched him in a chokehold, and even as he clamped his mouth shut, it flooded through his nostrils, down his throat.

Drowning him.

His panicked thoughts teetered like a sinking ship.

The lack of air, the agony of it.

Hendry, gone.

Gavin, defenseless.

How close they were to breaking the tournament, how direly he wanted to see it.

The pressure building in his lungs, so great he might burst.

Hendry, promising him he'd be okay.

Hendry, urging him to fight, to live.

In a desperate gamble, Alistair summoned the Giant's Wrath and, with the last of his strength, wrenched his arm down against the water's force and flattened his palm on the wall behind him. He seized the thought of his brother, an anchor, and focused. The stone buckled, and he was thrown backward as the wall collapsed. He slammed painfully atop granite, then immediately pushed himself on all fours as liquid poured from his mouth, one choking spate after the other.

Sounds rang out ahead, but Alistair barely registered them. Reality only returned when air did, and he shakily rose to his feet, panting, his entire torso sore from coughs. Around him, the Castle's cellar was submerged in a thin layer of water, rocky debris scattered about. Sunlight streamed in from the hole he'd blown through the wall.

He stumbled toward it, tripping twice and falling once. Then, after he scaled the Landmark's broken foundation, he froze.

Across the moat, Walsh prowled toward Gavin. Curses exploded between them, and glittery remnants hung in the air, so blinding that Alistair had to shade his eyes with his hand. Gavin, merely a silhouette amid the glare, had managed to heave himself to his knees, and though he was fighting, casting, he was also losing. The enchanted restraints had yet to unravel, and the Spikeshield armor glowing around him was fractured, crumbling away piece by piece.

At Alistair's approach, Walsh whipped toward him, and his eyes widened, as though he'd already thought he'd finished him off. Scrunching his face in fury, Walsh turned back to Gavin, and the crystal dangling around his neck gleamed as he summoned its curse.

Bright.

Powerful.

Deadly.

When Alistair Lowe made the final choice of his life, he harbored no delusion that it was noble. It was too instinctual, too ruthless, and no decision born from such a place inside him could be anything other than wicked. Not even if it would save someone else.

He stretched his hand out toward the spellmaker, and the ring he'd worn for so long as a trophy, as a promise to himself, flared with magick. He could almost picture his grandmother's disgusted sneer as she realized what he was doing, that—unlike the Giant's Wrath breaking the wall—this curse was no gamble. Casting it would, without a doubt, kill Walsh.

And it would kill him too.

As he summoned it, heat ignited in his stomach, so searing that he gasped, and smoke flitted from his mouth. The curse roiled within him, ravenous, seizing on all Alistair's emotions so that it could feed. First it consumed his rage, his fear, and molten light shone from his abdomen even through the soaked wool of his sweater. Then it swallowed his grief, swelling from the size of it.

Soon it blazed so powerfully that Alistair had to brace himself on the ruined wall to hold himself upright. Embers kindled on each of his fingertips, and sweat poured down his temples. Yet still, he let it feast. He gave it his shame, his want, his hope. He gave it everything he had.

Finally, just as he swore his skin might blister, he squeezed his fist and cast the Demon's Pyre.

The raw magick hovering near Osmand Walsh fled from him in all directions, as though sensing what was to come. The spellmaker hesitated at the sight of it, confusion—then horror—creeping over his face.

A moment later, his body ignited.

Alistair barely heard Walsh's scream. His already frantic heartbeat careened into a fever pitch, and the heat snuffed out all at once, a dreadful cold clutching him in its place. It was colder than the water, the winter, colder than anything he'd ever known.

He crossed the moat and collapsed onto the grassy bank. Pain shuddered through him, and he raked his nails into the mud, arched his back beyond the point of what felt like stretching, fracturing.

The Reaper's Embrace had consumed him.

"Al!" Gavin shouted, and a second later, he seized Alistair, pinning his arms down and pulling him into his chest. But it all did little to steady him. Alistair shook in his grip, his breaths sputtering, his gaze blurring in and out of focus. And as his pulse gradually slowed, each remaining beat of his heart sent an agonizing spasm through his body, more excruciating than anything he'd ever experienced. It transformed every sensation into torture: the lashing of the wind, the sun scorching against his skin, and—worst of any of it—Gavin squeezing him. But nothing, not even death, would be enough for Alistair to break away from the one good thing he had left.

"No, no," Gavin moaned, struggling to hold Alistair upright. "You can't—you shouldn't have—"

But Gavin couldn't finish his words. Unable to contain it any longer, Alistair threw his head back and screamed, hoping it was the last breath he'd ever let out.

Brutally slowly, the pain lessened, his heartbeats fading into murmurs. He slumped against Gavin, his forehead pressed against his shoulder. Below him, his reflection stared back from the water's surface. Apart from the dark of his pupils, any color or life in his face was gone, consumed entirely by the cursemark. He looked frightening, grotesque. A monster.

When Alistair swayed, Gavin hoisted him upright. "Y-you need to give me Hendry's spell. I'm going to heal you."

Alistair laughed weakly. "It won't work."

"It *will*. It has to." He clasped Alistair's hand and, without bothering to waste time prying off the ring, intertwined their fingers. At his touch, the yellow crystal on Alistair's pointer blazed bright and ready.

But Alistair ignored it. He had barely any breath remaining, and he wanted his last words to be good ones.

"I couldn't have killed you," he choked. "I'm sorry I tried. I'm sorry I . . ." His voice slurred into a groan, and his vision—so radiant moments before—blackened. But it didn't scare Alistair. He knew this feeling, having nearly died twice before.

Then a sudden warmth settled over him, and he jolted—Hendry's spell, filled with his brother's own life magick, soothing as a blanket. But, so Alistair had expected, the sensation faded, and he shivered as the same cold seeped over him.

"No." Gavin seethed, sounding angrier than Alistair had ever heard him. "There has to be a way."

But there wasn't. The tournament's curse wasn't broken, and the wrongs Alistair had committed couldn't be undone.

Gavin must've realized the same thing because he let out a sob. It startled Alistair, who had never expected anyone to cry over his end, especially not him.

"I'm sorry," Gavin forced out, over and over, as though he'd somehow failed Alistair after being the only person beside his brother who'd stayed with him, who'd believed in him despite everything he'd done. With despair, Alistair realized that he'd wasted his last words, apologizing to his enemy when he should've been thanking him. If not for him, Alistair would've certainly faced this same awful end, but he'd have faced it alone.

He squeezed Gavin tighter, willing the touch alone to suffice.

As though in response, Gavin cupped Alistair's cheek with his other hand and pressed their foreheads together, and despite Alistair giving all of himself to the Demon's Pyre, a paltry fragment must've remained, because desire still twisted in his gut—cruel and excruciating. After everything he'd gone through, one thing remained unchanged: He'd always want what he'd never have.

Then his mind slipped—not into nothingness—but into madness. Because as he inhaled his final, feeble breath, he felt Gavin press his lips to his.

This fantasy didn't resemble any he'd conceived before. Gavin trembled against him, in grief instead of want or fear. And though his hand on Alistair's face trailed lower, it stopped before it could reach his throat—instead gently lifting his chin.

Yet it could only be a fantasy. Because barely two days before, Alistair had knelt over Gavin and nearly taken his life. They were born to opposing sides of the same, bloodstained story, one of them always fated to die in the arms of the other. And if his enemy's lips were the last, fatal touch Alistair ever felt, then so be it. He would gladly welcome his demise.

Something stirred in his stomach, comforting and warm, but Alistair dismissed it. Even *his* imagination wasn't potent enough to trick him. Hendry's spell had long since sputtered out.

And yet, Alistair sighed what should've been his dying breath and kissed his enemy back.

The empty blackness behind his eyelids brightened, and his heart sped up, the pain he'd felt with it gradually releasing its hold. New details snuck into his fantasy, vivid enough to be real. The water from his sopping hair dripping down his cheeks. The way Gavin tasted, like salt and smoke. The Castle moat lapping at their ankles.

"Is this real?" Alistair rasped.

Gavin's breath hitched, and he responded by unlacing his fingers and snaking his arm around Alistair's waist. He pulled him closer, crushing him against him, as though Alistair might disappear otherwise. Alistair countered, wrapping his hands behind Gavin's neck. He kissed him fiercer, deeper. Soon, the only pain was Gavin's nails stabbing into his sides, his teeth biting against his lip, and it dawned on Alistair that this was no fantasy. He was alive, saved by the very person who'd wanted to kill him most.

Gavin broke away and whispered against Alistair's cheek, "Open your eyes."

Alistair did, taking in the glare of the sun, the glint of relief in Gavin's bloodshot stare. Then he saw his hands, pink and pale. His breaths—many in number now—stuttered out in shock as he untangled himself from Gavin enough to peel up the bottom of his soaked sweater, to wrench up each of his sleeves. The cursemark was gone.

"I-I don't get it," he stammered. "The tournament isn't broken. Hendry's spell couldn't have . . . How did you know that would work?"

"I didn't," Gavin answered breathlessly. "But the Reaper's Embrace was *cast* with a kiss, and I've . . ." He swallowed. "I've wanted to do that for so long."

Alistair was so used to distrusting Gavin that he narrowed his eyes, scrutinizing Gavin's grave expression, searching for the lie. Then, in another dangerous gamble, he smiled and leaned his head to the side, letting his lips hover over Gavin's ear.

"Longer than you've wanted to kill me?"

Gavin shuddered against him. "Sometimes, I wanted both."

Alistair's body, though no longer afflicted by the Reaper's Embrace, was far from healed. His back ached from where it'd slammed into the Castle's wall, and as his adrenaline waned, the exhaustion of his arduous night caught up to him—and the painful events of the day before.

But he didn't care. He was alive, and he didn't want to think of what pained him, what threats still loomed in their future. Even after one of his most treacherous fantasies had been fulfilled, he still harbored far, far more.

He kissed a trail down Gavin's neck, and he felt a low, yearning sound rumble in the other boy's throat. Gavin lowered him into the grass, and for several minutes, Alistair thought of nothing except the dangerous thrill of having his enemy against him. He had never tasted a sweeter poison. Never so happily let himself drown.

Until the wind changed direction, and a nauseating odor made both of them stiffen.

Gavin sat up, frowning, then his gaze drifted to the right. With a start, Alistair remembered the spellmaker, the screams that had long since gone silent. As his truer, darker reality settled in, Alistair turned his head to look, but Gavin caught his face in his hands, holding him steady. "Don't."

But Alistair didn't listen. He tore away and rolled to the side, taking in the charred husk that had once been Osmand Walsh. Though most of him had disintegrated—a heap of ash within the grass—some shape of him remained. A bulge that might've been a scapula. A disfigured blackened hand reaching toward the water, its spellrings fallen and tumbled into the shallows.

"He would've killed me," Gavin murmured. "Either of us. All of us."

"I know." But that made killing him no easier to swallow.

Numbly, he let Gavin take him by the hand and lead him back up the hill toward the drawbridge, and though Alistair had entered the Castle before, only now did it occur to him how closely this place resembled the Lowes' stories. Since slaying his family, Alistair had used each of their favorite curses. He'd hurt, tortured, murdered.

Cured or not, there was no end to the monster story if, all along, the monster had been him.

BRIONY THORBURN

"The question no longer seems to be if they can break the curse, but how—and what it will mean for the rest of us."
98.6 Local Broadcasting Beat

B riony and her allies emerged from behind Reid's wards with their best defensive spells already cast, bracing for an ambush—only to find a deserted alley. Sirens wailed around them, and people rushed in all directions on the nearby street, shouting. Some carried luggage, others toted protest signs. No one paid them any mind. The strangeness only continued once their Here to There spells dropped them in front of the Castle.

Briony, who'd cast three such spells so easily a day ago, felt weakened after a night spent guarding the wards and a morning spent donating her life magick. She didn't normally care what she looked like, but she'd caught the worry on Finley's face and investigated her reflection in the bathroom mirror before they'd left. Her skin appeared nearly jaundiced, and the veins threaded around her temples stood out starkly against her sallow complexion. But the bone-deep weariness within her concerned her the most. Her muscles ached, sore and pinched, as though she'd finished a workout and skipped the cooldown stretch. Yet she was determined not to show it.

"What happened here?" Briony gawked at the uprooted landscape, squinting into the unfamiliarly bright daylight. Part of the Castle's foundation had collapsed, along with a stretch of the moat; large chunks of earth had been tossed aside as though little more than pebbles.

"The spellmakers probably attacked them, too," Isobel said gravely.

"Look at this." Finley pointed a quivering finger at a heap of charred bones. Stray spellstones glimmered in the moat beside them. Briony's stomach lurched.

"Whose body do you think that is?" she asked nervously. It was impossible to tell, although the Castle's wards still shimmered around the extended drawbridge, suggesting the survival of at least one champion. Reid blanched at the sight of the corpse, then white-knuckled the makeshift Crown.

"Only one way to find out," he muttered, jerking his head toward the Landmark.

Briony couldn't believe she'd donated life magick to create a Relic as noble and lauded as the Crown . . . only to wind up with a hat that looked like it had been abandoned in a lost and found box. But the three spellstones set into the beanie's side glowed, proof of what they'd done.

As they treaded carefully down the drawbridge into the Castle's stony embrace, the wards parted at their approach. She could only hope that meant both boys were still in one piece—and that they were all still on the same side.

The Castle's interior contained the same decor she remembered. If anything, it looked nicer than ever, the suits of armor gleaming, the curtains and tapestries vibrant and beautiful.

They found Alistair and Gavin in the throne room, sitting side by side on the steps leading to the dais, in the shadow of the pillar that stood atop it. At the others' approach, they rose, setting aside what looked like a very haphazard, unappetizing meal. Alistair had changed—the bone white of the Reaper's Embrace was gone, his cheeks now flushed with color, his eyes shining gray and clear.

Isobel gasped. "Your curse. Did you . . . is it . . ." She started toward them, but Gavin stepped protectively in front of Alistair.

"It's okay," Alistair murmured, placing a hand on Gavin's shoulder. Gavin backed away, although his cautious stare still bored into all of them. "It's gone. Gavin broke it."

Isobel's gaze darted between the two boys. What looked like dozens of questions flitted across her face, before her expression collapsed into one of relief.

Briony had questions, too, but Reid got there first.

"How?" the cursemaker asked in disbelief. "Breaking it would take . . ."

"Something powerful," Gavin said pointedly. "Something good."

From the tone of Gavin's voice and Reid's visible surprise, Briony could tell that his words held significance to all three of them.

"Gavin's cured, too," Alistair added.

"How did—oh, never mind," Reid muttered. "Our Relic comes with a time limit." He held up the beanie-Crown. A loose thread had already unraveled from it, dangling in the air. "If we're going to break the curse, we need to do it *now*."

Alistair let out a noise of derision. "You turned a Relic into . . . that?"

Reid frowned. "I've gotten a lot of wear out of this hat."

Gavin rolled his eyes. "And it's about to be destroyed, anyway."

"Let's get started," Briony said. "All six of us should be able to do this trial pretty fast—"

Alistair cleared his throat. "The trial's not our only problem. We found out what the spellmakers and the government are planning."

A horrified hush descended over the group as Alistair and Gavin explained all they'd learned. Briony had known her family was in-volved in something twisted and despicable. But the thought that they'd been so willing to trade one curse for another, all while experi-menting with other peoples' life magick, made her already-weak body feel as though it were about to give out. She shuddered and swayed, steadying only when Finley snaked an arm around her shoulders and led her to a table in the corner.

"We can't let them cast that curse," she croaked, sinking into a chair.

"I agree," Isobel said firmly.

"Then we need to split up," Finley said. "Some of us break the curse; some of us stop the spellmakers and the government."

"If they're going to try and claim high magick, they'll do it at the Champions Pillar." Reid paced back and forth by the dais. "That's the spellstone at the center of all this."

"But it'll be swarmed," Finley countered. "It already is. We watched the news all night—people are either fleeing the city, or staying to fight for high magick."

"What about the resistance?" Briony asked. "They'd help us, right?"

"They would," Finley said. "But they want control of high magick too, Bri. They might not be trying to cast a new curse, but aren't they just members of the families fighting for it all over again?"

"When high magick comes back to Ilvernath, *everyone* will want it." Isobel perched on the edge of the table and tapped her nails anxiously against the stone. "Not just our families, not just the government, not just the spellmakers."

"Not just Ilvernath, either," Reid warned. "The Blood Veil's broken, and the whole world knows about the tournament. Anyone who wants high magick is about to get a chance at it. *Anyone.*"

"You're saying this could start a war," Gavin said. He and Alistair remained beside the dais. Even from a distance, Briony noted the matching bits of mud and soot crusted across their clothes; the dark circles beneath their eyes. Although they were both cured, they still looked exhausted.

"I would argue it already has," Finley said darkly.

Briony had seen enough of the news to know he was right. Once high magick returned, people would battle for it the way Ilvernath's champions had. There would be a far higher death toll—and far greater consequences.

She rose to her feet. "Stopping the government and the spellmakers won't be enough, then. We need a plan for what happens to high magick."

Isobel slid off the table and strode into the center of the room, her footsteps echoing across the cavernous space. "I think we should destroy it. For good."

All six of them fell silent. Blood poured from the pillar behind the throne, pooling on the dais and dribbling onto the floor. The tapestries shivered and shook in an invisible wind. The sunlight streaming in through the windows was pure, untarnished, the sky a disarmingly vivid blue.

Briony thought of a world where every moon was a Blood Moon. Where an army's worth of people would be made to throw their lives away for power most of them would never use.

"I'm in," Alistair said immediately, his words high and shaky.

Gavin spoke a heartbeat later. "So am I."

"Same," Briony said, not wanting to be outdone by the people who'd fought for high magick more than anyone else there.

"Me too," Finley added.

"Reid?" Isobel arched a brow. The cursemaker leaned his head back, his gaze fixed on the slopes of the vaulted ceiling.

"Oh, I'm in," he drawled. "I'm just thinking about the best way to pull this off without us all dying."

The enormity of their decision settled over Briony. Maybe it was a choice they had no right to make. But they were the ones who'd experienced firsthand the price people were willing to pay for power. The ones who'd risked everything to end the tournament.

Yet even ending the tournament wouldn't be enough to stop the slaughter.

"Does that mean you have an idea?" she asked Reid.

Reid steepled his fingers. "If we assume high magick works like common magick, then the same cursemaking theory applies. When the tournament breaks, all the high magick in Ilvernath will be drawn toward the Champions Pillar like a magnet, since it was the focal point of the curse. If we can destroy the pillar once that happens, we can destroy high magick with it."

"That's easier said than done," Finley murmured. "The whole city will have swarmed the Pillar by now."

"Could the resistance help us?" Isobel asked. "If we and several others cast spells on the Pillar at the same time, it would break."

"We shouldn't tell anyone what we're doing, the resistance included," Briony said carefully. "If we really do destroy high magick, no one outside this room should *ever* find out it was us. I—I know what happens if you try to go public with stuff like this now. It would make us targets for the rest of our lives."

"She's right," Finley said quickly.

Isobel swallowed, then nodded. "Reid and I can craft an oath spell after, then. We'll keep it a secret. But that means destroying the Pillar's on us, and us alone."

"We've done the rest of this alone, haven't we?" Gavin pointed out.

The others nodded gravely.

"All right, then," Briony said. "Who's going where?"

"I'm staying here," Alistair said. "This is my family's trial, so Gavin and I will be here to see it through."

"Actually . . ." Gavin turned to Alistair. "Al, I don't think I can do this with you."

Alistair's eyes widened. "What?"

"I'm sorry. But it feels like my fault that the spellmakers got this far."

Alistair grabbed him by the wrist and yanked him toward the dais. They hovered in front of the throne, arguing in low, worried voices.

Isobel, meanwhile, strode to Briony and propped a hand on her hip.

"I want to be at the pillar," she said. "Destroying high magick was my idea."

Reid appeared beside her a moment later. "I'm coming with you. Although I need to refill some spellstones first. Do we have time for that?"

Isobel frowned. "A few minutes, maybe. There's probably some raw magick in a storeroom down the hall."

Reid handed the beanie-Crown to Briony, then hurried off, so fast he was nearly running.

"If Gavin's going, Briony and I should stay here," Finley said. "Three and three, right?"

"Makes sense." Briony gave his hand a reassuring squeeze. "We were there for the first trial—I'd like to be there for the last one, too."

"Then it's settled," Isobel said. "Gavin? Are you coming with us or not?"

"Yeah." Gavin turned away from Alistair, who still gnawed on his lower lip. "I'm ready."

Briony looked around at all of them—these people who'd come here prepared to kill one another. They weren't exactly friends now, but they had more than a common enemy: They shared a common cause. And they were ready to fight for it.

But before they did, there was one more thing she wanted to do. Once upon a time, a boy had freed her from a dungeon and given her faith when she'd had none left. Now, she could finally thank him for it.

She tugged her hand away from Finley's and walked to Alistair, then held out the makeshift Crown.

"It's your family's Relic," she said. "I know I didn't trust you, before. I can't fix that. But I just wanted to say I'm grateful for what you did the last time we were here. And I think you should be the one to start the trial."

He blinked at her, surprised, then took the beanie and carefully turned it over in his hands. "I can't wait to destroy this place."

"Me too," Briony said. They were so close to victory, she felt dizzy.

All six of them had schemed and fought and betrayed one another, and then, somehow, they'd changed.

They'd found another way. They'd told a better story. Now they would end it. Together.

ALISTAIR LOWE

"As ludicrous as it is to say, it's almost a good thing that the Lowes are gone, isn't it? They've been killing their own kids every generation. They'd have sooner murdered all the champions than let the tournament fall."

Champion Confidential, WKL Radio

Alistair wordlessly approached the Castle's throne, the makeshift Crown in his hand.

As a child, he'd fantasized countless times how it would feel to sit upon it, to clutch the gilded armrests and sink into the velvet cushion. In another story, another life, this throne was meant for him.

He couldn't wait to see it fall.

"Are you just gonna stare at it?" Briony didn't sound impatient, but her voice reminded Alistair of how long he'd been frozen there. He tore his gaze from his forsaken birthright and craned his neck up at the pillar that rose behind it. The cracks he'd examined two mornings before had deepened into gouges, molten with crimson light. The rivulets of blood streaming from it ran down the chair's grooves and into the mortar between the floor tiles, as though the Landmark's heart was truly threaded with veins.

"I'm trying to figure out how to crown a giant rock," Alistair lied. "With a beanie."

"I thought you wanted to do the honors," Finley said.

"Yeah, well, I forgot to read the instruction manual."

Feeling foolish and awkward—and relieved Gavin wasn't here to witness this—Alistair climbed onto the chair, first atop the seat and then the armrest. Gripping the pillar tightly so as not to fall, he stood on his tiptoes and stretched to place the beanie upon the peak.

It took balance—far more than he had. As soon as he let go of the Relic, his fingers slipped on the blood-slicked stone, and he crashed onto the floor. The sound of it echoed down the hall.

Then, after far too long of a pause, Briony and Finley leaned over him and burst into laughter.

"Menacing," Briony choked, clutching her abdomen.

Alistair's face burned, and he resisted the urge to snap. Though Briony had offered him a truce, though the Reaper's Embrace no longer marked his skin, Alistair wasn't sure he deserved any salvation, when the body of his latest victim still smoldered outside.

He told himself he didn't care. What mattered was that they'd granted him this chance to destroy his family's legacy once and for all.

Ignoring Finley's offered hand, Alistair rose to his feet. But no sooner had he straightened than the ground began to quake, and the three of them stumbled to catch their balance. One by one, the daylight beaming through each of the windows blinked out, as though the Castle had been plunged into the throes of night. Every torch and candelabra in the chamber flared with scarlet flame, and a phantom breeze wafted through the air, smelling of ash.

"Brace yourselves," Finley warned.

Alistair tried, but despite how ardently he wanted to bring the Castle down, dread seeped through him like icy water between his bones. It was a fear worse than the first sight of the Blood Moon, than facing Elionor in the woods. Because of all the nightmares he'd endured, he could imagine no horror greater than one tied to his family.

A thunderous sound tore through the Castle, seeming to rattle the fortress down to its very foundation. The three champions jolted and covered their ears.

"What the hell was that?" Briony demanded, wincing.

"It couldn't be . . ." Finley looked at the ceiling. The sound had come from inside the Landmark, somewhere on a high, faraway floor.

But Alistair knew what it was with terrible, absolute certainty.

"A roar," he rasped.

Gradually, new noises joined it. Whispers carried in the air, caressing the bare skin of Alistair's neck. Screams cried out, muted and distant.

Briony hesitantly descended the steps in front of the throne, holding her palm out in front of her. Gray snowflakes drifted from the ceiling, the same as the day that Hendry had reappeared. Alistair brushed one off his sleeve in revulsion. They looked like flakes of skin.

"What is this?" Briony asked.

Finley let one fall onto his fingertip, then licked it. "It's ash."

Above them, the ceiling rumbled. Footsteps, so tremendous that the wood and cast iron chandelier overhead swayed.

"Are we about to fight a dragon?" Finley asked hoarsely.

"Not just a dragon," Briony breathed. "Look."

Down the corridor, figures advanced toward the throne room in a slow, haunting procession. Their forms wisped and flickered, transparent as smoke, yet their features remained unmistakable. The cruel set to their brows. The hollow curves of their cheeks. Their widow's peaks, dagger-sharp.

They were Lowe champions, the same ones who'd glared disdainfully down at him for sixteen years from their portraits in his home. Alistair even recognized some of them. Aunt Alphina, with her narrow, bony shoulders so like his grandmother. Ellar Lowe, without his usual eye patch, revealing only an empty, dark socket. Rowanne Lowe, one of the few non-victors, her skin mottled from the burns of a fiery curse.

Their gazes slipped over Briony and Finley to Alistair and, despite being specters, no realer than the figments of a Conjurer's Nightmare, Alistair swore they recognized him. And how could they not? The matching gray of his eyes, the cold weight of his stare. He was unmistakably one of them, and they'd punish him for defying them, no different than in his mother's story.

Instantly, the other champions readied themselves for battle. They bolted back up the steps to the dais, seizing the high ground. Briony cast a shield spell, and a shimmering wall of prisms materialized in front of them. As the specters drifted through the open double doors at the mouth of the hall, Finley threw a lance of crackling blue light at Ellar, who exploded as though a cloud of smoke—only to reform moments later, undeterred.

"How are we supposed to stop them?" Briony asked.

"What are you doing, Alistair?" Finley demanded. "Move! Get up here!"

Instead, Alistair stepped toward the specters. All his life, he'd scrutinized these faces, hoping to be worthy of them, and despite all the blood he'd spilled, he hadn't been sure he'd succeeded. The fear inside him had never faded, and maybe it never would. But now, he could prove himself. He could defeat them, just like he'd defeated the rest of his family.

With both arms stretched in front of him, he cast a Phoenix's Forge.

The floor in the hall's center buckled, and a fissure split through it from end to end. Lava erupted from it into the air like a geyser, until its waves crashed over the ground, separating the chamber into two halves with a moat of magma. Alistair held his breath as he watched it sweep toward the specters, eager for them to burn.

But to his dismay, it did nothing to deter them. Even as the wooden chairs along the wall burst into flames, Alphina walked on, unfazed.

As the specters continued to advance, Alistair had no choice but to flee up the stairs to join Briony and Finley. He released the Phoenix's Forge, and the lava hardened instantaneously into rock. But the temperature in the room had skyrocketed. Sweat dribbled down his temples, his arms. Behind them, low, ominous growls reverberated from the stairwell as the dragon made its way toward them.

They were trapped.

Briony wiped her glistening forehead. "This is worse than the skeletons."

"Are you surprised?" Alistair drawled.

"Focus," Finley told them desperately. "What happens when they reach us? How are we supposed to stop them?"

The first of his questions was answered a second later as Alphina ascended the steps toward the throne. The moment she passed it, her body—once solid and lifelike—became transparent, and her curls wisped around her like tendrils of smoke. She reached a trembling hand out, fingers pointing toward Alistair as though casting some kind of spell. An eerie wind tore at them, and though it tugged at Briony's hair and ruffled Finley's clothes, it was Alistair who gasped. Alistair who brought a hand to his neck, who fell to his knees as the air was torn from his lungs.

A wraith, straight from his family's stories.

Beside Alphina, Rowanne's shape transformed. Her spine elongated, her rippled skin hardened into scales. In heartbeats, what was once a girl became a snakelike creature, who loomed over Finley with a sinister hiss. A leviathan.

Every Lowe, transforming into a different monster.

Alistair's terror intensified a hundredfold. He couldn't breathe, and the very creatures he'd spent a lifetime fearing now surrounded them, realer than any training exercise, than any nightmare. But as he frantically examined each set of fangs, each husk, each grotesque face, a realization dawned on him. For years, he'd clung to his family's tales so fervently that their words might as well have been etched on his skin. But in the very stories designed to hone him into a monster, the Lowes had unwittingly given him the key to their undoing. He knew how to defeat a wraith—he knew how to defeat them all.

He cast the Dragon's Breath, and fire spewed from his mouth. With a shrill, bloodcurdling scream, Alphina ignited as easily as paper. She snuffed out, gone.

As the air rushed back into Alistair's lungs, he jumped to his feet and spun toward the leviathan. Finley's enchantments ricocheted off the serpent's scales, and, after a final blast of a fiery curse, the beast wrapped around him, constricting him.

Alistair didn't waste time to aim. He cast a Thunderstrike, and a bolt of lightning shot from the ceiling and struck the leviathan in its stomach. It shrieked and dissolved, and Alistair raced to Finley's side as he collapsed to the floor, retching onto the granite.

"Are you all right?" He carried a single healing spell, but the only broken bones he'd ever mended were his own.

"I-I'm fine." Finley grabbed Alistair's shoulder and hoisted himself to standing. "Thanks."

"Don't mention it."

Something slammed behind them, and they whipped around. Ellar Lowe had seized Briony by the neck and thrust her against the wall, raising her a meter into the air. She kicked and thrashed at him, but it was no use. He placed a sharp claw against her abdomen, intending to unzip her.

It would take an Iridescence to defeat a shadowling, but Alistair didn't have one on him.

"A glass bottle," he gasped at Finley. "Hurry. *Hurry.*"

Finley's hands quivered as he overturned his pockets and pulled out an empty magick flask. He uncorked it, and Ellar wailed as he was ripped away from Briony, the vortex sucking him down, down. The moment the last of him whirled into the bottle, Alistair snatched it from Finley's grasp and threw it against the floor. It shattered, and Ellar disappeared.

Briony staggered toward them, shaken but upright. "How did you know what to do?"

"Never mind that." With the two other champions gawking behind him, Alistair cracked his knuckles and prowled toward the other monsters.

He was going to enjoy this.

Goblies, vampires, nightcrawlers, and changelings. One after the other, the Lowes fell, and Alistair's fear, his ever-present companion, finally, wholly vanished. After his family had slain his brother, Alistair had blamed himself for being too weak a champion for them to believe in him.

Oh, how wrong they'd been.

His family had built their legacy on horror and sacrifice, and the soft, frightened boy they'd once scorned was more powerful, more monstrous, than they ever could've imagined.

As Alistair impaled the final beast, a banshee, on the point of his Vampire's Stake, the footsteps in the stairwell thudded closer, and the dragon at last crawled into the throne room.

It looked every bit like the creature Alistair had romanticized as a child. Its enormous size, its marble-white scales as sharp as blades. Huge spikes protruded down its spine and shoulders, a mace of bone, and when it locked eyes with each of them, its irises burned a hollow, eerie silver.

Smoke billowed from its nostrils.

"Oh shit." Alistair sped away, Briony and Finley at his heels. They ducked behind the columns near the far wall as the dragon breathed out a blast of fire that rendered Alistair's favorite curse paltry by comparison.

"What do we do?" Briony asked Alistair, coughing as smoke plumed around them.

"A sword pierced through the heart," he answered.

Finley squeezed his hand into a fist, the spellring on his pointer glowing bright. "A sword I can manage."

"No," Alistair said. "It should be me."

"This isn't about pride," Briony growled. "It's about finishing this. The dragon waited until we'd slain all the other monsters, so this has to end when we kill it, right? Then we'll— Hey! Wait!"

Alistair ignored her and dashed out from behind the column. The dragon sighted him, and it reared its head back, preparing another blast. But it wasn't fast enough. With a triumphant cry, Alistair summoned the Night Blade and pierced it through the dragon's chest.

Its end wasn't as satisfying as he'd hoped. No blood spurted from the wound, no final growl tore from its throat. Instead, it slumped forward, and Alistair slipped out from beneath it before it could crush him.

He threw up his arms, smiling wickedly. "There, happy now?" he called to his companions.

But Briony's mouth hung open in horror. "It's not—you didn't—"

Alistair didn't hear her finish. Something heavy and hard slammed into his side—the dragon's tail—and he was hurled through the air. He struck down below the steps, and as he rolled limply across the floor, the dragon roared, so loud the windows above him shattered. Dizzy, he braced his arms over his head as shards of glass rained down, though daylight never streamed inside.

Then brightness flashed in front of him, and when Alistair painfully lifted his head, the dragon's flames surged toward him. His fear returned to him all at once, and he clamped his eyes shut, bracing to be burned.

Except several more heartbeats passed, and when he peeled his eyes open he saw Briony had sprinted in front of him and summoned a new gigantic shield. The fire jetted off it and sputtered out.

"Th-thanks," Alistair told her.

"Just returning the favor," Briony said, casting him a sideways grin. Then, in an organized, fluid tandem, she and Finley fired attacks of their own. Finley's electric lance struck the dragon in its left wing, impaling it, and Briony's hailstorm of conjured daggers grazed the side of its head. It reared back with a violent, ear-splitting screech.

But their success was fleeting. Barely an instant later, the dragon regained its focus. And to Alistair's horror, its wounds began to shine with ruby light—and knit closed.

"How are we supposed to slay it if it *heals*?" Briony asked.

For once, Alistair had no answer, but he *should* have. How many times had he and Hendry reenacted this story, Hendry the knight, and him the dragon?

He staggered to his feet, swearing under his breath. Of course battling the truth of his family's story wouldn't be so simple. But he didn't understand—he'd slain every champion who'd come before him. What other Lowe could he have left to face?

Then he realized it—the scales as white as bone, the choice of creature, the sick twist of it all. A single Lowe champion *did* remain.

Him.

Heart pounding, Alistair heaved himself up the steps to Briony and Finley. He cast every curse he could think of—the Basilisk's Gaze, Gorgon's Locks, Kraken's Whip, Revenge of the Forsaken—until he swayed from exertion. No matter which of his enchantments struck the dragon, no matter how wrathfully it cried out, its wounds healed in an instant. Barely ten minutes ago, he'd prided himself on being the most powerful monster of any Lowe, and he was right. This beast was the accumulation of every cruelty he'd committed, every villainous role he played in his family's story. And now he'd be slain by the very monster he'd wanted to become.

"What do we do now?" Briony strained as the dragon's serrated tail whipped against her shield. Twin trails of blood trickled from her nostrils.

"You can't hold that much longer," Finley warned her, and Briony shot him a withering glare in response.

They both looked to Alistair, their terror as plain as his own.

"I-I don't know," he stammered. In his lessons, there had always been some kind of trick, some test, and though Alistair knew his grandmother hadn't devised the danger before them now, Alistair had once sought her approval above anyone else's.

He reconsidered the dragon's appearance. Briony had suggested it'd waited because it was significant, the final foe they had to defeat. But they had heard its roar before any of the specters had arrived, from some far tower or room in the Castle. Maybe it was that place that held significance. And the longer he stared at the dragon, the more he realized it hadn't moved from its position in front of the stairwell.

His thoughts immediately took him to the vault in the Lowe estate—the family's hoard.

"It's not the dragon that matters," Alistair choked out. "It's what it's guarding."

Finley's eyes widened, and he nodded at the steps. "You mean we have to go up there?"

"Would've been nice to know that earlier," Briony grunted. "But we need a way to get past that thing."

Alistair swallowed. Once upon a time, there was nothing he'd wanted more passionately than to destroy his family's legacy—and so he'd done it. He'd acted on vengeance and fury, and it hadn't fixed him, it hadn't banished his nightmares, hadn't made the ache of Hendry's death and their betrayal ever fade. Instead, it'd made him into *this*, a monster more terrifying than any other he'd feared. A monster he could never defeat.

And though he wished otherwise, Alistair couldn't abandon Briony or Finley here to fight the creature for him. This was *his* battle, as it always would be. Because even if the Lowes were gone, their harm would forever live inside him. But he didn't have to surrender to it. Alistair might not be the hero who unmade this curse, but in his own story, the hero wasn't the person who chose goodness because it was noble. They chose it because, even if it went against their nature, even if it was a test to be endured every single day, the alternative was to be the epitome of everything they despised.

He didn't know if he could succeed, but his brother had believed in him. Gavin had believed in him. And maybe that would be enough.

"Go," Alistair said. "Grab the Crown. I'll hold it off."

Briony gaped at him. "But—"

"Go!" he shouted, seething, then he burst through her shield to the left wall.

The dragon's gaze followed him, and it extended its wings and let out a piercing screech, one that rattled him down to his bones. He summoned another Night Blade and stalked threateningly toward the monster. It loomed over him, snapping at him with its fangs. The enchanted iron struck its teeth with a clamor. He swung, again and again, until he was left panting. Finally, his sword swiped across the dragon's eye, and as it recoiled, Alistair charged.

For the second time, he stabbed the monster through the heart.

Its wings sagged, and, shoulders heaving, Alistair glanced at the stairwell with relief. He'd done it. Briony and Finley were gone, and they'd taken the Crown with them.

But he knew not to take his eyes off the monster for long, and so he withdrew his sword and staggered back. This battle might never end, but at least, through this choice, he knew that he had won.

The dragon's silver eyes shot open.

ISOBEL MACASLAN

> "Traffic sits at a standstill on the T9 and Q7 as thousands of vehicles flee the city of Ilvernath in fear of the curse's collapse."
>
> *98.6 Traffic & Weather Reports*

Isobel, Reid, and Gavin staggered as their Here to There spells deposited them in an alley downtown. To their left was a dead end, and to their right, a queue of cars rumbled at a standstill on an intersection. The air seemed to vibrate with the impatient honking of their horns and the screeching of tires. One van had even parked lopsided up the curb, doors open, abandoned amid the traffic. Now that the Blood Veil had fallen, Ilvernath's residents could finally flee the city.

"Come on." Gavin jerked his head toward the street. "The Lead the Way needs daylight."

After casting their cloaking spells, the three of them emerged from the alley's mouth, and Isobel gaped as she examined the shopping district. Stores normally bright with neon signs were dark, each of their doors marked CLOSED. Twenty-four-hour cafés and fast-food chains had shuttered their windows. The few pedestrians walked briskly, their heads down, bags slung over their shoulders. Like ants skittering for cover before an oncoming storm.

"Is this the part where the zombies show up?" Reid muttered.

On the sidewalk below them, their shadows elongated and shifted to the west despite the afternoon sun.

"This way," Gavin said, and as they followed the direction their shadows led them, it dawned on Isobel that the path they were taking was a familiar one. Soon they passed storefront displays of glittering crystals, artfully arranged on towers or silken pillows. The corner she turned every morning on her walk to school. Finally, the pastel green awning of her mother's spellshop came into view, the blinds lowered. Their shadows stretched unmistakably toward it.

"This doesn't make sense," Isobel said. Based on Gracie's message, she'd expected to meet the resistance in some basement, some deserted school auditorium. Not here, not at home.

"You think it's a trap?" Gavin asked warily.

"No, but I . . ." Isobel didn't know why she was surprised. Of course her mother wanted the curse broken; she'd always hated the tournament, had begged Isobel not to be champion. But those were precisely the reasons Isobel hadn't worked up the nerve to face her again. "It'll be fine."

"It will be," Reid said reassuringly.

Still, Isobel braced herself as she grasped the knob. Same as when she'd last visited, the lock spell disengaged at her touch, and she hesitantly swung open the door.

The shop was crammed tightly with people, its glass cases shoved against the walls to make room. No sooner had she taken in the faces of Gracie Blair, Innes Thorburn, and Fergus Grieve than a voice cried out.

"Isobel? *Isobel.*"

Honora Jackson swayed as she stepped toward her daughter. She wore an ensemble Isobel only saw her in on lazy weekend mornings: a sweatshirt and yoga pants, her long blond curls drooping from a haphazard bun, her face makeup-less. Not even the deep violet that rimmed her eyes had been enchanted away.

"Mum," Isobel whimpered, and simultaneously, the mother and daughter ran to each other. Isobel buried her face into her mum's shoulder, breathing just to soak in the comforting gardenia scent of her shampoo.

"You're here," her mother gasped out. "Oh, I can't believe I'm holding you. I can't believe it." She tightened her embrace until it was almost painful, but Isobel didn't dare move away.

"What are all of you doing here?" Isobel asked.

"Helping you, of course. All of you. We don't have much time, but I . . ." Honora's voice cracked, and finally, she pulled away enough to cup Isobel's cheeks. Her brow furrowed. "You're freezing. And you're . . . Oh, honey. I have you. I have you now. It's all right."

Isobel hadn't meant to cry, but even after all the nights she'd spent imagining it, hearing her mother say those words still hurt more than she ever could've prepared for. And as sobs wracked her, she tried to find some way to explain that it *wasn't* all right. If her mother knew what she'd done to herself, the choices she'd considered to stay alive, then she would realize this person she was holding was barely her daughter at all.

"I'm not—" Isobel choked. "I'm not the same, and if I tell you . . ."

Her mother shushed her, then she drew back and wiped away Isobel's tears with her thumb. Her eyes roamed over her as though checking for bruises or scrapes, the sort of wounds that were visible. "All I see is my Isobel."

Isobel blinked away more tears, hoping that she meant it.

Someone cleared their throat behind them, and Isobel swiveled to spot Abigail and Pamela Blair. Like her mother and the rest of the room's occupants, they wore casual clothes: jeans and sweatshirts and trainers, and Isobel noticed several others clutching posterboards or disposable coffee cups.

"I'm sorry, Honora, but where is our son?" Abigail asked breathlessly. "Where are the others?"

Gavin released his younger brother, who'd broken through the onlookers to wrap him in a hug. "Alistair, Briony, and Finley are at the Castle, dismantling the last Landmark as we speak," Gavin explained. "We decided to split up. The government, some of the spellmakers, we know they're—"

"Since when has there been a 'we'?" Pamela demanded. "If the Lowe boy is at the Castle, Finley and Briony could be—"

"We're helping," Gavin snapped. "All of us, we're on the same side."

In the room's corner, Callista Payne spoke up, "If the others are already bringing down the Castle, then we don't have much time."

"She's right," said Wen, another local spellmaker. "We need to get moving. The moment the tournament comes down, they'll cast their curse."

"You know about the curse?" Isobel asked with surprise.

"I figured it out," said a girl she recognized from school—Diya Attwater-Sharma, one year above her, who Isobel knew from their advanced spellmaking classes. "I've suspected they were planning something for ages, but after I talked to you"—she nodded at Gavin—"I broke into Walsh's shop and found his work. It's seven people at each point on the septogram."

"But Walsh is dead," Gavin said. "He died this morning."

Diya blinked, stunned. "Oh . . . Th-that's—"

"Good news," Pamela finished for her. Around her, several people began to fish for their car keys or file toward the back door. Honora slipped on her autumn jacket. "But we have to assume they'll replace him. They're in a rush and they have a very limited window of opportunity. Once the tournament is broken, it's believed that high magick will gather at its central point—the Champions Pillar—before dispersing. *That* is when they'll cast their curse. And if they lose that chance, it will be far, far more difficult to stop the people of Ilvernath from finding and collecting raw high magick."

"But not impossible," Gavin pointed out, stepping beside Isobel.

"No, it's not," added a new voice, and Isobel gaped as her father stood. He'd been sitting in the corner, far from her notice—maybe deliberately so. When he locked eyes with his daughter, she couldn't read his expression. It might've been disappointment—a few weeks ago, she'd assured him she was capable of winning for her family, and clearly, she'd broken that promise. But Isobel knew her father's disappointment well, the way it sharpened his already hard features. This was a countenance she didn't recognize, one she hoped—perhaps naively—was shame. He had always asked too much of her.

Which was exactly why his words stung.

"So we gotta act immediately. They've cast a powerful ward around the Champions Pillar, but if we break it, if we rob them of this chance to cast their curse, then by the time the Cursebreaking Division and the spellmakers figure out how to construct a new one, the high magick will already be ours. And even if they try to take it, we'll fight for what belongs to us."

Isobel winced as though struck in the stomach. Because of course, his presence wasn't about her, it was about his greed, about *all* of their greed. They'd gathered here, not to help the champions, but to prepare for battle, and even though she'd braced for as much, it still hurt to confront that truth. That their families had sent their children to die in a war of their own design, and now all they wanted was to start another one.

But rather than voice that, Isobel swallowed and cast a meaningful glance at Gavin. Briony had been right to caution them against telling anyone—sharing the full scope of their plans could transform their allies into their enemies in an instant.

"Then the three of us will help you," Isobel told her father. "Whatever you need."

Abigail frowned in confusion. "The three of you?"

"The three of . . ." Isobel turned around.

Reid was gone.

"Where the hell did he go?" Gavin stomped toward the door and flung it open, but the street was all but deserted except for the traffic. He whipped around and met Isobel's gaze with wild eyes.

Isobel frantically wracked her memories for when she'd last seen Reid. It'd been here—right outside the door to her mother's shop, but she'd been too distracted with her own thoughts to notice if he'd entered with them. Her mind conjured countless scenarios, each more chilling than the last. He wouldn't simply leave—he wouldn't.

"D-does anyone have a tracking spell?" she asked, and Wen slipped a topaz crystal from her hand and gave it to her. Clenching it tightly, Isobel spoke, "Reid MacTavish."

The light in the stone sputtered and died.

She knew she didn't have time to panic, to stall, and so she groaned with frustration and practically threw the stone back at its owner. "Why didn't it work? Where is he?"

"Somewhere he can't be tracked," Wen answered. "Behind a ward—a powerful one."

Though wards had once protected Reid's shop from such spells, they'd be long depleted by now, and he hadn't refortified them last night—she would've seen. A Landmark's ward would conceal him, yet he had no reason to return to the Castle.

But, so her father had mentioned, there was now another powerful ward in Ilvernath.

"It seems to me that they've found their replacement spellmaker," Pamela said dryly.

Isobel had heard the woman, had come to the same conclusion herself, yet the truth of it still struggled to take shape in her mind.

Reid, whom she'd saved at the Cottage, who'd rescued her in return. Who'd stopped her from making her greatest mistake.

Whom she'd trusted with the worst parts of herself.

Who'd touched her like she wasn't cold or cursed or broken.

Who'd once told her how desperately he wanted high magick.

Who'd mutilated himself in pursuit of his obsessions.

Who'd abducted her.

Who'd written the book that had ruined her life.

How cruel it was that her heart could break but still not beat.

Behind her, Gavin seethed and pounded his fist onto the door, making the blinds rattle. "I'll kill him."

Isobel shuddered, her gaze immediately sweeping to her mother for comfort. Yet as she took in Honora's worried eyes, she realized this was not the time to fall apart, on the day she needed to be stronger than any other.

And so, her voice hoarse with rage, she asked, "When does the plan begin?"

A crowd thronged outside the Ilvernath banquet hall.

When Callista Payne had described protestors gathered not far from the Champions Pillar, Isobel had pictured the small crowds who'd stationed themselves outside the Tower shouting expletives and demanding retribution on Alistair's behalf. Instead, she stepped onto the front lawn and took in a sea of jostling people, protest signs brandished in the air like weapons raised for battle, their jeers and chants indecipherable amid the havoc. To their right, two teenagers stood on the hood of a parked minivan, a banner raised above their heads reading OUR CITY, OUR MAGICK.

Behind the marble architecture of the hall, a shimmering dome rose—a powerful shield, reinforced with what must have been dozens of enchantments. Uniformed agents stood guard at every entrance point to the Champions Pillar's courtyard, each street and alley blockaded with traffic cones.

"Are you still sure about this?" Gavin asked her. "The plan makes sense, but how do you know they'll follow you? You're not exactly . . ." At Isobel's pointed stare, he shifted awkwardly. "Popular."

"That's why I have you, right?" When Gavin opened his mouth to argue, Isobel turned and strode ahead. Her Burial Shroud spell seeped over her, rendering her invisible, and despite his grumbling, when she peeked over her shoulder, Gavin trailed after her, donning a spell of his own.

In the streets behind them, the resistance followed. Her mother, carrying a ridiculous sign. Her father, along with a pack of her relatives. Innes and Gracie, dressed entirely in neon, for some reason.

In a few more steps, Isobel and Gavin slipped through the crowd, and though several protestors glanced their way, confused about the phantom bump against their arm or shove at their side, no one noticed they'd reached the front until Isobel cast the Rocket Flare. The curse whizzed like a firecracker toward the blockade spell, then both enchantments exploded in a burst of glittery white magick.

For several seconds, the crowd lurched back, their chants slipping into startled screams. Then Isobel and Gavin materialized ahead of them, approaching the uniformed agents of the Cursebreaking Division, and everyone silenced to watch.

"You can't . . ." one agent started, then his eyes widened in recognition. He shakily raised his fist to his face and spoke into one of his glowing spellrings. "Sir, two of the champions—Isobel Macaslan and Gavin—"

Before he could finish, Gavin cast a strange curse. Two gigantic fists appeared before him, glinting as though solid titanium. Before either agent could react, the hands swatted them aside like they were little more than gnats. They slammed against the wall and crumpled, heads slumping onto their chests.

Behind the two champions, Innes and Gracie were the first to charge forward, and—exactly as Isobel had predicted—the crowd followed. To a trumpeting of shouts, the hundreds of onlookers and reporters poured down the street toward the shield that engulfed the town square.

And the battle began.

Immediately, more agents rushed to confront them, any attempts for peaceful restraint abandoned. Stunning curses bulleted from all directions, and Isobel hastily cast an Exoskeleton. Her spell protected her from the worst of the enchantments, but she still winced as several hit her—two in her arm, another a sharp blow to her stomach. Ignoring the pain as best she could, she ducked to the square's edge, where gray cobblestones met the grass of the tree line.

She had a shield to bring down.

Though the ward wasn't opaque, its surface rippled, rendering the seven figures within it too distorted to discern. All she could make out were the white lines of chalk traced onto the ground in the shape of a septogram, and at its center, the Champions Pillar, so cracked that the once tall and magnificent stone now leaned on a tilt, as though a strong wind might blow it over. Each fissure shone, transforming the Pillar into a beacon of crimson light.

"Cover me?" Isobel asked Gavin, then she cast a second Rocket Flare. Her curse struck the shield with a hiss, like a drop of water splashing on a hot iron. Briefly, the barrier thinned, allowing her a clearer glimpse within. Across the square, she spotted Calhoun, a spellmaker whose shop stood catty-corner to her mother's. Two agents had claimed the points of the septogram to his either side.

Then, on the point closest to her, was Reid. Though he glanced over his shoulder, before he could meet her eyes, the barrier thickened once again, and he returned to no more than a mangled shape, a blur of his black shirt over gray jeans.

Beside her, Gavin swore. Despite the cold, sweat glistened on his forehead from the effort of maintaining his armor.

"It's going to take more power than that," he said darkly.

Isobel cataloged her most powerful cursestones: a Poisonous Pincers and a Mantis's Flight, both class nine, and one of Reid's own recipes, the Belladonna's Bane, class ten. But she couldn't afford to drain such powerful crystals on a futile strike.

Behind her, the blinding light of a curse shot past, and she hastily strengthened her Exoskeleton. "Go find whoever you can and bring them here," she told Gavin. "If we each cast something at the same time, we can break through this."

The moment Gavin lowered his shield to run, another curse whizzed toward her, and Isobel cried out as it grazed her thigh. On the sidewalk, one of the agents advanced in their direction. Blood dribbled down the left side of his beard.

Gavin hesitated, clearly preparing for a fight.

"Go," Isobel snapped at him. "Go."

Finally, he took off, and Isobel cringed as she touched her thigh. Blood wet her fingers from the wound, and though it burned, it was shallow.

The agent fired another curse as he approached. It ricocheted off her Exoskeleton and left a smear of chalky white as it skidded across the flagstones. The man grimaced, but before he could ready himself to cast a more powerful curse, Isobel summoned the Mantis's Flight. Magickal swords spun toward him like the blades of a ceiling fan. He tried to duck out of their path, but they sliced his enchanted armor, which exploded, and he dropped to the ground.

"Isobel!" a voice called across the square—Innes. "Now! Now!" In between them, Gracie summoned a shimmering white mace in her hand, preparing to strike.

Steeling herself, Isobel faced the barrier and glared at Reid's murky figure on its opposite side. Of all the wounds carved into her, she hated that this one stung the most. More than Briony naming Isobel the first champion. More than Alistair abandoning her the moment he sighted his brother. And she had no one to blame but herself. Because after everything she'd been through, she should've known better than to trust anyone, let alone someone like Reid.

Together with Gracie, with Innes, with Gavin and her mother and a half dozen others, Isobel cast the Belladonna's Bane.

The shield rumbled as enchantments pummeled it on all sides, and a victorious thrill gripped her when a small hole ruptured beneath her curse.

This time, Reid was already looking at her. As their gazes locked, he stiffened, and Isobel hoped he could see the rage burning in her eyes as clearly as he'd seen every other piece of her. Yet instead of the smug satisfaction she expected, his face tightened in alarm, and though she no longer trusted her own ability to read him, she swore his expression was almost pleading.

He pointed at her, then at himself—so subtly and quickly Isobel could barely be sure she hadn't imagined it.

Her curse fizzled out, and she watched in horror as the hole in the wards sealed, as though it'd never been there at all. Then a rowdy protestor knocked her in the side, and she tumbled onto the cobblestones. More agents streamed toward them from the opposite end of the square. Realizing they were outnumbered, many of the protestors fled toward the trees.

Dizzily, Isobel clambered to her feet, and even amid the havoc, she couldn't stop replaying Reid's expression in her mind. She swore that he was trying to tell her something.

To her left, Gavin and Abigail took on a pack of four agents. But despite their barrage of cursework, one of them slipped past—running straight for Isobel.

Isobel froze. She had few curses left to waste.

Yet she readied them anyway. But no matter how hard she tried to concentrate, her focus slipped back toward Reid. She didn't know if she could trust him, and even more painfully, she didn't know if she could trust herself.

Her desire and her instincts warred with each other. She'd never been one for faith, but she had made this mistake before, in this very spot. And even if it cost Isobel her survival, even if every conversation between her and Reid had been a lie, *he* was the one who'd told her to make choices out of hope instead of fear. And so, she would. What little foolish, fanciful faith she had, she would put in him.

She summoned the Poisonous Pincers and aimed them, not at the agent racing toward her, but at the barrier. The moment it struck, another flash of light joined it—Reid, casting a curse from inside. The ward split, and their enchantments collided in a maelstrom of wind and smoke. Isobel shrieked as she was thrown backward, smacking into the agent behind her, and both of them rolled across the patchy grass and roots near the tree line.

Isobel lifted her cheek from the dirt. Ahead of them, the shield was gone, destroyed. With a wave of cheers, her allies stormed inside the septogram, and the square brightened with whizzing cursefire.

But as she tried to push herself to her feet, the agent clasped her wrist, yanking her down. Isobel screamed as her back slammed into the earth. With wild eyes, the man pressed his other fist against her clavicle, his cursestones biting into her even through the fabric of her sweatshirt.

One of his crystals flared, and Isobel thrashed, too panicked to focus enough to cast another enchantment. But she didn't have to. Before the agent could finish summoning his spell, a curse blasted into his back. He swayed, gasping, as blood began to pour from dozens of wounds across his body, streaming down his face and blooming in splotches over his clothes. He screamed and fell to the side, and Isobel scrambled away just as Reid raced over to her.

He held out his hand, and she gratefully accepted it.

Only to shove him back. "What the hell was that all about?" Even if he'd helped her destroy the barrier, he'd still run off without telling them. She didn't know what to think.

"Remember when the Cursebreaking Division and other spell-makers kept trying to call me after Hendry returned?" Reid asked. "After the six of us figured out their plan, it wasn't hard to deduce that I was originally supposed to be a part of it. And with Walsh dead, I knew I had an opening, that we'd have a better chance if we had someone on the inside."

"So you just *left?*"

"I would've explained, but I couldn't risk it—not if they cast truth spells on any of you." He lifted his T-shirt, revealing the spellstone reimplanted in his abdomen, far messier than it'd been before. The light inside it pulsed like a heartbeat, and webby black veins tethered it to his flesh, mottled with dried blood. "I was careful."

She didn't know whether to be more horrified or relieved. "You call that careful?" she demanded, yet now she leaned into him instead of pushing him away. "They could've hurt you, you know. If you ever stopped to th-think . . ."

Her voice stuttered and trailed off, and she latched onto Reid's arm as the ground beneath them began to shake.

BRIONY THORBURN

"Protestors have flocked to the Champions Pillar, some advocating for the return of high magick, others warning of its many dangers. As a reporter, I remain impartial."

Special correspondent, *SpellBC News*

Briony bolted into the stairwell, Finley a step below her. Behind them, roars echoed through the throne room. A blast of fire licked at their heels, and a searing heat chased them upward, smoke billowing around them as they ran. Briony gasped for air and careened onto a landing, then stumbled into a corridor.

She heaved between breaths. "Do you think . . . we're safe now?"

Finley wiped soot from his brow and cast a nervous glance over his shoulder. "I think so."

Castles and dragons featured heavily in the Thorburns' bedtime stories, as fortresses to defend and monsters to fight. But Briony had learned that her family's imaginary foes paled in comparison to their own villainy. And the boy who was supposedly the biggest monster of all had freed her from the Castle's dungeon—then stayed behind to slay the dragon.

Briony turned away from the stairs and examined the hallway, which was lined with flickering torches and ended in a grand, intimidating door. A few months ago, Briony would've charged recklessly down it, but now she hovered at its edge.

Her body ached from her donated high magick and the strain of battle. She caught Finley anxiously studying her face and swiped at her upper lip. Her fingers came back bloody.

"What do you think is waiting behind that door?" she asked him, pushing down a wave of light-headedness.

He frowned. "After everything we just saw? Probably another monster. How does the Crown look?"

Briony flipped it over. The top of the beanie was unraveling, fast. "It's okay for now, but we need to hurry."

They'd done this before, in the Crypt, in the Tower, in the Cave. She trusted everyone in her alliance now, but she trusted Finley most of all.

"One more time?" she asked, reaching for his hand.

"Bri . . ." His grip tightened around hers. "Are you sure you can do this? It's been a really long day, and you're—"

"I've been stronger, I know that," she said, pushing down a flutter of nerves. "But it's not like we have any other choice."

He sighed. "All right. One more time."

Together, they strode forward, past the first row of torches, and suddenly the corridor warped around her until it stretched a dozen times longer, until Briony could barely see the door at the end. The torches extended and blurred into a crimson wall of flame. Then the floor beneath her trembled, then moved, wrenching her hand away from Finley's. She stumbled ahead as the hallway spun, struggling to keep her balance. Something *yanked* at the Crown, tugging it forward, and she clung to it desperately as it dragged her along in its wake.

She collided with the door, crying out with surprise, then scrambled backward. The pull had stopped. She straightened and stared at the Crown, still clenched in her hand. Then she whirled around.

"Finley?" she shouted. But he was gone. So was the hallway, replaced by a wall that hadn't been there before. A single torch protruded from it, common magick floating around an enchanted flame. She banged on the stone with her fist, then cast an Avalanche, then a Ten of Daggers, each to no effect. "Finley!"

"I'm okay!" The voice was muffled but unmistakably *his*. Briony sagged with relief. "I can't get through, Bri. This is all made of high magick."

"I can't get through, either," she said hoarsely. Now that her initial panic was fading, the truth of her situation began to sink in. "I . . . I think I'm stuck here."

"You have the Crown," Finley said, his voice deceptively calm. "That must be why you're trapped."

"You're probably right. But the door's still shut."

"Do you see any way to open it?"

Briony examined the door, which was far more unsettling up close. Carvings of leaves and bramble twined around its edges, cluttered with thorns. A small iron scythe with a wickedly sharp blade jutted from the center. There were no knobs or keyholes. She pushed against the cold metal, but it didn't give.

"No," she called back.

"Then let's think," Finley said. "What else do we know about the Lowes?"

Briony ran through their reputation in her mind, their cruelty, their greed. "You remember that interview Alistair gave? There was something in it. Some . . . gross family saying?"

His response came a moment later, his tone reluctant. "Blood before all."

Briony eyed the scythe, then the beanie, and then the spellrings clustered on her fingers.

"I know what to do."

She couldn't see Finley's face, but she could picture it. "Be careful, Bri. Please." The tenderness in his voice made her heart clench.

"Go help Alistair," she told him. "That dragon was vicious."

"I wish you didn't have to do this alone."

Briony pressed her hand to the wall. "Me too. Now *go*."

She sniffled and turned around, glaring at the scythe. Its tip gleamed threateningly in the torchlight. Briony knew she would need every bit of her bravery for whatever lay ahead. She drew her strength around her like a shield, then exhaled shakily.

"So you want blood, huh?" She touched her pointer finger to the scythe's blade. She felt a prick, and then a drop of crimson ran down the iron. The tip of the weapon shimmered, then the blood disappeared, as though the door had sucked it in. Briony felt a second rush of wooziness, like she'd stood up too fast, but she quickly shook it away.

A moment later, three small indents opened along the rim of the scythe. Each of them was shaped like a spellstone. Briony pressed the Crown's three crystals into the empty divots, and with a great, awful groan, the door creaked open.

The dragon's hoard inside the small, circular chamber was not gold or silver—it was piles of spellstones in every cut and color imaginable, each pulsing with magick. They were the lone source of light in the windowless space. Briony could hear nothing of the battle taking place downstairs—only her own footsteps, her own breathing. The door slammed shut behind her with a nasty *thud*. She jumped and whipped around, but yet again, there was no visible way to open it, just another scythe and those creepy carvings, a perfect mirror image of the front. She gave it a half-hearted push, but knew in her gut that the door wouldn't let her out until she finished this. Whatever *this* was.

In the center of the chamber was a small table, laid with a white cloth. Two items sat atop it: an elegant iron stand and an empty spellstone, clear and colorless as glass. Briony knew what to do with at least one of them. She took the Crown, which was halfway unraveled at this point, and draped it haphazardly over the stand.

Then she studied the spellstone.

It was the only one in the room that wasn't glowing.

The Castle surely wanted her to fill it—but why? How? She could try and siphon common magick from one of the stones on the floor, but that didn't feel worthy of a trial. Briony took a deep breath and tried to think. There was something else Alistair had mentioned in his interview that had felt too horrific to believe, even though Briony had witnessed the evidence of it each time she'd encountered Hendry Lowe.

The Lowes won because of sacrifice.

This spellstone wanted her life magick.

"Shit," Briony muttered.

She had no idea how to provide that. She wasn't a spellmaker like Isobel or Reid. She wasn't as clever as Finley or Gavin. She wasn't Alistair with his family's dark, twisted secrets to draw upon. Out of all the champions, she was the least suited to this challenge.

A challenge that could end the tournament—or seal all their fates six feet under, buried facedown.

Briony picked up the empty crystal. She could sense the enchantment inside—some stronger, stranger version of a Skeleton Key.

When Isobel and Reid had taken her life magick to make the Crown, they'd hurt her to extract it. If she could find some way to replicate that . . . She rifled through the nearest heap of spellstones, but each curse was far too twisted and dangerous to attempt on herself.

When Briony looked at the Crown again, her heart lurched in despair. The three spellstones draped pathetically against one of the prongs of the stand; black yarn uncoiled around it, limp strands tumbling to the table below.

She was running out of time. They were going to die, and it would be all her fault.

Briony gulped and looked at the door. At the scythe.

She walked up and pressed her finger to it once more. Again, her blood sank into the iron; again, she felt that dizzy rush. But this time, she paid attention to the slight tendrils of magick shimmering around the scythe's tip. A round shape opened in the blade, like an empty eye socket. And the scythe itself protruded fully from the door, the iron melting into gleaming, razor-sharp steel. Briony snatched the spellstone from the table and slid it into the slot. It was a perfect fit.

Then she grasped the handle with her fingertips and pulled. The scythe came free from the door seamlessly, without making a single sound.

"You already took life magick from me, didn't you?" Her words hung heavy in the air. "How much more do you want?"

But it didn't matter, not really. Not when so much was at stake. Briony sat cross-legged and braced her back against the door, trying not to think about how torturous this had been the last time. Then she hefted the blade in her hand, inhaled deeply, and brought it down in a perfect arc across her outstretched palm.

Blood oozed along her lifeline, and pain jolted up her wrist, then her arm. She shuddered at the familiar burn of it, as though something had cut into her from the inside out. Green and purple flared beneath her skin, like that strange septogram she'd seen before Isobel healed her. White strings of magick shimmered around the blade, then sank into it as the stone began to glow. Her life magick filled it in a steady stream until the blade stopped drinking her blood.

Briony wondered uneasily how many years it had taken. But life magick regenerated over time. She'd be fine.

She stood and faced the door. When she returned the blade to the iron, it sank in silently. The spellstone flared.

The door clicked, then began to open . . .

Behind her, something crashed onto the table.

Briony turned—and gasped.

The Crown was nothing but thread now, its three spellstones scattered across the cloth. Every one of them was dull and dead, completely devoid of power.

The Relic was broken. Her life magick was gone. Which meant this trial wasn't finished, which meant all six of them were dead.

Thankfully, Briony was at her best under pressure.

She grabbed the scythe and yanked it out of the wall again, pleasantly surprised when it gave way. Then she pried out the spellstone, heedless of the way it tore at her now brittle fingernails, and replaced it with one of the Crown's empty ones. The crystal didn't quite fit, but it stayed.

The cut on her palm hadn't even begun to scab. It was no trouble at all to slice it once more. Blood dribbled into her hand; the scythe drank it greedily. Green and purple coursed up her arm. This time, the pain was worse. Spots bled at the edge of her vision, but she blinked them stubbornly away.

"Please work," she mumbled. *"Please—"*

The spellstone winked back to life. Briony whimpered with relief as the stone filled with her life magick. She could still fix this—she *had* to fix this.

Briony finished the first spellstone and fetched the second. The scythe bit into both of her palms before the crystal was satisfied. Purple and green pulsed beneath her forearms; an ache rose into her shoulders, then coursed through her chest. She coughed, then wheezed, groaning. Her arm trembled so badly, she could barely hold the weapon.

When she pried the spellstone from the scythe, she didn't recognize her hands. They were withered and mottled. She lifted them to her cheeks and felt sunken, papery skin.

Briony cried out in horror. The scythe tumbled into a pile of spellstones as she collapsed to the floor, wrapped her arms around her knees, and pressed her forehead against them, shaking. All she could picture was the photograph of that body in the *Ilvernath Eclipse,* a lifeless, drained husk.

She had given this Relic more than the ten years Isobel and Reid had taken from her. Far more. And there was still one spellstone left.

Briony was exhausted and terrified. She wanted to go home—but there *was* no home, not the Tower, not her old bedroom. She'd destroyed them all in pursuit of this moment, this ending.

She thought of what Finley had told her, about throwing her life away. But the tournament needed to end for good, and high magick along with it—not just for the champions' sakes, but for the rest of the world. She had to see this through, no matter what it cost. She could cast like no one else. She could fight like no one else.

"You can handle this," Briony whispered.

Then she reached for the third spellstone and pushed it into the scythe. Briony slashed the weapon across one palm, then the other. Blood pooled in both of her hands, far more than should've come from such small cuts. Her body twitched, then writhed. Hair drifted to the floor around her in chestnut-brown clumps; she spit out one tooth, then another. Agony shot through her limbs, searing hot. Yet still she held firm, unflinching, as the spellstone filled and filled until at last it was satiated. Briony barely had the strength to pry it from the scythe.

She crawled to the table, then grasped the other two spellstones and the tangle of black yarn. Briony wrapped it all together and cupped the remnants of the Relic in her bloody palms.

For a long, long moment, nothing happened. Then, just as Briony was ready to abandon all hope, the yarn began to wind around the stones. Each of them blazed, renewed by her life magick. And something materialized in her hands, something solid—not the beanie, but a pointed iron crown. Briony clutched it to her chest and rolled onto her side, wheezing. The mountains of spellstones around her blurred, then faded into nothing.

Briony Thorburn had believed she was prepared for what victory could cost her. But the truth was that she wasn't. That she was terrified to face her final moments, that despite all she'd sacrificed, she wasn't ready to surrender. And so she fought for every gasping breath, even as excruciating pain wracked her withered body. Yet death was something not even Briony could battle, a force stronger than hope, and faith, and stubborn will.

She thought of Isobel, her truest friend, who'd seen her at her worst and chosen to stand by her anyway. Of Finley and everything they'd fought for together, everything they'd become. And of Innes, the only family she'd truly loved. She'd hoped that after the tournament, they would get a second chance.

But there would be no after for her. There would be no happy ending.

Her story—heroic or villainous, triumphant or tragic—was over.

The Crown clattered to the floor and rolled to the side, knocking against the bottom of the door.

On the pillar in the throne room, a thin white line slashed through the name *Briony Thorburn*.

And with a great, heaving groan, the Castle walls began to crumble.

GAVIN GRIEVE

"It is our recommendation that citizens of Ilvernath who have not already evacuated shelter in place until the Curse Collapse warning has been formally lifted."

SpellBC News, "Breaking News: Dispatch from Mayor Anand's Office"

The earth below the Champions Pillar quaked, then buckled, sending a wave of cobblestones rippling outward. The ground roiled so violently, Gavin felt as though the world had been thrown sideways. He fell painfully onto his shoulder and tumbled across the ground.

Screams rang out across the square, punctuated by the shattering of windows and the blares of distant car horns. It was as though he'd fallen into a sea of bodies—his head banged into someone's shoulder; a hand clawed at his arm. He shook them away and rose into a crouch, then spotted Reid and Isobel only a meter away.

"What's going on?" Reid mumbled, disoriented.

"I think it's breaking," Isobel gasped. Gavin agreed. One way or another, the curse was ending, which meant it was time to prepare for the destruction of the Champions Pillar. Threats still surrounded them on all sides, and although the crowd was distracted, they wouldn't stay that way for long.

"Next time you pretend to double-cross us, warn us first," he told the cursemaker.

"If I'd had any other choice, I would have."

The three of them peered forward, struggling to balance on the still-trembling ground. The barrier that had once concealed the pillar was fully broken now, and the six other people who'd stood at each point of the chalky septogram had been thrown every which way, along with those who'd swarmed them in an attempt to disrupt the curse. Gavin gazed beyond the chaos at the Pillar.

"But I think I know how to stop them," Reid continued. "They're each using a flask of life magick to bind themselves to the tournament. If we can destroy those, they'll fail."

"We'll tell everyone on our side about this, then," Gavin said. "But we're still ready to do what we really came here for, right?"

Isobel and Reid nodded firmly.

Just then, the red lights inside the pillar pulsed so violently, they all had to squint. And a *crack* split through the air, deafeningly loud.

Gavin braced himself for the fissure to slice down the wrong side of the stone, obliterating their names—and their lives—in one fell swoop. But instead, it opened on the side with the stars.

Pain engulfed Gavin's left pinky. The scarlet light in his champion's ring flickered, faster and faster, brighter and brighter, until the crystal shattered. The band vanished from his skin, and below them, the earth finally stilled.

"Th-they did it." His voice trembled. "They broke the curse."

Beside him, Isobel choked out a sob, while Reid broke into loud, slightly unhinged laughter.

The tournament had ended. The tournament had ended, and all six of them were *alive*.

Gavin couldn't comprehend the enormity of it. He wanted to yell with joy; he wanted to find Alistair and kiss him again, this time without the weight of their survival on their shoulders.

But he pushed away the instinct to celebrate. They weren't finished yet.

Gavin stumbled toward the Champions Pillar, squeezing past the throng of yelling, confused people. And then, through the chaos—a piercing scream.

"Look at her name," Innes Thorburn wailed from beside the Pillar. "Briony's dead, Briony's *gone*—"

"No," Isobel murmured, clambering to her feet.

Gavin reached the Pillar a moment later. Their names were so small on the list of hundreds of others, many rendered illegible by the cracks. But it didn't take him long to find it.

~~Briony Thorburn~~

He didn't expect her death to feel like a blow, but it did. They'd barely been on the same side through all of this, and he hadn't particularly liked her. But Briony had fought for this with everything she had. He couldn't deny that. And if *she* had fallen to the Castle's trial . . .

Heart pounding, he checked the other five names—but they remained untouched.

Alistair was still alive. Gavin needed to believe he would stay that way. He turned back to the people gathering around the Pillar, searching for the government agents and spellmakers who'd scattered into the crowd. But as he did so, a drop of water struck his shoulder, then his hand.

Except it wasn't water at all. The liquid was thick and warm. And red.

Blood poured over the city skyline. It matted his hair and soaked through his shirt; it dribbled down his cheeks, like tears. He knew this sanguine rain had to be an illusion, no different than the blood oozing from each of the Landmarks' pillars. But that knowledge did nothing to quell how *real* it felt—or how horrific everyone around him now looked.

The people around him screamed and rushed in all directions; someone bumped into him, and someone else pushed him away, sending him windmilling into the crush of bodies. He skidded across the newly slick ground, lost, before a hand shot out of nowhere and pulled him into an alley.

"Are you all right?" Isobel demanded. Reid hovered behind her. Both of them were doused in crimson.

"Yeah." Gavin shuddered. They'd lost ground, but not much—he could still make out the hulking rock through the downpour. "We need to get back to the Pillar—"

"Look," Reid breathed, pointing upward.

As he spoke, the rain began to lighten into a delicate drizzle of scarlet, twinkling like stardust. High magick. It sparkled in every sliver between the cobblestones. On the outstretched arms of the empty tree branches. On the poles of parking meters, on windowsills, in the sewer grates. And all of it was drawn toward the Champions Pillar, like thousands of tiny moths collecting around a flame. The air around Gavin became so dense that he had to swipe his hand in front of his face to see. He didn't dare inhale, lest he choke on it.

If it hadn't been so horrible, he might've felt wonder. But there was no time for awe. The people around them became even more frantic, some bolting away, some rushing to collect high magick. Curses fired through the chaos, sending people scattering. Gavin readied himself to rush back into the battle as their screams crescendoed into a high, terrible roar.

But before any of them could move, two figures appeared in the white light of a Here to There spell. They staggered, colliding with the alley walls before toppling into a heap at Gavin's, Reid's, and Isobel's feet. Finley, his arm slung around Alistair's shoulder, both smothered in soot.

Gavin could've cried with relief. He was on Alistair in a second, grasping frantically at his tattered sleeves. "What happened?"

Alistair gasped. "What happened to *you*? You all look like hell—"

"She was still in there!" Finley shouted, shoving Gavin to the side and grabbing Alistair by his collar. "We could've saved her!"

"Her name was struck out on the Castle's pillar," Alistair hissed, trying to squirm out of his grip. "I *saw it happen*."

"You still should've let me go after her—"

"What, so you could die, too? The Castle was collapsing!"

Finley shuddered, then released Alistair and staggered against the wall. He clawed at his chest, as though he couldn't remember how to breathe. "Did you know it was some kind of trap? Did you send us upstairs to die?"

Alistair blanched. "I would never—of course I didn't—"

"We don't have time for this!" Isobel's voice cracked. "Briony's name is crossed out. We saw it, too. She's gone. But this is the one chance we have to stop the new curse."

"She's right," Gavin said. "If we're going to destroy high magick before the government takes it, before this city eats itself alive, we need to do it *now*."

Reid filled Finley and Alistair in on the situation as Gavin squinted through the haze of magick. He made out one, then two, then three figures standing oddly still around the Pillar. They were about to try again.

"Reid and I will focus on taking out the septogram," Isobel said. "I know we were all originally going to cast curses on the Pillar, but it'll have to be just a few of us."

"Al and I can destroy it," Gavin said firmly, and Alistair nodded beside him.

"Finley?" Isobel walked to the other boy nervously. He stared blankly at the alley wall, trembling. "Bri wouldn't want—"

"I know what she wants—what she wanted." His face contorted with anguish, but then he seemed to shake his misery away, a cool, controlled expression in its place. "I'll help you and Reid."

The five of them split up, disguised by cloaking spells. Even without them, Gavin would've lost track of the others immediately. There were simply too many people, shouting, fighting, fleeing. With everyone drenched in blood, it was hard to tell who was on whose side.

Alistair cast a Shrouded from Sight, then gripped Gavin's hand, including him in the enchantment. The two of them wound through the chaos—past a sobbing Innes Thorburn, shielded by Gracie Blair. Past several Macaslans and Paynes whose magickal battle with government agents had devolved into a fistfight on the cobblestones. Past reporters and their crimson cameras, past protestors now using their signs as makeshift weapons, past people rushing around with open flasks of magick, trying to coax the scarlet glimmers inside before they collected around the Pillar.

"How close do you need to be to cast your spell?" Gavin called out. He already had the perfect curse in mind to add to Alistair's.

"Close enough to make sure it doesn't hit anyone else."

As they drew closer to the Pillar, a different battle took shape. Resistance members grappled with government agents, undeterred by the haze of high magick. Isobel and Reid traded cursefire with Agent Yoo. Gavin even caught sight of Diya, casting bursts of golden flame at Calhoun.

A small tornado of high magick had appeared above the Champions Pillar, funneling it into the stone. Twinkling bits of crimson seeped beneath the cracks and moss. Soon, all of it would be absorbed.

If Gavin and Alistair struck then, before the government could collect it, they'd have a chance of destroying it for good.

"We'll only have one shot at this," Gavin said, turning—but Alistair's only response was a surprised *oof* as a bout of cursefire knocked him on his back. He skidded across the cobblestones, then righted himself.

"I can hold a shield *and* a Shrouded from Sight," Alistair grunted. "You destroy the Pillar."

"Do you really think only one curse will work—"

"It's gonna have to." Alistair stood behind him. Back to back. Just like they'd fought for the Medallion. A moment later, the Exoskeleton settled over them both, a series of plates resembling the chitin of beetles laid over each other, so powerful that it felt as though the rest of the world was behind a thick wall of glass. The sounds of battle grew distorted and muffled.

Gavin stared at the cursering on his thumb. It was his class ten Triumph of the Fallen, and when he'd asked Osmand Walsh to craft it for him all those weeks ago, he'd thought it would be the key to his victory. He'd been ready to do anything to win the tournament then, no matter how desperate or depraved.

The last of the high magick disappeared into the stone.

Gavin's ring flared brightly. For a moment, he felt a rush of doubt—he was weak, untrained. The blowback from this could kill him. He should've let Alistair cast the curse instead.

But Gavin knew now that those thoughts came from the wound that had festered in him all his life. The belief that no one else believed in him. That his existence was a waste—was *nothing*—unless he forced the world to see otherwise.

There was no spell or curse that could grant him self-worth. Only Gavin could do that.

He smiled, then cast the Triumph of the Fallen.

Tendrils of mist gathered around the Pillar, spiraling and swirling. They sank into each crack and groove, creeping beneath the moss, tunneling into the ancient stone. A great pressure built inside Gavin's mind as the curse grew stronger and stronger. Dark spots bled into the edges of his vision. And then, like a dam bursting, the pressure *broke*.

The lights on the Champions Pillar flashed, bright as a beacon. The entire stone shivered. Then it rumbled. And then, just as Gavin leapt away from it—it exploded. Tiny chunks of debris flew everywhere, raining like meteors onto the crowd. Gavin flattened himself on the ground beside Alistair, cocooned in the other boy's spell. Rocks battered the shield, weakening it; Gavin placed an arm over his head, too drained to cast anything else, and waited.

The Exoskeleton cracked. The sound of the explosion faded out, and the world faded back in.

When Gavin lifted his head, the Pillar was almost completely gone. All that remained was a chunk at the bottom, curved upward, like a piece of broken eggshell. The last few remnants of high magick winked out inside it, crimson fading into ashen dust.

"No!" cried Calhoun. The courtyard burst into questions.

"What happened?"

"Who did this?"

"Where did it *go*?"

Gavin rose to his feet in a daze as the government agents slipped away in a flurry of Here to There spells. As spellmakers and families devolved from panic to confusion. As a blue, cloudless sky shone above them, free of rain, free of any magick at all.

"It's over, isn't it?" Alistair asked from beside him. Tears shone in the other boy's eyes.

"Yeah," Gavin said hoarsely, wrapping him in a bloody embrace. "I think it is."

They had done the impossible. They had done what countless newspapers, what experts, what Gavin himself had never believed they could do. And even if the hundreds of sacrifices the curse had taken over the centuries were still meaningless, the story that had claimed them was finally finished.

ISOBEL MACASLAN

Her death leaves behind more questions than answers. The extent of her culpability in her family's alleged criminal activity remains unknown, as do the exact circumstances of her untimely demise. Her family and her fellow champions have refused to comment further. The world may know her name, but the real Briony Thorburn will forever remain a mystery.

Ilvernath Eclipse, "Obituary: Briony Thorburn, 17"

Isobel Macaslan stood alone on the hill overlooking the graveyard.

There was no funeral in Ilvernath the Macaslans didn't attend, but for once, they hadn't claimed their typical station at this spot. Bundled heavily against the cold, she savored her anonymity as she watched an enormous crowd traipse across the brittle grass below. Reporters had come in throngs, and now that the Blood Veil had fallen, they'd journeyed from afar to capture the conclusion of the story that had seized the world's attention. They stood at a distance from the Ilvernath locals—classmates, townies, and of course, the families. Despite this funeral being the final of the three that had occurred this week, the number of mourners hadn't dwindled; if anything, it had swelled—the grandest audience for the grandest show.

The Darrows arrived first, always precisely punctual. Isobel was surprised they'd come to the memorial of the girl who'd killed their champion, not a day cold in the ground.

Next were the Paynes, looking bitter and tight-lipped. The Grieves and the Lowes arrived together, so few in number they could've been missed, and the Macaslans followed. Though still in their typical white, they'd dressed uncharacteristically subdued, with no flashy gold jewelry to be seen.

Then came the Blairs, and Isobel winced when she spotted Finley walking at the front. His face was unreadable, as it had been the four times she'd visited his house. Each instance had been awkward, even trite. *Are you planning on going back to school? How has your family been now that you're home?*

Isobel waited several moments longer, shifting from side to side. Apart from Innes, the Thorburns were notably, despicably absent. And though she knew Briony had severed ties with her family, wouldn't care that they'd stood this up, Isobel felt a flare of righteous fury on her friend's behalf. Briony deserved better.

Four chairs were arranged beside the grave, barely visible behind the elaborate display of bouquets and wreaths sent by sympathizers across the world, and Isobel descended from the hill only when hers was left unfilled. She removed her knitted hat and scarf as she walked, exposing her easily identifiable red hair. As people turned to stare, she struggled with how to mold her expression. In the year since she'd risen to accidental fame, she'd never managed to stop the performance. It wasn't that she wanted to please, but that she had no idea how to be candid in such a public setting, with the entire world watching, forming judgments.

Which was why she didn't cringe, seeing that her chair was next to Alistair's. Knowing the glee the reporters would have with that.

"Hey," he said quietly.

"Hi." Isobel sat down, then glanced at Finley on her other side. His gaze was fixed on the closed casket. She didn't have any words to offer him that she hadn't already tried, so she squeezed his hand. He didn't say anything, but he squeezed back.

On the other side of the casket, Innes's face was blotchy and swollen. Isobel wondered how she and the other champions must look in comparison. Unfeeling. Cold. Resolute.

Exactly as Ilvernath had made them.

She didn't think Briony would've been. Briony would've forgotten about the world watching altogether. She would've cried for any of them.

Ilvernath's mayor, Vikram Anand, led the ceremony, but Isobel spent most of it lost in her thoughts. She met her mother's eyes through the crowd, who'd come makeup-less, prepped for tears. Then she stared for a long time at the flowers. When left with no other recourse, she picked at her cuticles.

She knew she was supposed to spend this time thinking about Briony, and it *was* hard not to. Ever since the curse broke, Briony's voice had played constant companion in Isobel's mind, urging her to check on Finley and to call Innes and to flick off the camera crew that had permanently parked themselves outside her mum's spellshop. She could hear Briony commenting on how many people her memorial had drawn.

Or maybe it was easier to pretend. Because it felt wrong to mourn her best friend and mourn her own future without her at the same time. Isobel got to live, and Briony didn't. Isobel got to try to put the tournament behind her, and Briony didn't. She wished she knew if these feelings made her normal. If they made her terrible.

But the four of them had all been terrible once, and it would take more than a few days to learn to be anything else.

When they lowered the casket into the ground, no raw magick dissipated from it.

Isobel's brow knitted together, and she stared, confused, as Innes cast a spell that shoveled the earth into the waiting grave. The only reason raw magick wouldn't appear was if there wasn't any left.

But before Isobel could make sense of that, the funeral ended. She itched to stand, but she didn't want to be the first to do so. Thankfully, Reid walked over, giving them a reason to get up from their seats. Since the tournament's conclusion, the five of them had only seen each other once, and the weight of that night hung between them.

"They should've given you a chair here," Finley said, the first words she'd heard him speak.

Reid flashed a sour smile. "I'm not sure that's true, but thanks for the thought. Where are you all heading?"

"My mum is hosting something at the spellshop," Isobel said. Finley nodded.

"You're all going to that?" asked Reid.

"We're not," Alistair said quietly.

"What did you expect us all to do?" Gavin asked Reid. "Go out for brunch?"

"Yeah, asshole. I came over here to invite you all to my slumber party, so we can watch movies and braid each other's hair." Reid shoved his hands into his pockets. "I got a call yesterday from my agent. My publisher wants to do another book."

"And *this* was the right time to tell us that?" Gavin demanded.

"Was there going to be a next time?"

Isobel admitted that Reid had a point. The five of them had everything and nothing in common. Inevitably, when the shock of it wore off, when Briony's voice faded from Isobel's mind, they had no reason to speak to one another again. Isobel wasn't returning to school—she could earn her diploma remotely. She and Finley had only ever been acquaintances of circumstance, and now that circumstance was gone. She and Gavin had never crossed paths before and doubtfully ever would again. Alistair looked at Ilvernath's spiry skyline as though trying to forcibly expunge it from his memory. And Reid . . . she had no idea.

It bothered her, even if it was probably easier this way.

"So, what, you've already changed your mind?" Gavin asked angrily. "We swore not to—"

Alistair shushed him. "Look how many people are here. Anyone could be listening in."

The night after the tournament ended, the five of them had met in Reid's shop, still exhausted and shaken, and cast the oath spell they'd agreed to with Briony that same morning. It'd only lasted a couple minutes, few of them speaking, none of them lingering—even Isobel. But it'd been too important to delay. Amid the chaos of the mob at the Champions Pillar, no one understood why the world's final vein of high magick had disappeared. According to the most popular speculation, destroying the tournament had destroyed the power along with it.

Maybe it didn't matter whether they'd see each other again. Their secret would connect them, always.

"I haven't changed my mind," Reid said sharply. "And I already told my publisher to fuck off, but I figured I owed it to you all to let you know."

"Yeah, you made the right call," Gavin snapped.

Then, when no one added anything, with seemingly nothing else to say to one another, Reid nodded stiffly. "Right. Well, bye then."

He walked away, and before Isobel could follow after him, she heard Finley's voice, "It's nice of your mum to do this. You, too."

"It felt like the least we could do," she said.

"Look I . . . I'm sorry I haven't been around. I don't mean to be avoiding people, and it's not you guys I'm avoiding." He cast a rueful glance at the journalists flocked outside the roped off area. "But my vote is for a next time. For a lot of next times, even. If that's what you all want."

"I'd like that," Isobel said, and she was surprised when Gavin also told him, "Maybe that's a good idea. Maybe it will make it all . . ." He gestured at everything around them, at nothing in particular. "Better than whatever this week has been."

Isobel had more she'd like to talk to them about, but when she peeked over her shoulder, Reid was almost at the sidewalk.

"I'll catch up with you later," she said hurriedly, then she sped after him.

Reid glanced back at her. "Oh, are we speaking after all?"

"What do you mean?"

"You don't return my calls. You've been to see practically everyone except me. If you don't want anything to do with me, you can just say so."

Isobel bit her lip. "I haven't been avoiding you on purpose. I just—"

"It's not breaking up if we were never together."

"Stop trying to be so cool and unbothered for one second," she snapped. "I just needed time to figure this out. And I've been with my mum, trying to figure out how to be a regular person again."

"Yeah, well, I've been alone at home all week, getting takeout, watching the same footage of us over and over again on national news, being too fucking freaked to leave my flat because now the whole world knows I wrote the book and has decided to hate me for it. So do you think we could make whatever we are halfway normal again so we can go back to being—I don't know—not alone, at least?" His words spilled out far faster and higher pitched than he'd probably intended. He furiously wiped his eyes on his oversized black button-up.

Maybe it shouldn't have surprised her that Reid was the only one of them to shed tears today. Reid hadn't been raised for this the way they had. Of all the countless funerals Isobel had attended, in not one of them hadn't she imagined her own. She'd pictured this same time of year. This same crowd. These same flowers. And the sudden knowledge that this funeral hadn't been hers, that she'd survived when Briony hadn't, hit her like a blow to the stomach.

"There was no raw magick when they buried her," she murmured. "What do you think that means?"

A shadow darkened Reid's face. "I saw, but we shouldn't . . ." A muscle in his jaw clenched. "It's better not to think about it."

"Why?" Isobel asked sharply. "Because it might be our fault?" When Reid didn't respond, she pressed on, her voice diminishing into a whimper. "What if the Crown didn't work? What if we messed up one of the—"

"But she did it—she finished the trial." Reid closed his eyes, his anguish perfectly mirroring Isobel's own. "I don't know what took her life magick, but I'm pretty sure Briony wouldn't want us to beat ourselves about it."

Isobel finally blinked back tears of her own. "I know that's true, but I still feel awful, especially because I feel *relieved*. We were so close to it being all of us. And that's . . . I shouldn't feel that way. It's not fair to her."

"I know," he said grimly.

"I—I never thought I'd be here, you know? In the *after*. I talked to myself like I did, but I didn't believe it. I never thought I'd have to do this."

Reid pulled her toward him, and she buried her face in his shoulder. She didn't sob, but her windpipe burned, and a pressure throbbed behind her eyes. She'd already cried so much in private that it ached.

"I'm sorry," he said. "It's not your job to hold us all together."

"I-I'm just scared. What am I supposed to do after this? My best friend is gone. Things have been weird with my dad, with my whole family. I can't go back to school. Even university . . . Five years, ten years, twenty years, people will still recognize me. I'll still be the person that this happened to. Mum said it might be healthier if we don't see each other, but what if we're all we have left? I spent the past year alone. I can't do that anymore."

"I get it. I don't think I can just move on and pretend it never happened."

It was relieving to talk to someone who understood. "I know. I don't want that either."

Reid cleared his throat. "You should probably move, if you prefer this not to be on camera."

Isobel let out a very wet snort into his shirt.

"I'm serious. I'm the one who told you to find Alistair, who altered Gavin's magick, who destroyed the Cloak, who fucked up the Crown. If it weren't for me—"

"I'd be dead if Alistair hadn't helped me." Isobel drew away and stared at him seriously. "Gavin would've probably died, too, if he wasn't a vessel. And if you hadn't destroyed the Cloak, we would've had no idea how to make the other Relics, and the tournament probably would've collapsed before the last Relics could fall. *And* we never would've broken that shield around the Champions Pillar if you hadn't gone inside."

"Even if all of that were true," Reid said, "I've watched a *lot* of the news this week. Enough to know that I'm the bad guy."

"None of us think that."

"Well, it's hard for me to believe otherwise when you're all avoiding me."

"Point taken. And for the record, I do want to have something to do with you, if that's what you want, too."

Reid grinned. "I was hoping you'd say that." Then he leaned down and kissed her cheek. "I'll actually see you then? Later?"

"Tonight," she promised.

"Tonight."

Isobel watched him walk away to the street. She swiped her fingers beneath her eyes, and they came back smudged with mascara.

"Please tell me he's nicer than he looks," her mother said beside her.

The comment was so normal and silly that she laughed. "Sure."

Honora wrapped her arm around Isobel's shoulders and steered her toward the sidewalk. "Our guests don't need to stay long. I know this morning hasn't been easy for you."

"It's fine. I'm glad we're hosting something. Briony deserves it."

"How are you feeling?"

"Okay, I guess."

"Your father called again earlier." When Isobel gave her a look, her mother continued. "I know, and I told him not to come today. I don't care if he's trying—he and his whole family took advantage of you. But he said he's dug up some research on the Roach's Armor. He's going to pass it all over to me, so the two of us and your cursemaker can look into reversing its side effects, if that sounds all right to you."

"It's the least Dad could do," she mumbled.

"That's what I told him."

It took twenty-five minutes to walk back to the spellshop, by which time Isobel was shivering from the cold. But as she turned onto her street, even that sensation faded into numbness. She gazed at the café where she and Briony used to do homework after school. The stores the pair of them had once haunted. And finally, as they approached their front door, she craned her neck up toward her bedroom window, obscured by sequined curtains, and her thoughts drifted somewhere else, somewhere a long time ago.

She didn't notice the camera flash.

The photograph was one of several on the front page of next morning's edition of the *Ilvernath Eclipse*, on the early talk shows, in the tabloids. And of all the moments they could've chosen to capture that day, it was the only one Isobel didn't hate. Her mum at her side. Her back to the camera. Her face in profile. An image that was unguarded, unbroken, honest.

GAVIN GRIEVE

Almost all those who evacuated Ilvernath in the immediate after-math of the Blood Veil's fall have returned. Classes have resumed at every school, local employees have ended tournament stress-related leave policies, and restaurants and shops have redecorated their storefronts for the winter season. Everyone seems deter-mined to put the past few months behind them.

Ilvernath Eclipse, "Finding a New Normal"

The interior of the Magpie was just as Gavin remembered it—dark wooden walls, dim lighting, air clouded with smoke and the tinny rock music blaring from the jukebox. He sat in the corner booth covered in a red-and-white-checkered tablecloth, nursing a beer. Gavin could almost forget how crowded the place had once been. But although the various cursechasers and report-ers had cleared out of town over the past month, the drinks had yet to return to their formerly low prices, and the pub hadn't removed their novelty Blood Moon cocktail from the menu. Gavin doubted they ever would.

He'd just taken the first sip of his beer when his companion ar-rived. Her cloaking spell was so powerful, he didn't notice her until she slid into the seat across from him.

"I'm glad we could do this." Diya's pixie cut had grown out a little, and her spellstone choker was gone. She tugged her leather jacket tightly around herself, looking nervous.

"So am I," Gavin said cautiously. Diya had worked with the spell-makers, but she hadn't gone along with their plans. She'd helped Gavin and Alistair. She'd even fought with the resistance, at the end. Yet in the weeks since the tournament had ended, Gavin had been hesitant to reach out. All of the champions were being watched, and he didn't want to make her a target. Based on the strength of her enchantment, she didn't want to be one either.

"How have you been?" she asked him.

"Alive," Gavin said. "You?"

"Busy." Diya fiddled with her spellrings. "I just finished finals week. And sent in all my uni applications."

It was such a mundane thing to say. Gavin wondered at the bizarreness of it all.

"Congratulations," he said dryly. "Are you going to study spellmaking?"

"I think so, yeah." She hesitated. "Things look a little different on the Spellmaking Society board these days. Nobody questions me being there anymore. But . . . I used to think it was important for me to be part of all this, so my family would know they'd made the right choice naming me as their heir. Now I'm just glad I didn't get in too deep."

"I don't blame you," Gavin said.

In the aftermath of the tournament, certain spellmakers had shuttered their storefronts. Others had received mysterious and lucrative opportunities in new cities. The Cursebreaking Division's involvement was only mentioned in whispers; as far as the official news reports went, any government interference at the Champions Pillar had been limited to protective measures. Meanwhile, the Thorburn family was walled up in their estate, fighting a legal battle against the murder victims' families. Gavin didn't doubt that whatever agreement they'd had with the Division meant the Kendalle Parliament would never be implicated for their crimes. He thought the whole thing was bullshit, but he'd learned a long time ago that life was inherently unfair.

"I was wondering, though." Diya met his gaze. "How's your tattoo treating you? I'd imagine the healing process would be quite complicated."

"Actually, it's been fine."

"No problems?"

"None at all. I guess I got lucky." Gavin didn't know how quickly his life magick was regenerating, but he had no access to it anymore. And thanks to all those exercises he'd done, his spellcasting was far stronger than it had been before the tournament.

A smile flickered at the edge of her lips. "Good." But then Diya's expression changed into something more solemn. She crossed her arms on the edge of the table and leaned forward. "I've been stalling. I didn't just want to catch up."

"I figured," Gavin said. Them meeting at all was risky. Diya wouldn't have asked for it without a good reason.

"I keep thinking about the day the curse broke," she continued. "So much happened so quickly, and then high magick was just . . . gone. And it makes sense, of course, that the tournament ending had unpredictable side effects. But I've heard some wild theories about it all."

Gavin kept his voice neutral. "So have I."

"What do *you* think happened?"

The question was delicate. Loaded. Gavin wondered if she'd try to cast a truth spell on him, but it wouldn't matter if she did. The champions' oath spell was too powerful. But none of her rings flared. She merely watched him, waiting.

"I think the simplest explanation is probably the truest," he said neutrally. "And honestly, now that the tournament's over, I never want to think about it again." He paused. "What about you?"

"I think there were a lot of spells and curses flying around that day. It's impossible to tell which ones hit their target on purpose, or by accident. Or what effects they were meant to have. Who could really know, for example, if a curse had struck the Pillar itself?"

"It's tough to say. I'm no spellmaker."

She gave him a small, knowing smirk. "I guess we'll never really figure out what happened, will we?"

"I guess not."

Diya glanced around at the rest of the pub. "I'm pretty sure my protective spells held for this conversation. But as long as we're both being watched, I'll be keeping my distance."

"I think we'll be watched for a long time."

"I agree," she said. "Oh, and tell Alistair I said hi. I assume you know he's two booths down, eavesdropping?"

Gavin nearly choked on his beer. "He was supposed to meet me *later*."

Diya chuckled. Her cloaking spell slid over her again, so strong Gavin could barely make out her silhouette. She stood and flitted back through the pub, like a ghost. A few moments later, Alistair slid onto the bench beside him.

"You could've joined us, you know," Gavin said.

"I didn't want to," Alistair said waspishly. He was dressed in a well-fitted suit that still managed to look all wrong on him, hair gelled back in some semblance of propriety. Gavin watched, amused, as he rumpled it, then loosened his tie. "I've been *polite* all day, and it was awful."

"Did the hearing go all right?"

"It went fine." Alistair slumped in the booth. "It's just . . . I hate sitting there, nodding, while a bunch of people who don't know anything about me decide what I deserve."

Since the tournament's end, Alistair had been tied up in a significant amount of legal red tape. The curse clause traditionally protected participants caught in unwilling enchantments from criminal prosecution, but no one had been sure how he and his dead brother murdering their family factored into that. Today's hearing had been meant to decide the terms of Alistair's settlement with the Lowe estate.

"They don't want me to see Marianne anymore, for her sake," he continued, tossing his tie onto the checkered tablecloth. "I . . . I don't know how to feel about that. It's not what Hendry would've wanted. But maybe they're right. It's better for her. And once I agree to that and the court-mandated therapy, they'll declare me legally emancipated."

Gavin thought of Alistair in counseling. He probably needed it. They probably all needed it, although he shuddered to think of what his own future therapist would have to endure.

"Maybe they can help you," he said. "With the nightmares."

"Yeah," Alistair muttered. In the month he'd spent recovering from the Reaper's Embrace, a healthy flush had returned to his cheeks, but he still looked haunted. They both did. It was hard to stop carrying curserings, to stop glancing over their shoulders, to stop imagining the phantom, metallic reek of blood. "Are you still having them, too?"

Gavin nodded. "Sometimes I can't believe it's over. I guess we lived a nightmare for so long, it's hard to wake up."

Alistair's leg shook restlessly under the table. "It'll be better when I get out of this city."

"When?" Gavin asked softly. "Not if?"

"They said it's almost a sure thing, once they finish their paperwork. I—I'll be able to leave Ilvernath. I know it won't all magickally get better the second I'm somewhere else, but . . . I have to believe it won't be as bad as it is here."

All the champions attracted unwanted attention everywhere they went, and probably would for some time. But the attention was particularly painful for Alistair. The press might've decided Reid was a bigger villain in the end, but the Lowes had been feared in Ilvernath long before the tournament's secrets came to light.

Gavin had heard Alistair talk again and again about how badly he wanted to leave. Yet the knowledge that it was so close, so certain, sank like a stone in his stomach.

"Have you decided where you're going yet?" he asked. Alistair had struggled to make up his mind. One day he wanted to start over in a small town on the northern cliffs, the next he wanted to go abroad, to a giant, bustling city. The only thing that remained consistent was a desire to disappear from the public view.

"That depends. Do you . . ." Alistair swallowed, then slid his hand into Gavin's. "Do you want to come with me?"

Gavin interlaced their fingers and squeezed tightly. He should've known on some level that this question was coming—but Alistair had never asked it before.

Gavin couldn't deny that he, too, had thought about leaving. It was tempting to consider a new life where no one knew who they were. Where their secrets could stay tucked neatly away, the ones they'd sworn to take to the grave and the others that were still too painful to talk about.

But while Alistair had made it clear there was nothing left for him in Ilvernath, Gavin felt differently.

"I can't," Gavin said. "I told Fergus I'd take care of him. I need to see that through."

He'd promised Fergus that he'd do everything he could to obtain legal guardianship of him the moment he turned eighteen—only a week away now. Originally he'd wanted to take Fergus far from Ilvernath, but his brother had asked him if they could stay. Awful or not, for him, the city was still home. Reid had split the royalties from *A Tradition of Tragedy* among the surviving champions, and so Gavin had used his first payment to rent a two-bedroom flat in Ilvernath proper, one with lots of natural light and a powerful security system.

He was determined to protect his brother from their parents, even if it meant staying in town a few years longer than he'd like. Callista had also offered to take Fergus in, but Fergus had chosen Gavin instead, and Gavin's relationship with his sister remained strained at best. He *was* grateful that she and the Paynes had decided to formally foster Marianne, whose interests had recently changed from bones to carnivorous plants. At least the girl had started to care about something living.

"I get it," Alistair grumbled. He tugged his hand away from Gavin's.

Both of them fell silent. Gavin thought of brothers, of Hendry—unlike the three funerals for the dead champions, his death remained unacknowledged by most. Alistair had told him that the Magpie was important to them. Gavin could only hope he found it comforting right now.

"Hendry deserved better," Gavin said quietly.

Alistair inclined his head. Errant curls tumbled across his brow. "He wanted to escape this place, too," he said bitterly. "Now he never will."

"I know," Gavin murmured. "But he'd be happy that you are."

Alistair shifted in his seat. "Would you come visit?"

"Of course I would. And it's not like I want to live here forever."

"You're not mad at me, for going?"

"Are you kidding me?" Gavin asked. "You clearly need this. It's just . . ."

"Just what?" Alistair asked sharply.

Gavin sighed. "If Ilvernath is causing you this much pain, I don't want to be a reminder of that."

Another ghost. Another specter.

Alistair met Gavin's eyes. Once, Gavin had thought the intensity in his gaze was hatred—but he knew better now. "You don't cause me pain," he said fiercely. "You're the only good thing I have left. So I want to try and make this work, if you do."

In answer, Gavin closed the distance between them. The first time he'd kissed Alistair, it had felt like the bravest, most dangerous thing he'd ever done. It still did, a little bit. He forgot the smoky lights of the bar, the too-loud music. All that mattered was the feel of

Alistair's curls twined in his fingers, the shiver that coursed through him as their mouths moved against each other, the tender, eager way the other boy kissed him back.

"I want this, Al," he whispered, drawing away. "I promise."

"Me too." Then Alistair glanced around the bar. "Hey—the pinball machines are free."

"You want to play?"

"Yeah. There's this one with a dragon . . ."

"Of course you like that one." Gavin raised a brow. "I have the high score on it."

"That's impossible," Alistair said. "I play it every time I come here. There's no way you're better than me at it."

"I guess that makes us rivals." Gavin paused. "But I'll win, you know."

Alistair flashed his sneer of a smile, and for a moment Gavin saw the boy he'd fought with for so long. Alistair might not be a villain—Gavin wasn't really sure there *was* such a thing—but there would always be something a little wicked about him.

"Come on, then," Alistair said, pulling him out of the booth.

The tournament had ended, but Gavin's story had only just begun. He wasn't sure yet what kind of tale it would be. All he knew was that it would be a future he wanted. A future he chose.

It was a prize far greater than anything he'd imagined.

ALISTAIR ~~LOWE~~

Designed by local artist Marcas Duff, the Blood Moon Curse memorial is a powerful and striking homage to Ilvernath history and to the hundreds of victims who have lost their lives to its violent cycle.

Ilvernath Eclipse, "Blood Moon Curse
Memorial Unveiling"

Exactly one year since the fall of the Blood Veil, the city of Ilvernath still felt like the setting of a haunted tale. Ivy clawed over each of the historic buildings, bare bramble scratching like fingernails over shuttered windows and doorframes. Its disorienting maze of cobblestone streets lured pedestrians into shadowed alleys and dead ends, as though a place designed to get lost in. Despite the months of exposure to the elements, flecks of dried blood still clung to the wrought iron lampposts, the plexiglass bus stops. Nightmares lurked here, nightmares that time alone could not expunge.

Alistair's heart hammered as he approached the familiar square at the city's edge. The Champions Pillar, long destroyed, had been replaced with a deep crater of smooth concrete. At its center rose a strange red pole, unveiled only an hour earlier.

"What the hell is that?" Alistair muttered, acutely unmoved. He hadn't expected to weep at the newly installed memorial, but he'd still expected to feel *something*.

"A joke," someone said to his right, and Alistair spotted Gavin strolling toward him.

Contrary to the accepted laws of physics, Gavin had managed to grow yet another few centimeters in the past year. Alistair, meanwhile, felt as though nothing about him had changed, nothing that mattered. He could shear off his hair or grow a beard or swap his whole face for a new one and somehow he'd still feel like the boy once drenched in blood.

"Where were you?" Gavin asked sharply.

"I . . ." Alistair had rehearsed several excuses on the walk here, but Gavin knew him too well to believe them. Since Alistair had finally been allowed to leave Ilvernath, he hadn't once returned. But he'd promised to, for this. And yet, despite traveling here, while the locals, journalists, and surviving champions had gathered for a commemoration ceremony, Alistair had lingered, petrified, in the train station, until the entire event had ended. "I'm sorry."

"Finley was pissed," Gavin said. "Isobel was worried something had happened to you."

"And you?"

Gavin sighed, then leaned down and kissed Alistair on the cheek. "I wish you'd warned me—I didn't want to do that bullshit alone. But I get it. I'm just glad you're here. How does it feel to be back?"

"Like I never left." Which was precisely what he'd feared. He shoved his hands anxiously in his pockets. "So how'd everyone look?"

"Isobel looked good. She and her mum and Reid managed to cure the side effects of the Roach's Armor. Reid looked . . . well, I guess. He was weirdly cheery. Guess he's thrilled the news cycle has found other people to hate or something. Finley said he likes uni. He made his life sound almost normal. Kept bringing up Briony, I think to make her feel part of it. Isobel and Reid seemed into it, but it's not like I have a million happy memories of her to make thinking about her not shitty, you know?"

Alistair understood, as he avoided dwelling on Briony at all costs. If anyone should've died breaking his family's Landmark, it was him.

"They asked about you, obviously," Gavin said. "I told them you were fine, that you've got your flat. But I mentioned how you've had to move a few times, that you were thinking of changing your name—"

"I already did it, actually," Alistair told him. "Got the papers just before I came here."

Gavin's eyes widened. "Wow. That's good, right? You feel good about it?"

At first, Alistair hadn't, had dismissed the notion for months, even as his government caseworkers suggested otherwise. Because as much as he loathed the Lowes, his name was one of the few things that tied him to Hendry. He'd already been able to live his life in a way his brother never would. But so long as he was Alistair Lowe, he still couldn't escape their family. Ilvernath's curse was too famous, and wherever he went, his notoriety always caught up to him. And even if it felt like nothing had changed, even if he still carried cursestones in his pockets and winced every time a traffic light turned red, he was tired of running.

"Yeah, I feel good about it," Alistair murmured.

Though the square had long since cleared out, a few stragglers remained, and one couple sat on the steps of the banquet hall—a young woman and a girl, watching them. Without the familiar face of Callista Payne beside her, Alistair might not have recognized his cousin. Instead of her usual haunted doll ensemble, Marianne Lowe wore blue jeans and a frightfully normal, even bland puffer jacket.

Alistair knew he wasn't supposed to talk to her—a decision he still felt was for the best. But if they'd waited, she must've wanted to see him, and so he gave her an awkward, distant wave. She waved back.

"She looks well," Alistair said, and he was glad for it.

"She is, from what Callista tells me," Gavin said.

After that, Callista and Marianne stood to leave, and Alistair jerked his head and started walking—not toward the city, but away from it. "Come on."

Gavin hurried to catch up. "Where are we going?"

"Somewhere I can think."

The pair stalked past the hideous, pointless art installation, over the sidewalk, and through the tree line. The air, once heavy with memories and secrets, seemed to grow crisper, clearer. And even though the branches and underbrush still careened out of his path, Alistair knew it to be the wind.

Maybe he *had* changed, and it had just taken coming back to realize it.

Gavin took his hand, and for several minutes, Alistair thought he'd be content merely to walk in peaceful silence, neither of them needing to glance fearfully over their shoulder. Then Gavin said, "Tell me a story."

"What kind?"

"One you haven't told me before."

That was hard, as in the countless late nights they'd spent on the phone or beside each other, he'd told Gavin all the stories he had.

Except one.

"Once there was a boy who wanted to be a monster . . ."

Alistair spoke for some time. Enough that they passed familiar places—crash sites like the footprints of giants crushed into the forest floor, the rubble of what might've once been a witch's cottage nestled in the trees. However, they never stopped, nor did Alistair pause his story—at least, not until he'd reached his final words, as he had to consider them carefully. Though this monster story had never been destined for a happily ever after, he had achieved something close to it.

". . . and no tale was ever heard of him again."

ACKNOWLEDGMENTS

Cowriting *All of Us Villains* and *All of Our Demise* has been an incredibly special and rewarding experience for both of us, one that's left us better writers and better friends than we were before. But releasing this duology wouldn't have been possible without the amazing group of people supporting us, and we're so grateful for every single one of them.

Thank you to our agents, Kelly Sonnack and Whitney Ross, the original champions of this series. Thank you to our editor, Ali Fisher, as well as to our fantastic team at Tor Teen, including Kristin Temple, Devi Pillai, Tom Doherty, Anthony Parisi, Isa Caban, Sarah Pannenberg, Eileen Lawrence, Saraciea Fennell, Giselle Gonzalez, Sarah Reidy, Lucille Rettino, Megan Kiddoo, Jim Kapp, Heather Saunders, and Michelle Foytek. Thank you to our team at Gollancz in the UK, including Gillian Redfearn, Rachel Winterbottom, Will O'Mullane, as well as to Will Staehle, Lesley Worrell, and Rachael Lancaster, who have designed the most incredible, striking covers for this series. We'd also like to thank Neha Patel and Grace Wynter for their invaluable insights on *All of Our Demise*.

Thank you to every writer friend who's been eternally supportive throughout this process. Rory Power, Janella Angeles, Mara Fitzgerald, Kat Cho, Allison Saft, Akshaya Raman, Amanda Haas, Axie Oh, Meg Kohlmann, Melody Simpson, Maddy Colis, Erin Bay, Tara Sim, Katy Rose Pool, Ashley Burdin, Claribel Ortega, and Alex Castellanos—we're lucky to know you all.

Thank you to Ben and Trevor, our partners, who have heard every possible ending to this story over the last five years.

And finally, our most heartfelt gratitude goes to our readers, whose support for this series as well as our other books is what made *All of Us Villains* possible. We hope the villains of our dark, twisted fairy tale have felt as captivating and real to you as they have to us. But, of course, all the stories in Ilvernath are true.